Essex-born Giovanna is an author, actress, blogger, vlogger and presenter. She is married to Tom Fletcher from McFly/McBusted and is mum to their two boys Buzz and Buddy. She spends far too much time on social media and/or talking about Nutella. Follow her on Twitter @MrsGiFletcher

Always with Love

A Billy and Sophie Story

GIOVANNA FLETCHER

PENGUIN BOOKS

PENGUIN BOOKS

UK | USA | Canada | Ireland | Australia
India | New Zealand | South Africa

Penguin Books is part of the Penguin Random House group of companies
whose addresses can be found at global.penguinrandomhouse.com.

First published 2016
009

Copyright © Giovanna Fletcher, 2016

The moral right of the author has been asserted

Set in 12.5/14.75 pt Garamond MT Std
Typeset by Jouve (UK), Milton Keynes
Printed in Great Britain by Clays Ltd, St Ives plc

A CIP catalogue record for this book is available from the British Library

ISBN: 978–1–405–91918–0

www.greenpenguin.co.uk

For you, the reader. Thanks for buying my books and allowing me to turn a love of mine into a 'job' . . . I now get to sit at home in my PJs while rewarding myself for productive writing days with spoonfuls of Nutella and chocolate Hobnobs. I'll be forever grateful (although my waistline may not). xx

PART ONE

I

'Would you like some breakfast?' someone asks me in the dark, startling me as they gently touch my shoulder and wake me from my slumber.

My hand flies to the black mask on my face and lifts it up a smidge, my brown eyes squinting as the light comes pouring in and blinds me momentarily.

'Erm,' I start, my mouth dry as I sleepily look at the air stewardess crouching down beside me. Her perfectly highlighted hair is immaculately swept back off her flawless face and her bright red skirt suit silhouettes her shape beautifully. I feel a state in comparison in my baggy black pyjama set. Beyond her I spot other people either still fast asleep in their individual pods or waking up and milling around the plane we're in.

Slowly, I remember where I am – on a Virgin flight to Los Angeles. In Upper Class, no less. Not that I actually paid for the luxury, though. Rather that the Premium Economy tickets I had bought us were kindly upgraded by the smiling girl at the check-in desk as soon as she saw who I was travelling with. Never mind the Christmas madness – there's always space for a VIP. We were whisked through fast-track security and into the gorgeous lounge fairly swiftly after that bump up. Not that I'm complaining – this is actually my first flight as an adult, so travelling in such comfort has certainly made the whole thing much more exciting. I'll admit that I was feeling pretty jittery and anxious when my mum and her new fiancé Colin dropped us off at the airport earlier. The glass of bubbles on arrival didn't quite make me blasé about being tens of thousands of feet up in the air (I still paid extremely close attention to the safety announcement and demonstration before we took off), but it certainly took my mind off it slightly.

I glance to my left but can't see over the seat divider in my horizontal position, so just gawp back at the air stewardess's smiling red lips in an undecided, hazy, fashion – as though the simple question of breakfast requires more than just a yes or no in reply. I'm clearly not great at functioning when my sleep is interrupted while travelling over time zones.

'He's already munching away,' she smiles, answering my non-voiced question and tilting her head to nod in his direction.

'Oh, great. Then, yes please,' I smile, rubbing at my face, which suddenly feels dry from the air conditioning.

'And what would you like?' she asks, her tone friendly, calm and warm – clearly used to jumbled exchanges like this with lethargic passengers. 'Cereal? Pastries? A bacon butty?'

'Ooh, bacon butty, please,' I coo, unable to resist – my rumbling tummy telling me it's still Christmas time and that it's OK to indulge. Well, it's only the day after Boxing Day, after all. 'Do you have ketchup?'

'Yes,' she laughs, standing upright. 'Tea? Coffee?'

'Tea, please,' I smile, removing the eye mask from my head properly and sweeping my hands back over my hair to smooth out my brown frizzy mane and collect it into a tidy ponytail – hoping it makes me look a tad more presentable.

'No problem,' she says, gliding off towards the kitchen in the sky.

I get on to my knees and look over at my companion, who's sat upright watching something on the TV screen attached to his seat, whilst wearing the same pyjama set as me (we were handed them when we boarded the flight in London), although he somehow manages to make them look far cooler than I do. But that's Billy Buskin for you – effortlessly brilliant.

'Morning sleepy head,' he winks, noticing me peering over while he chews on some toast – the small table in front of him buried under empty bowls and plates. 'Got hungry,' he admits, his dark chocolaty brown eyes endearingly screwing up as he laughs, causing them to twinkle.

'So I see,' I smile, finding him utterly adorable. 'Did you sleep?'

'A bit,' he nods. 'Then I started watching a film and that snowballed into me watching a couple more.'

'You must be shattered.'

He draws his hands across his face and stretches out the skin around his eyes, looking completely knackered. 'Great films though.'

'Clearly.'

'I watched *Deserted*. It was so intense and awesome. Hardly surprising Ralph Joplin got Best Director at the Oscars for it – it's incredible,' he sighs, shaking his head in awe at the screen, as though he's still watching it.

He might as well be talking to himself.

There was a time in my life when my desire to watch a film over reading a book was usually led by whether Jude Law made an appearance in it or not. But then gorgeous Billy Buskin entered my life with his big booming laugh, stylish quiff and purple Converse trainers and helped change that. Everyone knew a film crew was rolling into the village to make an adaptation of *Pride and Prejudice*, but when Billy wandered into the shop one day I wrongly assumed he was one of the crew . . . I didn't realize he was starring in the film as Mr Darcy and that he was arguably the biggest actor of our generation. Gosh, it makes me cringe just looking back on our first few exchanges, but for some reason Billy loved my jittery ways and swept me off my feet.

Needless to say, dating a film star has increased my liking for cinema, broadened my tastes and made me watch things I wouldn't normally pick (I also talked him into letting me watch the *Halo* trilogy and *Twisted Drops* – films he actually stars in). I still don't have the foggiest who he's on about when he talks of directors, producers and all the hundreds and thousands of people who work the other side of the camera, though. It's such a huge industry to get my head around and even though I'm enjoying building my love for something Billy is passionate about, I have to admit that *The Holiday* is still my favourite film of all time. Yes, my love for Jude lives on – especially as I got to meet him just after Billy won a BAFTA for Best Actor in *Twisted Drops*. Somehow I managed to stay calm, cool and collected when talking to Jude, even though all I wanted to do was shriek in his face and tell him I loved him. That being said, Billy had just given the most romantic acceptance speech of all time, so I was probably still shell-shocked from that. I don't think my mind could handle any more dramatics.

'Did you watch anything?' Billy asks, raising his eyebrow at me – already knowing the answer.

'No . . . I read my book,' I smile.

'Of course you did, my little bookworm,' he grins. 'And what was it this time?'

'*Little Women.*'

'Again?' he laughs.

'It's a favourite,' I shrug, knowing he's not actually poking fun at me and my desire to read the same books over and over again. There's a reason such stories have become classics and are still bought in bookshops today, and it's not just because kids are forced to read them in schools – if anything that's detrimental to their enjoyment factor. 'How long do we have left?' I ask, leaning over and running my fingers through his thick dark hair. He still wears it in the quiff he had when we first met, although right now it's floppy and product-free, meaning he doesn't mind me playing with it.

'Hour and a half, maybe?' he guesses, closing his eyes and enjoying my touch.

'Wow. I must've slept for ages,' I note.

'You did,' he nods, opening his eyes and peering up at me. 'Even heard you snoring.'

'I did not!' I gasp, horrified as I snatch my hand away.

'Talking too,' he grins, clearly enjoying himself. 'Telling the whole of upper class about your desire to join the mile high club.'

'Oh really,' I say, raising my eyebrows at him, now knowing he's definitely trying to wind me up.

'I know. Everyone was quite surprised,' he exclaims, his eyes glittering. 'Never would they have thought sweet Sophie May would come out with something like that. Little do they know she can be a total vixen when she wants to be.'

'Oh, shush you!' I blush, getting up, grabbing my bag and change of clothes from beneath my seat and making my way to the loo.

When I get to the tiny cubicle I turn to see Billy shaking his head at me in mock disgust. 'I'm not doing it,' he mouths, pursing his lips in protest, his dark eyes wide with objection.

'What?' I mouth back, thoroughly confused.

He gestures towards the toilet door with a frown.

I frown back.

We stay like that for a few seconds before his face breaks into a grin and lights up with amusement.

Mile high club.

Cheeky monkey.

I roll my eyes in his direction and head inside the small box of a space – horrified to see I've had black mascara smudged around my eyes, that my pale skin is now bordering on ghost white and that I look puffier than normal. This is what I looked like during the whole exchange with Billy and the air stewardess. They were both clearly too polite to mention the state I was in – and there I was thinking it was just my hair that needed taking care of.

It's only when I've freshened up, got changed into my own clothes (a pair of thin jeans and a plain mint-coloured t-shirt), whipped my hair back into a giant turquoise hanky and am back in my seat, biting into my bacon roll, that reality hits and the nerves start to seep in. I'm about to meet Billy's family for the first time.

Even though we've distantly been in each other's lives for almost two years, our paths have never crossed beyond the occasional Skype chat – so I guess it's perfectly natural to have a tummy filled with a million manic butterflies . . . right? Especially as my family consisted of just me and my mum after my dad was killed in a hit-and-run accident when I was just eleven. My quiet home life was miles away from Billy's upbringing with his four siblings (older twin sisters Jenny and Hayley, younger sister Lauren and little brother Jay – the baby of the house who's just turned twenty-one). I can't even begin to imagine what a family of seven must be like, although it can't be too dissimilar to the mayhem *The Waltons* portrayed, right?

The Buskins all live stateside, something that the family, originally from Surrey, all decided was for the best once Billy started having success in Hollywood, thanks to him playing the lead role in *Halo* – a huge teen movie which turned Billy into a heart-throb overnight. With *Halo* dominating the teen market and Billy becoming highly sought after for future projects in LA, it looked like he was set to live there indefinitely and, understandably, his mum wasn't too keen on letting her young son move across the Atlantic without her. After much thought the Buskins decided that they'd all make the move with him. Leaving their jobs, friends, extended families and schools behind, they started a new life for themselves in a big family home in sunny LA and haven't looked back since, it seems. From what Billy's told me they all settled in extremely quickly and loved the sudden change of pace.

Several years after they all made the upheaval, Billy's job took him back to London – although this time it was decided they would stick with the sunnier climate as Billy was bound to be back in LA working again soon enough. They clearly weren't banking on him meeting me and declaring a break from the big bad world of fame soon after, choosing instead to live a peaceful existence in the place where I grew up, the tranquil village of Rosefont Hill in Kent.

I wonder how they feel about that. It wasn't something I ever pushed for or encouraged, but I did welcome it. I was thankful to have Billy by my side, declaring I was all he'd ever wanted. What girl wouldn't go weak at the knees to hear someone they loved give themselves over so completely? Obviously I've spoken to his mum and dad since and they've been nothing but lovely, but I wonder if the relaxed reaction to the whole thing is actually how they felt . . . or if they'd rather Billy was still 'playing the game' with one of his fellow actors, like the disastrous Heidi Black (his ex, who's more than a little psychotic). Or maybe I'm being pathetic and overthinking things. It wouldn't be the first time I've done that. It seems to be a hobby of mine if I'm honest. I guess I'll know more in about an hour and fifteen minutes when we touch down in LAX. My tummy is in knots at the thought.

'What's the frown for, baby?' Billy asks, peering over the seat divider.

'Oh, nothing.'

'Getting nervous about meeting the in-laws?' he asks correctly, causing me to flounder in response. 'They love you already,' he grins.

'Just trying to stay calm,' I breathe.

'Don't you go having a panic attack on them. It might've charmed me but Mum will get in a right tizz and be flapping around you no end,' he jokes, making me think of the first time we met in the teashop, when I shamefully had a little episode. Luckily, they've tailed off and I haven't had one in a while, but I always feel like there's an extra little shadow following me around. No matter how sunny and bright my day might be, it's just there ... lurking. Waiting. 'You know they'll be just as nervous about meeting you,' he adds with a wry smile.

'As if. There's an army of them and just one of me.'

'True. But I can guarantee Mum's been driving everyone mad with her worrying, wanting to make sure everything's perfect for your arrival. She'll have been bossing everyone around. Dad will be out in the garden making sure there's not a rose out of place, the girls will have been scrubbing the floors with toothbrushes and poor little Jay has probably had to tidy his own room for the first time ever. I'm telling you, you're causing pandemonium in the Buskin household.'

'You have staff,' I laugh.

'Yeah, but saying the maid's been working overtime doesn't set quite the same image,' Billy grins. 'You eating that?' he continues, looking greedily at the food in my hands.

'Yes, I blooming am,' I laugh in response, taking a bite out of my bacon butty and chewing on it with gusto, feeling a little less apprehensive than before and thankful that the man I love knows how to calm my worrisome ways.

2

'You excited?' I ask, once we've been escorted through passport control by the awaiting ground staff, reclaimed our baggage and are about to walk through the arrivals gate, finally on our way to leaving the airport and meeting Billy's family.

'Ecstatic!' he beams. 'Can't wait to relax in some hot weather. Christmas on the hill has been amazing, but I need some vitamin D! Plus, it'll be nice to just chill out and do nothing with my family.'

'I work you so hard,' I tease, knowing that my words are actually full of truth.

As it was my first Christmas as the owner of Molly's-on-the-Hill, I wanted everything to be just right. Left to me in my old friend Molly's will, I was determined to make sure the shop ran at its best with every mince pie cooked to perfection, every Christmas pudding boozily soaked to the max and festive cheer seeping from every nook and cranny. Having worked in the shop for almost ten years and Molly passing on everything she knew, I think I managed it.

The whole thing was made even more special when Colin asked my mum to marry him in the most surprising and romantic proposal ever in the shop itself (I'd even, unwittingly, been an accomplice to his plans, thanks to him anonymously emailing and asking for my help). They were both still in a giddy bubble when we left them, a state I'm thrilled to see my mum in.

Actually, I'm blooming grateful for the two of them. I'd arranged for Billy and me to go to LA as a surprise Christmas present, but it's only been made possible by them volunteering to step in and run the shop for the two weeks we're away. I'm sure Colin's children, Aaron, who's ten, and Charlotte, who's eight, will lend a helping hand too. They really are the cutest little humans. It's been lovely getting to know them more over the last few months. Funny how easily I've slotted into the role of big sister – I feel so protective of them already.

'I'm just looking forward to having a bit of Sophie May time away from cakes and pretty bunting,' Billy nudges, pulling my thoughts away from my life in Rosefont Hill and all the people I've left behind for two whole weeks.

'And I'm looking forward to having some Billy Buskin time away from all of your fans in the village,' I laugh as we step through the doors and into the arrivals hall.

We're welcomed by the frantic sound of clicking and lights flashing manically as a dozen or so paparazzi surge forward and stick their cameras in our direction.

'Brilliant timing,' winks Billy, his eyes widening as he holds his elbow out for me to grab on to while he pushes our luggage trolley towards the rabble – going through them is our only way out.

'Billy Buskin, what brings you here?' one yells, his camera hiding his face.

'Good to have you back!' says another.

'You here for filming, Billy?' asks a woman, sticking a

dictaphone in his face, clearly hoping for a quote. 'Or is it just for the holidays?'

Billy does nothing but stare ahead, ignoring their calls and questions.

Meanwhile, I try my best not to look baffled and horrified by the whole thing. I'm not one for attention and would much rather blend into the background unnoticed, away from the judgement of others. Although I should have realized there'd be a hubbub waiting for us when we got here. It is, after all, Hollywood – the land of movies.

Above the commotion we hear a shriek and see arms madly waving behind the heads of the photographers. It's only as the paparazzi part (through fear of getting run over by the huge metal trolley Billy's ploughing towards them) that they reveal Billy's family excitedly waving at us. His mother Julie is gripping hold of her husband Clive's arm, her eyes shiny with tears at just the sight of Billy standing metres away from her. Clive nods as his son approaches, his face joyously pinging into the same wonderful smile as Billy's. In fact, looking at the siblings, that's the one facial characteristic they all share – gigantic toothy grins from their big mouths. They're rather infectious.

Billy stops and just stares at them all, echoing their happiness with his own brilliant grin. He visibly relaxes, and his body literally softens from the comfort of being surrounded by family, even though the press are still just a few feet away from us all.

'You're here!' sighs Julie breathlessly, her hand on her heart, her face full of pride and almost disbelief, as though she never thought the day would come when Billy would be back with them.

The twins jump on Billy first. They're identical and unified in their look, both appearing chic in their boho style of floaty clothes, which is complemented by wavy light brown hair cascading over their slim shoulders in perfect symmetry. I imagine they really enjoy getting ready together in the mornings.

Julie and Clive step forward next, with Julie literally bashing the others away to clear the path to her oldest son. Not one thing about her screams 'mum'. Instead, she's elegant, graceful, pampered to perfection and long-limbed. She looks incredible for her age without a single wrinkle on her agelessly smooth, tanned skin and her blonde hair seems so soft in its tousled waves that I experience a sudden urge to touch it. Clive, on the other hand, still looks like a plumber from Surrey with his baggy jeans, light-blue buttoned t-shirt and trainers. A fact that makes me smile, even though I'm sure the whole lot is probably now designer clothing rather than stuff found on the high street. I like the fact that he's still so clearly connected to his roots and is true to the man he was before he came here. It makes me instantly warm to him.

When she's finally in front of him, Julie grabs Billy by both cheeks and pulls her face into his.

'God, I've flipping missed you,' she whispers without even moving her jaw. She then gently pulls his cheeks forward and back in a way I can imagine she's done since he was a young boy – it's incredibly endearing to watch. The whole reunion is enough to bring tears to my eyes.

Billy doesn't share quite the same emotion as me; instead

he pulls a face as though he's embarrassed (something I know he's doing for comic value) and backs away slightly, grimacing at his dad.

'Get used to it,' Clive laughs in response, patting him on the shoulder as he steps forward and gives Billy the manliest of man hugs. Although he too seems unable to stop himself from literally breathing Billy in.

Billy's younger sister Lauren is the first to acknowledge and greet me, not that the omission from the others worries me at all. It's clear they're far too caught up in having Billy back in their company to see the girl standing a few feet from his side. But not Lauren. She doesn't head towards him like the others, instead she flings her arms around me as though we're best friends, her sweet floral perfume tickling my nostrils. I'm usually one for boundaries and keeping my personal space (even my own mum rarely hugs me), but it seems this family are a tactile bunch and that there's going to be a lot of touchy-feely behaviour over the coming weeks. Something I make a mental note to prepare myself for.

Despite the invasion, I instantly like her. Lauren's dark brown eyes twinkle in the same cheeky way Billy's do, although her face is far more delicate and feminine than his. Her nose is thinner and more button-like, her cheeks are rosier and her lips are a wondrously shiny red. Besides the lipstick, she looks as though she's ready to hit the beach at any moment. Not just because she's in sandals but because her white bikini is peeking out beneath her pale denim hotpants and round her neck under her cropped pink vest top. Her dark hair is pulled back into a messy top bun, on top of which sits a pair of black

Ray Ban sunglasses. She looks cool, relaxed, approachable and kind.

'I can't believe you're here,' Lauren sings, hopping from one leg to the other while her arm is still draped around my neck.

'Is this the first time you've met her?' calls out one of the photographers, having overheard and decided we've had long enough to enjoy greeting each other without being interrupted – they've got a job to do, after all.

'Get together and face us. Give us a happy family shot,' another barks in a less than polite manner, as if it's something we're required to do. We're not, although his outburst draws my eye to their attention and the drone coming from the cameras as their shutters close and open at quick speed – a sound that has been so continuous since our arrival that I hadn't even picked up on it.

'No chance,' Lauren says flatly, raising an eyebrow at him before taking me by the hand and pulling me towards the rest of the family so that my back is turned to the photographers and the gathered crowd.

I love her for sensing my discomfort and being a physical shield.

'Sophie,' Julie sighs with a smile as she spots me, her head flopping to one side as she says it. She reaches out an arm and drapes it around me. I'm surprised at the softness of the embrace despite her thin frame. 'Thanks for bringing him back.'

'I think Billy could've booked a flight if he really wanted to see us, Mum,' grins one of the twins who I'm guessing is Hayley simply because her face is ever so slightly fuller than Jenny's – a sneaky tip Billy gave me in telling them apart.

'I feel like we know each other already,' Julie continues, ignoring her daughter who's grinning behind her. She grips hold of my shoulder and gives it a squeeze, her skin remaining flawless as she smiles at me.

'Where's Jay?' Billy asks, looking around past the group and further into the arrivals hall.

'Oh, you noticed,' says Julie, her lips pursing in disdain, clearly hoping Billy wouldn't ask after his youngest sibling who he seemed so excited about seeing.

'Of course. Where is he?' he asks, frowning at her.

'Still in New York,' offers Hayley (the ever-so-slightly chubbier twin), bored of waiting for their mum to spit out his whereabouts.

'What?' asks Billy, his face dropping. 'Why? Didn't he know I was coming?'

I watch as Billy looks more hurt with each question he asks.

'He did, but . . . things are hectic for him there,' Julie reasons, looking at Clive to see if he'll help her explain. He looks down at his trainers as though he's not even a part of the conversation.

'So he's not going to be in LA at all while I'm here?'

'No, he's not,' Julie sighs, before looking back at Billy with (what is clearly) a forced smile, 'You know what it's like – final year of uni while juggling a job. He really wishes he could be here though. Phoned us on the way.'

'Right,' Billy nods, managing to smile back. 'Understandable.'

He might be a world-class actor, but I see the sadness in his eyes at the absence of his little brother and it pains me greatly. I've never heard Billy say anything but sweet things about Jay, so I'm not surprised he's disappointed when he's spent the last few days thinking they were going to be reunited. It's got to sting a bit to know he hasn't made the effort to see him – not that I know anything about his situation.

'Shall we get out of here before it gets crazy?' Lauren asks, breaking the awkward tension that's descended upon us.

I look around and spot two more paparazzi join the crowd with their cameras poised in our direction.

'Yes please!' groans Billy, already pushing the trolley towards the exit.

'I'll get that,' his dad says, taking over and ignoring Billy's protests. 'James is out front waiting.'

'But I drove us kids,' says Jenny, waving around her keys.

'New car?' asks Billy.

'A G-wagon. It's totally awesome,' she grins.

'I bet.'

'You're coming in with James,' Julie says hastily, nodding towards the exit door while giving Billy a warning look. 'You're not getting away from me that quickly, young man.'

'Fair enough,' he shrugs, raising his eyebrows at me. 'See you guys at home, though. Yeah?' he calls after his siblings.

'Yep,' answers Hayley with a grin, before following her twin who's already started floating off through the terminal building towards her brand spanking new car.

'I'm coming with you,' smiles Lauren, jumping ship from the kids' car to the one with her parents and us. It's only when she tugs on my arm excitedly that I realize she's been holding my hand the entire time.

'Who's James?' I whisper to her, not wanting to offend anyone in case I've forgotten the name of an uncle, grand-dad or distant relative that's residing with them over here. I'm pretty sure he doesn't have a relation called James, but it's best to be sure rather than get myself in an awkward situation.

'The driver,' she says simply.

'Oh yes,' I nod, still finding the fact that they have staff hilarious. 'So weird.'

'Everyone has a driver,' says Lauren flatly, her eyebrows knotted, looking confused as to why I might find it an alien concept. Surely she's not forgotten simpler times in England when they didn't have such a luxury. 'Besides, everything's so far apart in LA. You're pretty screwed without a car.'

'I see. Well, I don't drive either,' I admit.

It's just something I never got round to doing. I did think about taking lessons in my early twenties, but then reasoned I could manage without it seeing as I'd coped that long without being able to, anyway.

'No, I have a licence,' Lauren says, looking shocked that I never got mine. 'And I have a car.'

'Oh?' I ask, suddenly feeling embarrassed.

'Yeah, I don't always use James,' she reasons.

'I see . . .'

'We have to share him between the lot of us, you know.'

'You're almost deprived,' I tease.

'Tell me about it,' she grins, pulling my arm so that our shoulders bash together.

Stepping outside the airport I'm hit by a waft of heat as the sunshine bears down on me. The intense warmth is a shock to my body – hardly surprising as it's been in freezing cold England and then on an air-conditioned flight for the last eleven or so hours. But the new warmth instantly soothes my body with a tingling sensation, the vitamin D quickly dispersing along my bare skin and working its magic.

'James,' Billy calls, ignoring the gaggle of photographers who have decided to follow us to the car.

A tall, burly man, dressed in a black suit and white shirt, nods in Billy's direction and opens the door of a huge blacked-out SUV for us all to climb into.

'Sophie, James. James, Sophie,' Billy gestures between the two of us, shaking James's hand before hopping into the car.

'Ma'am,' he growls kindly, nodding his head.

'Hi,' I say, relieved to meet the first person here who isn't going to require a physical greeting to accompany the verbal one we've exchanged.

'Sir, allow me,' James offers, leaving us in the car to help Clive with our luggage. I feel guilty leaving them to it – especially when all I keep thinking about is how hot James must be in his suit in the sunshine. Although having said that, I spend my days fully clothed in front of a piping hot oven while I bake cakes. Working in unbearable heat and keeping a smile on your face is something I know all about.

'I'm so glad you're here,' sings Julie from behind us once we're all in the car and it's silently started rolling off, away from LAX airport and the prying paps.

Unsurprisingly, a few of them hop on to waiting motorbikes and ride alongside us, but as the glass is totally blacked out it's pretty pointless of them. They're probably hoping we're heading somewhere other than Billy's house, which I know is thankfully set back behind gates. Having said that, from what I know of these vultures they'll probably camp outside for the duration of our stay and see what they can sneakily grab through the bushes or as we're coming and going. I don't know how Billy stands it, but he always does so without much of a grumble, and thankfully we've managed to stay fairly secluded back at home and don't feel too watched all the time.

'You OK?' I whisper, running my fingers up his bare forearm, gutted that Jay's absence has put a dampener on our arrival.

He nods and grips my hand before taking it to his lips and kissing the back of it. 'You?'

'Knackered,' I say, smiling at the gesture.

'All that reading,' he grins, looking up at me.

'You have to tell me some good books to read!' Lauren says enthusiastically, leaning into my side and gently nudging me. 'I've been working my way through the *Pretty Little Liars* set but I'm almost at the end of it.'

I love her a little more in that second. Seeing as Billy isn't a reader (he once made himself sit and read all of my favourite classics but has since returned to his former status as a non-reader), I've never really had someone my own age to talk books with.

'Sophie reads proper books, Lozza,' says Billy, rolling his eyes.

'I read proper books too!' she retorts.

'They're a bunch of crap.'

'I bet they're not,' I say, not sure what really qualifies as a 'proper' book – reading is reading after all.

'They're not,' she says, her eyes widening. 'And what would you know? You've not read them.'

'They're based on an MTV show,' he shrugs.

'No they're not!' squeals Lauren. 'The books were written first and then made into a series by ABC. But even then, it's only loosely based on them, anyway. Get it right.'

'OK you two, cut it out,' sighs Julie.

'Tell *her*,' he moans.

'Tell *him*,' she whines.

'Listen to you both,' I find myself cutting in. 'We've only been here for half an hour and already you've regressed into the stereotypical annoying older brother role.'

Billy's mouth drops in surprise at my words.

'You don't have any brothers or sisters, do you?' asks Lauren, instantly calming down, as though a switch has been flicked, and looking amused at my observation.

'No.'

'This is standard behaviour,' she shrugs. 'He winds me up and then I retaliate. Wait until the twins get involved later. There's never a dull moment with us kids around.'

'A constant battle of who can wind the other one up the most,' nods Billy in agreement, the two forgetting their spat as they explain their interesting family dynamic while cheekily grinning at each other.

'You must love each other really,' I say, looking at the pair of them as though they're slightly bonkers and wondering why they can't just be nice.

'Of course they do. Be lost without one another,' says Julie for them, calling over from the seat behind us.

'Oh totally,' nods Billy, looking across me to Lauren and pulling a silly face. 'She's just so annoying.'

'Ditto,' she replies, rolling her eyes before leaning back and looking out the window. 'God, it's good to have you back!' she mutters.

I lean my head on Billy's shoulder and squeeze my arm around his, drawing it into my body, so thrilled to be here with him in the comfort of his family who clearly love him as much as I do – even if they have an interesting way of showing it.

3

We seem to be driving for ages. Not that I mind, as it's lovely to look out and get a grasp on Los Angeles and where Billy's family lives. It's huge, just like the car we're sitting in, and seems to just carry on for miles without any clear definition of which neighbourhood we're in. It all seamlessly merges, although some areas are clearly nicer than others. As I'd hoped, there are palm trees everywhere – even on the side of the motorway (sorry, freeway). LA appears to be mostly flat, although peeping up from the horizon in almost every direction are huge mountains.

'The Hollywood sign!' I gasp when I catch a glimpse of the iconic landmark sitting up high in the Hollywood hills.

'Yep,' says Billy, grinning at me and pulling me in for a kiss.

'Bizarre to think of that as your normal,' I say out loud to the rest of the car once he's released me. It might be old-fashioned, but I can't help but feel weird about having a PDA in front of Billy's parents. I know we're both adults and free to do as we please, but as this is the first time he has taken me home to meet his parents, I feel a rigidness overcome me and my cheeks flush, making me squirm like an awkward teenager. Hugs are fine, but kissing? Eek!

Billy clearly notices my apprehension as he has a little

chuckle to himself and softly places a hand on top of mine, patting it gently.

'Yeah . . . you know what,' Lauren replies to my earlier comment, thoughtfully staring out of the window. 'I hardly even notice it's there any more.'

'Same here,' says Clive in the back, who's stayed silent during the rest of the journey while everyone else has been nattering away. I have a feeling that (besides Billy), the women lead the majority of conversations in this family and that the guys just fill in the gaps or dive in whenever they can. 'You know what it's like, you see something every day and it's difficult not to take it for granted.'

'Forget its beauty,' agrees Julie with a sigh.

'That's sad,' I say.

'I still feel the magic, though,' Julie adds quickly, as though not wanting us to think she's bored of being over there. 'It's brilliant out here. Waking up every day with the sun shining and blue skies above – hard not to get excited about that.'

'Don't miss the rain at all,' mutters Lauren, subconsciously pulling on her halter-neck bikini strap.

'I'm telling you, Sophie. Within a day or two you'll be planning on moving out here yourself,' says Julie, reaching over the seat and touching my shoulder.

I laugh and give a little shift in my seat.

'I wouldn't be so sure about that one, Mum,' smiles Billy, winking at me when I look up at him. 'You've never experienced the magic of Rosefont Hill.'

'Yes. Well . . .' Julie replies shortly, removing her hand. 'It's great that you've decided to have your work hiatus in such a magical setting.'

'Just like you then, Mum,' retorts Lauren.

A silence I can't decipher falls over all of us. Doing my best not to overanalyse the moment, I continue to look out the front window. Turning right on to a road called Vermont Avenue we're greeted with what looks more like a high street, with a post office, independent coffee shop (not just another Starbucks – of which I've spotted loads since landing) and even a little book shop which I can't help but twist my head to get a better view of.

'Trust you to sniff that out,' Billy whispers in my ear, making me smile.

Two minutes later the car starts travelling uphill along a winding road. We go higher and higher, past a row of houses with their cars parked outside, and continue to climb. When James slows the car down and waits for some electric gates to open, I'm surprised at the modest appearance of the white-painted home that I can see in the distance, up another steep incline. Not that I thought Billy would be living in some blinged-up mansion, but it's a little smaller than I'd expected. In fact, now that I think of it, none of the houses on the way up here screamed out in the overly flashy manner that I've come to imagine when thinking of LA, but I guess that's because we're not over in Beverly Hills, the residential Mecca for Hollywood's rich and famous.

Billy grins at me excitedly. 'What do you think?' he asks, once we've pulled up outside and have started getting out of the car.

'It looks lovely.'

'Wait until you see inside,' grins Lauren, walking past us and opening the huge wooden front door and heading inside.

'I'll just grab my suitcase,' I start to say, turning to the boot of the car before noticing that James has already removed them and is currently taking them through the garage.

'After you,' Billy smiles, holding his arm out towards the house and waving me inside.

Walking in, I realize I was completely wrong about the house being small and discreet. It's actually a flaming TARDIS! Seriously, it's huge. I suddenly feel like Kate Winslet in *The Holiday* when she arrives at Cameron Diaz's mammoth home and can't quite believe her luck, a comparison that makes me feel extremely giddy.

Although Billy's home might appear to be single storey from the front, you actually walk down a swooping staircase into the main section of the building and the space opens up dramatically into a huge living area which leads to further rooms. The size of this room alone is not far off that of the entire floorplan of the childhood home that I still live in with Mum and Billy, and that's no exaggeration. But, just like Billy's amazing flat in Hyde Park, it's been decorated in a way that makes it homely and inviting – just with an extra bit of something to make your jaw drop as soon as you walk in.

Exposed brick lines the room, adorned with photographs of the family throughout the years (almost the exact same collection that I've seen in Billy's flat but with additions from newer adventures). Chunky and earthy wooden beams run beneath my feet, but it's not any sort of wooden flooring (and certainly nothing like the kind Mum and I bought from our local DIY store a few years back to lay in the kitchen). No, this actually looks like it's come directly from a forest – it's perfectly rugged with every ridge and knot visible, giving it far more depth and beauty. Plush gold and cream sofas gather in a group around a charcoal black-and-biscuit-coloured tapestry rug, on top of which is a coffee table, made of glass and sculptured fanned wood (it looks more like a piece of art than a safe place to rest a mug of tea). Nevertheless, this luxurious area calls to be sat in, especially as it faces out to the main feature of the room – a never-ending black-framed window that stretches along an entire wall, giving the most amazing view of the city spread out in the distance.

Walking towards it to get a closer look, I spot the swimming pool below and spy Lauren already stripped down to her white bikini sitting on a nearby sun lounger, talking animatedly on her phone. She really was itching to get back out there as soon as she could.

'What do you think?' asks Billy from behind me.

'Wow,' I breathe, looking back up to the impressive skyline. 'Just wow.'

'Indeed,' laughs Julie, walking past us and heading off into one of the adjoining rooms, which I'm guessing is where everyone congregates if they're not sprawled out next to the pool.

'I can see exactly why your family like it here,' I admit.

'If I'm honest I forgot how incredible it all is,' he laughs, putting his arm around my waist as he stands beside me and looks out in awe.

'Have you missed it?' I ask, feeling a lump forming in my throat as I wait for his answer, not wanting to hear that he has and hoping he's not suddenly found himself regretting falling into the modest life he has with me.

'Ask me that again at the end of our stay . . .' he says, looking down and winking at me, kissing the top of my head.

I close my eyes and take comfort from his warmth. We're a team, that's something I never find myself doubting any more.

'Come see my room.'

I can't help but laugh.

'What?'

'We might live together but hearing you say that in your parents' home suddenly makes me feel like a naughty teenager doing something wrong.'

'Oh really?' he asks, raising his eyebrows at me as a cheeky sparkle lights up the brown of his eyes. 'Is this going to be a problem?'

'No!' I giggle.

'Good, because it's my house. I own it,' he growls playfully, tugging on my arm and pulling me through the lounge towards the hallway, which has another sweeping staircase leading down towards the bedrooms. Unfortunately the doors are all shut, meaning I can't have a snoop, but the hallway is grand enough. Textured cream wallpaper with flecks of gold covers the walls and half a dozen pieces of artwork are hanging proudly. Down here, it's all London themed. London buses, red telephone boxes, Big Ben, Buckingham Palace, The London Eye – even the British flag, all painted in vibrant, bold colours to show them off in their optimum glory.

'God, I've heard about these pieces,' Billy sighs, stopping to look at the painting of the London bus. The bus itself is in focus, but it's been painted as though it's in motion with the lights of Piccadilly Circus and the crowds of people on the streets blurred and streaked around its sharp structure. 'Mum had an art dealer come to the house. She phoned me up delirious about this collection, saying it made her feel like she had a part of our old home here in LA.'

'That's sweet.'

'Not really,' he scoffs with a little eye roll. 'We've never lived in London as a family, I've never been on a red bus or made a call in a red telephone box.'

'You've not lived!' I exclaim, thinking of the trips me, Mum and Dad used to make when I was a child into Trafalgar Square, and the fact that there's still a red telephone box in Rosefont Hill that I'd continued to use until I finally got my first mobile phone a couple of years ago.

'That's something coming from Sophie May,' Billy laughs at me, giving my elbow a gentle nudge with his.

'Exactly!'

'Come on,' Billy says, moving away from the offending paintings and towards the end of the hallway. He opens the last door and takes a deep, satisfied breath as he walks inside with a smile spreading across his face, clearly happy with the room he's finally reunited with.

And I'm not surprised.

Billy's room is ridiculous. Actually, it's not a room, it's basically a flat minus a kitchen with two beaten-up tanned leather sofas creating a lounge area in front of a television, a walk-in wardrobe where his clothes have all been divided into different categories using fancy lighting, an en-suite bathroom that's triple the size of our single family one at home (complete with two sinks, a hot tub and multi-headed shower), and the biggest four-poster bed I've ever seen.

Seriously, it's huge! I'm surprised not to see more of Billy's personality stamped into the décor, but I guess the majority of his stuff would have been moved to his London flat. Instead, the minimalist cream, gold and black theme from the rest of the house continues throughout.

Although the room doesn't need much to be viewed as incredible, the best bit is the two entire walls that mirror the main feature in the lounge upstairs. Floor-to-ceiling windows allow us to get another glimpse of the astounding city view, as well as some glorious greenery to one side, which I'm guessing is Griffith Park as we saw lots of signs for it as we were driven up here.

'Seriously?' I ask, looking around in awe and comparing it to my own tiny, pink bedroom. 'Are you joking?'

'Epic, right?'

'Well, I'm glad you're not trying to play it down.'

'It is just a house, though,' he says.

'A flipping amazing house.'

'Yes.'

'And you have a driver,' I remind him with a smile, James popping into my head.

'James has been with us since my *Halo* days,' he shrugs. 'Dee has only been with us since we moved in here though.'

'Dee?'

'His wife.'

'Of course, the housekeeper,' I say, remembering that they live in a modern version of *Downton Abbey*. I puff out my cheeks and exhale loudly. 'This is another world.'

'You know, it's not. Don't think of it in any other terms than my family and our home. It's no different to the bricks and mortar that make up your house.'

'Slightly more exuberant maybe . . . fancier materials.'

'Maybe,' he smiles, looking bashful, before throwing himself on to his bed and kicking off his shoes.

'But don't you feel weird about having strangers in your home?' I ask, scrambling next to him and sighing as my head melts into the insanely soft feather pillows beneath me. It's as though I've literally climbed on to a cloud.

'They're actually like family,' Billy states. 'They even come over for Christmas dinner.'

'Oh . . . really?' I ask, surprised at how personal it sounds. 'I guess it's just a set up I'm not used to.'

'It might seem odd to you, but it works,' he says, pulling himself up on one elbow and leaning next to me, his fingertips gently stroking the bare skin on my forearm. 'It means my mum is chilled out over here and not spending her days cleaning up after the lot of us when she could be out enjoying herself in the sunshine. Life's too short for that and she did enough of it back in Surrey. It's my way of giving back after they all changed their lives for me.'

'Fair point,' I say, smiling up at him. 'It's great how everyone has really embraced living here. They all look so happy.'

'Exactly – and nothing matters more in life than making those we love as happy as possible,' he says, his head lowering, allowing him to place his lips on mine, his kiss gently pulling me closer into him.

'I couldn't agree more,' I sigh. 'It's a shame about Jay.'

'Tell me about it,' he says, shaking his head in disbelief. 'I'm surprised he's not here, but it's no big deal.'

'You sure?' I ask, wanting Billy to know he can open up.

'Absolutely. This is going to be a fun trip,' he whispers.

'It is!' I agree as my tummy gives a little unexpected somersault.

'Good. Glad you think so, too,' he says, shifting slightly away and looking directly into my eyes. 'Promise to just enjoy it for what it is? Don't go throwing weird meanings on to things or overthinking anything.'

'As if I'd ever do that,' I smirk, making him laugh.

'Live for now and enjoy it,' he says, coming closer, his nose nuzzling against my cheek. 'And don't forget to talk to me if anything freaks you out.'

'Like what?'

'I don't know. Just anything.'

'I will,' I say, wishing I could willingly stop my analytic self comparing our different worlds, and hating the fact the Billy knows exactly how my complex brain works. So what if his family lives in a mansion with a driver and housekeeper; that doesn't actually change anything. We're all just humans at the end of the day, milling around in an attempt to do the best we can at this thing called life, right?

'I just need to settle,' I admit quietly.

'OK,' he says, giving me another kiss, although this time it lingers a little longer and his hand creeps slowly up my thigh, his thumb slipping under the hem of my top and running along my skin.

'Billy Buskin,' I start with a giggle, slapping his hand. 'We can't . . .'

'Not my parents' house,' he purrs with a grin, eagerly diving over me to lock the bedroom door before bouncing back on to the bed and resuming his position. His lips move to my neck. His gentle, barely-there kisses quickly make my head light with pleasure, as a tingling sensation speeds through my body and instantly throws out all thoughts that aren't to do with Billy's mouth.

I push him off me, my body following his as I straddle my legs either side of him, giving my hips a little playful wiggle, making Billy smile, his eyes sparkling at me as a hungry look flashes across his face.

'Don't try telling me you weren't even tempted by the mile high club,' he murmurs, licking his lips, his hands grabbing hold of my bum.

A giggle escapes from my mouth as I pull my t-shirt up over my head and swiftly unhook my bra.

4

My eyes are heavy and my head is groggy as I force myself out of sleep. Daylight is flooding through the windows, telling me I shouldn't be snoozing, that I should be up and awake. Yes, it's the middle of the day, no matter how much my body wants to protest against that fact and would love to cosily drift back to my dreams.

I know I shouldn't have napped. So many people warned me to stay up and live on LA-time straight upon landing so that my body adjusts quicker. That was what I'd intended to do, so I don't even know how it happened.

I'm surprised Billy didn't wake me.

Saying that, I feel so knackered still that I'm sure I'll sleep through tonight anyway. Well, as long as jetlag doesn't chase me down to steal my dreaming hours: I need the sleep.

I sit up and painfully force myself out of Billy's comfortable bed with a groan as I wonder where he's gone. Throwing my discarded t-shirt back on, I take a proper look around his amazing room. It feels so surreal to be here in this lavish home, mostly because I know Billy to be incredibly grounded, down to earth and not in the least bit superficial. The character profile that I have on him doesn't fit this house, but that's not necessarily a bad thing. It just shows that he's unaffected by the wealth of Hollywood. And I completely agree with what Billy said, it's just a bunch of bricks and cement . . . a bunch of bricks and cement that (once I push my worries aside) I'm going to love staying in for two whole weeks.

Hearing a noise outside, I go to the window and look out to the pool. Splashing about are Billy and Lauren. I watch as they wrestle in the water and challenge each other to swim underneath for as long as possible without catching a breath. There are some games you're never too old for.

I must have been watching for five minutes, totally absorbed in their fun when Billy spots me and waves frantically, beckoning me to join them.

I hold my hands out to the side and shrug, reminding him that I've no idea how to get out there and watch as Lauren hops out of the pool, grabs a towel and heads towards the house. Clearly coming to get me.

Leaving the window, it occurs to me that I also have no idea where my suitcase full of clothes is, but quickly spot a pair of my well-worn jeans hanging in the dressing room along with the rest of my clothes which have been expertly hung up and displayed in a perfectly organized fashion. I don't know when Dee managed it, but I'm surprised when it sends a flurry of excitement through me. Perhaps Billy's right. Just being able to exist and enjoy life might be quite lovely. Although, when I spot my knickers all neatly folded and piled up I do experience a slight knot in my stomach at the thought of someone else handling them and spotting the embarrassing holes and faded colours of them all. I've been meaning to get some more but it's been so chaotic with the shop and the run-up to Christmas that I just haven't had a chance. Having said that, I should probably ditch the lot and buy something a bit nicer for Billy to look at anyway – though he doesn't usually seem at all interested in what's covering up the bits he wants to get to. They're just a hindrance to him that he can't tear off quickly enough.

Funnily enough, our relationship never used to be this sexual, but it seems to have ramped up a gear since he made his big move to be with me, which I hope isn't just down to the boredom of village life. I wouldn't say I've ever thought of myself as an overtly sexual person – in fact, quite the opposite. Yet having someone actually want me in that way while being in a loving relationship is something I've only ever had with Billy. Not that I was a virgin before he came along, but what I'd previously experienced was nothing compared to what we have now, something I realize more and more with the wonderful thing called hindsight.

Grabbing my blue polka-dot swimsuit from the drawer, I whip off my top, quickly step into the leg holes and start pulling it up. I've lifted it just as far as my knees when the door flings open.

'You're awake!' Lauren sings, bursting into the room without a single knock or ounce of warning. I'd stupidly assumed it was still locked.

'Whoa,' I yelp in shock and yank the stretchy material upwards, getting flustered as it gets stuck over my butt. Hastily trying to cover up my naked body, my face flushes instantly bright red as I turn into a sweaty panicking mess.

Lauren, however, doesn't bat an eyelid as she continues into the room and throws herself on the bed, even though she's still dripping wet. In fact, she's totally unbothered by the fact that she's seen my naked breasts, bush and bum (I stupidly turned around while covering myself up, meaning she's caught a glimpse of the triple whammy). Lauren's indifference must be the result of having two older sisters. Needless to say, my upbringing as an only child who shied away from any sort of human interaction and a mother who had her own demons to deal with means I'm absolutely horrified and not at all aloof about being found so incredibly naked by anyone other than Billy.

'Great swimsuit,' Lauren praises.

'M&S,' I mumble, tying the straps in a knot behind my neck and turning back round to face her.

'Killer body, too,' she says with a grin, looking me up and down.

'Thanks,' I blush, making a mental note to make sure the door is locked any time I'm changing in future, while wrapping myself in the white robe I spot folded on top of a chest of drawers.

'How do you eat all those cakes and still have a figure like that? I only have to look at a cupcake and I've already gained ten pounds. I'm seriously contemplating gluing my eyes shut – think it's for the best.'

The way she delivers her comment with such flippancy makes me laugh. She's funny. Naturally so. Plus, she still manages to give off this friendly, chilled-out energy even though she's seen me butt naked.

'I don't eat loads of cakes – I just bake them,' I admit, pulling my fingers through the knots in my hair and tying it back into a ponytail.

'How can you cook but not eat them? That's ridiculous.'

I laugh. 'Don't get me wrong, I do have days where I

just sit and scoff, but those days are few and far between . . . and usually instigated by Billy.'

'I bet,' she tuts, rolling her eyes at the thought. 'You have to make us some while you're here. Billy says your cakes are amazing.'

'Well, he does love his cake.'

'He's got such a sweet tooth.'

'He does,' I smile, thinking back to when he first came into the shop and ordered a slice of lemon drizzle cake. 'Well, I'll make you something. Is it OK to use the kitchen, though?'

'What do you mean?'

'Will Dee mind me going in there and using it?' I ask, not wanting to step on anyone's toes.

'You've not met her yet, have you?'

'No.'

'She's the sweetest little thing ever. Completely goes with the flow and doesn't get het up about anything. Anyway, it's *our* kitchen. We're not barred from it. It's our home. Believe it or not we're allowed to go in and help ourselves whenever we like, too. We don't even need to ask,' she might be being sarcastic, but it's enough to get her point across – which is the same as Billy's. They're not living in some upstairs-downstairs arrangement like in all the classic books I read (which is possibly why I've been resistant about the whole set up). This is modern-day service, where everyone is considered a human and can integrate on a personal level.

'That's good to hear.'

'Come on,' she says, shuffling herself off the bed and towards the bedroom door whilst pinging the waistband of her bikini bottoms (it seems to be a habit of hers). 'Grab your sun cream. You might have a body to be envious of, but that lily-white skin is going to burn quickly if you're not careful.'

I take her warning on board, while managing to stop myself from blushing at her compliment, and grab my sunglasses and a bottle of SPF50. Better to be safe than sorry, I can't remember the last time my body saw sunlight.

'You're awake, finally,' shouts Billy when we walk out of the double doors on the ground floor and into the swimming pool area. Like the rest of the house, it's seriously beautiful. The pool itself goes right up to the edge of the garden and seems to just stop, giving a lovely contrast between the calm, tranquil water and the busy-looking city ahead. White sun loungers and umbrellas huddle around the water's edge on cream stone flooring, and to the left, on a huge wooden decking area, is a barbeque, bar and more cosy seating space, all surrounded by pretty pink, purple and red flowers. Dipped into the decked area, towards the front, is a hot tub that bubbles away and still manages to look inviting even though it's a scorcher of a day.

'I can't believe you let me sleep!' I say to Billy, dropping my sunglasses case on a sunbed and squirting some cream on my hand before rubbing it into my legs, the sun's piercing heat on my back and shoulders reminding me that it really is a necessity.

Lauren wastes no time in getting back into the pool. Stretching her arms along its edge, she leans back and faces her head towards the light. She looks like a Hollywood film star.

'You looked too cute to wake up,' Billy says, his smile growing as he squints up at me, looking ridiculously handsome in the glow of the Californian sunshine.

'Pass me a bucket,' mocks Lauren, pretending to be sick in her hands as she waves them in front of her mouth. The spell of glamour breaks.

'I'll give you a bucket,' replies a grinning Billy, bouncing through the water and grabbing hold of her foot. He tugs on it, causing her to let go of the side and her face to dunk into the pool.

She splutters and wipes the water from her face, then quickly retaliates by jumping on his back and forcing him under the surface.

I gasp, thinking they're being too rough with each other (Lauren's a girl, after all and extremely dainty compared to Billy) but clearly I'm the only one that thinks so as the two eventually come up for air, cackling with laughter.

'You're such a git,' Lauren shouts, scooping a handful of water in his direction.

'You asked for it,' splashes Billy, running his hand along his face and wiping the water off with a flick, before shaking his fingers through his hair and sweeping it all back out of his eyes. 'Coming in?' he asks me.

'Not if you're going to do that to me,' I warn, unwrapping myself from the dressing gown and dropping it next to me.

When I glance back, Billy is looking at me with a cheeky smirk.

I squint at him against the glare of the water, as I gently nibble on my bottom lip.

He takes a deep breath and dives under again, completing a couple of laps before coming back up for air. He's laughing when he wipes the water from his eyes, unable to wipe the saucy expression from his face.

'I've booked a table at Little Dom's for dinner,' calls Julie a few minutes later, peering out from one of the windows above. 'That OK with everyone?'

'We've got an event we're going to,' says Hayley, coming out of the house with Jenny in tow, each of them having changed into matching floaty kaftans that sparkle and blow gently in the LA breeze.

'Tough,' barks Julie, not missing a beat. 'Your brother has just got back.'

'What's the point in asking if it's OK with us if you're going to tell us we're coming anyway?' retorts Hayley, her hands on her hips as she swivels around to look up at her mum with an eyebrow raised.

'Just being polite,' Julie smarms back, letting her oldest daughter know that it's non-negotiable. She might be outnumbered by her offspring, but she's certainly still in charge and the boss of the household. 'Table's booked for seven,' she calls out to the rest of us. 'Didn't want to do anything too late as I guessed you two would be jetlagged.'

'Thanks Mum,' calls Billy.

'Can we go out afterwards?' asks Jenny with an innocent little shrug, her eyes glancing over to Hayley with hope. It's clear that these two have a very close bond, but that they also have a good cop/bad cop thing going on. One fights mean, the other treads softly afterwards and restores order. I can't help but wonder how that makes Lauren feel. She's not privy to their exclusive twin gang and surely that must get lonely.

'Only if Billy doesn't mind,' Julie replies, her head ducking back indoors.

Both the girls' heads swivel round to look at Billy with wide imploring eyes.

'Of course I don't mind,' he laughs. 'I'm going to be eating for England though, so don't expect to be going anywhere fast,' he teases, pulling himself up on to the pool's ladder and out of the water.

'Erm, dad bod,' scoffs Hayley, looking him up and down.

'Erm, what bod?' he snorts, rolling his eyes as he heads over to me. He grabs a neatly folded black towel from one of the sunbeds and shakes it out before wrapping it around his waist, looking uncomfortable at the scrutiny his body is receiving.

'You've been away far too long,' she retorts with a raise of the eyebrow and a practised pout of her lips.

'It's when male actors relax and gain a bit of squidge,' Jenny clarifies as the duo perch on adjacent sun loungers in the shade. 'Somewhere between a six pack and a beer belly,' she continues.

'I do not have a beer belly,' mutters Billy, clearly offended.

'No, guys with dad bods don't have beer bellies,' shrugs Hayley, as if her comment is meant to be far from the insult it was delivered as.

'Don't fight it – it's fashionable, big bro,' laughs Lauren from the other side of us, picking up a magazine and flicking through its pages.

'Can't wait for a bit of Little Dom's. It's been ages,' Billy shrugs, choosing to sidestep the topic as he unwraps his towel to expose his body once more, proudly standing with his hands on his hips and, in my eyes, looking pretty darn perfect.

'Meatballs?' asks Lauren, knowingly.

'Of course.'

'Yuck. How can you do that to your bodies?' asks Hayley with disgust.

'They're both on a gluten, meat, sugar, everything-that-tastes-good free diet. Like most girls in LA,' Lauren whispers to me with a smirk.

'We heard that,' says Jenny, looking put out.

I'm just about to start some small talk and move the conversation on to something away from food and body type when I feel Billy's arms squeeze around my waist before lifting me up and waddling the pair of us over to the pool.

'Billy, what are you doing? Put me down!' I shriek through laughter, just as Billy steps from the edge and our bodies splash into the cool water. 'It's bloody freezing,' I gasp as I come back up for air and push my hair out of my face.

'You'll get used to it,' Billy laughs.

He's right. The more I kick and move around the less my body shivers at the chill around me. In fact, it's actually not that cold, just a lot colder than being sat on a sun lounger in the sunshine.

Still holding on to my waist, Billy pulls me closer to him and guides us to the furthest part of the pool so that we're facing the gorgeous city skyline and away from the house and his family.

'I'm so glad you're here,' he whispers, kissing my wet shoulder. 'Sod doing this without you.'

'You said it was all sibling teasing,' I say, leaning my head lightly on his.

'Yeah, but too much of this and I'll end up with a head-ache,' he laughs, straightening his head while giving it a little shake. 'I'd forgotten what it's like.'

'What?'

'Being with my loving family,' he says, throwing his head back and letting out a big laugh.

I smile at the sound, loving the warmth of it.

'Bloody dad bod,' he huffs.

We perch there with our arms resting on the side of the pool, quietly looking out at the busy city below and enjoying the peace around us. We're up here in paradise and I'd be lying if I didn't say I'm loving every second of it – even the spikiness of family dynamics. It beats growing up in a household of despair and misery. At least they had family members to wind up. I was left with only one member and I was too scared to even talk to her in case she broke.

But this?

This is much more pleasant.

5

Dinner is amazing. Little Dom's is incredible. I've never been to Italy, but this restaurant is like being given a chunk of it. The smells, the tastes, the friendly waiters with their thick Italian accents and bushy moustaches, it all feels authentic, cosy and inviting. I love it.

As soon as we sit down, an array of goodness is carried out to the table on direct orders from the chef. Having heard Billy is back in town, they're clearly bending over backwards to give their VIP guest extra special service. They politely fuss and ensure we have everything we could possibly want and more. Likewise, the guests in the restaurant all show Billy a spot of love too: 'welcome back' drinks are discreetly sent over, business cards are exchanged and friendly conversations shared. It feels as though a bubble of excitement surrounds Billy – something I'm not used to seeing back in Rosefont Hill, where he's largely managed to blend in with the locals. This feels alien to me, but I can't help but smile at the friendliness of it all.

The chatter between the Buskin family seems to have simmered down and is a lot calmer and more enjoyable too. For a start, the twins are in much higher spirits (even though they've sat and watched everyone but Julie eat plates of delicious meatballs) and no one appears to be trying to wind anyone up. It's lovely.

'So what do you want to do while you're here, Sophie?' asks Clive, who has managed to splatter tomato sauce everywhere, decorating his white shirt in bright red freckles (much to Julie's dismay). Not that he seems at all fussed – he's far too laidback to worry about how he might look.

'Oh, I haven't really thought about it. Just get to know you lot,' I smile sheepishly, looking back down at my plate, while kicking myself for feeling shy around Billy's family.

'That's it?' asks Jenny, screwing up her face in dismay. 'We're fairly boring.'

'That's fine by me,' I shrug, realizing they're probably all aware that I'm not the wildest girl Billy's brought home to meet them.

'There must be something you want to see. The Hills, Rodeo Drive, Venice Beach? The Walk of Fame?' suggests Julie, listing the various tourist sites with her fingers.

'Or there's Disneyland?' shrugs Lauren.

'Oh, yes!' says Julie, seeming surprised she hadn't thought of it before.

'I thought Disney was in Florida,' I say.

'This is the original one,' nods Julie, eagerly.

'It's magical,' adds Lauren.

'Aren't you a bit too old for all that?' asks Hayley grumpily.

'Disney is for all us dreamers in the world who believe anything can happen . . .' smiles Lauren.

Hayley raises an eyebrow in response but remains quiet, clearly biting her tongue.

'It's a wonderful place,' declares Julie, siding with her youngest daughter.

'You hate it there,' Billy exclaims, looking at his mum as though she's gone mad.

'No, I don't!' she gasps. 'I used to hate going there with five screaming children who all wanted to go in different directions, but me and your dad dip in every now and then and take in the atmosphere . . . it's really quite magical watching people's faces light up in wonder.'

'That's so sweet,' I say, imagining the two of them wandering hand in hand in front of the iconic castle.

'Vom,' says Jenny, unable to stop one side of her mouth rising into a smile.

'I always wanted to go to Disney in Paris when I was younger, but . . .' I stop, realizing the reason we didn't end up going on the holiday that so many children dream of was because my dad died. I look at the people I've only just properly met with my mouth wide open, pausing mid sentence. '. . . but we never got around to it,' I mumble into my glass, hoping my discomfort hasn't resonated too loudly among the group.

From the silence that's descended on this usually chatty bunch I guess they've managed to fill the void of my sentence for themselves anyway. These days everyone knows my heart-breaking past thanks to it being used as a piece of idle gossip in the tabloid papers last year. It's common knowledge now. Just an incidental fact about the girl Billy Buskin is dating.

'Billy!' we hear someone shout across the restaurant, thankfully deflecting the attention from my awkwardness. I look up to see a grey-haired man in his late fifties striding over to our table, his face pink and jolly, clearly excited to be bumping into Billy.

'Richard,' Billy smiles, standing up briefly to shake the man's hand. 'How are you?'

'I'm good, buddy,' he says, gently patting Billy's arm as he smiles at the rest of the table. 'I heard you were coming home for the holidays.'

'Well, here I am,' Billy laughs. 'This is Sophie,' he adds, placing a comforting hand on my knee. It's a gesture that, I'm guessing, is either to do with me never getting to Disney or to reassure me that he doesn't see LA as home, that part of him is now fiercely loyal to Rosefont Hill. Either way it's soothing.

'Of course,' Richard replies, smiling at me and throwing a friendly wink in my direction. 'Pleasure to meet you, Sophie.'

'You too,' I smile back.

'And you know everyone else.'

'Sure do. Julie, Clive, not so kiddy kids,' he says, nodding his way around the table with a warm grin. 'It's been too long folks. The studio's not the same without you guys.'

'Richard was exec producer for *Halo*,' Lauren says in my ear, making the situation a little clearer. Basically, he's one of the bigwigs in film.

'Any chance we can tempt you back any time soon? I'm working on some great projects.'

'You always are,' Billy praises back with a laugh, clearly attempting to bat the conversation away.

'True, but you'd be perfect for one of them . . . it's a guaranteed smash,' he teases, smirking at Billy as he tries to suss out his reaction.

'He's having a little break,' calls Julie from across the

table, waving her hands at Richard, as though telling him not to bother Billy right now.

'A break, Julie? What's that?' Richard laughs, slapping Billy on the back. 'You just be sure to give me a call when you're well rested.'

'I will,' Billy nods, tapping Richard's elbow.

'Well, I'd better get going, my wife is going to be wondering where I've got to. But I'll see you in a couple of days. We can catch up then,' he says with a nod, before leaving us as we were.

Billy throws his mum a questioning look.

'Oh I know you said you didn't want a fuss made of you being here but I thought, seeing as it's New Year, it would be nice to have a party. Nothing big and fancy, mind. Just something small and chilled.'

'You don't do small and chilled,' says Billy flatly.

'He's got you there, Mum,' agrees Hayley, stifling a giggle.

'Remember the low-key party she threw for our eighteenth?' asks Jenny, causing the other kids to laugh at the memory.

'Or the relaxed Christmas dinner where she ended up inviting fifty people over to join us for our intimate family gathering?' chimes in Lauren, her expression wide and disbelieving.

'Let's face it, there doesn't even have to be an occasion . . .' adds Hayley innocently, raising an eyebrow in Julie's direction. 'One of us could have simply put the trash out and she'd be there ready to celebrate the mammoth event.'

'Oi!' Julie reprimands them lightly, though not disagreeing. She turns to Billy, her expression softening at once. 'At least this way you'll get to see everyone in one go. Then you can spend the rest of your holiday in whatever way you wish . . . Oh, Billy, I'm just so excited to have you here. Please let me just do this one thing?' she pleads.

'Fine,' Billy says, shaking his head at her, but unable to stop himself from smiling, clearly quite happy that a fuss is being made of him.

'Sounds lovely,' I offer, realizing that the last New Year's Eve party I went to was the one Molly and I threw in the shop. I'm not usually keen on celebrating New Year's Eve, especially as I feel the whole night is based on the unrealistic promise of new beginnings, but it was lovely to be surrounded by great people. Obviously, I won't really know people here aside from Billy's immediate family, but Billy will, and it'll be nice to understand his Hollywood life a little bit better. No doubt Billy will be the centre of attention, and that'll give me time to work out the lie of the land while blending into the background, something I've always prided myself on being rather good at. 'I'll have to do some baking for it,' I offer, knowing that I'll love being hidden in the kitchen in the build up.

'Yes!' hisses Lauren gleefully.

'Dee will love that,' says Julie, looking extremely pleased that I'm up for the get together, making me wonder how much she knows of me being a borderline recluse. 'Dee's a great cook but English desserts are just not her forté.'

'You'll have to teach her,' suggests Clive.

'You'll have to tell me your favourites,' I beam back at them both, thrilled that my offer has been accepted so warmly and that I'm able to do something for them in return for having me to stay.

Billy squeezes my leg under the table, which I take as a sign that this meeting with his parents is going well. Which is always good.

A little later, as we exit the restaurant and head towards James, who's sitting across the road in the car, a homeless man walks by. His skin is thick with wrinkles, and heavily tanned from the California sun. His grubby jeans and brown check shirt hang off his bony frame, and a structure made of tinfoil sits on his head. He taps at it while talking to himself in an animated fashion, as though he's communicating with some extra-terrestrial life form.

When he spots us looking at him he shares a big toothless grin.

'Evening, folks,' he sings, as he continues on his way, stopping by the rubbish bin and peering inside to see if there's anything of value he can take, or possibly even looking for food.

It's heart-breaking to watch, but I can't take my eyes off him even though I know I shouldn't stare and I'm being rude.

My attention is pulled by someone jumping out in front of us with a camera held up to their face, followed by the sound of repetitive clicking and the flashing of light. I'm disorientated momentarily and freeze to the spot, unsure what to do.

Billy's hand finds mine and pulls me towards him, reminding my legs how to function as he casually continues walking towards James.

The flash of the camera keeps bursting bright light through the car as we all get in and put on our seatbelts, but it fades behind us as we pull away and head towards the safety of the house.

During that five-minute car ride no one references the incident with the paparazzo. There's not a tut, or a hint of annoyance at the lack of privacy. There's not even a joke made about the ordeal.

But I guess it's different for them. This is the life they lead. To them it's mundane and commonplace, whereas to me it's invasive and horrific. Especially when pounced on from the darkness without any warning . . .

6

When I wake up the following morning I feel as though I'm dreaming. I experience a moment or two of confusion when I'm not entirely sure where I am, but when I roll over and see Billy, everything falls into place.

'You up?' he mumbles, his head turning towards me.

'Yeah. You?'

'No, I'm talking to you in my sleep,' he chuckles, rolling over and placing a heavy arm around my waist.

'This bed is amazing,' I sigh, closing my eyes and enjoying the way my body has sunk into it.

'It's a good bed,' he agrees.

'It's an amazing house, too.'

'A long way from our three-bed place in Surrey,' he laughs, his hand circling my bare skin. 'Not sure how that happened.'

'Because you're talented,' I say, throwing one of my legs over his and moving closer to his chest, getting in there for a little snuggle.

'Because I'm *lucky*,' he says, a disgruntled frown line forming between his eyes.

'Because you work hard,' I smile, poking him in the ribs, not at all surprised to hear he's not giving himself the credit he deserves.

'Look, I'm not one of those actors who's going to pretend their job is draining and demanding,' he says, raising his eyebrows at me. 'Yeah, all right, we have to put in long hours for a few months of the year while filming and then travel around doing press junkets, but we're not doctors. We're not saving or sparing lives on a daily basis. We put on other people's clothes and we play around. When you put it into perspective like that, you've got to look at this place and laugh. It's madness. Why on earth do I get this when some homeless man has to sleep rough on a park bench? Or in a shop doorway that he'll eventually get shooed from? It doesn't make sense.'

'God . . . it's awful, isn't it,' I say sadly, my thoughts going back to the homeless man the previous night. I'd almost forgotten about him thanks to the paparazzo's intrusion.

'Doesn't really fit the image of palm trees and sunshine that comes with the place, does it?' Billy asks with a hint of sarcasm.

'I guess not. The pap thing was a bit freaky, too,' I say, feeling my chest tighten as I bring it up.

'Have you forgotten what it was like in London?'

'I don't remember it being like that.'

Thinking back, I'm sure there were only a handful of times we were caught out on the street (the worst being when I was walking along in my *Coffee Matters* uniform), or without us even knowing (like when our relationship was global news thanks to us having an innocent kiss goodbye outside the shop).

'You're forgetting because we've been cocooned in Rosefont Hill for so long,' he frowns. 'But yeah, I guess LA can be a bit heavier . . . You OK, though?'

'Yes. Yeah. Completely.'

I'm not sure what makes me lie and act as though I'm totally unperturbed by the whole thing. Billy is usually so good at sensing when things make me feel panicky that I rarely have to explain myself . . . although, actually, our tougher times as a couple have come from our different viewpoints on what is socially acceptable. I hope we're not about to encounter something similar with our different outlooks on life here.

'Just part and parcel of being in LA. That's what makes it crazy and enthralling,' he shrugs, making my heart sink. 'Breakfast?'

'Yes, please,' I say, my voice an octave higher than normal. I instantly leap out of bed and pull on a little blue summer dress, my head not wanting to ponder too heavily on what we are each willing to consider as normal.

'Have you seen the pile of stuff upstairs?' asks Hayley, after briefly knocking on the door and walking in wearing gym gear. The slight blush in her cheeks suggests she's been doing some kind of workout – I look more exhausted, bedraggled and puffed out after my simple walk to work each morning.

'What is it?' asks Billy, putting on a t-shirt.

'Flowers, baskets, boxes – all addressed to you. It's in the kitchen,' she says, lingering in the doorway.

'Must've arrived when we were out last night,' Billy says to himself.

'We were both so exhausted when we got back. We literally came in here and collapsed immediately,' I say to Hayley, suddenly feeling like I really want her to like me.

'We're heading up now,' Billy says, leading us all out of the room and up the stairs.

'The press are having a field day, too,' she says, her eyes wide with excitement.

'Really?' I ask.

'You've both caused quite a stir,' she laughs, clearly enjoying telling us what she knows. 'There are the obvious rumours that Billy's back for work, that you two have secretly organized to get married here – plus, one website is claiming you're up the duff and have come to break the news to Mum and Dad.'

'Nice,' I mumble, my heart instantly feeling heavy and deflated. Even though I know it's all nonsense, I hate people talking about me. I always have. I thought it was bad enough being in a tiny village back home where everyone likes to have a little whisper here and there, but there's something about papers and journalists writing about us that's even worse. They don't know me, yet they're clearly willing to write complete rubbish to sell papers or get people clicking on to their website. It's horrible.

'All a load of crap,' Billy shrugs, seemingly unbothered. But then, he's used to being in the tabloids every day – and not always for good reasons.

'Wait until you see what's in there,' Jenny calls out as we pass her in the hallway. She's also in her gym gear (of course they would have worked out together) but she's stretching out her legs while bending her body in half.

We all walk into the kitchen to find the central island overflowing with bunches of flowers, baskets of food (muffins, brownies and a couple with healthier alternatives like fruit – although they're naturally accompanied by a top-of-the-range juicer), bags of designer clothes, boxes of gadgets, cards, invites and letters . . . it's like a crazy version of Christmas Day. Utterly bonkers.

'Who on earth sent all of this?' I ask in shock.

'Anyone who's seen the news and knows Billy's back,' laughs Hayley. 'People in the industry wanting to welcome him home and suck up. Plus, if he is about to get married, they'll be wondering where their invite is.'

'The clothes will be from PRs hoping Billy will be spotted out wearing something of theirs,' says Jenny, grabbing a lemon from one of the baskets, slicing it on a marble chopping board and putting some into a glass. 'They know he'll get papped loads here.'

'It's madness,' laughs Billy, looking both impressed and embarrassed at the lavish gifts sitting in front of us.

'You also have invites from nearly every exclusive restaurant, bar and club in the city,' Hayley says, looking delighted at the stir his return has created.

'Have you been snooping?' questions Billy.

'As if you're going to sit here and open everything,' she scoffs, raising an eyebrow at him.

'You're more likely to get Dee to sift through it all and send it off to charity,' says Jenny.

'Such a Good Samaritan,' Hayley laughs, leaving me undecided as to whether she actually thinks it's a good idea or not.

'Jeez,' mutters Lauren as she sleepily enters the room wearing a crinkled long baggy t-shirt that barely covers her knickers, her hair dishevelled and last night's make-up smudged across her face. 'Is it someone's birthday?'

'Billy's back,' shrugs Hayley matter-of-factly, as she and Jenny saunter out of the room.

Lauren rolls her eyes at us, a huff escaping her body. 'Have you seen the photos from yesterday?'

'No, and we won't be looking,' tuts Billy, walking past his abundance of gifts and heading to the fridge.

'Well, those two are flipping loving it. Anyone would think they were the megastars the way they play up to the cameras. But then, they are the Buskin twins,' she says, with a hint of jealousy lining her sarcasm. 'Happy to coast on the wave of their little brother's success.'

'That's not nice,' says Billy feebly, while continuing to nose about the fridge's contents.

'Just frustrates me,' she sighs, looking a little hurt that Billy's not backing her up in her quest for a little bitch about their older siblings.

Having brothers and sisters seems far harder than I'd ever imagined . . .

7

It takes a few days for me to completely unwind and relax. Probably because the busyness of the festive season wore me out before flying over here, and since we landed there's been the added worry about my unfamiliar surroundings, the stress of meeting Billy's family and anxiety over feeling so on display by Billy's side. I just wanted a nice holiday with my boyfriend . . .

If I'm honest, nothing much has changed. I still feel knackered from the jetlag, desperate to impress the Buskins and judged by the press. But now, sitting on a plush blue sun lounger on a gorgeously remote beach in Malibu, in a red polka-dot bikini with my hair wrapped in a matching scarf, it's hard to let anything other than happiness tingle its way over my skin. Some of what's been weighing me down evaporates, and a feeling of contentment washes over me instead.

It's heavenly.

I actually can't remember the last time I sat on a beach and did this. Maybe I never have. But, perhaps, as my shoulders loosen and my body melts into the calmness, this should be something I do more often. Well, certainly allow myself a break now and then, in any case.

'You looking forward to getting back into the kitchen tomorrow?' asks Billy, who's sat forwards on his sun lounger, watching the waves break and crash into foamy nothingness.

'Of course I am,' I grin.

'You can take the girl out of the teashop, but you can't take the teashop out of the girl,' he laughs, glancing over at me.

'Exactly,' I smile back, proud that my love for the shop is so ingrained in my being. 'What about you? Looking forward to your party?'

Billy rolls his eyes as though dreading it.

'Don't give me that!' I laugh. 'I'm the shy and retiring one. You're the people person.'

'Do I have to be?'

'It's what you were born to do,' I grin.

'I'm not so sure . . . I'm out of practice.'

'Don't you think it's funny that your mum's not even hiding the fact that she's throwing it especially for you?' I ask, aware that I've heard Billy's name mentioned a million times over the last few days.

'She's not really,' he laughs, squinting back at me. 'You heard the others – any excuse. I'm just providing the latest reason for her to be the hostess with the mostest. It's not really about me. Just a chance for her to get out the posh crystal glasses that have been gathering dust.'

'Right . . .'

'Like we said, it's not going to be a small gathering,' he says adamantly, toying with his sunglasses between his fingers before putting them on. The dark lenses make him look every inch the Hollywood star who's known by millions of teenage girls around the world. 'Knowing Mum, she'll want to turn it into the party of a lifetime. One that people will be telling their friends about.'

'Really? Why?'

'This is LA. Being talked about for the right reasons is extremely important.'

'Right . . .' I say, aware the calm feeling I'd finally welcomed is rapidly seeping away from me.

'It'll be lovely though. Just not small. Think big and fancy, then you won't be too surprised.'

'Well, I'm not sure how a Victoria sponge cake will sit within all that grandeur.'

'Who cares? I'm going to love it!' he exclaims as a waiter comes over with our lunch – two buckets of crispy fried calamari and chips. A complete over-indulgence on our behalf, but we are on holiday, and it is still Christmas . . . so we keep telling ourselves, anyway.

'Your mum is so excited about it,' I say, munching on a hot, salty chip, as an image of matriarch Julie carrying around a mammoth 'to-do' list in a notepad flickers across my memory from earlier.

She's a lady on a mission.

Ever since Richard spilled the beans (we'd probably still be kept in the dark if it wasn't for him), she's been ticking off every minute detail from her list and barking out orders to get the things that aren't done sorted.

The poor staff.

'She loves a party,' Billy grins, shoving food into his mouth before wiping his hands on a blue cotton napkin.

'Perhaps we should've stayed and helped?' I say.

'And done what? We'd have got in the way,' Billy shrugs, clearly thankful not to be a part of the whirlwind his mum is creating. 'Besides, you're doing your bit tomorrow.'

'You're helping, too,' I frown.

'Of course,' he smiles, reaching over and placing a reassuring hand on my calf.

Having met Dee, I know that she's every bit as lovely as Billy described her. The curvaceous and pint-sized Filipino lady is extremely friendly, hardworking and bubbly. So far I've not heard her complain once about the millions of extra chores being passed over to her. If anything, she seems to thrive on the chaos that Julie brings her way.

I'm looking forward to showing her a few recipes, knowing that'll she'll pick them up with ease, but I'd still like Billy to be there with me in the kitchen that I don't know – even if it's just to pass me baking trays or to find the baking powder and butter.

'Are you having fun?' Billy asks over the top of his glasses. 'Do you like LA?'

'Of course I do. It's impossible not to enjoy the sun, the food and meeting your family,' I say, sticking a ring of calamari into my mouth.

'They can be overpowering.'

'They're great,' I say, although tempted to completely agree with him.

'That too,' he smirks.

'Do you think they'd ever move back?'

'To England?' he asks with surprise, even though it's a topic he must have thought about before, having spent the last few years apart. 'Maybe kicking and screaming,' he laughs.

'They certainly seem nicely settled,' I agree with a nod, picking up a lemon chunk and squeezing it over the top of my lunch.

'I think Mum's the one who'd find moving back most

difficult. It's not even that she's settled here, but her life is so hugely different.'

'The staff?'

'No!' Billy laughs. 'Well, in part. She's just got no stress. No responsibility. Sometimes I'm not sure if what I did for them is a blessing or not. Fancy placing someone on a permanent vacation. I think I'd go mad.'

'Excuse me?' asks a young girl in an orange bikini, flanked by a younger boy who could possibly be her sibling. Her eyes widen when Billy looks up at her, clearly nervous now she's dragged his attention away from his lunch. 'Sorry to interrupt your food, but can we grab a quick selfie with you?'

'Sure,' Billy smiles happily, wiping his hands on the napkin and jumping off his sunbed as though it's not an inconvenience at all, even though we're halfway through a conversation and eating our lunch.

The two youngsters are gone within seconds, but their coming over seems to have sparked the interest of other sunbathers who'd previously been unaware of Billy's presence amongst them. They are now peering across at us over their phones, or through their dark sunglasses as though trying to be inconspicuous. Maybe they're deciding whether it's actually him, making judgements on what he looks like in the flesh or wondering whether to come over.

A few do. All pleasant and lovely people, of course, but our cosy day for two on the beach quickly turns into Billy being surrounded by a dozen or so other sunbathers. I still find it completely odd, unable to marry together the public perception of Billy with the man I love. Back home,

Billy can walk through Rosefont Hill with ease, but over here he's watched like an animal in a zoo. What an odd way to live. Not that he seems to mind. Despite his protests, it's clear that part of Billy enjoys the attention. Not in a big-headed way, of course, he simply exudes a humble warmth that draws people to him and makes him instantly likeable. And that's what makes him wonderful.

He doesn't really complain about this side of fame. He takes it all with a pinch of salt. I, on the other hand, am the one who finds it all alarmingly scary.

We quickly finish our lunch and decide to head to the privacy of his home.

8

'Now, I can make a bed in ten seconds flat, I can polish silver so hard you'll be able to see your reflection in it for weeks – but one thing I cannot do is make those pesky English cakes,' Dee declares in her thick accent while grinning widely and welcoming me into the kitchen.

It's the morning of New Year's Eve and before the chaos reaches its peak, Dee, Billy and I have gathered to whip up some treats for the party, while teaching Dee how to make a few home comforts for the Buskin family in the process.

'There's nothing to worry about, Dee. It's easy. Even Billy can do it,' I say, nodding in his direction as he climbs up on to a bar stool and sits at the kitchen counter.

'Him?' Dee shrieks, letting out a howl of laughter at the thought of it.

'Hidden talents, Dee,' he grins, looking pretty impressed with himself.

'I'd say,' she nods, wiping a rogue tear from her eye. Clearly the thought of Billy baking is too much for her, a fact I can't help feeling some pride in. It's nice to know he's picked up the surprising skill because of meeting me.

'I got all the ingredients you said we'd need,' Dee says, motioning over to the kitchen side where flour, sugar, fruit and all sorts of colourings and flavourings have been piled.

'Looks perfect,' I say, walking over and inspecting the products in American packaging I don't recognize.

'I don't know why you're so scared of baking,' says Billy, shaking his head at her.

'I'm not scared now I know you can do it,' she retorts with a grin, looking back at me expectantly, letting me know she's ready.

'We'll start with Billy's favourite,' I say, pulling out a few packets of different ingredients and moving them over to where they're waiting.

'Lemon drizzle,' Billy says, licking his lips as he nudges a glass bowl and a set of electric scales in my direction.

We bake for hours – churning out a bakewell tart, Victoria sponge, Eccles cakes, custard tarts, a rich fruit cake, marbled mint and chocolate cake and two dozen classic Chelsea buns. We even make up a batch of Molly's signature scones, which will be nicely displayed with a variety of English jams and clotted creams that have been flown in especially for the occasion – highly excessive for my liking, but no one else seems to think so.

It's a mammoth baking session, with me talking Dee through all the tiny but significant methods that could have led to her previous baking disasters. For instance, the importance of lining a tin, pre-baking your pastry when cooking tarts (no soggy bottoms here) and the necessity of finely cutting fruit into smaller pieces to encourage even distribution throughout a sponge.

I'm in my element. For the first time since being here I feel as though I have a purpose and that I know what I'm talking about. I don't feel lost or nervous. If anything, I revel at being the one in charge. I love it. Although it does make me miss my little spot behind the counter in the shop more than ever . . .

'You know the hardest part?' Dee asks, while checking on the scones in the oven for the millionth time and eyeing up the finished treats on the side.

'What?' I ask, drying up a washed baking tin (I wasn't going to leave her with all the mess too).

'Not being able to eat them. Not for my own greed, I assure you, but just to check they're ready and taste good.'

'You'll just have to make sure you try it all later,' I tell her.

'I'll be a bit too busy to eat cake,' Dee tuts, glancing again at the oven.

'You're off tonight, surely?' asks Billy.

'Oh,' Dee says, waving her hands about as though it's no problem. 'I'm not officially on duty, but you never can trust these people they have in. Agency staff,' she says with horror. 'I like to have an eye on them and keep them on their toes.'

'Well, just as long as you get some time to celebrate too,' Billy frowns, clearly unhappy with the idea of Dee not being able to let her hair down for the night.

'I will, Billy,' she winks, highlighting the fact that the relationship they share is more than the removed one usually seen between staff and employer. It's far friendlier, and makes me warm towards her even more.

'What's that smell?' asks Hayley, floating into the kitchen with her nose curled up in disgust.

'Nothing for you, that's for sure,' smirks Billy as Dee breaks away from us to put away some of the used ingredients.

'There is going to be food for me and Jenny too though, right?' Hayley fires back, her hand finding its way to her hip in a fierce attitude.

'Have I ever left you to starve before?' asks Dee, with saintly patience.

Before I can interrupt and say that we've actually made them a couple of everything-free cakes, Hayley shoots Dee a damning look before turning on her heels and walking out the door.

'Whoa,' Billy whispers, echoing my thoughts. 'What's her problem?'

'She's hungry,' Dee replies flatly, clearly used to being spoken to like that.

I'm nervous as I get ready for the allegedly small and intimate gathering (that's actually going to be a gigantic party containing nearly everyone Billy and the Buskins know in LA).

I decide to go for a simple dress and heels combo, all items that I brought along with me from home. Lauren did offer to take me out for a bit of a shop on Rodeo Drive to see if I fancied buying anything new, but as none of the people here (aside from Billy) have seen me in the burnt orange knee-length dress that I have with me, I decided there wasn't much point in splashing out unnecessarily. I certainly didn't fancy having a *Pretty Woman* moment while being laughed out of some fancy designer shop. That said, knowing that all the other women in the household have purchased something new has left me slightly worried that my outfit might not be up to scratch. Still, there's not much I can do about that now – and, besides,

I'm still scrubbed up compared to my normal appearance. There's not a speck of flour on me anywhere, a clear improvement.

'Oh, I love you in that,' Billy says, coming out of the bathroom amidst a waft of his aftershave – a gorgeously musky and woody aroma that never fails to linger on my clothes and body long after he's left a room.

'Is it right for tonight?' I ask, feeling insecure about my choice as I run my hands over my hips and back up my stomach.

'It's perfect. Just like you,' he grins, taking my hands and leaning down to give me a kiss.

'Smooth talker,' I laugh, enjoying his praise and getting to have him all to myself for a moment.

The kids weren't lying when they said Julie doesn't know the meaning of a small gathering. The huge main lounge area is already rammed when Billy and I walk in ten minutes later. An arrival that doesn't go unnoticed thanks to Julie shouting out, 'Here he is,' as soon as she spots us.

The room stops momentarily and everyone looks across, all eyes on us as we venture towards a waitress with a tray of champagne flutes and help ourselves. Billy turns and raises his glass to the crowd before taking a gulp. In response, they continue to natter and mingle, merrier now they know the promised VIP guest has arrived.

'It would be really helpful if you could explain the butterflies in my stomach,' Billy mutters in my ear, while smiling and nodding at someone who's caught his eye across the room.

'Welcome to my world,' I grin back, taking hold of his

hand and firmly squeezing it. It's unusual for me to be the most composed but, bizarrely, knowing Billy is nervous makes me feel more confident. I even feel my spine straighten a touch in response.

'I don't know how you cope,' Billy grunts.

'Sometimes I don't . . . but a simple panic attack should get you out of the situation,' I joke, knowing my words will make him smile.

They do.

He grins into his glass before taking another swig. 'Knew it was all an act.'

'You're just out of practice,' I remind him.

'I miss Rosefont,' he whispers, causing me to beam proudly over the fact that my little village has captured his heart so much.

I put my arm through his and clutch hold of it.

'Billy!' says a guy about our age, holding his arms out wide, scooping towards him for an embrace. His hair has been entirely shaved from his head, although the majority of his face is extremely hairy with a thick dark beard covering it.

Billy looks at him for a second before reacting, as though he isn't able to place him straight away. 'Johnny Trew! Dude, it's been ages,' he booms in the guy's direction, the wide cheeky grin on his face telling me he's clearly pleased to see him.

'Tell me about it, man,' Johnny says in a thick Kiwi accent, wrapping his arms around Billy's shoulders for a hug before turning to me with a little nod, wink and mischievous grin – an expression that I've seen Billy wear a million times.

'What's this?' Billy laughs, grabbing hold of his beard and giving it a little tug.

'For a movie I'm shooting. Pretty far out, hey?' he says, his fingers running along it to check it's smoothed down, or perhaps it's a new habit he's picked up to accompany the facial hair.

'I'd say,' Billy says, shaking his head at the thick wiry mass. 'You look bonkers.'

'My poor wife and kids had to sit through Christmas dinner with me looking like this.'

'Hopefully it won't scar them too much,' Billy chuckles, placing an arm around my waist. 'This is Sophie. Sophie, this is Johnny – the craziest and most ridiculously talented actor in Hollywood.'

'Only 'cause you ain't on the scene right now, mate,' he smiles, shrugging off the compliment before reaching over and giving me a kiss on the cheek. 'Pleasure to meet you and nice to see I'm not the only settled heart-throb around,' he jokes.

'With kids, without kids – you'll always be my pin-up,' chuckles Billy, before turning to me. 'We shot a little independent film together years ago. I don't think it's one you'd have seen. Not really your sort of thing. It's about a gang of FBI agents gone AWOL. Lots of swearing and guns.'

'Nice,' I laugh, knowing it's certainly not the sort of film me and Mum would have sat on the sofa and watched together as we munched on a takeaway on a cosy Friday night in.

'You've not made her watch that one yet, then?' Johnny asks Billy, looking confused at his omission. 'I always used to whip out the back catalogue on a first date. Worked a total charm with the females every time,' he says, unable to contain his laughter.

'No wonder you bagged Cherise,' nods Billy with a grin, tucking into a mini canapé that he's just grabbed from a beautifully designed golden tray carried by one of the waiters. The room smells delicious.

'Exactly!' Johnny laughs. 'One glimpse of me in a cop's outfit and that was it. Done deal. Think it helped that I took my kit off in it too. I had great abs back then. Remember, mate?'

'I still dream about them,' jokes Billy.

'I take it you didn't actually show her your back catalogue, then?' I ask, deadpan, as though I'm in need of clarification.

'Of course not!' Johnny says, looking at me as though I've lost the plot.

I grin back and enjoy watching him figure out I was only playing.

'Ah, you Brits and your humour!' he laughs, wiping tears from his eyes.

'She got you there,' Billy smiles, winking at me.

I feel oddly triumphant at cracking a joke and making one of Billy's friends laugh. It instantly makes me feel cool and with it, a feeling I'm not at all used to. I'm much more accustomed to being on the outside and not having the foggiest what or who anyone's talking about.

'So what's the scoop, big man?' Johnny asks, clamping a hand on Billy's shoulder whilst looking around the room like he's an undercover investigator. He raises a questioning eyebrow at him.

'What do you mean?' Billy smirks, patting him on the back.

'What's new? What are you doing back here?' Johnny asks quietly, almost conspiratorially.

'It's Christmas.'

'Yeah, but you're here, there's a party . . .' he says, his voice trailing off.

'Yeah?' Billy replies, raising an eyebrow at his friend and encouraging him to finish his sentence.

'I figured you were going to announce you're ready to hit the scene again, you know?' Johnny says, looking confused as he glances around the room. 'I'm only here to see first-hand whether I'm going to be out of work next year or not. The Mrs sent me along especially – I'm to be home with a full report within the hour.'

'It's only been a few months!' Billy laughs. 'I'm enjoying the quiet life for now.'

'For now . . . I like that,' he smiles, nodding at the pair of us while looking a little relieved. 'Well, Cherise will be pleased,' he winks. 'Shame I'm heading back up to Canada in a couple of days, otherwise it would've been great to catch up properly.'

'I know, I've not seen the kids in so long . . .' Billy comments, looking genuinely gutted that he's missing them.

'Mate, they've grown so much since you saw them in London!'

'I bet.'

'How old are they?' I ask.

'Jasmine is four, she's the oldest, and little Noah is one and a half.' He pulls out his iPhone and brings up an image of a beautiful smiling woman with dark brown corkscrew hair (I'm guessing she's Cherise), awash in sunshine with her arms draped around the shoulders of two adorable dark-haired children. The girl is wearing a pink tutu and wellies and has her face pressed up against her mother's, while Noah, the little boy, is grinning at the camera and holding out a fluffy brown teddy bear. It's such a loving photo. They all look incredibly happy and picture perfect.

'They're so cute,' I gush, peering closer at the screen. 'Still babies, really.'

'You say that, but as soon as they're out of the Babygro stage the Mrs is on about expanding the brood.'

'Already?' asks Billy, his eyes wide.

'I'm telling ya, mate, they're addictive little mites.' Johnny shoots an infectious grin at the pair of us.

I like him. Like Billy, Johnny gives off this energy that's endearing, intriguing and electric. Their auras are so inviting and charismatic. I momentarily find myself wondering whether all successful Hollywood actors are like them, but then remember Heidi Black (Billy's bitch of an ex) and decide it must be quite a mixed bag. Nonetheless, it appeases my worrying heart to know Billy has good influences over here and that there are great people mixed in with the madness.

9

We manage to talk to Johnny Trew for a good half hour before we're interrupted. I'm amazed it didn't happen sooner, although I assume everyone is just warming themselves up and letting the drinks flow first, knowing that Billy will be available to pounce on all night.

We're just about to head over to grab a bite to eat from the buffet table, looking for something more substantial than the delicate canapés, when Richard stops us.

'Billy, Sophie!' he says, his arms open wide to engulf the two of us at once. I'm surprised to be included in the warm welcome but am chuffed that he's remembered my name. 'Great to see you both again. I'd love you to meet Ralph,' he says, his hand moving backwards to find the shoulder of the man he was standing alongside just moments before. 'He's working with me on the new project I was telling you about. You've heard of Ralph Joplin, I take it?'

'Of course I have,' Billy gushes, as the willowy frame of a clean-shaven, crisp yet tortured looking soul steps forward, holding out a hand for Billy to shake before offering it to me.

While this is happening, I glance over Richard's shoulder and spot Julie with another group of guests, although she's not paying them any real attention. It's clear she's focused on watching the encounter from over the top of her champagne flute instead. Her eyes are squinting, as though she's desperate to know what's going on. Despite not knowing, the sides of her lips curl up ever so slightly – something I notice with interest. When she spots me looking at her, that expression broadens into a grin before she turns and answers a question the lady to her left has asked.

'It's such a pleasure to meet you,' says Billy, grinning at Richard and Ralph, while looking a little caught off guard. 'I actually watched *Deserted* on the way over here, didn't I, Sophie? Couldn't stop banging on about it,' he laughs, without needing me to verify anything.

It doesn't take me long to put the pieces of the puzzle together. Ralph's the director of the moment. The one with the Oscar. No wonder Billy seems so in awe of the weathered-looking stranger. Funnily enough, I've never really seen this side of my unflappable partner, usually it's him sending others into a flap.

'What a film,' Richard nods, looking pleased with himself as he glances between the two men.

'So, you're directing Richard's next project?' Billy asks, swallowing a gulp of liquid from his glass (straight after it's been refilled by a waiter), clearly eager to find out more now that the seed of intrigue has been well and truly planted.

'That I am,' says Ralph, giving Richard a respectful nod. 'You'll have heard nothing about it yet as we've kept a lot of it under wraps, but it's the only project I've felt this hungry and crazy for since *Deserted*.'

'Really?' Billy asks, clearly drawn in deeper.

'Totally. I've just got this feeling under my skin that

won't go away . . . it's so intoxicating it keeps me up at night.'

'Explains those dark bags under your eyes,' Richard says above a whisper, whilst nudging me on the arm.

'Quite,' sighs Ralph, drawing his hand up over his forehead and running his fingers through his unruly hair. 'I don't think you'll be complaining about them when people are congratulating you on the best film you've ever produced, though.'

'That's what you'll find over here, Sophie. Everyone is just far too modest,' laughs Richard, unable to hide the excitement from his own face.

'Welcome to Hollywood,' Ralph fires back, his eyebrows slightly raised. 'But unlike some, I'm not promising a load of hot air,' he says to Richard, not caring that me and Billy are watching them, listening to their every word. If anything, it goads him on further. 'This isn't just going to be a film that gets a few heads turning. It's going to be the film of the century. The highlight of both of our careers.'

'And I thought it was my job to sell it. Looks like you're doing OK with that one yourself. Wouldn't you say so?' Richard asks Billy.

'I'd say . . .' Billy agrees, his head bobbing up and down eagerly. 'You've certainly got me interested.'

A pregnant silence hangs over our little group as I get the impression Billy has said exactly what the two men wanted to hear.

Richard glances around the room, winking at a few familiar faces, Ralph stares into his empty glass before a waiter approaches to refill it with fresh bubbles, and Billy seems in a total daze. I just stare at the three of them, wondering what's going to be said next, my mind starting to predict where the conversation is leading and already feeling nervous over its outcome.

'How are you finding England?' Ralph asks, surprising me by abruptly changing the subject.

'Beautiful as ever,' Billy beams, winking at me. 'It's home.'

'Nowhere like England at Christmas time. So pictur-esque,' says Richard, his eyes widening in delight. 'Spent many Christmases there with relatives growing up – mince pies, lots of holly and mountains of snow.'

'Sadly, there was no snow this year, though,' I chime in, enjoying his fond description.

'Shame,' says Ralph, smiling kindly at me. There's another pause. With an audible intake of breath he turns to Billy in what can only be described as a 'drum roll' moment. 'You know, we've been trying to get hold of you for quite some time.'

'Really?' Billy replies, unable to hide his delight.

'Eesh, I told you, the kid's not interested,' Richard says with a frown as he rolls his eyes for Billy's benefit and waves his hand around as though getting Ralph to back off.

It's a gesture I, sadly, don't believe as it's practically identical to what we saw Julie do to Richard the first night we met him. But Billy laps it up anyway – keen to hear more.

'I didn't know that. I don't actually have a manager at the moment,' he shares, making me think back to his smarmy ex-manager Paul, who used to permanently undermine me and make me feel like utter crap. The worst bit was that it was usually done with a smile and Billy used to think he was nothing but nice. In fact, he idolized the horrible man.

Thankfully for me, Paul showed his true colours to Billy when he put his foot down about a few things he was trying to make him do career-wise, like continue filming with his ex, Heidi Black, who very nearly tore us apart by setting Billy up and selling a story on their fake reconciliation to the press. It still makes me fume just thinking about it. During that turbulent time, Paul threw some pretty big verbal grenades that I'm glad to say were unforgivable, thus ending their working relationship and thankfully removing Paul from our lives.

'I split from Paul a few months back,' shrugs Billy, still unable to hide the hurt from his eyes. I know how highly he values trust in the people he works with and it's clear to see he's still affected by the betrayal.

'Oh, we knew you weren't with him any longer. Must say, I was quite pleased about that one – he was a nightmare to negotiate with,' says Richard, slowly shaking his head. 'I mean, I know you deserve the best, but what a terror.'

'We contacted your agent, though,' Ralph says, glancing at Richard to check what he's saying is right and to move the conversation away from bad-mouthing Paul – quite right, as I'm guessing it's always better to err on the side of caution in the entertainment business. You never know who's going to be the next flavour of the month, or who someone's going to be relaying your words to.

'I've told my agent not to contact me,' Billy reveals.

'So I heard,' Ralph says, raising his eyebrows. 'Multiple times.'

'Now *they* are a loyal bunch,' approves Richard. 'Nothing I said would make them budge and pick up the bloody phone to you. Annoying for us, but great for you lapping up the quiet life with Sophie . . .'

'I guess I was quite firm about wanting time off,' Billy laughs, looking a bit sheepish.

'Well, I didn't have your English number, so I ended up doing the obvious thing and phoned your mother!' grins Richard.

'My mum?' asks Billy, looking confused as he glances over at her.

Julie is in a throng of yet another group of people, playing the role of hostess brilliantly as she makes her guests giggle at some tale she's sharing.

'She didn't say anything . . .' Billy continues.

'Of course not. She reiterated your agent's stance on things and said you weren't to be bothered,' Richard winks.

'Right,' nods Billy. 'And then she invited you over here tonight?'

Richard shrugs, unable to remove the grin from his face. 'We're old mates. New Year should always be spent with the mates that you want to carry through with you into the next year. Metaphorically and literally.'

'Look, I'm not expecting you to drop everything without knowing more,' says Ralph, taking control of the conversation while holding his hands to his chest in an earnest manner. 'I've left a script with your housekeeper. Take a look and give me a call when you're done.'

Despite knowing he's been ambushed and that tonight has probably all been a ruse to make this meeting occur, Billy seems flattered as he shakes his head with a smile.

'No pressure,' says Richard, patting him on the back. 'Just read it.'

'I will,' Billy promises.

'You too, Sophie,' suggests Ralph.

'Oh?'

'Why not? It's always good to keep everyone in the loop. I think you'd be a good ally,' he smiles kindly. 'Right, we should be off,' he says, clapping his hands together and widening his eyes at Richard.

'Already?' asks Billy.

'You're not staying for the countdown?' I ask, sure that it's the most important part of New Year's Eve.

'Afraid not,' smiles Ralph without explanation.

'You don't want us overstaying our welcome. Everyone else will do that,' adds Richard, raising an eyebrow at the rest of the room in a knowing way.

'Very true,' Billy laughs.

After several handshakes and hugs the two leave us in the middle of the party to mull over what's been said.

Billy looks utterly bewildered.

'Did that actually just happen?' he sighs.

'I think so,' I say, biting my lip.

'Madness,' he nods. 'I don't know what to make of it all.'

I find myself giving Billy a pensive smile – pensive because I don't really know how to digest the previous conversation either. We've both become so used to our cosy little life in Rosefont Hill, even though it's only been a few months. It's mindboggling to think that one little conversation with someone who's practically a stranger could turn that on its head and potentially completely change the life we've been living. Obviously, we don't know any of the facts about the project, like where it's being filmed or how long it could take, and Billy hasn't even read the script yet (he could hate it), but the prospect of there being something on the horizon that could alter our lives so dramatically is . . . unsettling.

Before either of us manages to digest what could potentially lie before us, we're accosted by a new group of people – this time friends of Julie and Clive. Thoughts of the conversation get pushed to the backs of our minds for the time being. Although I do notice that Billy seems brighter than he did at the start of the night. He seems more confident, and happier to be there, as though someone has just switched on a light within him and given him a confidence boost.

As though someone has just given him purpose and belief.

The night whizzes by as we bounce from conversation to conversation and greet everyone who's come along to join in the celebrations. Unsurprisingly, the Buskin clan seem to be rather good at mingling. I watch as each of them work the room and schmooze their way around. Julie is clearly a pro at hosting parties like these and looks more radiant than ever, the twins stay side by side, elegantly floating in and out of conversations, and Clive just seems happy to have a cold bottle of beer in his hand and talk to whoever he ends up next to.

The only one who seems slightly less interested in keeping it up for the whole night is Lauren. Julie has allowed her to ask her own friends along, so she doesn't overly bother with the rest of the guests after a polite amount of mingling early on. I find myself rather jealous when I spot her curled up in a corner with a couple of mates, nursing a glass of wine while looking out at the glorious view of the city that's lit up below. Being chilled and on the periphery of a party is far more me (actually, not being at a party at all is far more me).

Before we know it our glasses are being topped up yet again, and little plastic party poppers (the sort I remember from when I was growing up, although a bit more bling and upmarket) are being thrust into our hands, getting us ready for the countdown.

'Everyone got some bubbles?' calls out Julie, looking like she's had her fair share of them already.

Clive puts his arm gently around his wife's waist and pulls her into him, kissing the top of her head as she giggles like one of the girls.

Their intimacy makes me think of my own mum and dad as an image of them doing the same many years ago flashes before me. My dad might be gone, but he's certainly not forgotten. Just like with Molly, thoughts of him pop up when I least expect them – catching me off guard but warming my heart at the same time, ensuring that he still lives on despite his absence.

I find myself wondering what Mum is up to right that second. Probably snuggled up in bed with Colin, thanks to the time difference. She usually wouldn't be too fussed about seeing the New Year in, but I know the pair of them promised Aaron and Charlotte that they could stay up and have a proper midnight feast with the mountains of treats left over from Christmas (Colin went overboard buying the goodies). I've no doubt they've remained in their magical cocoon since getting engaged too, still giddy with the promises the new year is bringing with it.

'You know what Richard said earlier?' Billy asks, draping an arm across my shoulder and rubbing the tip of his nose against my loose hair.

'Which bit?' I ask, my insides suddenly lurching forwards in suspense.

'About New Year?' he whispers, kissing my cheek. 'And spending it with people you want to take through with you into the year ahead?'

'It was something like that,' I laugh softly, feeling relieved that the conversation isn't going elsewhere.

'Well, I'm going to have you by my side every single New Year from now on – because I don't want a single year to go by without you in it.'

'Year?' I ask, raising an eyebrow at him. 'So as long as you see me once every year you'll be happy?'

'Month, week, day, hour, minute, second – I want them all to be spent with you, baby . . .' he whispers, his hand moving to tilt my chin upwards so that his lips can find mine. 'You're my forever Sophie May. My always. I'll be happy as long as I have you by my side.'

It's a lovely thought.

It's the perfect plan.

But as the crowd around us starts counting down to the start of a New Year and letting off their poppers while cheering with drunken merriment, I can't ignore a nagging worry that this is all too good to be true and our happy little bubble is about to dramatically burst . . .

10

By the time we get to bed that night, I've almost forgotten our earlier chat with Ralph and Richard. It's so late and my body is utterly knackered, and as soon as we climb under Billy's duvet I instantly fall fast asleep.

Hours later (though it feels like minutes) I force my heavy eyelids open, screwing my face up in disgust as my head pounds. I feel like I'm lying on a bed of hard stone, rather than the fluffy white-feathered pillow I know Dee would have spent ages plumping up to perfection.

'Ouch,' I groan, as I painfully twist round to look across the bed at Billy, who disappointingly looks rested and handsome, sitting propped up and looking at his phone. Clearly he's not feeling the same way I do.

'Head?'

'Why do people do this to themselves?' I cry, covering my face with my hands and peering at him through my splayed fingers. 'I didn't even think I'd drunk that much. I had the same glass all night . . .'

'The same glass that kept magically getting topped up?' he asks with a grin, putting his phone down by his side and leaning over to get a better view of my scrunched-up face. 'Those waiters are like ninjas. You think you're on top of how much you've drunk, but really they're dodging and scheming their goods into your glass with stealthy perfection.'

'Urgh . . .' I mutter. 'Why are you so chirpy? And why do I feel like this and you look like you're in some sexy underwear ad. You look deliciously unkempt. I just look . . . unkempt.'

Billy laughs. 'You look cute.'

'I don't feel it.'

'Drink your water. It'll help.'

'No, I think I need . . . oh, I don't know what I need,' I grumble, unable to collect a fully formed thought or detect what my body craves, other than to be out of this pitiful state.

'Want me to go rummage around in the kitchen? Dee might've cooked something,' he offers.

'Mmmm . . .' I smile, throwing the duvet back over my face and sinking further underneath the covers.

'I'll be back in a tick,' he laughs, rolling out of bed. A collection of coins and keys jangles in the pocket of his jeans as he pulls them on, making my head ache even more before he exits the room and leaves me in silence.

I lie there feeling sorry for myself.

After a few minutes have passed I realize I can no longer ignore the need for a wee that's been silently irking me since waking up. I decide to splash my face with some cold water too, which seems to help momentarily. At least it makes me feel fresher.

It's only when I'm on my way back to the inviting bed that it dawns on me that Billy's been gone for quite some time. I'm about to throw on some clothes and brave my way to the kitchen when Billy bursts back in red faced and, rather disappointingly, empty handed.

'You OK?'

'Of course,' he nods, not looking at me. In fact, weirdly, he seems to be avoiding eye contact all together. 'Want to go out for breakfast instead?'

'If you fancy,' I say, mildly disgruntled that I'm not going to be able to just curl up in a silent, unsociable ball for the next couple of hours. 'Although I'll have to wear some sunnies. Even if we sit indoors. I don't think I can face daylight. Or anything bright.'

'Deal,' he agrees with a forced laugh. 'Let's just chuck on some clothes and go.'

'Fair enough. Should we see if anyone else wants to come? Are they all up?'

'Mum and Dad are,' he replies, pulling a black t-shirt over his head and grabbing last night's discarded socks off the floor. 'But let's leave it as just us.'

'I guess we're seeing them all later at lunch, anyway,' I say, trying to get my brain to function so that I can get into some clothes. I decide on one of my summer dresses and chuck a hoodie over the top. It might not match, but I'm not particularly bothered right now. 'Is your mum still making a roast?'

'Already in the kitchen,' Billy mumbles, leaning over to slip on his black Vans trainers.

'Well, does she need any help?'

'Sophie,' he sighs, straightening up, suddenly looking exasperated. 'Dee is usually running around after them all. I think Mum will be fine with cooking this one meal on her own.'

His tone stops me. Billy is never snappy with me, and that was most definitely on the verge of being so.

'Are you sure you're OK?' I ask again.

'Sorry,' he replies regretfully, running his hand through his hair. Something has clearly aggravated him in the last ten minutes as he was in high spirits when he left the bedroom before. 'Let's just get out of here.'

We finish getting ready in silence and leave.

Fair to say it doesn't feel like the best start to a new year.

Billy remains silent and brooding as we climb into his 1969 baby blue Chevy Camaro, a car he's banned anyone else from driving when he's not around, and make our way down towards the rest of civilization. Usually I feel like an old-fashioned movie star in this beautiful piece of vintage machinery, but today I barely think about it. I'm too busy wondering what Billy's thinking about to take in the beauty of my surroundings.

'Are you absolutely sure you're OK?' I repeat, when we're finally seated outside a little restaurant that looks like an actual house – homely and cosy, complete with mammoth trees that make you feel like you're in an enchanted garden. 'Has something happened?'

'Mum. My *mum* happened,' he says cryptically, looking at the menu.

'What's she done?'

'Meddled . . .'

'Is this about Richard and Ralph?' I dig further, trying to get him to just say whatever it is that's on his mind. 'I'm sure she just thought she was being friendly by inviting them along.'

'Sophie, even you know that wouldn't be the case,' he says, raising an eyebrow in my direction, as though daring me to say otherwise. 'There was more to it than that.'

'But you loved meeting Ralph. At least, you looked like you did last night.'

'No, I did,' Billy says, raising his hands in protest as he allows a flicker of delight to cross his face. 'Honestly, that bloke is one of the best, if not *the* best, director in Hollywood right now.'

'Then what's the problem?'

'Nothing,' he exhales, pursing his lips at me.

I can't help but feel frustrated as he's clearly stopping himself from sharing whatever is on his mind, even though it's put him in a funny mood and is ruining our day.

'It'll all sort itself out, I'm sure,' he shrugs.

'Right,' I frown, hating his ambiguous reply. 'And have you given what they said any thought? About filming?'

'Sophie May, I'm on a break!' he says with indignation before laughing. 'Now, what do you fancy for brekkie? I'm torn between the pancakes with a side of bacon and the traditional eggs Benedict.'

'Tough one,' I sigh.

Him changing the subject obviously shows he isn't going to let me in on what he's thinking just yet, so I decide there's no point pushing it. His flippant replies will only aggravate me further and that's the last thing I want.

'I think I might go for the granola,' I say, dropping my menu and looking around the beautiful space we're in.

'Are you kidding me? All this amazing food on offer and you're going for a healthy granola?'

'Got to get some goodness back in me,' I moan, finding myself laughing at the screwed-up face he's pulling. 'I might even get a banana on the side.'

'Sod that. I'm going for pancakes,' he grins, looking a little happier with himself as he bangs the menu back down on the table in front of us and looks around for a waiter.

'You folks decided?' asks a young guy, who looks incredibly trendy despite being in his staff uniform of a black t-shirt with a white logo on the front. He taps on the notepad in his hand with his pen, seeming impatient. I can't help but wonder if he too had a heavy night and is feeling a bit resentful and tetchy about having to work today. I definitely wouldn't be able to cope with having to give service with a smile after last night. No chance. I think I'd have to just open the door and let the customers help themselves for the day while I slept in a corner, feeling sorry for myself. No doubt my wonderful regulars would actually find the whole thing amusing, seeing as it's completely out of character for me, although they'd probably be talking about it for months afterwards.

'Fancy seeing you two here,' we hear, just before we're able to place our order with our new impatient, and possibly hungover, friend.

Looking up we see Hayley and Jenny, both immaculate as always in another floaty pair of matching outfits – identical white dresses with long, thin straps that make them look effortlessly chic and glamorous. My guess is that it's something in the Buskin genes that means the whole family fail to ever look bad, which is great news for any future kids we might have (here's hoping), but rubbish for me who'll always look crap in comparison.

'You joining us?' I ask, reaching out to grab the empty seat next to our table and pull it across.

'No, no. Don't worry,' smiles Hayley, stopping me. 'We were actually only nipping next door to pick up a quick smoothie but saw you two in here . . .'

'So, Mum's on the warpath!' Jenny states, looking directly at Billy.

'She is?' I ask.

'Don't know what you've done but you'd better fix it soon,' warns Hayley. 'She's hell to live with when she's on one.'

'Yeah, well . . .' Billy sighs, looking downtrodden once again, giving me proof that this was the reason for his dramatic change of mood earlier, too.

'Great. Looks like this afternoon's going to be a barrel of laughs, then,' says Hayley with a sarcastic roll of her eyes – something they all do far too much here for my liking.

'Well, we'll catch you guys at home later,' says Jenny, turning to leave.

'Laterz,' adds Hayley, waving her fingertips in the air as she goes.

I turn back to look at Billy, who's shaking his head while watching his older sisters.

'Don't,' he moans, looking up at our waiter who seems to have perked up now he's realized who he's serving. 'Just don't.'

Apparently, whatever has happened with his mum is something he really doesn't want to talk about. Unfortunately, given our plans for lunch, we both know he'll only be able to put it off for so long . . .

11

Julie has instructed everyone to be back at home by three o'clock for a late family lunch. It would seem that Billy wants to spend as little time back at his LA home with his loved ones as possible right now, because we end up arriving back there without a second to spare after a meandering drive through the surrounding hills.

We walk in to find the rest of the family already seated in the dining room – another gorgeous and airy space that matches the grandeur, yet cosiness, of the rest of the house with its cream chairs, solid glass table and shaggy rug below our feet. Six vases of long-stemmed blush-coloured roses sit on the dining table and on a cabinet that runs the length of one whole wall, their luscious flowers giving off the sweetest of scents.

Yet, even their exquisite nature can't hide the ugliness that's lurking in the atmosphere.

The reception we receive as we walk in is a frosty one, which is largely due to the fact that Julie is storming in and out of the kitchen, slamming down plates and trays of food with a face like thunder.

'Anything we can help with?' I ask brightly, trying to act like I'm unaware of the tension and the steam that's practically gushing from Julie's ears.

'No, thanks,' she barks quickly as she marches past, a lady on a mission.

'She's got it all under control apparently,' replies Clive, who is sitting sheepishly at the head of the table, watching along with everyone else as Julie charges back and forth.

'Lovely,' I say with a forced smile, taking a deep breath as I lower myself into a chair next to Billy, opposite the three girls.

Me and my mum hardly ever argue. In fact, I can't remember the last time we bickered about anything. She might go into a quiet little bubble every now and then when something troubles her, but she'd never act like Julie is right now. She's visibly chucking her toys out of the pram over something and acting like one of the kids. The situation is completely alien to me, so it's hardly surprising that I find myself feeling rather anxious over what's going to happen next.

I take a deep breath to steady my inexplicable nerves, a feeling I'm not used to having around this family who have been largely nothing but welcoming to me so far.

I hate feeling like this, on edge and uncomfortable. I'm wondering what's about to happen and dreading the explosion that's sure to erupt any minute.

I glance at Billy and see a bemused expression on his face as he watches the Buskin matriarch rage through the house. Once he senses my eyes are on him, though, he does his best to dissolve that look so that he can smile at me. Perhaps he's trying to pretend nothing's going on, or hoping it's all going to blow over and that the lid of this simmering pot is not about to be blown off.

'Good luck, everyone,' Lauren whispers before Julie enters the room once more, this time with a jug of gravy in hand.

She places it on a mat in the centre of the table and looks around at our empty plates with an irritated expression.

'Serve up,' she practically barks before sitting down between Clive and Billy. 'Don't let it get cold. I haven't cooked all day for it to get ruined.'

Hands are thrust forward instantly, jumping at her command.

'Where's ours?' mumbles Jenny, her eyes seeming to search the table, even though she's been eyeing up its contents for the last five minutes.

'What's that?' asks Julie, looking red faced as she bats some loose strands of hair away from her face and calmly places a cream napkin over her lap.

'Our nut roast?' Jenny asks meekly, nervously glancing at Hayley, sensing that their mum is on the verge of a Hulk-like outburst.

Julie glares at the food on the table in silence, as hot air audibly blows from her nose.

'It's fine, Mum,' shrugs Hayley, visibly elbowing her twin. 'There's enough for us to eat here without it.'

Julie still doesn't respond. Instead she stiffly spoons a small pile of roast potatoes on to her plate along with two sprigs of broccoli. Clive, trying to be helpful, goes to serve some chicken alongside it but she roughly pushes his hand away, choosing to just nibble from the feeble portion in front of her instead.

Everyone else spoons food on to their plates and passes the bowls and platters around, clearly not put off by Julie's mood. Their appetites seem to remain unaffected, unless they're hoping that seeing us all enjoying the fruits of her labour will appease her somewhat. I fear they're fighting a lost cause there.

When we've been eating for a couple of minutes and Julie has managed to shift the little bits of food she has on her plate from one side to the other three dozen times, she breaks her silence. 'Everything OK with the food?' she asks in a high-pitched squawk, as though daring any of us to pick a fault.

'Mmmm . . .' is the general reply.

'It's great,' grins Lauren.

'Delicious,' says Jenny, her face bright and cheerful as she says it.

'Best roast you've made in this hou—' starts Clive, but Julie interrupts.

'I just don't know what you're thinking, Billy,' she suddenly snaps, lowering her knife and fork on to her plate with a clatter, clearly unable to bite her tongue any longer and wanting to voice whatever is troubling her.

'Here we go,' mutters Lauren, not caring that she's sitting opposite her mother and can probably be heard. I would have said she's the feistiest of the bunch, but Julie is currently giving her some stiff competition for that title.

'Julie, not now,' Clive, forever the peacemaker, says under his breath.

'Why not?' she shouts, slamming her hand on the table and making everything on it wobble precariously. 'When *is* a good time? It's a family matter, Clive. It concerns us all. We should talk about it. Here. Now.'

'Jeez, can't we just eat first?' asks Jenny with a sigh, before neatly placing a potato into her mouth and munching on it. It's the first piece of white starchy carb I've witnessed her eat since we arrived. I'm guessing the tension has led her to comfort food in order to get her through whatever is about to occur.

'I didn't raise you to be selfish, Billy,' Julie continues, ignoring her daughter's request, as her voice goes up a few decibels. She might be talking to Billy, who's next to her, but she's not looking at him. Instead her comments are fired out towards the group.

'I'd hardly call him selfish,' says Lauren, unsurprisingly leaping to Billy's defence straight away.

'Oh really?' asks Julie, snapping her head up to glare at her youngest daughter with wide angry eyes.

'What's he done?' she challenges, looking from her mum to Billy.

'Nothing,' replies Billy, somehow remaining calm amidst the chaos.

'Exactly,' nods Julie, rather manically. 'Nothing. No-thing.'

'Right, glad I asked, then . . .' sighs Lauren, looking across to her dad who's looking dumbfounded, even though he clearly knows more about what's going on than any of us do.

'Ralph Joplin,' cries Julie, putting her head into her hands before bringing it up again and repeating the name to the heavens. 'Ralph Joplin.'

'Should we know who that is?' asks Jenny, her tone fighting to remain light and upbeat.

'*The* director. Well, he wants Billy to star in his next film,' explains Julie.

'That's cool,' nods Hayley, flashing Billy a wry smile. 'Congrats.'

'Oh no, no need to congratulate him. He's turning him down,' she snaps.

I turn to look at Billy, who is looking expressionlessly at his plate of food.

I thought he didn't want to talk about it because he was considering taking up the offer, not because he was thinking of turning it down.

'Well, he *is* having a break,' says Lauren, with a hint of nervousness lurking behind her bravado.

'A break you were all more than supportive of me taking,' Billy chucks in coolly, as though reminding them of the stance they took just a few months ago when he told them he needed time away from the madness of showbiz, for his mental health more than anything else.

'Do you know how much we sacrificed to come here all those years ago?' Julie seethes, her face screwed up in disgust. 'I left my mum behind, and my sisters.'

'I didn't ask you to,' Billy shrugs.

'There wasn't a choice,' she snaps back, slapping the table between them again with the palm of her hand in rage. 'We're your family. We were there for you. But if you throw in the towel now, Billy . . .'

'I'm not throwing in any towel – I've not quit acting, Mum,' he sighs, sounding exasperated. 'I'm just giving myself a break like I said I was.'

'But for how long?' Julie pleads, her body turning to him. 'You might not get another opportunity like this, Billy. Considering what happened last year you should be thankful Ralph wants you. You walked out on a prestigious director halfway through filming. To be frank, I think Ralph is taking a serious chance on you.'

'Thanks,' Billy laughs back bitterly.

'It's no laughing matter. The work might not be there when you decide you want it again,' she shrieks.

'Again, thanks Mum.'

'You've got to be realistic, Billy,' she breathes, her tone starting to soften now that she's exploded, or maybe she's trying a different tactic to see if it'll work better. 'You know how this business and those people work. It's fickle! I'm not saying it to be unkind, but you can't be out of the game for too long. They'll move on to fresh meat.'

'I thought we agreed my sanity was worth more than some movie role,' Billy frowns.

'It is,' Julie says, dramatically throwing a hand to her heart, as though devastated that he could assume anything else.

'Well then, who cares what I'm doing as long as I'm happy? If I don't land an acting role when I decide I'm ready to take it up again, then I'll do something else that makes me happy. I'll do some charity work, or some gardening.' Billy shrugs in such a flippant way that he might as well be waving a red rag at an angry old bull.

'Oh really?' Julie (the bull) spits, getting riled again. 'And what will happen to this house and your family when you're out rustling around in other people's shrubbery and getting grass stains on your jeans? What will happen to *us*?'

'God forbid we have to go out and get actual jobs,' gasps Lauren, placing her hands theatrically over her own heart, echoing the action her mother made seconds before.

'Will you shut it?' Julie orders her. 'You're not helping.'

'Helping what? Billy wanted some time off,' she argues,

leaning back in her chair and not complying with Julie's demands at all. 'Seeing as he's the only one of us that's done a day's work since getting here, I think he's entitled to it. Although let's not discredit Jay, poor thing gets so compared to Billy all the time that he's had to move all the way to New York just to get away from you.'

'Go to your room!' Julie screams, leaping to her feet and thrusting a pointed finger to the door.

'I'm not five!' Lauren frostily replies.

'Clive, tell her,' Julie says to her husband, gesturing towards Lauren.

'It's OK, Loz,' says Billy, shooting her a small smile and clearly grateful to have someone vocally on his side. Obviously he knows he has me, but there's no way I could get involved in this dispute and I'm sure he knows that. 'Mum, I don't think this is the best way to deal with things. You throwing a wobbly isn't going to make me want to do what you so desperately want me to. In fact, it'll push me even further the other way. Just . . . just calm down. This is ridiculous.'

'So that's what I am to you now, is it? Ridiculous?' she asks, her eyes visibly welling up with tears.

'Mum, I didn't say that,' Billy says patiently. 'Come on, you've twisted my words.'

'I'm done,' she sobs, dramatically shoving her chair back from the table and storming out of the room. Seconds later we hear her bedroom door slam shut.

'I'll go,' sighs Clive, giving the table a tight smile before following her.

'What the fuck just happened?' asks Jenny, her face looking utterly confused.

'Mum's lost it,' says Lauren matter-of-factly, raising an eyebrow and throwing down her knife and fork as she leans back in her seat.

'I'd say,' replies Jenny.

'You OK?' Billy asks, putting his hand on my knee.

'That was . . . eventful,' I exhale.

'Never seen anything like it?' asks Hayley with a grin.

'Nope,' I admit.

'The lady has five children to deal with. It's no wonder she blows. We've seen this dozens of times before. She simmers for a few hours, explodes, cries and eventually goes back to being vaguely reasonable,' shrugs Hayley, not seeming at all bothered about what just occurred.

'Right . . .' I say, surprised they all seem to have such an understanding of their mum. But then, I know and understand my own mum far better than she thinks I do. Perhaps all mums think of their children as switched off to their emotions, not really giving us the benefit of the doubt.

'She'll be more embarrassed that you've seen her like that,' says Jenny, looking at me.

'Oh, she doesn't need to worry about that . . .' I mumble, putting down my knife and fork and leaning back in my chair.

'We'll clean this all up,' says Lauren, standing and collecting up the plates around her. 'You two go off for a bit,' she says to Billy and me, gesturing towards the door.

'You don't have to do that,' I start, leaping to my feet and grabbing a couple of plates.

'We'll be in my room,' says Billy, taking my hand away from the delicate china and leading us out of the room and downstairs.

'I'm so sorry,' he says as soon as his bedroom door is shut. 'I can't believe you had to see that.'

'You don't have to be sorry,' I say, giving him a hug and holding him close.

'It's bonkers . . .'

It is exactly that, I think to myself. Utterly bonkers that his mother would act in such a way and clearly try to emotionally manipulate the situation so that Billy ended up doing what she so badly wanted. And the fact that she tried to get the rest of the family involved too . . . what did she hope would happen? That they'd all gang up on him and he'd bend to their will? Would they be happy knowing he was only doing the film for that reason? That his heart longed to be elsewhere but felt forced to comply with their wishes? It seems a horrible way of getting what you want.

'I can't believe she spoke to you like that,' I say.

'She's my mum. She loves me more than anything. I know she only wants the best for me,' he replies, shrugging in my arms.

'Of course.'

'She's not that lady. She's just passionate about us kids.'

I don't respond, knowing it's not my place to speak badly or question his mother's motives. Back when his ex-manager Paul was, in my opinion, being manipulative over Billy, us, and his career choices, I did question it a few times – which didn't go down too well. Billy is a loyal soul, and would definitely be protective over his family, especially his mum. Criticizing the family of your partner should never be done in a relationship. I might not be the most experienced when it comes to relationships, but even I know that.

'What are you going to do now?' I mumble into his chest.

'Wait until tomorrow and talk to her calmly.'

'You're not going to talk it over tonight?' I ask, my head moving away from him so that I can see his face. I can't believe Billy will be able to sleep later knowing his mum is so upset, even if she's that way because she wound herself up so badly. I also don't believe Billy will be able to simply brush off the incident and snooze soundly. It's horrible trying to sleep with that agitated undercurrent bubbling away. He knows it's something I try my best to never do.

'Fine, I'll wait a couple of hours for it all to dissipate and then I'll go talk to her.'

'That's better,' I say, cuddling into him again.

'God knows what I'm going to say . . .'

Yes, I sigh to myself, but I'd rather not think about it.

'Do you think it's true what Lauren said about Jay?' I ask.

'Feeling compared to me?' Billy asks with a sigh. 'Must be flipping hard being my brother. The girls can avoid that to a certain extent, but not him.'

'Do you think that's why he's not here?'

'Don't know . . . I definitely think that's part of the reason he's working so hard to achieve something away from us all.'

'So you could argue that being compared to you has given him drive and passion?' I suggest, knowing he's still upset that his little brother isn't here, but trying to put a positive spin on it.

'Maybe. Want to go for a swim?' he asks, nodding

towards the window, indicating he's done with the discussion for now. 'Might help your hangover.'

'You know what, I'd completely forgotten about that.'

'It's amazing what a family drama can do,' Billy laughs, heading off to get changed.

12

It feels odd to be outside enjoying the warmth of the day with Billy when we know Julie is inside feeling awful. However, the swim does help to shake off the grogginess I woke up with and the anxious feeling that's been building inside me all day. The stretching of my weightless limbs as they glide through the water, combined with the sun beaming on my back, helps bring a sense of stillness.

'You've been in there for ages,' Billy calls from the side of the pool, his legs dangling in the water. In contrast, he's been sunbathing on a lounger, or possibly stewing over what he's going to say to his mum when he next sees her.

'I'm on one hundred and twenty-eight laps now,' I grin, as I swim past him.

'Good going! How many you doing?'

'Two hundred? Or one-fifty?' I breathe, as I realize I'm already fairly shattered. I didn't mean to swim so much, but I've just kept going, enjoying the feeling it's stirred in me.

'Nice,' Billy nods, smiling at me. 'I'm starving.'

'Me too,' I admit. Julie might have cooked an impressive roast dinner (minus the vegan dish), but none of us really felt up to eating much while all the arguing was going on, or once the battle had been fought.

'I'm going to go see if I can rustle up something in the

kitchen,' Billy says, getting to his feet. 'You keep going and come in when you're done.'

'Will do,' I say, putting my head back under the water and ploughing through my tiredness, wanting to get to a round number.

When I get to a hundred and fifty, I'm spent. There's physically no way I can reach two hundred today. Maybe it'll be an aim of mine while I'm here, I decide, as I wrap a towel around me and dry off.

I sit on the corner of a sun lounger and wait for my heart to steady itself. I might be on my feet all day in the shop, but I'm still a bit slack when it comes to doing regular exercise, and my body is currently making sure I know it. In stark contrast to how I felt in the water, I now feel heavy and lifeless. Although, bizarrely, it actually feels quite pleasant and grounding.

Once the late rays of the afternoon sun have dried me off and my body has semi-recovered, I stand, slip my feet into my brown Havaianas, and decide to venture towards the kitchen to get some grub.

I'm about to walk through the door when the sound of talking stops me.

Julie is in there with Billy. Despite what happened earlier, I'm glad they're trying to discuss the matter.

'Mum, honestly, I know where you're coming from and I know you might think I'm being ungrateful, but –' I hear Billy say, as though reasoning with a child.

'I don't think you're being ungrateful,' Julie says with a big sigh. 'Well, part of me thinks you're being utterly absurd and childish, but,' she breathes, clearly stopping herself from getting irate again and trying her best to talk in a calmer fashion. 'It's my place to worry. I'm your mum, Billy. And all I ever want is what's best for you.'

'I know that,' Billy replies softly.

'I don't want word getting round that you've turned down Ralph. It could be detrimental to everything you've spent so long creating. You're the charming soul who's hardworking and dedicated, who's worked relentlessly to win the respect you've gained,' she says. I might not be in the room, but it sounds as though she even has a smile on her face. Clearly, the atmosphere is totally different now they're on their own and a couple of hours have passed. 'Don't forget how hard you had to work to shake off that teen image you had. You did it. You won a BAFTA, Billy. Who'd have thought that would've happened five years ago.'

'Tell me about it,' he laughs in response.

'I understand that you needed to take time away, and if I ever see that Heidi flipping Black I'll show her what for, but you've got the accolade you strived so hard to achieve. You'd be foolish not to follow that up with a great piece of work, to show your fans that you're still here and to really hit home that you're the actor to be watched. The actor of your generation.'

If anything, it's touching to hear her give Billy credit in such a heartfelt exchange. Talking about the decision in terms of what it'll mean for him and his career, rather than how he'd be a disappointment to the family if he didn't take part.

'Mum, films are being made all the time,' he says, still trying to make her see his point. 'Not taking this one doesn't mean I won't secure something electrifying when I'm ready.'

'You don't think you're looking a gift horse in the mouth?'

'No . . .'

'Because I'd hate for you to look back and regret your decision.'

From where I'm standing at the other side of the door (ridiculously rooted to the spot), I can't hear an audible reply from Billy, but there seems to be a pregnant pause hanging over them while Julie's words linger in the air.

'And another thing – now, don't be cross at me for talking about this – but you're so young. Too young to be throwing your life away for a girl.'

I feel as though I've been smacked across the face, stunned that I've even been brought into the conversation. My chest tightens, my body stiffens and my breathing stops – eager, yet petrified, to hear exactly what's going to be said next.

'Mum,' he says in a low and pained tone, as though he's warning her to stop.

'What? Where do you see it going, Billy? Do you think you'll end up marrying her?' she asks, as though the idea is absurd. 'I mean, Sophie's a lovely girl but perhaps it was a bit of normality you craved so much.'

'Don't underestimate normality, Mum. Or Sophie,' he says dryly, his voice low and steady.

'Oh, I know she seems very sweet and I'm not surprised you were so drawn to her,' she says, seeming to back off of her argument before deciding otherwise and continuing. 'But does she understand the business? In the long run, how will she cope with you travelling around filming in different locations while she's stuck at her shop.'

I bristle at that – there's nowhere in the world I'd rather spend my time than at Molly's-on-the-Hill, and I was beginning to think Billy felt the same.

'We'll cope together,' Billy brushes her off.

'Really?'

'I love her.'

'Enough to throw away your dreams?'

'Enough to chase love and happiness,' he says flatly, causing tears to prick at my eyes as I bite down on my bottom lip.

'They're big words, Billy,' Julie says, theatrically taking a huge intake of breath. 'I just hope they don't come back to bite you in the arse.'

'They won't.'

'How can you be so sure?'

'Because you brought me up properly and I know what's important in life,' Billy says softly, appealing to her romantic side.

'And what if she's not the one? What if this is all for nothing?'

'Then at least I'll know I did the best I could. That I acted decently – always with love.'

'I see,' Julie sighs.

Part of me wants to crumble on the spot and sob, the other wants me to make my presence known to them both. Yet I'm unable to do either. Instead I remain standing and listen to the silence that's fallen between them.

'And what about us?' Julie eventually asks meekly, almost inaudibly.

'What do you mean?' Billy asks, his voice soft and caring.

'Oh, nothing,' she murmurs, before breaking into quiet sobs.

'Mum . . .'

'Just don't forget about us,' she weeps.

'Mum, I couldn't.'

'And don't think we don't want anything but the best for you . . .'

'Mum, why are you being like this?'

Having heard more than I should have, I tear myself away. Tiptoeing back along the hallway, I go down to Billy's room. When the door is finally closed behind me, I gasp for air, my chest heaving in panic.

I shouldn't have stood there so long. I shouldn't have listened to their conversation. Because now I've heard things I can't un-hear and sadly I know just how little Julie thinks of me. I know she doubts my ability to cope and that she's failed to see me as a permanent fixture in Billy's life.

It's crushing to hear the mother of the person you love question what you share and value, as though me and my *normality* have been just a phase for Billy. A phase that he'll probably soon tire of and regret . . .

But she's been so nice and welcoming to me since we arrived. Surely that can't have been all an act to get me on side?

I can only imagine the stream of girls Billy has brought home in the past, some, undoubtedly, with dubious intentions to further their own careers. With that in mind I can understand her being a little cautious, but surely she knows I'm not like that. Right? I'm not looking to gain anything from our relationship and I'm not looking to pin

Billy down and stop him from doing what he loves. I love him. I want him to flourish in life!

I hate that she thinks I'm a huge part in his decision not to do this film with Ralph and Richard. I mean, I know I'm a part of it, but I'm not the *whole* reason, surely? He wanted time away from everything. Time to be himself . . .

But what if that decision drove a wedge between him and his family? What if it grew into something irretrievable? How would I cope knowing I had a part in causing that?

Although I hate to admit it, some of what Julie said made sense. Billy has worked hard – first of all to get into one of the biggest teen movie trilogies of all time, and then to break the mould and be recognized for his indisputable talent away from that genre. Is a break now the best thing? Has he really thought it through beyond worrying that it would hurt me? I saw the way he was practically drooling over Ralph Joplin last night and I'm not sure he could guarantee he wouldn't hate seeing someone else playing the role they so desperately want him for. I'm not sure I could cope knowing he missed out on such a huge opportunity, just so he could head back to Rosefont Hill and bake cakes by my side for the next few months.

I decide to have a shower, wanting to be actively doing something whenever Billy inevitably notices I haven't reappeared and comes to find me. I know I can have a good cry in the glass cubicle without being seen or heard – and if I can only keep those tears at bay for so long, I'd rather spill them alone.

13

'I think you should rethink,' I blurt when I come out of the shower and see Billy sitting on a sofa looking longingly out of the window, with two ham and cheese sandwiches on a plate next to him. Once again, I find myself not hungry.

Billy looks up at me with a confused expression.

'Ralph and Richard. The film. You haven't even read the script yet,' I say with a shrug, trying to sound more determined about this than I feel. 'Read it before making a decision. You don't want to wake up one day and regret not being part of the "greatest film ever made".'

'Ralph's words?' he asks, giving a sad smile.

'He clearly believes in it. Just read it before refusing.'

'Where has this come from?'

'Nowhere. I've just been thinking, that's all,' I lie, not wanting him to know that I overheard his chat with his mum and have just spent the last twenty minutes having a mammoth cry over it.

'No one's said anything?'

'To me? I've not seen anyone . . .' Well, it's not a lie.

Billy looks at me and sucks in his cheeks before blowing them out again. 'It doesn't mean anything if I read it.'

'Exactly,' I shrug, as though it's no big deal.

He nods thoughtfully, clearly tempted by the idea of giving the script a once over. A sigh follows, and I know he's warming to the idea.

'I don't want you thinking –'

'I won't be thinking anything,' I interrupt, not wanting him to feel he has to apologize for something I'm talking him into doing. 'Might as well see if you like it before we all get into a flap.'

'Wise words,' Billy says, leaping from the chair and giving me a kiss, before heading out of the door with a spring in his step, presumably eager to retrieve the script from wherever Dee has put it.

I grip the sofa to steady myself and take a deep breath. Even though I know I'm doing the right thing I can't stop the fear from forming and trying to take over.

Two hours later, when I'm on the sofa trying to read Thomas Hardy's *Jude the Obscure* (and failing to block out thoughts of Billy and the movie, as he silently reads next to me), Billy turns over the last page of the script and exhales loudly.

'Bloody hell . . .' he whispers, looking at the blank back page.

'Good?' I ask casually over the top of my book, though my heart is pounding.

'Unbelievable,' he says, his face moving into a thoughtful frown as he lifts the bound manuscript and cradles it in his arms, looking extremely protective over the thing he wanted nothing to do with just hours before.

'Thoughts?' I ask, longing to know more about whether or not he's going to take this role – and whether we're going to be forced into being apart.

He shakes his head, unable to look at me.

'It's all right,' I say, nudging his leg with my own. I need him to know that, whatever happens, I'm still going to be supportive. After all, reading the script was my idea.

'Shit . . .' Billy mutters, looking desperately torn as he shakes his head and burrows his face into his hand.

'Billy . . .'

'I shouldn't have read it,' he mumbles.

'Yes, you should've.'

'I should've burnt it or –'

'You did the right thing, and I think you'll do the right thing again now you've read it.'

'But it's filming here,' he says, unable to hide the panic and desperation in his voice. He seems paler than ever as he stews over what I've been thinking about since he turned over the first page of the script for *The Pious*.

Of course, I suspected it was going to be every inch as fantastic as they said. Their passion felt like more than just cocky industry talk, even to an outsider like me. That's why I knew he had to read it, because I didn't want Julie to be right and for Billy to forever resent the time he took off to spend with me.

'Billy, we'll cope,' I say. Resting my hand on his thigh, I give it a little squeeze of reassurance.

'It won't be easy,' he says, looking up at me with his dark Bambi-like eyes.

'Nothing worth having ever is,' I shrug.

'You sure you'd be OK with it, though? I won't be leaving you in the lurch at the shop?'

'You were only really there as eye candy. It'll probably be a lot quieter without you anyway,' I joke, making him smile.

'And you won't be able to just stay here with me?' he

asks sadly, knowing the answer before he finishes asking the question.

'If Molly was around she'd be packing my suitcases and kicking me out the door straight away,' I laugh. 'But things are different now. I have to be there. It's my business,' I say, smiling pensively. I realize Julie was at least right about one thing – I'm pinned down and unable to just mindlessly follow him around. Not that I'd find much happiness in that scenario, anyway.

'I know . . .' he nods, reaching over to tuck some of my hair behind my ear, his warm hand resting on the back of my neck. 'Let's not panic until we know more.'

'Always good to know what there is to worry about first,' I nod.

'Exactly,' he agrees, still looking torn, his own words clearly not making the decision any easier for him. 'You would tell me though, if you really didn't want me to do it?'

'Billy!' I sigh, taking his hand and cupping it in my own. 'I made you read the bloody thing, didn't I?'

'I just want you to be happy.'

'And I want *us* to be happy. It's no good just having one happy person in a relationship. That's not how they work,' I say, hearing the truth in my own words.

'Fair point.'

'So, what happens next?' I want to move the conversation forward before I have a chance to backtrack on everything I've said. Or cry again.

'I guess I call Ralph or Richard. See if they still want me,' Billy half laughs, shaking his head.

'And then you'll have to tell your mum. I'm sure the

news will cheer her up,' I smile, remembering I'm not meant to be aware of anything that's happened since she stormed off at lunch.

'Thank you, Sophie,' he says, putting the script down and throwing both arms around me. 'I promise I'll do anything I can to make this as easy as possible for both of us. I meant what I said last night. You're my forever.'

'And you're mine,' I smile, although there's a cynicism in me that's grown over the years, that's taught me that forever usually comes with a limited timespan. Look at Molly, Colin and my mum. They all thought they'd found their forever loves. In reality, forever only lasts for as long as it's allowed to, until something else steps in and stops it from existing. Although that's a dangerous train of thought to dwell on – it's much better to embrace the now and live within whatever moment I'm in. 'So what's it about?' I ask, tilting my head towards the script.

Billy blows air through his lips in response and leans back into the sofa.

'Sounds great,' I laugh.

'There's just so much to it. It's like *The Matrix* meets *Avatar*, meets . . . I actually don't know how to finish that sentence. But, I guess it's about having a purpose beyond our expectations.'

'Right.'

'You have to read it.'

'I will,' I promise, hoping I'll be able to get my head around the concept. 'So what first? Your mum or Ralph?'

'Ralph!' Billy says, reaching for Ralph's business card that was paper-clipped to the front of the script. 'Mum can stew a little longer.'

'I'll leave you to it,' I say, grabbing my phone and walking out the door.

Not wanting to be in the house where I might bump into people, I head for the decked area next to the swimming pool, the section with the comfier chairs. It's dark, but lit with the soft glow from subtly placed (and expensive-looking) lamps. I unlock my phone, scroll through my contacts and call my own mum.

'Hello?' she croaks, sounding apprehensive and distant.

My first instinct is to worry that something's happened, that something has set her off balance, but then I remember the time back in England. 'Mum, I'm so sorry,' I whisper.

'Sophie, it's you,' she breathes, allowing me to hear the smile that's formed on her lips from hearing my voice.

'I forgot about the time . . .' I mutter sheepishly.

'Don't you worry, I couldn't sleep anyway.'

'Really?'

'No, and I missed actually speaking to you at midnight,' she continues. 'It didn't feel right not talking to you again.'

As we were seeing in the New Year seven hours after the UK, I managed to speak to them just before *their* midnight. I'll be honest, I was surprised they were all awake still but they seemed to be on a total sugar high.

'How was your night?' she asks.

'Great. Really lovely, actually.'

'And today?'

'Good,' I fib, realizing my mum doesn't need to know about Julie's meltdown (the fewer people who know about that the better) and that she really doesn't need to hear that she doesn't think I'm a good fit for her son. 'What about you guys?'

'Colin talked us all into getting fish and chips and we've had yet another day walking about in the cold and relaxing on the sofa in front of the fire.'

'Sounds heavenly,' I smile, a huge part of me wishing I was there doing the same. 'Crap, I've not woken Colin too, have I?'

'No,' Mum laughs. 'He took them back to theirs tonight.'

'Oh thank goodness,' I sigh, feeling less guilty.

'I'm going to meet him at the shop tomorrow. I think the kids are going to come in too as they're still off school.'

'Lovely,' I say, trying to ignore the pang of longing that hits me, from wanting both to be with my family, and to be back in my safe haven of the shop.

'Although we have started talking about a few important things . . .' Mum continues hesitantly.

'Like what?'

'Like where we'll live,' she says, pausing for a reaction.

'Oh?' is all I can manage.

'We've not made any set plans or anything like that, but we know that we don't want to be living apart once we're married. It would be nice to be under one roof.'

'Well, I guess that's a fairly normal thing to happen for a man and wife.'

'Yes. Daunting though, isn't it? Very . . . final.'

'You don't need to sell the house, Mum. And there's really no rush to do anything either,' I say, not wanting to think too heavily about the possibility of having to say goodbye to my pink bedroom and my childhood home.

'Oh, I know. Just have to give myself some time to get my head around it,' she says slowly.

'Yes, and remember why you want to do it. We're moving forward, Mum. And that's always a good thing,' I say, reassuring myself as well as her.

'No point just living with the ghosts from the past, got to let some humans in too,' she chuckles, a sound I'm happy to hear. 'How's it been there, anyway? Is it beautiful?'

'LA is stunning and hot,' I say, looking out at the stunning view, with the lights of the city laid out in front of me.

'I'm so jealous. It's miserable here.'

'No snow yet?'

'Just rain,' she grumbles. 'Wish we'd hijacked your holiday.'

'You should've done,' I say, finding myself thinking about how differently I'd feel if I had my supportive patchwork of a family by my side.

'Is Billy loving it?'

'Yes,' I nod. 'It's so funny seeing him here. It's a different world to Rosefont, that's for sure.'

'Bad different?'

'No,' I say, thinking about the fun I've managed to have here already. 'It's just not a quaint little village tucked away in the countryside. It's huge for a start and we have to drive everywhere because it's all so spread out ... Then there's the press.'

'They're not hounding you, are they? Because I keep seeing lots of pictures everywhere. Looks like they're permanently on your case.'

'It's not that bad. Just not what I'm used to ... but the place, the food, the people – that's all great,' I add quickly.

'So you'd be happy to go back there? You've not been scared off?'

'Of course,' I find myself saying, failing to tell her that it's likely I'll be back out here sooner rather than later thanks to Billy's new opportunity.

I must have fallen asleep at some point, as I'm woken up by Billy placing a blanket over my body and squishing in next to me on the chair, his arm wrapping around me as his face nuzzles into my neck.

'How'd it go?' I murmur, slowly waking up.

'Brilliantly. I spoke to Ralph – he was chuffed.'

'Ha! There's a surprise,' I smile.

'I didn't realize, but they're keen to get the ball rolling as quickly as possible.'

'Really?' I ask, his words waking me up more.

'Now they've got me on board they're hoping everything else will slot into place.'

'So when do they think they'll start filming?'

'March, but they've asked if I'd be here for some screen tests with other actors they've already seen, and then come back for training in February . . .'

'Training?'

'There's lots of stunts. It's quite physical.'

'Sounds full on,' I say, trying to sound as positive as possible. 'When are they doing the screen tests?'

'There's the annoying bit,' Billy sighs. 'They were hoping to contact a few agents and get people in before we head back, but I'm not sure that's going to be possible, so I might have to stay out here for another couple of weeks.'

'So I'd have to fly home without you?' I practically squeak.

'Soph, I'm so sorry . . .'

'No, no – that's fine. I just wasn't expecting it. I thought these things usually take a bit more time to arrange,' I say, though inside I feel as though something's breaking. I hadn't realized I'd talked him into doing something that would have such an instant effect on our lives – I thought I'd at least have a month or so to prepare.

'I'm sure they could reschedule a bit –'

'I think they've been chasing after you quite enough,' I say, not wanting to make things any more difficult for him or them. 'We'll cope.'

'Well, we still have at least a week here before you have to go home, anyway. I promise I'm not letting you out of my sight the whole time you're here,' he says softly, kissing me on the cheek.

'There's a lovely thought,' I reply.

Suddenly I feel a pressure on me, immediately making me want to change the subject and do something else. Although I think it's more the conversation and reality of what's to come spurring me into action, I sit up in the seat, wrapping the blanket tighter around me.

'I spoke to Mum,' I say, still rearranging myself.

'Is she OK?' Billy asks, looking at me with a concerned expression on his face.

'Fine – she's talking about selling the house so that she and Colin can live together.'

'Blimey. Are you OK with that?'

'I'm an adult. I need to be,' I shrug, realizing I'm deflecting the discussion of one issue by talking about another. 'It's just bricks and mortar.'

'You and I know your attachment to the place goes a bit deeper than the décor,' he says, sitting up and taking my hands in his.

'Very true,' I sigh, comforted by the fact Billy understands that my childhood home is one of the last remaining ties to Dad, especially my bedroom, which I have fond memories of us painting together. 'To be honest, it's probably time I stopped living with my mum anyway. It just means there'll be a lot of changes happening this year.'

'Change isn't a bad thing,' he offers.

'I know, I just like the security of knowing exactly how things will be. I'm not good in limbo,' I confide.

'Maybe don't think of it as limbo, though. Maybe it should be more about possibility, and that, this year, anything could happen?' Billy says, his fingertips tracing along my cheek.

'Anything could happen . . .' I think, mulling over the words. 'It's a nice, but terrifying, idea.'

Billy laughs. 'Well, I promise that wherever you're limbo-ing, I'll always be right behind you, ready to catch you if it gets too much.'

'Thank you,' I say, turning my head and kissing him as I try to ignore the feeling of doubt niggling away in my chest.

I adore hearing him declare his love so freely, though I'm also aware of how the last few hours have caused a huge shift to occur in the lives ahead of us. I felt so whole and content before coming here, but now I look into the future and see uncertainty threatening its way into view.

It's a scary sight. One I wish I could ignore.

14

Julie is like a completely different person when I see her the next morning at breakfast. Whereas yesterday she looked angry, haggard and desperate, today she seems joyous, flawless and serene.

'Sophie,' she calls, getting up from the kitchen counter as soon as we walk into the room. Seeing as the family cook hardly any of their own meals, they sure spend a lot of time in here. Even with staff it seems to have remained the hub of the house.

Julie wraps her arms around me and gives me the tightest hug I've ever had.

'Billy told me I have you to thank for changing his mind,' she says, releasing me from her grasp and taking hold of my hands instead so that we can see each other's faces.

'Oh, not really,' I say with a bashful smile, hating the fact that I feel shy of her now I know she doubts our relationship, and wondering if this is just for show.

'Put her down, Mum,' Billy laughs, shaking his head as he goes to the cupboard and pulls out a few boxes of cereal.

'It's wonderful news,' she grins, before sighing heavily as her face becomes more serious and sorrowful. Unexpectedly, she starts to stroke the back of my hand. 'Sophie, I am so sorry about yesterday. I'm sure the other kids have told you that it's completely out of character for me to act in such a way.'

I decide not to say anything to the contrary and listen instead, nodding my head in agreement. It would be a shame to push her back into the demonic mood I witnessed before and I'm really not one for any sort of confrontation.

'I think I was exhausted from all the party planning and just found myself looking at the family future with uncertainty for the first time in a decade. I know we're very fortunate to have Billy providing us with such a beautiful life, but it's not usual for parents to have the control taken from their hands and given to one of their children. I panicked and I acted appallingly. I'm so sorry.'

'Please, don't worry,' I say, somehow managing to clamp my lips into a smile.

'I know this is going to be a worrying time for you, knowing that your relationship is about to go transatlantic,' she whispers so that Billy can't hear, while leaning in really close and squeezing my hand. 'But, I just want to reassure you that I know Billy loves you more than anything.' She smiles warmly, pulling me in for another hug – one that is, thankfully, not as tight as before. 'It'll be over before you know it and then Billy will find his way back to you,' she whispers, almost conspiratorially.

'Baby, what do you fancy?' Billy asks, turning to me and rubbing his tummy hungrily. His pouty lips save me from having to dwell on what'll happen beyond the next week and the fact that I have no idea how to deal with his mother.

'Actually, before you do that ... now, don't kill me,' Julie says, grimacing, her chest caving in as though she's nervous of sharing whatever she's about to.

'What have you done, now?' asks Billy, looking up from setting two bowls on the kitchen island.

'Bought us some tickets,' she grins, her face brightening up. 'I thought we'd take Sophie somewhere exciting.'

'Where?' I ask.

'Disneyland,' she giggles, putting her hand over her mouth to control the girlish noise. 'You need to see it before you leave.'

'What? Really?' I flounder, my insides torn between loving the idea of having a childhood dream fulfilled and hating the fact Julie's doing this to counteract yesterday's terrible behaviour.

'Today?' Billy asks, filling both bowls with Lucky Charms and milk before handing one to me.

'Yes. It's high time Sophie had her first experience of wearing sparkly mouse ears on her head,' Julie beams, clapping her hands together in excitement.

'Well, thank you,' I smile, the thought of me and Billy running around like children making my heart soar as I munch on a spoonful of colourful sugary cereal.

I look at Billy with a huge grin on my face and notice that he's not quite as pleased as I am.

'Are you OK?'

'Of course,' he shrugs.

'He's worried about the crowds,' Julie says knowingly, pursing her lips.

'Oh,' I reply, feeling instantly deflated.

Billy has an extraordinarily passionate fanbase, so it

makes sense that he'd get swamped in a public place like Disneyland. I can't believe the thought didn't cross my mind straight away.

'Well, we don't need to go,' I shrug feebly, my bottom lip puckering outwards. I feel like a small child who has, quite literally, been told she might not be going to stand in front of the princess's castle of dreams after all. It won't be half as magical if I'm being pushed around while Billy signs autographs.

'Oh, don't be like that, Billy. It's all sorted,' says Julie forcefully, waving her hands around to let us know we're worrying over nothing. 'James is coming along with some extra security and a couple of their staff will be taking care of everything, so that we don't have to stay in one spot for too long.'

'Wow,' I say. 'That's nice of them.'

'Stops it being a security hazard, too,' Julie replies, with an insightful tilt of the head. 'Don't want people getting crushed or trampled on trying to get to this one,' she says, grabbing hold of Billy's shoulders and giving him a shake. 'Which did actually end up happening a few years back when we took a family trip to another theme park, alone. One poor girl broke her ankle.'

'Sounds awful.'

'These things happen,' Julie shrugs, shaking her head sadly. 'Not today though, these guys are on it. So organized and professional, but then, they're used to dealing with A-listers. It's LA. The Beckhams, Ramsays, Kardashians – they all venture there with their little ones and love it. '

'Great,' I smile, feeling elated again as I continue to munch on my moreish breakfast.

'Who's coming?' Billy asks.

'Just us and your dad,' Julie replies with a pinched smile. 'Thought it might be easier and the girls can go whenever they like, anyway.'

My elation wavers slightly. The last thing I want to be doing is spending time with Julie after yesterday, but it's obviously her intention to have Disneyland sprinkle its magic wand over us both.

'It'll be nice,' Billy nods, appearing happier now he knows we're going to be looked after, although I find myself wondering if he's thinking about yesterday at all.

He obviously doesn't know I'm aware of what Julie said, but if my mum had been so negatively vocal about my partner I don't think I'd be able to simply brush it off and forget. In fact, it would definitely make me question my relationship . . . is that going to happen with Billy? Now that I've pushed him into remaining in LA and shooting this movie with Ralph, is he going to become distant and aloof? What if Julie keeps on sharing her doubts? How long until they resonate with him and become his own thoughts?

'Honestly Sophie, nowhere does this time of year like Disney – even in the sunshine!' Julie squeals.

'I can't wait,' I smile, trying to brush off the thoughts clamming up my brain.

'Good. Now you two go get showered and ready,' she bosses, taking our bowls and pushing us to the kitchen door. 'Ooh, we've got to stay for the fireworks, too! They're beyond anything you'll have seen before, Sophie,' she adds, calling after us.

'Come on,' Billy says brightly, wrapping an arm around

me and holding my body into his. 'Let's go have the best day ever in the most magical place on earth.'

And just like that my heart leaps in my chest.

I've always heard that Americans do things bigger than anywhere else in the world, but now I can fully understand and appreciate the truth in that saying. As soon as we arrive at the Disneyland entrance I'm hit by the fun and mayhem as romantically magical and festive music pumps out through the speakers. Little girls and boys run around in the costumes of their favourite characters, all excited at the prospect of meeting their idols. There's literally a buzz in the air as both children and adults crowd to soak up the electric atmosphere – and that's all before even getting through the ticket machines and inside.

Our newly assembled team of security (dressed in normal clothes but with official looking earpieces wedged into their ears) and two staff members inconspicuously walk alongside the four of us. We're guided straight down the central road into the park, Main Street, which has a gigantic Christmas tree (decorated with more baubles and bells than I've ever seen) at one end near the entrance, and the iconic Disney castle at the other. Garlands and wreaths shaped into Mickey heads, complete with two ears, hang between the row of shops looking particularly festive, decked out with luxurious giant red bows.

'Where do you want to go?' asks Billy, turning from Aly, the girl hosting us who's dressed in her Disneyland uniform of a navy skirt, white shirt, red checked waistcoat and name badge (which tells us she's originally from

Louisiana). Billy squeezes my hand that's already firmly in his grasp, letting me know that now he's here he's just as giddy as me.

'I've no idea,' I shrug. 'Everywhere!'

'I'll see what I can do,' grins Aly, before talking into her walkie-talkie.

She does a remarkable job of giving us the full Disney experience with little fuss. We silently slip on and off rides while avoiding the queues and even find a nice spot to watch the afternoon parade as all the famous characters appear on floats and make their way around the park. I find myself grinning and waving manically at the familiar faces, not caring that I probably look like a loon and feeling thrilled each time one of them waves back. I do notice a few of the princesses, and even Peter Pan, clock Billy, their eyes widening slightly in delight as they continue by, spreading their joy and probably looking forward to getting off their floats at the end so they can have a good chinwag about whether it was him or not.

We are stopped every now and then by fans of Billy asking for autographs and I find myself laughing hysterically (mostly from absolute horror) when we see quite a few of them holding pictures of us on some of the rides, complete with one of me and Billy screaming on the Space Mountain roller coaster. It's sneaky, yet quite ingenious when you think about how quickly they've cottoned on to the fact that Billy's photo would be with everyone else's in the souvenir shops, but it's not as though it's possible to get angry in a place like this. Anyway, the security team manage to keep the interruptions to a minimum, so, thankfully, we're able to just stroll around and enjoy the beauty of the place without feeling like we're in a fishbowl.

In the afternoon we hop over to the Disney California Adventure Park which has a few of the bigger rides for some more thrill seeking (complete with more hilarious snapshots for others to enjoy) before heading back to the Disneyland Park for dinner.

I'm shattered by the time we're standing in a little VIP area waiting for the fireworks to start by the castle. Shattered, but happy from having done something completely different with the day.

'I can't believe we've been here almost a week already,' Billy says.

'I know, it's flying by.'

'Before we know it, it's going to be time for you to leave me here sad and lonely,' he pouts, resting his arms on top of my shoulders and leaning in to brush his nose against mine.

'Do you two want an ice cream?' Julie asks, cutting in. 'Your dad wants one, Billy.'

'I'm up for that. Sophie?' he asks, breaking away from me.

'Yes please,' I nod, thankful that I don't own bathroom scales at home after indulging for the last few weeks nonstop.

'What do you guys want?' asks Clive.

'Anything that looks good,' I reply, rather unhelpfully.

'I need the loo anyway, so I'll come with you,' says Billy, kissing me on the cheek before wandering off with his dad, a couple of the security men and Aly.

'Are you having fun?' asks Julie, looking out at the castle.

'Loads. Thank you so much for organizing today.'

'It's nothing. You can't come all the way over here and not experience this delight,' she shrugs. There's a pause. 'You clearly make Billy very happy,' she adds, turning to me.

'I do?' I'm pretty sure there's more shock in my voice than there should be at her statement, but as I've heard her voice a slightly different opinion, it's hardly surprising my reply comes out a little squeaky.

'You know you do,' she says, giving a light and playful laugh. 'It's nice to see he's had good people looking after him while we've been over here. It's not been pleasant having so many miles between us.'

'I'm sure,' I nod.

'I really hope this visit is the start of many more, Sophie,' Julie says, taking my hand and giving it a squeeze. 'Because I know you'd make a lovely addition to our family . . .'

The gesture takes my breath away, probably because it was the last thing I was expecting from her today. My heart is torn, wondering whether I'm able to simply draw a line under the unfortunate events of yesterday and move forward. After all, part of me still seeks her approval and longs to be let into the Buskin fold. Plus, the way she said it, it's as though she's welcoming me as a daughter-in-law. Isn't that what I've been wanting? The days leading up to us coming here, my anguish on the flight, my trepidation coming through the arrivals terminal at the airport – all I wanted was for them to like me. Could I have achieved that?

It could be the hangover lingering from New Year's Eve, but I find myself quite tearful.

'You're really something,' she says softly.

My head is confused at what is truth and lies. Could it be that Julie was playing devil's advocate yesterday in a bid to help Billy weigh up his options better, so that he could see what he actually wanted? Was it really a dig at our relationship or was she just trying to make sure he wouldn't regret whichever decision he made? Does she actually like me?

I feel a little lost.

I quickly wipe away the tears that have managed to escape just as the rest of the group return, armed with ice creams.

I take a big lungful of air to steady my wobbling emotions.

'You were quick,' sniffs Julie, busying herself with rifling through her bag.

'Perks of having Aly with us,' Clive winks. 'It's not only the rides she can get us seen quickly for.'

'See, it's totally worth dating me, just for this,' Billy laughs, handing me my huge frosty treat – a cone with at least two flavours of ice cream, drizzled with chocolate sauce.

'You all right?' he asks, glancing at his mum before looking back at me.

'Of course!' I say with gusto and a little shrug, as though questioning why we wouldn't be. 'Now, talk me through this,' I add, licking the brown top while making a sound of delight as its thick warmth hits my mouth. It really is sweet and delicious, so there's no acting required there.

'You've got rocky road and cookies 'n' cream, topped with hot milk-chocolate fudge,' he grins, sucking on his own enormous treat which looks just as tasty as mine.

'This is so good!' I exclaim, the job of tackling my ice cream stilling the more pressing thoughts that were on my mind mere seconds before.

The park is suddenly plunged into darkness and the gathered crowds around us whoop in delight, letting us know that the fireworks are about to start. Orchestral music booms from nearby speakers as the castle starts twinkling beautifully. My body tingles when the display bangs into action, as some of the most loved Disney characters are projected on to the front of the castle while nostalgic songs from my childhood are played out. Memories of being with Mum and Dad on the sofa at home watching those old movies fill my heart and I feel choked with emotion as I think how wonderful it would have been to come here with them all those years ago. We would have loved it . . .

When 'Let it Go' from *Frozen* starts playing I burst out laughing as adorable little Charlotte, my soon-to-be stepsister, pops into my head. I know she'd be in her absolute element if she were here, singing along at the top of her lungs.

It's a sensory overload – the music, the fireworks exploding in the air, the display of pretty lights on the majestic castle – all with the man I love by my side. I lean into Billy and put some of my weight against his chest.

'I love you,' I whisper, keeping my eyes fixed on the captivating display.

'And I love you, baby,' he replies, kissing me on the side of the head. 'For always.'

'Always . . .' I grin, feeling warm, gooey and whole.

'We're going to be fine,' he says softly, squeezing me tightly across my chest.

I blink back the emotion those few words stir within me, realizing that they aren't said just to comfort me, but also to reassure him.

PART TWO

15

'Where's Billy?' asks Mrs Sleep as soon as she walks through the door of the shop wheeling her shopping trolley behind her. In my absence she's clearly treated herself to a little pampering, as her short grey hair has had a fresh rinse and perm and now looks immaculate.

She looks around the place with wild disappointment and a touch of mild panic.

It's been ten days since The Big Decision and now I'm back in Rosefont Hill and my familiar shop. I spent the rest of my stay having a wonderful time in Los Angeles with Billy, and getting to know his family a bit more. Julie remained loving and kind for the rest of the trip, although I'm still undecided as to what to make of the whole thing. And then I flew home, alone.

The flight went as expected – I had a little cry, even had a glass of bubbly, then read a book to try and stop my brain from thinking about how I was going to break the news of Billy's slight change of heart about living in the village to everyone back home. To be honest, Mum was the only person I was really concerned about telling. I didn't want her worrying over me worrying (ironic), which is why I decided to say nothing until I stepped back through Arrivals as a solo traveller.

'You OK, love?' was obviously her first question, but I think that's because I must have looked a bit forlorn as I was trying to work out what to say. She was more confused over the fact I hadn't told her sooner, as she completely understood that Billy had to make the most of the fabulous opportunity offered. I think her unfaltering attitude towards the whole thing made me see it in a slightly different light. There's no denying the craziness of LA turned it into a bigger and scarier thing than it should have been – he's an actor, he's had some work come in. It's that simple. In theory. I think it was just the way it all happened that marred how I dealt with it.

As I only got home last night, the news of Billy temporarily staying Stateside hasn't reached the rest of the village yet. That's why a Billy-less shop is a flabbergasting sight for my elderly friend who's always had a soft spot for my dreamboat of a partner.

'He's staying out there a little longer,' I say, flashing her a smile as I make up a pot of English breakfast tea for her.

'But, why?' she asks, her wrinkled hand gripping on to the counter. She usually takes a seat straight away and we head out to serve her at her table, but clearly Billy's absence is making an impact already. I almost feel bad having to break the news to her. 'Is everything OK?'

'Of course it is,' I say, finding it sweet that she cares so much. 'He met this amazing director over there who wants Billy to be in his next film, that's all.'

'But he's meant to be having time off,' she sighs, looking ever so worried.

'He'll be back next week.'

'Oh, that's good,' she says with relief, with one of her signature girlish giggles.

'But then gone for a few months from February,' I grimace.

'What?' she gasps, the news causing her to take a few steps backwards, as though I've said something horrific or scandalous. 'But how will we cope?'

'Like we did before he arrived,' I laugh, putting the pot and a china cup and saucer on her tray. 'Anything else to go with that? I've made a pecan toffee cake.'

'Oh go on then,' she says sadly, clearly hoping a slice will help her get over the distressing news.

I'm tempted to sit down and scoff the whole thing with her. Billy would be amused to hear that we've all turned to comfort eating in his absence.

Once Mrs Sleep has had her fill and left, most people arrive that morning seeming to already know I'll be behind the counter on my own; clearly my old friend has shared the news on her way back down the hill. There's no voiced shock or disappointment as they enter, although perhaps a few glum faces at discovering the rumours are true. And there I was thinking they were all going to have missed *me*. Damn Billy and his charming ways.

I've just placed a granary ham and mustard sandwich in front of Miss Peggy Brown when my mum bursts through the door, out of breath and not at all her usual composed self. Her hazel eyes are full of concern and her face is crinkled up with worry.

'You OK?' I ask, smiling politely at Miss Brown before heading over to her. Whatever it is, I don't want my dear old friend overhearing. That's how rumours are spread in a little village like this, although I'm sure she'll be watching closely and making up her own facts anyway.

I used to really fret about people in the village talking about me, but now I think I've just learnt to accept that it's part of the joys of living in such a close-knit community. I still try, wherever possible, to give them nothing to talk about, though.

'You've obviously not seen the papers or been online today,' Mum says, fretfully rubbing her hands together.

'Not yet. I've been manic,' I frown, although guessing whatever it is that has made her like this is bound to have something to do with my relationship with a certain someone whose every move outside of Rosefont Hill appears to be tabloid fodder. 'Billy?'

She nods, her lips apprehensively pursing together.

'What does it say?' I ask, going to get my mobile phone from my bag where I left it when I arrived this morning. I haven't had a chance to dig it out since, and usually people phone me on the shop's landline if they know I'm here anyway. Well, when I say people, I mean Mum and Billy.

Looking at my phone I see my lockscreen is filled with hundreds of Twitter and Instagram notifications from names I don't recognize, although dozens of them are a play on Billy's name or that of his fictional character Sid Quest with usernames like @BuskinForever135, @Buskinshalogirl and @QuestforBilly.

Ignoring them for now, I unlock my phone and go straight to one of the gossip sites I abhor and am instantly greeted with pictures of me walking through LAX airport on my own looking forlorn and miserable, while Billy is pictured elsewhere looking equally glum. They were probably taken on his way back to his car having dropped me off for my flight. I let out a sigh when I see the headline and brace myself as I start to read the article that follows.

BUSK-OUT

Fans of Billy Buskin will be relieved to learn that it appears the former lothario is back on the market after hitting rocky times with girlfriend Sophie May.

The two had supposedly flown over to Los Angeles at the end of the year to tell his parents Clive and Julie about their plans to get married, however it seems those discussions didn't go according to plan. Our exclusive photos show a somber Sophie flying home alone while Billy has remained behind with his British-born family, including twins Hayley and Jenny Buskin who are regulars on the LA party scene.

Of course, this wouldn't be the first reported split between the rocky pair, as they parted ways earlier last year when Billy was linked to his former *Halo* co-star Heidi Black – a reunion he has since venomously denied despite being caught in a steamy clinch with the well-known beauty. After several months apart, and Billy vowing to curb his acting career, Sophie and Billy reunited and seemed perfectly happy.

However, the on/off duo have become extremely private about their relationship in recent months. Something which doesn't match with Billy's overtly gushy outpouring of love for Sophie when he won his BAFTA at the start of last year, or how open and honest he appeared on Bernard Sharland's chat show, hoping to rekindle their relationship.

Could it be that his old stomping ground has lured Billy back into the temptations of Hollywood? Has Sophie dug her heels in and fought against moving across the pond? Or perhaps the two have realized how difficult life is when one of you craves the spotlight and the other seeks the shadows.

We've reached out to representatives but no comment has been made at this time. However, while we wait to find out more, here's a recap of Billy's relationships over the years, and how it looked like Sophie May was set to change his bad boy reputation for good . . .

Having read enough I look up and gawp at Mum.

'I can't believe they're allowed to write this rubbish,' I hiss, shaking my head, yet unable to stop myself from looking down at my phone again, as though part of me is hoping the article won't be there second time round.

'Anything you can do to let people know the truth?'

'Not without adding fuel to the fire,' I sigh. 'I don't think so, anyway.'

'And you didn't know your photo was being taken?' Mum asks.

'Does it look like it?' I reply. Although even if I had, I doubt my facial expression would have been any different. It's not as if I've suddenly started playing up to the cameras and smiling at them after all this time. They're a part of dating Billy that I truly do not welcome – nothing but intrusive and invasive. It's horrible thinking you could be being watched and documented like this at any time without having the foggiest idea. It shouldn't be allowed. Surely I should be given the choice to opt out of having my photograph taken, and as for writing this article about me, there must be more gripping and important world news out there for them to report on? 'I don't know who I blame more – the paparazzi at the end of the lens or the journalist sat at her desk fabricating the whole thing,' I say to Mum, feeling myself getting more and more riled up at the indecency. It's one thing to have people you know gossiping about you, but something entirely different to have people who don't know you at all spreading lies.

'So everything *is* OK with you and Billy, then?' Mum asks, apparently needing clarification and clearly not listening to me when I've said not to believe everything she reads.

'Yes, Mum,' I sigh, sneaking a quick glance at Miss Brown who's trying to look as though she's not listening in to our every word. I'm sure I caught her turning her hearing aid up.

'For a second I thought you might've . . . oh I don't know,' she tuts, placing her hands over her eyes. 'I know how you like to protect me from this sort of thing.'

'I would've told you, Mum. You saw me last time,' I say, rolling my eyes as I recall the mountain of tissues I buried myself under in my heartbreak. 'There's no way I could've kept something like that from you.'

'True, you have been quite composed,' she laughs, a sound that seems a trifle forced and more for my benefit.

My phone starts flashing in my hand as Billy's face pops on to the screen. It's first thing in the morning there, so I'm guessing he's woken up to the news, or maybe one of the twins has been in and told him before their early morning workout.

'Billy's calling,' I say to Mum, as an unexpected wave of nerves passes through me.

'Well, you go out back and talk. I can look after the shop for a bit. It's quiet down at the library anyway,' she says, reaching for an apron, looping it over her head and tying it behind her back.

'You sure?'

She nods and turns away from me before picking up a cloth and setting about wiping imaginary dirt from the kitchen counter.

I walk past the well-used oven, grab my coat and duck into the tiny courtyard out back. It's a spot that I hardly ever venture into but feel I need some privacy away from the shop for this chat.

'Hey,' I say softly.

'I thought you weren't going to pick up,' Billy says, sounding relieved to hear my voice.

'Sorry. Mum's here,' I explain. 'Just thought I'd find somewhere to chat out of earshot of Miss Brown.'

'You seen?'

'Yeah . . .'

'I'm so sorry,' he starts.

'It's not your fault,' I mutter, rubbing my hand against my forehead in frustration. I'm feeling overwhelmed by the whole thing but I know that this is only the start of things to come now that Billy is being thrust back into the public eye.

'I know it's not, but it's not nice to be written about. You wouldn't have to put up with rubbish like that if it weren't for me,' he says, clearly feeling guilty.

'I'm not going to lie, it's pretty tough knowing everyone's now going to think there are problems between us,' I huff, hating the part of me that refuses to appease his worry, even though I know it's not his doing.

'It'll be someone else they're writing about tomorrow,'

he says, as though knowing there's a constant stream of fabricated nonsense makes it any easier to handle. It doesn't. Not really. This is relevant to us. To me. I don't care who else they spend the rest of their time writing about.

'People will still think things are bad with us,' I frown.

'Sophie, you know there's nothing I can do,' he huffs.

I can tell he's annoyed, but I'm not sure whether it's at the article and the situation or at my reaction to it. I'm sure past girlfriends would have revelled in having their pictures out there for all to see.

'It's part of who I am. You've known that from the start,' he continues sadly. 'It's not like it's something new. I can't change it.'

His words still me. It's true. I knew who he was before we started dating. I'd also Googled him, so knew he'd previously been written about a lot so that shouldn't have come as a shock. I just had no idea I would be pulled into that side of his world and that our relationship would be hauled out as public property for people to talk and write about. But I'm also left feeling frozen because his words echo an argument we had last year when I was uncomfortable about him having to get physical with a co-star. The comparison to that dark time saddens me.

'Sorry,' I find myself mumbling, hating it when we argue. It's horrible having an air of hostility between him and me. It's not who we are, it's not us. Not when we were cocooned in our safe little haven of Rosefont Hill, anyway.

'No, baby . . .' he exhales faintly. 'I'm sorry. It's not you. It's just hard being so far away from you and not being

147

able to help you deal with this stuff. I forget how daunting it all is.'

'Actually, it's somehow a bit easier to read it when it's not true. It was harder when they were sharing difficult facts about my life as though they were meaningless,' I say with some resolve, trying to laugh at the situation but failing.

'God, yes. This is nothing compared to that,' he says, recalling the day photos of my dad and I were plastered across various tabloid front covers.

'Exactly,' I say in agreement, happier that the atmosphere between us has softened. Neither of us is in the wrong and we have to stay unified in that knowledge.

Although, as I stand there in the middle of a tiny village in rural Kent while Billy is thousands of miles away and about to begin a completely contrasting lifestyle (again), I realize there are certain facts in that seemingly insignificant and trash-filled article that do ring true . . . We are two completely different people with differing sets of ambition, wants and desires. Those are thoughts I've already battled with myself when seeing him thrive in the alien surroundings of Hollywood. I guess I just need to work out if those differences mean anything. Surely no couple can want completely the same things out of life? Surely it's all a game of compromise and give and take . . .

'I'd better go,' I find myself saying.

'You OK?'

'Yes, the shop is just getting busy,' I lie.

Peering through the window I can see it's still only Mum and Miss Brown in there, but I find myself just wanting to get off the phone.

'Will you call me later? On your way home?' he asks.

I agree, hoping the weight that's bearing down on me will have lifted by then.

'So, how is everyone?' Billy asks when I phone him a few hours later.

Thankfully I do feel a little better, having busied myself in the shop all afternoon. That said, I'm sure a few customers were probably whispering about the gossip behind my back and I still haven't managed to work up the courage to go back online. I think I'd rather ignore all the tweets and messages for now and not have to read them – something that's easier to do now I've worked out how to turn off the notifications.

'They're all good,' I say, making my way from the High Street on to the brightly lit path through the park, a route I've walked thousands of times over the years but that never fails to strike me with its beauty. 'Devastated that you're not here, though.'

Billy laughs down the line, knowing the effect he's had on the women (and some of the men) in Rosefont Hill, though he's eternally bashful about it. I know I've not really met many other actors, but sometimes he really can be the shyest hotshot superstar I've ever come across. Being adored doesn't seem to come easily to him, even though he dishes out charm by the bucketload and oozes this effortless aura that instantly makes people warm to him.

'I'll be back before you know it,' he says.

'Try telling them that,' I smile back. 'It's like there's been a death.'

'Don't say that, you'll make me feel guilty,' he cries.

'Poor Mrs Sleep. She was heartbroken earlier when she realized you weren't there to help her to her chair,' I half-joke.

'Well, tell her I miss her,' he replies seriously.

'That'll cheer her up no end,' I smile.

'Good . . . How are the kids?'

'Aaron is bummed you're not going to be teaching him how to ollie on a skateboard. Apparently his friend at school got one for Christmas and has been showing off doing all sorts of tricks on it, and Charlotte wants you to be her penpal.'

'Well, tell Aaron I'll be back next week and don't say anything to Charlotte. I'll just surprise her with a letter.'

'That's sweet,' I say, remembering the excitement I used to feel when any post arrived on the doormat for me. It made me feel so grown up and important. I used to sign up to fan clubs for that reason alone.

'It's so weird here without you,' Billy says with an almighty sigh, as I imagine him sprawled out on a sun lounger in the sunshine.

'Oh behave, you lived there for years without me, now it's just gone back to normal for you,' I say, surprising myself by accompanying my words with an eye roll – something I never used to do but have clearly picked up from Billy's family.

'My normal is with you,' he says softly. 'Without you I am abnormal . . .' There's a pause on the line. 'I don't like it.'

'So I offer you just a piece of normality?' I ask, finding myself mindlessly echoing the words Julie used and feeling a little sick as a result, the uneasiness of earlier returning.

'You say it as though it's a bad thing,' he replies, sounding confused.

'Isn't it?'

'I wouldn't say so.'

'Well, that's good,' I reply, feeling silly for saying anything when he's clearly just trying to be romantic. I change the subject. 'So when are you in for the screen tests?'

'Looks like Thursday or Friday,' he says, sounding excited, and I'm thankful that he is allowing himself to be now that he's sure I don't secretly hate him for taking on the role. 'Ralph wants to take his time and whittle it all down a little further before getting me in the room with anyone.'

'Because you'll be a distraction?' I smile.

'Because they're still trying to keep my involvement a secret until they announce it,' he laughs.

'Makes much more sense.'

'It might mean I'm here until the middle of next week, though. I imagine, if things run to schedule, that there'll be some sort of follow-up meeting once a few decisions have been made.'

'I see . . .' I say, my heart sinking.

'Is that OK?' he asks.

I imagine the frown of concern his face is wearing and feel guilty for not acting totally unperturbed by the whole thing. But I know I'll miss him, and I can't hide that fact.

'Yeah,' I say, trying not to sound too sad as I leave the path and turn on to my road. 'You do what you've got to do.'

'Have you put out an ad for part-time staff yet?' he asks.

'Give me a chance, I've only just got back.'

'Oh yeah. It just already feels like you've been gone ages,' he chuckles, before sounding more serious. 'I don't want you overworking yourself though. You work hard enough as it is.'

'Colin has said he'll help out when he can.'

'The joy of being self-employed.'

'Exactly,' I agree. 'He's like my Fairy Godmother. I'll just need to sort someone a bit more permanent for when you go in February.'

'Am I losing my job?' he asks, genuinely sounding worried.

'If I find someone who can actually bake then you might,' I tease, loving the fact he can make me smile even when he's thousands of miles away.

'You said I was good!' he says.

'We are talking about baking, right?'

'Ha!'

'You're the best,' I smile, lingering outside my house now that I've arrived home.

'I think I might need that in writing.'

'Deal.'

'I'll frame it,' he says seriously, making me giggle, thankful that things feel more normal between us.

16

The following week I arrive home from a long day in the shop after a birthday party. The group of ten women all had afternoon tea – something I've only recently introduced but is going down a storm – to find Mum, Colin, Aaron and a very giddy Charlotte watching *Frozen* for the ten-millionth time. Although Colin has his eyes shut and Mum is flicking through bridal magazines.

I love walking in on them like this. The content family atmosphere they create never fails to pull me in, making me feel secure and loved. Funny to think there were times I felt quite the opposite in the Buskin household, even though there's a public perception of them as an idyllic family from little old England. I guess no such thing exists. We all have our cracks and flaws.

'Guess what I got today!' Charlotte squeals, jumping up from the sofa to greet me, with her Minnie Mouse cuddly toy and a piece of paper in her hand.

'What?' I ask, removing my coat, scarf, gloves and hat, then giving myself a little shake to rid the cold that seems to be glued to me even though I'm back indoors.

'A letter from Billy!' she gushes, opening up the piece of paper. Her delighted brown eyes give it another good look, before she passes it to me.

'She's not put it down since she opened it,' says Colin, sending me an appreciative wink.

'Wow, this is amazing,' I say, rubbing her back as I read it.

'He said he's going to be my penpal,' she grins with excitement, roughly pushing a strand of long brown hair from her face. 'I'm going to write back tonight. Dad said I can use my new purple pen. Even though I'm only allowed to write in black or blue at school. I might use some stickers too.'

'It'll look beautiful. He'll love it,' I say, cherishing how such a small and simple thing has made her so happy and that she has thought so creatively about what to send back.

'Your dinner is in the kitchen, Soph,' Mum says, starting to get up.

'Don't worry, you sit down. I'll go get it,' I say, gesturing for her to relax. I'm not the only one who's been at work all day. 'What is it?' I ask, turning to leave.

'Chili con carne. I've already plated it up for you,' she calls after me. 'Oh, and there's some post for you on the side too, love.'

On my way to the kitchen I pass the side table in the hall and pick up the two letters addressed to me. One looks like a boring bill, while the address on the other is handwritten and has an airmail sticker on it. Along the seam of the closed envelope, in familiar handwriting, is written 'Always with love'.

Billy.

Placing my dinner in the microwave to heat up, I shut the door and rip open the envelope.

Dearest Sophie,

I know you're all modern these days with your phone, laptop and the fact you're even on blooming Twitter AND Instagram (when I'm not) but I thought we could take things old school and act like we're in one of those old books you're permanently reading. It'll give our grandchildren something to be amazed by when we're long gone. No doubt they'll stumble upon a dusty and weathered box in the attic and open it with delight as they realize how much love we once shared . . . or how bad my spelling, grammar and punctuation were. Either way, it'll be insightful.

In short, I know I've already agreed to be Charlotte's penpal, but I thought having something tangible being shared between the two of us might help bridge the gap that's about to be forced upon us just a little bit more. So please be the leading lady of my handwritten love story and reply.

'He waited day after day, saying that it was perfectly absurd to expect, yet expecting . . .'

You probably recognize that one, it's from Jude the Obscure. And NO, I've not read the copy you left here, but decided to Google it on my phone to see if there was a good quote I could nab to make you think I did. This was all I could find that could possibly work in a letter without it looking like I've lost the plot entirely . . . looks like a bleak book, Miss May!

Anyway, I digress.

See you in a few days!

Always with love,

Your Billy Buskin

xxx

I feel as though I might join Charlotte and carry the letter everywhere with me – keeping it close by so that I can have a little look when the pangs of being apart get too much. This first week has been quite difficult, especially as the press haven't exactly helped matters. The first story might have disappeared like Billy said it would (not that I've been looking), but that hasn't stopped the pitiful looks I've been attracting from locals whenever they see me.

But this letter, it makes my heart smile.

Billy's right, it's so nice feeling like I actually have a piece of him in my possession. Knowing that he's handled, thought about and created this little note especially for me is incredibly special and heartwarming.

What a romantic thought, I think to myself as the microwave pings to let me know my food is ready. Before retrieving it, I take out my phone and send a text.

Thank you for putting a smile on my face. I love you. xxxx

I get a reply within seconds.

You kids and your modern technology! ;-)

I grin as I grab my plate and a fork, and walk in to join the others.

17

Dearest Sophie,

I'm writing this on the plane heading back out to LA. Yes, I know I've only just left you, but it feels so strange not to know exactly when I'm going to be seeing you again. Going from working and living together to being miles apart and in different time zones is going to kill me. I hope you know that. I hope you know how difficult it was saying goodbye today. Please don't think it's easy for me.

I actually cried as I made my way through security earlier. Totally acted as though I had something in my eye, though. I think I managed to style it out. My escort asked if I wanted to stop off in Boots for some eyewash . . . I went along with it and bought some. Ha!

I'm so glad you've finally got an extra pair of hands in the shop. I know Colin and your mum (and Charlotte and Aaron) do all they can to help out, but I think having someone permanent will definitely lighten your load. Plus, you'll feel less guilty about taking time off to come and see me . . . I'm not going to push you on this one as I know how busy you are and that you have more than me to worry about — but just know I'd love to have you back in LA with me. I want you by my side, baby. Hopefully it won't be too long until you are.

Always with love,
Your Billy
xxx

This letter arrives at the shop with Postman Steven just before eight in the morning – meaning I, thankfully, don't have to wait until I get home to find he's written. It really helps lift my spirits.

Billy came back home for a few weeks and everything was great again. Back to normal even, just with added movie chat from everyone in the village. Needless to say they were all chuffed to see him back on the High Street and to quash those pesky break-up rumours that were floating around. The newspapers also backtracked on their gossip slightly, although they made it seem more like we'd reconciled rather than admitting they'd got it totally wrong in the first place. It doesn't really matter though, as I've promised myself not to look any more at whatever they choose to write. It's not like anything positive can come from me reading a bunch of extremely loose facts about myself.

It was gorgeous having Billy back in our tranquil little bubble . . . I think we were living in utter denial to be honest, but the weeks flew by and before we knew it he was saying goodbye to us at Heathrow, promising both me and Charlotte that he'd continue to write.

He's right, it's horrible not knowing when we're going to be together again. Although I know that, realistically, it's up to me to find the time and make the journey. I can simply organize cover for the shop and go, whereas his schedule is dictated by a huge team of people who have paid an obscene amount of money for him to be there.

But things are changing here too. Last week was the start of a whole new chapter for me because it was the first week I've actively hired an employee and not roped in

Billy or a family member to help. I've hired Rachel, who is a mum of twin boys and the wife of Shane – a guy I dated a very long time ago. To others this could be an embarrassing set up, but there's no escaping some sort of history when you live in a small village like ours. You'd end up with no one to talk to. Plus, our history together was years ago and I *really* like Rachel.

I didn't actually make the connection between them at first because I heard they'd moved away before getting married and having children. However, they then decided to move back to the area, as we have excellent little schools round here.

When I reopened the shop after Molly passed away, Rachel used to come in with her boys Nathan and James and some of her mummy friends every Wednesday morning. She then started coming in on her own more often once the boys started school, enjoying a bit of time to herself once she'd dropped them off at the gates. No doubt she was rejoicing at having time for a quiet cuppa and a guilt-free slice of cake, without having her two munchkins to fuss over (or share said cake with).

I was quite surprised when she asked about the position the day I put a little handwritten advertisement in the window a couple of weeks ago.

'I was just wondering,' she asked, her mouth twitching as she spoke. 'How many hours were you looking for?'

'Pardon?' I asked, trying not to get too distracted by Billy fist pumping the air behind her as he went to deliver a ham and pickle sandwich to Mrs Wallis.

'The job?' Rachel frowned, pointing towards the window.

'Oh!' I laughed, feeling like a twit. 'Ideally full-time and doing five days a week if possible.'

'Right . . .' she replied thoughtfully, clearly thinking something through.

'Were you . . . ?'

'Well, yes. I've been looking for something now that the boys are at school. It's great that it's local, but I'd have to see if I can work around the hours.'

'I see,' I said, looking at her pensively. 'Why don't you have a chat with Shane and I'll have a little think too. See if we can work something out between us.'

'Really?' she asked, a beaming smile on her face. 'Will I need to come in for an interview?'

'Molly never believed in them. Finding the right person was more important than putting someone on the spot and making them feel inadequate,' I smiled, thinking back to when Molly had first employed me at eighteen.

'Well, thank you. I'll be back first thing tomorrow as soon as I've dropped the boys off.'

And she was. The next morning she bounced into the shop and told me that she and Shane had talked it over and spoken to both their mums. The idea was that she could work eight until four in the week if everyone else helped with taking the boys to and from school, but only if I didn't need her to close up the shop.

I was thrilled and went one step further, saying she could alternate her days and sometimes start earlier and finish at three so that she could pick up the boys too – meaning she wouldn't feel the mummy guilt or like she was missing out. I didn't mind closing up the shop on my own, or dealing with the influx of schoolgirls at around three thirty. They only ever want skinny cupcakes and herbal teas anyway.

The key to making the whole thing work with Rachel, we decided, was flexibility. I liked her and knew I wanted to make it work, if possible. Obviously I still had the problem of getting someone in on Saturdays (we've always closed on Sundays, but that's village mentality again), but I hoped Mum or Colin would like to get involved for now while I found a local schoolgirl who wanted to earn a bit of cash. Rachel has said she doesn't mind doing the odd Saturday here and there either, so that's helpful.

I felt relieved the position was snatched up quickly and by someone who seemed so willing and, more importantly, competent.

So last week marked the start of that new friendship and working relationship. I'll openly admit that I am extremely naff at being around new people (though I am getting better at it), but I somehow found myself looking forward to the new arrangement. I never thought that would happen after years of preferring my own company, although Molly and the shop definitely helped to rid me of most of my unusual ways.

'Morning,' Rachel sings, as she comes through the door and joins me behind the counter.

'Good night?' I ask. One week in and this seems to be the standard rapport we start our mornings with.

'Both the boys were in bed by seven-thirty and Shane was out with his cricket lot, so I treated myself to a glass of wine and a bath. I feel fab,' she shares, her blue eyes shining brightly. The indulgence has clearly done her good. 'Love letter?' she asks, peering at the paper in my hand.

Even though it's from Billy I feel myself blushing before I fold it up and put it into my back pocket.

'How romantic,' Rachel smiles, walking past me to hang up her coat and bag, before pulling a stripy green apron over her faded blue jeans and white t-shirt and tying her blonde hair back so that it's off her face. I haven't tried to make her wear a headscarf like the one I wear each day, although maybe I should at some point. It used to be part of my uniform when I first started working for Molly, but now I do it out of habit rather than anything else.

As I continue to work my way through the morning's batch of treats and delights, I watch as Rachel goes about her own list of morning tasks with confidence and ease, not having to be reminded how to do anything I've shown her. In fact, she does what I've asked and more. Even just one week in she really has shrunk my workload dramatically, making me wonder why I didn't employ someone else from the start. Saying that, I really wanted to show myself that I was capable of doing more than I thought. I succeeded in that mission but am now thankful to be relinquishing some responsibility.

'Do you miss being out in LA?' Rachel asks, once the cakes have been displayed in the cabinet and she's organized all the corresponding labels correctly — little cards that detail what the cake is, what's in it, and how much it costs.

'I miss Billy,' I reply. 'The place I can take or leave.'

'Really?' she asks, sounding shocked as she selects the

shop's playlist on the iPod and Nina Simone's magically soulful sound is released into the room, listing all the things she 'ain't got'.

'Well, it's just not what I'm used to,' I try to explain, because I wouldn't say I disliked it at all.

'Vastly different to here, then?'

'Definitely!' I laugh. 'Everywhere is spread out, meaning getting anywhere on foot is pretty impractical for a start.'

'Doesn't sound too bad,' she shrugs, leaning on the counter. 'And nothing beats a bit of sunshine.'

'You say that, but I found myself gagging to be back here, wrapped up in my coat and gloves,' I confess, hearing how ridiculous that sounds.

'You've got to be kidding me?'

'No!' I laugh. 'It was winter. Winter should be cold and cosy with knitwear, not filled with skimpy bikinis and kaftans.'

'Have you ever lived away?' Rachel asks, standing next to me and helping to spoon cake mixture into little cupcake cases. Something she does without needing to be asked.

'I moved with Billy to London once,' I share, thinking back to last year and feeling surprised when I realize it wasn't even that long ago. I already feel like an entirely different person now.

'How'd that go?'

'Parts of it I loved, parts of it I didn't.' I pause to remember. 'It's chaotic!'

'I bet California is more laidback than that, though.'

'Oh, definitely,' I say, comparing the two in my head

and realizing that each probably has its perks that I just hadn't allowed myself to fully absorb while there. 'I think I just like to be doing something. I'm not very good at going somewhere and not having anything to do.'

'That right there sounds like my idea of heaven, Sophie,' Rachel gasps, placing a hand on my arm to emphasize her point. 'You should be making the most of those times before you have children. They'll quickly get sucked away and turned into a distant memory. In fact, they become so distant they almost become a myth,' she laughs, in a way that tells me she's really not joking but can, thankfully, see the funny side of her manic life.

'Yet here you are adding more to your crazy days . . .'

'Stops me having to think about the empty void that's been left now they're not by my side every waking hour of the day,' Rachel glumly admits, her lips pinching into a downward smile. 'Funny that. I yearned for some time to myself for years, but having it now just feels barren. I had to get a job before I decided to have more children. Time alone can make you think the absurd.'

'Well, yes, and I'm the same in my own way. Minus all the kid chat.'

'Fancy that, two women at completely different stages in their lives, feeling the same void if left without a purpose for too long,' she muses, mostly to herself. 'I wonder how many other women feel that way?'

'And men . . .'

'True. Best not be sexist,' she mutters. 'We're all just looking for a purpose. Something to help us get up in the morning.'

'Hmmm,' I nod.

'Sophie, I honestly can't thank you enough for letting me work in here. I hope you know how much I love it. Sure beats sitting at home and watching the hours tick by until I need to pick up the boys. Plus, and I know this'll sound totally crackers, but I feel like I'm starting to find myself again. When I'm here I'm not Shane's wife or the mum of twins. Not all the time anyway. I'm Rachel. People talk to me. I'm not some bystander in the life of others.'

'I only gave you a job.'

'Is that all it is?' she questions, just as the door opens and in walks the first customer of the day. Ending our conversation.

18

Later on, once Rachel's gone to pick up her boys and the afternoon customers have left, Mum pops in.

'Everything all right?' I ask, halfway through wiping down the tables. I did think once about discarding the mismatched PVC floral tablecloths and leaving the wooden tables bare, but it's amazing how different it made the place look. It felt more like a pub almost, so the tablecloths reappeared and I've made a promise not to ditch them ever again.

'Of course,' she replies, sighing as she pulls out a chair and sits down. 'Just thought I'd wait for you so we can walk home together for a change.'

'Lovely,' I smile, realizing it's something we rarely do, even though we only work at opposite ends of the high street. 'Would you like a drink while you wait?'

'I'll get it,' Mum says, standing up and walking behind the counter. She pours herself a boiling mug of water before adding a camomile teabag. 'So Colin and I talked a bit more at lunch.'

'About moving?' I ask, feeling my chest tighten. The conversation hasn't been brought up again since I got back last month. A part of me was (naively) hoping the topic had been parked and forgotten about.

'No. About the wedding, actually,' she replies, walking back to her seat.

'Oooh!' I say, relief allowing me to giggle as I remember the emotional night Colin proposed in this very room.

'Now, you're probably going to hate the idea, so please say no if you don't want to,' she says, looking pained and excited all at once. 'But, I'd really like you to give me away.'

'Oh.'

'What?'

'I thought you were going to ask me to be a bridesmaid,' I admit, although even the thought of that made me feel a little queasy.

'Are you disappointed?'

'No . . .' I say, shaking my head and trying to work out exactly how the question has made me feel. 'I just hadn't thought about you being given away.'

'It's more of a traditional thing,' Mum says into her mug as she dunks her teabag in and out of the water.

'It's quite a symbolic moment, Mum.'

'Well, yes. But there's no one I'd rather have by my side . . .' she says, looking up at me with an imploring expression on her face.

'I see.'

'It would mean the world to me, actually, to have you walking me from one life into the next. As though you're making that transition with me. That would mean so much,' she says wistfully. 'I'm not leaving you. I'll always be yours, Soph.'

'Oh Mum,' I say, a sob escaping from nowhere. 'I know you're not going anywhere, and I can't tell you how honoured I'd be to lead you into Colin's arms,' I add, knowing my words are true and not just to appease her worried heart.

'Thank you,' Mum says, her own eyes brimming with tears as she stands and walks over to me, pulling me into an embrace. 'I love you.'

'And I love you, Mum,' I sniff, enjoying our physical closeness.

We stay in that hug for a while and I breathe in the familiarity of her. I try my best to savour the moment, to make the most of it.

Mum kisses me on the forehead and backs off with a sigh, grabbing a chair and taking a seat.

'Have you talked any more about a date?' I ask, catching my breath as I wipe down the last table.

'Yes. We're thinking May or June this year,' she reveals with a shy smile as she sorts through the sugar sachets on the table and rearranges them back into colour order. 'I know it's soon, but it's only going to be a small thing. You, me, Billy, and then Colin, Aaron and Charlotte.'

'That's it? You're sure?'

'Absolutely,' she nods, looking up at me. 'All we care about is having you lot with us. You're our beacons of hope. Our family.'

'Our patchwork family,' I smile, thinking of something Billy once said to me, and of the wonderful patchwork quilt he got me for Christmas last year.

'Yes,' she smiles. 'And afterwards, if it's OK with you, we'd love to come here for a little celebration.'

'Really?'

'Why not,' Mum asks. 'It's the perfect place – understated, full of love, and it already holds special memories for us all.'

'It'll be lovely,' I say, finding Mum's smile infectious.

'Glad you think so.'

'What are you going to wear?'

'Nothing traditional. I'm not going to be dressed in a big white meringue, but I thought it would be nice to go shopping with you and Charlotte at some point. Find something special that I won't feel silly in,' she says, putting the sugar pot back in its place and sipping on her tea. 'I think it's important to include Charlotte.'

'I agree. She'll love it,' I smile, thinking how excited she'll be to have a girls' day out.

'I do hope so,' Mum says thoughtfully. 'I hope I'm not going to be a failure to them both. A wicked step-mum who they both hate and despise.'

'Mum! They adore you,' I laugh, shocked to hear this is a genuine concern of hers.

'Oh, I know they like me, but I'm not their real mum. It's such a tricky situation.'

'Well, I for one think you and Colin handle the whole thing in such a beautiful way,' I say, leaning in front of her so that she can see that I mean what I'm saying. Mum breaks eye contact with me and sighs into her cup.

'What?'

'I just wish I'd done the same with you.'

'We coped, Mum,' I say, grabbing her hand.

'Eventually,' she adds, looking up at me with a sad smile.

'We still coped. Those kids are lucky to have you, Mum,' I say passionately. 'And I'm so thrilled to be welcoming them and Colin officially into our family. We work. All of us together living in the present and moving forward. We work. It's something you don't need to question.'

'You're right,' she says with a deep breath, seeming a tad happier now she's voiced the thought.

'Now, let's stop nattering and get finished here. Otherwise we might never get home and I'm starving!' I laugh, giving her a kiss on the cheek before heading behind the counter, grabbing my coat and switching off the coffee machine. I loop my arm through hers and we head for the door.

Monday 22nd February 2016

Dearest Billy,

Is that too formal? I feel like I'm really channelling my inner Jane Austen when writing to you and it always makes me giggle. I hope you know I'm putting on an accent in my head when I write these. I'm like a 1950s radio announcer, speaking in heightened RP. Terribly posh, you know, with all the Ts and Ds present.

I want to start by saying that Rachel is great. Sadly this might mean that you've lost your job, but there is still a Saturday position available, so all hope is not lost (just the majority of it). My only worry is that she'll say it's all too much and quit, but it doesn't seem the case at the moment. If anything, she says it's given her a newfound energy. I love that the shop is still providing people with such life-affirming realizations. Molly would certainly approve.

In other news, Mum's asked me to give her away. I know . . . WOW! I was slightly shell-shocked at first, but now I'm thrilled to be taking on such an integral role and to be there for Mum right up until the pinnacle moment.

They're planning on a wedding in May or June, which is perfect as you'll be back by then. If everything runs to schedule at least! Also, they're going to have a little party afterwards in the shop – just us lot. I might ask Rachel if she wants to help set up and then serve though. I'm sure she won't mind and it'll mean we can all just enjoy the day.

As for me coming to see you, gosh, it's a tricky one. I want to make sure Rachel feels comfortable with everything in the shop first. She's got her own chores perfected, but it'll take some practice for her to do my load as well. Although the good news is that she can definitely bake! Hopefully I won't feel too bad at the thought of leaving her once she's had a bit more time here. Saying that, I know Colin would help out too. It's not like I'd be suddenly asking the poor woman to run the place alone . . .

Sorry, went off on a tangent.

I hope you're having a wonderful time there and that the sun is shining.

Send my love to your family. Oh, and tell Lauren I read one of her books and really enjoyed it. It might not be what I'd normally go for, but it certainly took me off into another world.

Missing you so much.

Love you,
Sophie xxx

Tuesday 1st March 2016

My dearest Sophie,

Now I also have a silly voice in my head when I write! Actually, the thought made me laugh so much that I've started reading them out loud as I write them, too. Although rather than someone prim and proper like Jane Austen I feel like Carrie Bradshaw from Sex and the City. You probably won't have ever seen that show (which is a little perplexing as it's definitely targeted more at you than me), but it's about four single women in NYC, one of which has a weekly column for a newspaper and can often be seen sat at her desk typing away while her highly provocative and enlightening words are voiced out loud. Gripping stuff . . . Anyway, I've started to feel like her.

Can't believe we've struggled to have a decent phone call since your chat with your mum. I hate being in a different time zone. It wouldn't be so bad if it weren't for my long days on set and them being a mishmash of days and nights. The hours are ridiculous. Seriously, Ralph is certainly getting his money's worth on this shoot. I don't stop.

Anyway, I just want to put in writing (for the record) that I think you giving your mum away will be such a beautiful moment for the two of you. I'd say me and my mum are fairly close (when she's not doing my nut in and trying to force me into things I don't want to do), but you and your mum have experienced so much more together. The respect and love between you both is something I truly admire. It's so special.

I'm chuffed to be ring bearer too! I was worried with Aaron there as best man (I still find that heart-melting stuff) and Charlotte there as The Boss of All Bridesmaids Ever (she told me that's her official title), that I'd be the only one without a role. Colin was such a blundering mess when he asked. I won't lie, it got me all choked up. Bless him.

So glad things with Rachel are working out. Not surprised she's taking to everything really easily – she's been running around after twin boys for years. Compared to that, being in the shop with you must seem like a doddle. I can't believe I've lost my job to her though. Damn her and her efficiency.

Things are ridiculous here. Since the announcement about the casting, the press have been really on at me. It's not nice at all. I'm just thankful to be heading to the studio every day, otherwise I think I'd quickly go mad. All the cast and crew are lovely, though. And Ralph is on a whole other level of genius compared to any other director I've ever worked with. He's so deep and profound – sometimes I just find myself nodding as though I know what he's on about but really I haven't a clue. I don't want to look like a total airhead. I'm getting away with it so far but I'm bound to trip up at some point.

We had a surprise visitor turn up last night – that little brother of mine. He's only here for a couple of days, but it's already been so good to see him and hear his news. New York is certainly keeping him busy.

Everyone sends their love. Lauren says she's halfway through Jane Eyre and is 'surprisingly' loving it.

Missing you silly amounts.

Please book a flight soon.

Always with love,
Your Billy Buskin xxx

Monday 7th March 2016

Dearest Billy,

Sex and the City doesn't sound like the sort of thing I'd watch with Mum by my side, so maybe I'll have to give that one a miss. Ha!

Amazing that Jay has been there with you . . . I bet you're loving having some male company in the house besides your dad.

I'm really missing you this week. I know that's silly, but it's suddenly hit me. I think I was in a bit of denial before, or caught up with the hilarity and excitement that I'm now someone's actual boss. OFFICIALLY!

It's lovely having someone in the shop with me, although it does suck that they're not you. I think I was absorbed in the novelty the first week, but the last two weeks I've been hit with the reality

173

that you're not here and that I don't know when I'm going to be able to see you next. It really sucks . . . and you're right, not being able to talk on the phone whenever we like really isn't helping.

Sorry if I seem a bit of a grump, I guess that's why it's taken me a while to write. I'm fine, honestly – just missing having you by my side to talk nonsense to all day long and to cuddle up to at night. But I'm going to the cinema tonight with Charlotte and Aaron to watch some Disney movie while Mum and Colin have a 'date night'. So I'm sure that'll cheer me up – those two never fail to put a smile on my face.

I probably shouldn't send this. All our letters have been light and bubbly so far and I don't want you worrying about me. But then I hate keeping things from you too. I'd want to know if you were down. Blah!

Love you always and forever!
Sophie xxx

I look at the writing on the page that I've just scribbled down. What is it about writing that allows feelings to find their way out of your head in a way that would be near impossible on the phone or 'face to face' on Skype? It just feels more permanent to lie in the written form, and it's tougher to put on a brave face even if you're more hidden than ever.

I think about not posting the letter, as I wrote, but somehow I find myself slipping it into the red postbox on my way to work the next morning anyway. I tell myself that I'll just have to warn Billy that a sadder letter is on its way to him, and not to take too much notice of it. We both have to face the reality of the situation we're in and get on with it.

19

Dearest Sophie,

I haven't received the grumpy letter you phoned to warn me about yet, but I hate to think of you so far away and down about the situation. Please know I'm not finding this easy either. I imagine it's simple to think I'm over here 'living the life' on a film set, but you know how boring these things actually are. I'm keeping my head down other than being there. My life is literally here at home, there on set, in the rehearsal room, or in my trailer. I'm enjoying the work though. I don't want you worrying about me either.

Now, I know you might tell me off for this, but you miss me (sounds like your letter is going to declare it quite plainly) so I'm hoping it won't make you too angry . . . I've phoned and spoken to Rachel, Colin and your mum. They've cleared a week for you to come and visit . . . SURPRISE! The flights are all booked. Once you get this I'll email all the booking confirmation over so you know all the details. I'll be honest, I was going to organize it for you to be here for two whole weeks, but figured you'd worry it was too long away from the shop — you are a businesswoman nowadays and I respect that you have your own life to lead and can't just drop everything as and when. I hope me helping plan it has lessened your guilt or worry though. So sorry it's you having to travel to me and not the other way round. Soon I'll be back in Rosefont — albeit jobless. ;-)

Hopefully you're wearing a great big smile now or dropping a few tears of joy.
I love you.

Always with love,
Your Billy Buskin xxx

Yes, his words make me smile and cry, but mostly they make me laugh. I can't help but giggle at the thought of finally seeing him as I cover my face with the letter he's sent me. Four weeks is such a long time to be separated from someone when you're used to seeing them every day.

I should have just booked the flights. I didn't realize just knowing I would be seeing Billy would bring me so much happiness. I should have known there was a simple solution and that Rachel and my wonderful family would selflessly help out. Besides, Rachel has been here a month now and has proved she's more than capable of coping without me.

I grab my phone, unlock it and tap on Billy's name. There's a short delay before the all-too-familiar international dialling tone starts. He doesn't pick up. Hardly surprising as it's after midnight over there and we've already spoken this morning. I opt to text him instead.

I just opened your letter – I can't tell you how excited I am. I want to know more. Wake up! Love you. Thank you!

'Something's certainly made you smile today,' smirks Rachel as she walks through the shop door a few minutes later. 'I can only imagine what.'

'You!' I smile, pointing my finger at her accusingly as laughter spills from me, causing my body to shake.

'What? What have I done?' she asks innocently, her hand on her chest in protest, unable to hide the knowing look on her face.

'Billy sent me a letter telling me he's spoken to you guys about looking after this place and that he's booked me a flight to America.'

'Finally!' she dramatically sighs. 'I've been so scared I was going to trip up and ruin the surprise. You wouldn't believe how many times something's been on the tip of my tongue and I've had to run off and stick my head in the fridge.'

'Well, I know nothing! I've tried calling Billy but he went to sleep an hour or so ago.'

'How useless!'

'So you have to tell me!'

'Really?' Rachel asks, her big blue eyes looking panicked. 'I'm not sure I'm allowed to divulge any information. I was sworn to secrecy.'

'But I know now.'

'True . . .' Rachel says with a pained expression on her face.

'Can't you just tell me *when* I'm going? That's not a big deal,' I shrug innocently.

A frown appears on her forehead as she looks at me and continues to size up the situation. 'I think you should call your mum or Colin. They'll know what they can tell you and that way I won't get into trouble.'

'Seriously?' I laugh.

'Absolutely.'

I chuckle as I pick up my phone once more and call Mum.

'Sophie! I'm just walking to work. Have you forgotten something?' she asks, slightly out of breath.

'No, I'm just calling because a certain little letter has arrived from a certain someone telling me about a certain trip he's booked me.'

'Ah!' she giggles.

'But Billy's asleep!' I say with exasperation.

'Oh . . .'

'Please give me a little more info. Rachel's proving to me that she's totally trustworthy by withholding any further information,' I say, causing Rachel to laugh as she organizes the chairs and tables in the shop, which were stacked up on Saturday night so that we could give the main floor a proper mop.

'Well that is a tough one . . .'

'Not you too!' I shriek, knowing another person is going to keep me guessing.

The shop phone rings, causing Rachel to stop what she's doing and dash to answer it.

'It's for you,' she says with an innocent shrug while her mouth splits into a beaming smile.

'Billy,' I whisper, realizing it's been days since I actually heard his voice thanks to his busy schedule and the time difference. 'Mum, I've got to go. Billy's called back,' I say, putting down the phone and leaping to the landline.

'What have you done?' I grin, feeling light and giddy, my breath rising to my chest.

'Ah, there's my smiling girl,' he chuckles sleepily, causing my heart to swell. 'I can't wait to see you this weekend.'

'This weekend?' I repeat with excitement, my voice high pitched and shrill. 'I'm seeing you this weekend?'

'If that's good with you?'

'It's perfect,' I sigh, laughing as tears spring from my eyes.

'You pleased?'

'Pleased doesn't quite cover it.'

'Good.'

In that moment I love him more than ever, and it's not because he's paid for me to fly out there, but because he's dealt with the whole thing. More than anything it shows that he must really be missing me as much as I'm missing him and that makes me so absurdly happy. Because as much as I hate to admit it, the distance between us has made me worry that I'll be forgotten, that Julie could be whispering in his ear again about the difficulties within our relationship. Or what if he'd realized he doesn't love me quite as much when I'm out of sight? Actually, it's not even like I've only been out of sight, we're in two different worlds living totally separate lives. So it's comforting to know I've not evaporated from his memory and that he's sticking to his word.

That afternoon my head, arms and the rest of my upper body are practically inside the glass counter display cabinet, giving it a good spring clean, when I hear the door open and heavy footsteps walk inside.

'Just a sec,' I sing loudly at the shadow looming in my peripheral vision, still feeling giddy from the morning's excitement and knowing I'll be reunited with Billy in just a matter of days.

'No rush,' says a deep, male voice, a sound I wasn't expecting.

I jump so high I bash my head on the glass above me and let out a strangled 'Ouch.'

'You OK?' asks the voice, sounding amused and just a touch concerned.

'Sorry,' I say, straightening up slowly whilst rubbing my head and turning towards the bronzed man who has entered. 'Peter!' I exclaim, taking in the face I barely know, yet feel has been present for a large chunk of my life. I can't believe I didn't notice how much he resembled his mum Molly the last time we met. Although that was such a sad time, having just said goodbye to my dear friend, I don't think I was up to absorbing much. But now I see Molly in the fine wrinkles around his twinkling blue eyes, in the sharpness of his nose and in the way his mouth opens to give such a welcoming smile. The similarity is pretty breathtaking.

'I thought I'd find you here,' he grins, ruffling a manly hand through his sun-kissed hair as he stands in the middle of his mum's old shop, looking dapper in his dark grey suit.

'Where else?' I say, reciprocating the grin. 'What are you doing here? Why aren't you in Australia?'

'Long story.'

'Want a cuppa while you tell it?' I ask, already grabbing a pot and two mugs. It's ten minutes before closing, so I know I'm fine to stop and chat. And although I know talking to near-strangers isn't like me, I feel as though a long-lost friend has just walked back into my life, making my heart feel light and giddy in his company.

'Oh, go on, then,' he says warmly with a touch of an Aussie accent as he pulls out a chair and sits on it. 'Love what you've done with the place . . . books!' he says, looking over at the cabinet that hosts a variety of my favourite reads for customers to pick up and enjoy. I wasn't sure they would at first, but it's proved very popular. Even with the teenagers.

'Jut a few bits here and there. Nothing dramatic,' I say, hoping he's not offended by anything I've changed.

'And the name?'

'Ah!' I smile. 'I wanted to acknowledge the fact that your mum's still a huge part of the shop even though she's not physically here,' I say, explaining my decision to change it from Tea-on-the-Hill to Molly's-on-the-Hill. 'Of course, it confuses people every now and then. A few times I've been called Molly and I've just had to roll with it. It stopped me in my tracks to begin with, though,' I admit.

'She'd have found that funny.'

'Seriously, I had to look behind me to make sure she wasn't stood there,' I giggle, making my way over to him with the tea and a selection of cakes.

Peter catches sight of the treats in my hands and laughs to himself.

'What?' I ask.

'Mum trained you well. A conversation's not worth having unless there's tea and cake.'

'She had a good point,' I reply, feeling my cheeks blush. 'So. Spill. What's brought you back?'

'Work. It's actually that simple,' he shrugs, while opening both his palms to the ceiling.

'You said it was a long story,' I frown suspiciously.

'I managed to condense it,' he laughs.

'So I see.'

'Basically, the company I work for has set up an office here and they wanted me to make sure everything was going smoothly. Apparently a British accent wouldn't make them feel like I'm someone from the Aussie team sent here to spy on them.'

'But you are?'

'Partly,' he says, pursing his lips together to stop himself smirking.

'And I hate to break it to you, but you've definitely got a twang of Aussie in there.'

'It's unbelievably catchy,' he laughs, shaking his head before exhaling a lungful of air. 'Ironic, isn't it? That I get sent here now Mum's gone.'

'Cruel, maybe,' I nod, knowing how much Molly would have loved a surprise visit from the son she talked about constantly.

'Don't make me feel too guilty,' he winks, before picking up a slice of cake and taking a large bite of it. It's a far cry from the delicate way my cakes are usually eaten. It's manly, rough and unexpected. I find it difficult to tear my eyes away.

'So, how long are you here for?'

'At the moment it's hard to say. Could be a month, could be a year. Or it could be their callous way of outing me over here without me kicking up a fuss. Let me get settled long enough that I won't grumble about not being back there in the sunshine with my surfboard,' he shrugs, taking another huge mouthful of cake.

'What about your life there?' I ask, surprised they've uprooted him and sent him to the other side of the world without a proper plan.

'Split up from my girlfriend over Christmas.'

'Oh, I'm sorry.'

'Nah, don't be – all she did was give me aggravation,' he says dismissively. 'I have a little bar near Bondi Beach that I own with some of my cousins, too, actually. Although, I think they'll be fine running it without me until I'm done.'

'So nothing to rush back for?'

'Just the sun and my board,' he laughs, the thought of the things he loves brightening up his face and causing his eyes to twinkle in a way that feels familiar. 'Missing it already and I've only been here a few days.'

'A few days in and you've already managed to escape from the office and head out to Kent by five o'clock? They'll be wondering what they're paying you for,' I joke, thankfully making him chuckle.

'First week,' he shrugs. 'They're being quite slack with the hours while we all get adjusted, so thought I'd make the most of that, get back here early and go see Mum's grave, you know . . .'

'Oh, right. Of course.' There's a heavy pause. 'How was it?'

'Like talking to a slab of concrete,' he says dismissively with a sniff, which fills me with sadness.

'I'm sorry you feel that way,' I reply, thinking of the comfort I've received in the past from visiting Molly and Dad at the cemetery, and the hours I've spent just sitting there talking about everything and anything. Each time I told myself I could feel a presence, convinced one of them was there with me.

'No, don't get me wrong, that's where her body is. I get that,' Peter continues, nodding his head in agreement with his own train of thought. 'But she's not there. Her spirit isn't there. She's here, you know? In these walls,' he gestures, looking around the shop.

The notion makes me smile. I've no doubt Molly and my dad are always with me, helping me make important decisions, or just sitting there as spectators of my life. Yet the notion that Molly is also somehow embedded in the fabric of the room we're in warms my heart.

'That's a wonderful thought,' I say, continuing to ponder it as I put half a lemon drizzle slice on a plate and fork some into my mouth.

'Well, that's the way I see it, anyway. Even the house isn't the same.'

'Is that where you're staying?' I ask, thinking of Molly's three-bed terrace house down the road where I know Peter spent his childhood.

'Never got round to selling it,' he shrugs. 'Maybe this was the reason. Some higher being knew I'd be back here sooner rather than later. The commute's not bad, mind.'

'Is it nice being back in your home?' I ask.

'I guess . . .' he frowns. 'It's so bare, though. So empty. I thought I'd feel something there, but I don't.'

'Oh,' I say sadly, again wishing his answer had been a little different.

'As with the grave, she's not there.'

'Right,' I nod, pensively.

'She's here, though. I felt it as soon as I walked through the doors,' he says, looking around the room. 'If I want to be closer to her I'll have to come in here.'

'Well, you're more than welcome here as much as you like,' I tell him.

'Thank you,' he smiles in response, before exhaling loudly and fondly looking around the shop once more. 'So how's it been with this place?'

'Great,' I exclaim proudly. 'Challenging, obviously. I've never run a business before, but I think I'm coping.'

'It's a place you know better than anyone else, so perhaps give yourself a bit of credit,' he says, holding eye contact with me while briefly touching my arm. It's a fleeting gesture, just a moment before he breaks away and reaches back for his cup. 'Have you got someone in helping you?'

'Well, Billy was here,' I say, his comment having caused an unexpected sense of pride to swirl around in my chest.

'Billy?' he asks, looking confused.

'My boyfriend.'

'Of course. Sorry. The actor,' he says, clicking his fingers as he remembers the information. No doubt Molly had told him all about our situation dozens of times on the phone.

'Yes, that's right. He was helping out but I've now got my first bona-fide member of staff,' I say, raising my eyebrows smugly as I nibble on a bit more yellow sponge.

'Wow, that's really something.'

'It is,' I nod, enjoying his reaction. 'I've introduced a

proper afternoon tea package, too. It seems to be going down a treat. I'm enjoying experimenting to see what works, like me and Molly used to do with our recipes . . . I'm still missing a Saturday girl, but I'll cope as long as my mum and her partner keep generously lending a hand during the busy hours.'

'Well, I can always help out if you like?'

'Really?' I say, trying my best not to laugh, which turns into me choking on a piece of cake that I accidentally suck down my windpipe. 'Sorry,' I say, once I've recovered. 'But you don't need to do that.'

'I can handle serving cake and tea one day a week,' Peter frowns.

'Thank you for the lovely offer, but we're coping at the moment.'

'Fair enough. The offer's there if you find you're stuck, though,' he says, raising his hands as though sacrificing himself. 'I'm only around the corner and I think it would actually be quite nice being here, doing what Mum used to do.'

'Well, I'll let you know, then,' I say, remembering what he said earlier about Molly being a part of the place.

'Great,' he says, as though it's a prospect he's really looking forward to.

'I'm away for a week from Saturday actually,' I blurt, without thinking.

'Need me to cover?'

'Well, maybe . . . perhaps,' I say, feeling cheeky as I say it. 'I'll give Rachel your number just in case. If that's OK?'

'More than OK,' he says, his face kind and friendly. 'Are you going anywhere nice?'

'LA. To see Billy.'

'Lucky . . .' he says, before trailing off. 'Well, thanks for the tea and cake,' he adds, standing and putting a coat over his suit jacket.

'It was nothing.'

'I promise I'll be back soon. Oh and here, take this.'

He puts his hand in his wallet and takes out a business card.

The tips of my fingers touch the inside of his warm palm as I take it from him, making my neck, cheeks and ears instantly and unexpectedly flame up.

'For when you want me to be your new Saturday girl,' he laughs, making to leave before turning to face me once more. 'Obviously you know the telephone number at the house, but that's got my mobile number on it. Just in case.'

'Thank you,' I smile, knowing that Molly's old landline number is, as he thought, perfectly drilled into my memory.

'Oh, and I'll be sure to keep this weekend free.'

'Great,' I smile, standing up to see him out. 'Take care.'

'You too, Sophie,' he calls, turning his back to me while waving his hand in the air and walking outside into the darkness of the late afternoon. 'Don't have too much fun in LA. See you when you get back.'

'Bye,' I sing.

I follow him to the door and flip the open sign to closed. Without thinking I find myself watching Peter bob his way down the hill, stopping to say hello to other shop owners along the way, all of whom know him from when he was younger and look delighted to see him again.

How wonderful to be part of a village community like ours where you can go away for months, or even years, and still feel so embraced by everyone when you come back. The thought makes me smile as I turn and get ready to go home.

20

Billy doesn't have a chance to pen a letter back to me before I fly over there because by the time I get on the plane he still hasn't received mine. Seriously, I know it's romantic and wonderful to have something tangible from each other, but occasionally the time spent waiting for a piece of flimsy paper to travel halfway across the globe is incredibly infuriating. I'm starting to question how any of the beloved characters in my favourite novels managed to hold on to their sanity waiting for a love interest to get in touch. I've always thought I was an incredibly patient person, but it turns out I'm not. Not really.

Then again, I know there are many more ways to stay in touch thanks to modern technology, but they also require you both to be available and not running a busy shop, filming intricate fight scenes on set or sleeping, thanks to your exhaustingly long days. So, believe it or not, those little letters have stopped me pulling my hair out at times.

Still, I'm relieved that we'll both be spending a whole week in the same time zone again – and in the same bed, too.

When I giddily arrive in LAX (having rather enjoyed myself on the flight this time – I guess it's something I'm getting more used to), Lauren is waiting for me, her hair scruffily tied back in a high bun and her lips redder than ever. However, this time she's slightly more covered up. There's not a bikini in sight, instead she's in jeans, a red t-shirt, black hoodie and leopard-print slipper loafers.

'Surprise!' she grins, throwing her arms around me and hugging me tightly. 'I'm so happy you're back!'

'So am I,' I smile, although my mind's already worrying whether the clothes I've brought will be warm enough (Lauren was never this covered up last time I was here), and also wondering why Billy hasn't come to meet me in person.

'Didn't he tell you?' she asks, pulling back and looking at my face as she picks up on my thoughts (and possibly senses my disappointment).

I won't lie, I was looking forward to a little airport reunion. Nothing that would capture the attention of other travellers, obviously, but simply that romantic first glimpse of him as the crowd between us parted. Watching his face light up as our eyes met, and feeling my heart lighten at the mere sight of his smile . . . That would have been delicious. It's fair to say that being greeted by Lauren doesn't quite conjure up the same emotional tug.

'What's that?' I ask her, trying not to sound glum and to just be happy that my second-favourite Buskin is here and so clearly pleased to see me.

'Billy. Obviously you weren't expecting to see me.'

'Well, no,' I admit, my cheeks blushing at her correctness. 'But it's a lovely surprise.' I smile, not wanting to offend her. It's sweet that she's come and James the driver hasn't just been sent for me instead.

'Well, he did leave in a hurry this morning, I guess,' she frowns, as though annoyed for me.

'Maybe my texts haven't come through yet,' I say, rummaging through my bag to locate my phone, but finding there's nothing from Billy. Just a goodnight message from Mum and one from a new US network service provider telling me about my tariff.

'Oh well! He was meant to have today and tomorrow off but got called into a meeting last minute. So I'm picking you up and taking you home. He might even be back by the time we get there. Hopefully.'

'Oh great,' I say, remembering the unpredictability of Billy's job and how plans can change quickly.

'To be honest, it's probably best I'm here anyway. You don't want the paps working their magic to fabricate a story out of nothing every time you arrive or leave. Plus, it's hardly the most glamorous photoshoot location, is it? The lighting is hideous. Shall we?' she smirks, already heading off towards the car park. It might not be Billy greeting me, but Lauren's mannerisms and confidence manage to put a smile on my face nonetheless. 'James has headed off with Billy so you'll have to put up with my driving. Don't worry, now that big brother of mine is back I've been having lots of practice at chauffeuring myself around,' she grins.

And she's right, she's not too bad – even if she does talk nonstop the whole way and look at me a bit too much rather than keeping her eyes on the road. It's great to have the lowdown on what's been going on there. The twins have been going to every celebrity bash possible now that the Buskin name is back in the limelight and the invites have been flooding in, Julie has remained serene and 'less of a bitch' while Billy's been there, and their little brother

Jay visited from New York for a few days, much to her delight. But the biggest news is that she's got herself a job as an intern at a fashion magazine. It's unpaid, the hours are atrocious and her boss sounds like a total dragon – but other than that it's wonderful, she tells me with a laugh. I assume the change of pace to her days is also what's caused the change in her attire. Gone are the days of sitting by the pool in her bikini, now she's on call twenty-four seven waiting for her boss to phone with an emergency. Funny to think of her running around after someone, but she insists it's all part of working her way up the ladder and seems incredibly happy at finding herself a job and giving her days some sort of meaning. A feeling I can relate to and fully understand the importance of. Plus, it's hardly surprising that things are less tense at home now that she's given herself a purpose and is juggling her own set of responsibilities. It would probably do them all good to do the same. It's interesting that the two younger Buskins have chosen to break away from hanging off Billy's coat-tails and are now flourishing as they strive to give some meaning to their lives. Bizarrely, I find myself feeling proud of the choices Lauren has made since I last saw her; there's no denying how much she's matured.

As soon as I arrive at the house, Julie and Clive engulf me in their overly familiar hugs with Julie leading the interrogation on how the past couple of months have been back in England. It actually feels lovely to be reunited with them both, and I'm happy to discover I feel nothing but warmth in their company.

That said, I welcome the tranquillity of Billy's room when I eventually walk in and dump my hand luggage on his bed (Dee snatched my case out of the boot before I'd even taken off my seatbelt). As it lands, I hear a crumpling of paper underneath and find my last note to Billy, which must have arrived that morning. Well, at least it got here, I reason. Thankfully, nothing's gone missing in the post so far. That would be a heartbreaking disaster.

I pick it up and read a few of my own words excitedly talking about Peter's return as I take it to Billy's bedside table, where I find the complete collection of letters from me and Charlotte. I run my hands over them. It's been just over a month since Billy flew back over here and already he has a sizeable wodge of our written thoughts. It's so lovely to think he sleeps with them close by, just like I do at home.

As Billy's not arrived back yet I make the most of being alone and nip into the shower so that I know I'll smell nice and fresh when he gets here, and not of stale plane air.

Ten minutes later, in a brilliantly clean The White Company dressing gown, I walk out of the bathroom to find Billy on a sofa at the window looking over a script and talking to himself. He's clearly learning lines.

Sensing me in the room, he looks up. As our eyes meet my insides melt – a sensation I'm pleased to feel after being apart for so long.

'There she is,' he beams, chucking the script on the floor by his side and striding over to me.

'God, I've missed you,' I say as he places his hands on my waist and lifts me into his arms, making me feel as light as a feather. I wrap my arms and legs around him, holding him closely, wanting him to understand just how much I've been craving this moment. No matter how difficult the distance between us has been so far, this closeness makes it all disappear.

'It's so good to have you here,' he breathes, his luscious brown eyes locking on to my own and holding my gaze, as though he's searching them for something.

'What?' I whisper.

'Nothing,' he says, looking down at my lips.

He kisses me then. Softly at first, breathing me in as his hands slowly glide along my back.

Quickly, the kissing intensifies and becomes passionately electric. My gown is discarded on the floor. His t-shirt is wrenched over his head and thrown aside. His belt unbuckled. His underwear pulled down.

Billy pushes my naked backside against the wall and runs his fingers along my bare chest, kissing my neck and making me groan.

I grab hold of one of his butt cheeks and pull his body towards mine.

He complies.

My head explodes with joy and satisfaction at being reunited with Billy.

My Billy.

'I'm so sorry I wasn't there when you landed,' Billy says later on, while running his fingers through the front of my hair – it was wet when I got out of the shower and has since dried. God knows what sort of state it's in now. I imagine it's wavy with plenty of frizz added in for good measure.

We're both still naked, but have found our way into Billy's bed. Our limbs are wrapped and knotted together, comfortably draped over each other. I feel utterly exhausted, but incredibly happy.

'My heart sank when I walked into Arrivals and didn't see you . . . I just wish you'd told me,' I reply honestly.

Seeing as I've been here a few hours already and no text or voicemail has made its way through to my phone, it's clear he hadn't actually got around to letting me know about the change of plans. Which wasn't very thoughtful of him.

'Sorry. I wasn't thinking. I got a call from the studio first thing and then your letter arrived . . . the morning just sort of disappeared,' he shrugs.

'Don't worry,' I say quickly, not wanting to create an atmosphere. There's clearly a rational part of me that knows these things happen thanks to his unpredictable working hours, and that there's little he can do to change that.

'I'm all yours for the rest of the weekend though.'

'Hurrah,' I say, turning and giving him a kiss, before snuggling back into his chest and enjoying the warmth of his body.

'Anything you want to do while you're here?'

'Nope. I'd be happy to spend the whole time in this bed with you,' I tease.

'Now wouldn't that be amazing,' he groans, running his fingertips gently along my side and making me giggle.

'How unlikely is it?' I ask, finding myself pouting like a little girl. I know the next thirty-six hours or so are all ours, but I greedily want more, knowing I'll be leaving him again next Saturday. 'Is next week jam-packed?'

'Yep. But you can come on set with me and hang out,' he suggests.

'I think I'd rather not. It's work. You'll be busy,' I shrug suddenly. My mood instantly changes, something that makes me feel stupid and childish, but I can't help it.

'Are you mentally scarred from the last time?' he asks softly, picking up on the slight edge to my voice that I wish I'd been able to hide a little better.

I take a deep breath at the thought. The last time I ventured on to a movie set was a total disaster. Billy had been shooting this film about a legendary rocker for a few weeks and it was finally time to capture the saucier moments in the script. I told him and myself that I was totally fine with the whole thing and that I understood it was simply part of his job. Billy even went out of his way to make me feel better by organizing for me to be on the set during filming so that I could see how mechanical it all was, even though all unnecessary crew had been ushered out for the day.

The fact is, I shouldn't have been there. I realize now that scenes like that are filmed on 'closed sets' with a limited number of crew present for a reason. A frustrating day led to a manic and goading director pushing Billy too far for my liking, which led to me seeing more than I'd ever want to in terms of Billy getting physical with another woman. I was embarrassed and humiliated. Especially when I had a near panic attack in front of everyone. Actually, it was more like a banshee having a breakdown as I let out an almighty wail and caused filming to come to an abrupt halt so everyone could turn and stare at me, the girl screaming because her boyfriend had just been forced to lick another woman's nipple. The thought of it still makes me shudder.

It's fair to say I don't want to go on to another film set

if I don't have to, especially as word has probably got around about my last visit to one. In fact, I'd be surprised if the people in charge and spending loads of cash on the film would let me anywhere near the studio anyway.

'You know there's nothing like that in this film,' Billy says gently.

'Yeah . . . I know,' I say, squirming at my inability to talk about what happened, even after all this time.

'Look, the schedule has been all over the place so far,' Billy sighs, starting to sound frustrated. 'Sometimes I'm there all day from six in the morning until ten at night doing different bits and pieces. I'll get to see you so much more if you come along.'

'I'm not coming.'

'Even though I've paid for you to travel all this way?' he asks, moving away from me so that we can properly see each other.

I stare at him open-mouthed.

'What?' he questions, raising an eyebrow at me and looking annoyed as he clenches his jaw.

'Are you actually throwing the fact that you surprised me with tickets back in my face? Because I didn't ask you to do that. And you paying doesn't mean I need to comply with everything you want me to do,' I retort angrily.

'No, you don't, but it would be nice considering.'

'I don't want to go,' I say adamantly, my face turning red at the memory of something which sadly still makes me feel extremely uncomfortable. Which I thought Billy of all people might have understood.

He sits up and exhales loudly. 'I thought we were past all that. We've moved on.'

'We have!' I say, stunned at his reaction, which is bordering on disgust.

'I thought you'd forgiven me.'

'I have.'

'Then why won't you come and spend time with me when you've flown all this way to see me?'

'Billy, it's not that simple,' I try to explain.

'It's not?' he challenges.

'You know me. I'm no good in those situations at the best of times.'

'So for as long as we're together you're not going to come with me on set?' he asks, his eyes wide and disbelieving.

'For as long as we're together?' I ask, feeling my face sting as though he's slapped me. 'What do you mean by that?'

'Nothing.'

'No. What did you mean?' I push, my voice becoming stronger as I tackle his choice of words.

'Nothing,' he says swiping his hands apart and shaking his head. 'We're arguing. I didn't mean that to come out the way it sounded.'

'Good, because it sounded like you were implying we're not going to be together forever.'

'You know I don't think that. My future is with you.'

'Right,' I say, our stances within the altercation shifting, with me suddenly becoming the one who's annoyed and him being the one needing to defend himself and backtrack.

'I think I'll just leave you to do what you have to and I'll chill here until you have time off. Or I'll go exploring. It's a big city with lots to see and do,' I say with finality, letting him know that there's no way I'm going to budge on the matter. Not right now, and certainly not after the way he's reacted.

The fact is, I'm a different girl to the one who was by Billy's side in London last year and, quite frankly, I don't want to put myself in a position I know I'll find uncomfortable. I now feel wise enough to decline such an offer, regardless of how much we want to make the most of our time together in the same city. As far as I'm concerned, I've seen one film set and that'll do for now. LA, on the other hand – that has far more to offer.

'Fair enough,' he says tightly, sounding disappointed as he gives up the fight.

We sit in silence for a few moments. I find myself wondering what he's thinking and whether he feels as rotten as I do. The money aspect aside, I have flown a long way to be here and am deflated that it's not all been rainbows and sunshine between us the first time we've been face to face in weeks. Part of me wants to grab my bag and go, just so I can avoid this uneasiness and pretend it's not happening.

This sucks.

It's so far from the beautiful reunion I'd been expecting.

'Sorry,' he mumbles eventually, putting his hand on my shoulder and pulling me towards him.

'No, I'm sorry,' I sigh. 'I'm over everything that happened, I promise. I'm just not ready for *that* yet.'

'I get that,' he nods.

'I'm fine, though,' I add, trying to sound slightly more upbeat now that we're both working to break down the tension that's arisen.

'Well, that's something,' Billy says softly, unable to

remove the sad smile from his face. 'I didn't mean what I said about the money thing.'

'No?'

'I'm just absolutely shattered.'

'Me too . . .'

'I hate it when we argue.'

'We didn't argue,' I shrug.

'No?' he asks, his eyes starting to smile and regain their sparkle.

'We just had a minor disagreement.'

'Oh, I see . . . so we're OK?'

'Absolutely,' I say.

'Good,' he says, leaning over and giving me a lingering kiss on the lips.

'Hungry, though,' I smirk.

Billy throws his head back as laughter erupts from his mouth. We're both clearly relieved at the change of subject.

'Well, we can't have that, Miss May.'

'So tell me everything. What have I missed?' Billy sings flamboyantly as soon as we've ordered dinner. At my request he's brought me back to Little Dom's and we're in a nice little booth in the corner. I've been dreaming about them ever since the last time I was here, so I've ordered the meatballs.

'Have you gone all LA on me?' I snigger, raising an eyebrow at him – although I'm thrilled the atmosphere has now totally dissipated and that we're back to having fun with each other.

'I don't know what you're talking about, sister,' he says in an American accent, as his hand swishes through the air in front of his face.

I cackle in response.

'Seriously, I can't tell you how much I'm missing the peace and tranquillity of Rosefont,' he says, taking a deep breath at the thought of my little village.

'So you will be coming back then?' I ask, not realizing I'd even been thinking he wouldn't until the question comes out of my mouth.

'Are you kidding me? It's like a second home. Actually, more of a home than this place.'

'Well, that's good to hear,' I say, an unstoppable smile spreading across my cheeks.

'Although . . .'

'Oh God . . .'

'No, don't panic. It's just I've been meeting a few people over here – new management and so on, and we're working out what I want.'

'What do you want?' I ask, feeling something clamp hold of my chest and my jaw stiffen. His comment from earlier is starting to rear its ugly head again.

'If I'm honest I think I hated the craziness before, although the further we get from *Halo*, the more I think it'll calm down. Like this project, yes, it's going to be huge –'

'I can tell you've been with Ralph.'

Billy laughs at my interruption.

'I know, I know.' He swallows. 'I just think it's going to be different without the teenage heart-throb title attached and without that stupid lothario image the tabloids had pinned on me before. I'm more grown up now. I'm settled. I look at it as my craft rather than something to get me into the LA hotspots. I want to be the best actor I can be. That and *you* are my main focus. Not the rest of the rubbish that can surround it if you let it.'

'So you're saying . . . ?' I ask, wondering exactly where his speech is leading.

'I wasn't going to do this on your first day here, but I'm trying to find a way of balancing everything,' he declares, reaching across the table and taking my hand in his. 'I know it's not ideal being away from you for long stretches of time, but I'm hoping, if everything is arranged properly, that I'll also be with you for long stretches of time.'

'Billy?' I ask firmly, wanting him to cut the fluff and not feel like he has to sugar coat how he's feeling.

'I'm not giving up acting,' he says, his shoulders relaxing as soon as the words are out of his mouth, as though he's been terrified of sharing them. 'But I'm not giving up on us either.'

'I didn't think you were.'

'Good.'

'And I certainly don't want you to feel like I'm holding you back.'

'Of course not. I don't . . . it'll all work out,' Billy says, continuing to nod his head as he squeezes my hand, making me wonder if he's saying this all for me, or if he's actually trying to reassure himself.

I look up to see Billy frowning at me nervously.

'Are you OK?' I ask.

'I've never felt for anyone else how I feel about you. I just want to get it right,' he whispers.

'We will,' I nod, blinking back the tears and hoping beyond hope that we can keep our word.

'I'll be home once shooting wraps on this. That's still

my plan. I might be back over here for a couple of months from September, depending on what projects come up. I'll definitely be home for the summer and then again for Christmas.'

'So you won't be missing Mum and Colin's wedding,' I say with relief. I know they'd be more than understanding but I think we'd all be gutted if he had to miss it.

'I'm ring bearer!' Billy exclaims, his eyes wide. 'I'll have you know that it's a very important role. Without me the wedding simply can't go ahead.'

'So you'll definitely be there,' I smile.

'I would never miss that,' he says seriously, holding my gaze for a few moments before looking away and shuffling in his seat. 'So how are the wedding plans coming along?'

The conversation is moved along and happily stays away from the uncertainty that looms ahead of us. On the one hand I completely agree with Billy – I've never felt the way I feel about him towards anyone else, so surely that means we'll be stronger in this situation than most couples might be. On the other hand, can a relationship really survive when there are thousands of miles between you both?

I guess only time will tell.

Perhaps this is another lesson in 'living in the moment', rather than worrying about what will or won't be.

All I know is it's worth a shot.

I'm sure of it.

21

The last time I was here Julie was trying to force the entire family into spending as much time together as possible, clearly trying to make the most of Billy being here and thinking they only had two weeks with him. This time, though, things are far more relaxed, with everyone just getting on with their own plans despite me being here, which for someone who doesn't like a fuss is brilliant.

They all seemed as though they were pleased when they saw me the previous day – I bumped into Hayley and Jenny as they got back from having their nails manicured and we were off out to Little Dom's. Other than that, though, there's been no talk of dinner or trips out together. It feels like I'm just lodging at the house and free to come and go as I please.

It might not be the family unit I'm now used to having with Mum, Colin and the kids, where our lives are nicely knitted together, but then they're a different bunch of people doing entirely different things with their days.

For various reasons – mostly because she's the most laid-back and warmest of the bunch – I could really see myself bonding with Lauren far more than anyone else in the Buskin clan. So it's a shame she's gone and got herself a job, as I'd like to have spent a bit of time getting to know her better while I'm over here again and largely going to be without Billy's company. I hope we'll find time to hang out together at some point, although it sounds like her boss is making the most of her free labour.

Billy and I don't discuss the shape of our future the following day, and I assume that's because there's really not much to talk about. Nothing has been set in stone yet and there are no solid plans, so it's hardly worth getting upset over something that could easily change or turn out to be far more manageable than I'd imagined in the first place. That's what my rational side is telling me, anyway. For now, I'm deciding to listen to that rather than dwell on any uncertainty.

Instead, we enjoy each other's company and don't venture too far from the house. The morning is spent lounging by the pool and then in the afternoon we head to Silver Lake – a little residential neighbourhood that's built around a gorgeous lake. The best bit? Heading to a shop called MILK and buying a gorgeous strawberry cheesecake ice cream to eat while we meander our way around the reservoir, going far slower than the dozens of locals we spot jogging the route either in groups, pairs or on their own.

'This is so nice and chilled,' I find myself murmuring as we head past a dog park, a place where dogs are free to run around lead-free and poop in a confined space away from everyone else.

'See? LA's not all parties, flashy cars and spotting famous faces.'

'Thank goodness. I think I'd hate it if it was.'

'So you don't *hate* it?' he asks, raising an eyebrow at me as he licks the side of his rum and raisin ice cream to stop it dripping down his hand.

'No.'

'Do you love it?'

'I don't think I've seen enough of it yet to know. It's lovely, though,' I say, giving it some thought. 'I do like coming here.'

'Well, I'm glad you've not been put off just yet.'

'Not yet,' I laugh, nudging into him as he reaches over, puts an arm around me and kisses the top of my head. 'So, what's Peter like?'

'Pardon?' I laugh, surprised at the change in conversation. 'What made you think of him?'

'I was just thinking about your last letter. You seemed pretty pleased he's back.'

'I don't really know him,' I admit. 'But he's Molly's son and seems like a nice guy.'

'Well, that's good,' he responds, his arm protectively squeezing me into his body once more.

'It's Rachel that's the total life-saver, though.'

'I knew she'd be great . . . not better than me, though,' he grins.

'Clearly. That would be impossible,' I laugh, poking him in the ribs.

On the Monday morning I get up with Billy when he goes to work. I know I should be making the most of having a lie in, but my body still hasn't got its head around the time difference. So when I'm woken by the sound of Billy's alarm it's difficult to drift back off to sleep.

Once Billy's left for the studio I slink into the kitchen, grab a fresh orange juice and a croissant and head back to

Billy's room where I sit on the sofa by his window. Snuggled up in my pyjamas, I watch the city awaken.

Growing up in the glorious countryside I never thought I'd find beauty in any city. They always seem so concrete and ugly, unchanging no matter the season, so I'm surprised when I take in this wonderful view. Perhaps it's because we're high up in the hills and therefore treated to an expansive sight, rather than hidden within a cluster of skyscrapers stealing the light from everything else in their shadows.

I watch as the sun slowly creeps up from one side, bringing with it the brightest oranges, the most luscious purples, vivid reds and perfect pinks. It's stunning. Simply beautiful and unlike anything I've ever seen before. The way nature frames the man-made city makes it look tropical, majestic and enticing.

Within minutes the sun rises higher in the sky, flooding the city below with its brilliance, declaring that a new day has officially begun. Having witnessed the transition I find myself quite taken by the city, so decide it's time to explore.

As soon as I'm showered and dressed, I grab my small rucksack and book an Uber into Los Feliz (Billy made me download the app which is apparently essential here in LA when I don't drive or have my own driver). The car arrives within minutes and takes me down to Vermont Avenue, the road where I spotted the little independent bookshop when we arrived in December.

I walk into Skylight Books and can't help but smile. It's small, unique and homely. In fact, it's a little like Mum's library back home, but LA-ified with the help of a tree growing in the middle of it. It's completely random but it adds an element of magic to the space.

I slowly work my way along the shelves, loving that nothing looks familiar. Almost every publication has a different cover to the ones I'm used to. They're all packaged differently for the US market which makes me feel like I'm discovering my favourite old classics all over again.

I leisurely pick up books and read a few pages of each before putting them back, feeling completely at home surrounded by the smells I know and love, even though I'm somewhere I've never been before.

Hours pass by in this way.

Before I know it my tummy's growling to let me know it's lunchtime. I buy a couple of books for myself, Lauren and Billy (he probably won't even try to read them, and she probably won't have time, but you never know) and head back out into the sunshine to a little café nearby where I order myself a chicken salad and green smoothie. I'd never get myself something like this at home, but there's something about being out in the heat that makes me veer towards a healthier option – my body craving more natural goodness now it's getting a huge helping of vitamin D.

It's only when I'm sitting down having a slurp on my drink that I take my phone out and realize Billy's called a few times as well as texted to see if I'm OK. Bless him. I send a quick reply assuring him that I'm fine and filling him in on my lazy but lovely morning, to which he tells me he's extremely jealous and that he hopefully won't be home too late tonight. Always great to hear. Instead of heading back home as planned, I continue to spend the afternoon mooching along the high street and the surrounding streets. I even find myself in a little park at one point and quietly sit and people-watch, which is fascinating because everyone is so different here.

I completely understand why Billy and his family ended up living West in Los Feliz rather than being isolated in Beverly Hills – although I'm sure even the Hollywood elite have a hubbub of activity that's just as intriguing as this.

Just like my last trip I'm struck by the amount of homeless people wandering around or gathered in groups drinking. They look happy enough, but the sheer volume of them is what alarms me. I remember seeing homeless people in London, but they were generally lonesome individuals or a rarity. Here it doesn't feel like that. It feels like a community, which just highlights the magnitude of their plight. Although none of them appear sad. They're just getting on with life in the town known for its rumoured stream of endless possibilities for the people who move there, longing for their dreams to be fulfilled. It's hard not to look at them and wonder what their stories are and how they ended up living on the streets. It's hard not to feel for them. Yet I bet the last thing any of them want or need is my pity. At least I'm not ignoring them, I guess. I'm not one of those who turn a blind eye to their existence.

When I've had my fill of watching the varied collection of people passing by, I decide to walk back up the hill rather than get a car. I'm in no rush to be anywhere, after all.

It turns out the walk is a bit further than I imagined

and that the hill is a little steeper than the one back in Rosefont. It takes far longer than I thought it would. When I arrive back on the front doorstep I'm a hot, sweaty mess and decide to head straight to the kitchen to get myself a cold drink.

Walking through the doorway I hear a load of voices in the house, but it's only when I'm on the sweeping staircase that I realize they're coming from the lounge below.

'Sophie,' Billy sings, as soon as he sees me. 'I've been calling you.'

'Really? Sorry, phone's in my bag,' I puff, looking at the other faces in the room as I make my way closer, wishing I could have quickly had a shower before bumping into anyone.

Julie and Clive are standing with Richard and a woman who looks like she could be in her forties, although I imagine she's a lot older – one thing I've really learnt here is that it's near impossible to guess someone's age. Framed by a fashionable below-the-shoulder blonde haircut, her tanned face is catlike, with taut skin gliding over her cheekbones. Her outfit is minimal and nondescript, yet stylishly decorated with the help of a dainty line of pearls around her slim neck. She looks professional, powerful and full of character.

'This is Rhonda Wilson. My new manager,' says Billy, gesturing towards her.

'Oh, gosh,' I stammer, looking down at myself and sweeping my frizzy hair back off my face. 'Sorry, I don't normally look like this.'

'Shame, I think you look fabulous,' Rhonda purrs,

holding out a hand for me to shake as her eyes twinkle in my direction.

'Not sure about that,' I mutter, feeling embarrassed at having her look even more closely at my appearance.

'Drink?' Julie asks, grabbing a glass and pouring some iced lemonade into it for me. 'Here.'

'Thank you,' I smile, taking it and enjoying the freshness in my mouth.

'Let's sit down,' Julie flaps, guiding everyone to the plush sofas. Bizarrely, she seems nervous, which is not how I'm used to her behaving at all, she's usually so calm and in control – well, when things are going her way that is.

I do as I'm told and go to the furthest spot on the sofa. As Rhonda gracefully sinks down beside me, I find myself sitting next to the new woman in Billy's life.

'Sorry we've popped in unannounced,' she says, her hands neatly folded on the tops of her thighs. 'I'm sure Billy's told you that we've been having a few meetings but now we've made everything official. I just dropped in so he could sign the contracts before he changes his mind. Now the boring bits are out of the way we can move forward.'

'That's great,' I reply, not realizing things had already progressed to this stage. A couple of nights ago he said he'd been having some meetings, but not that things were at the stage where contracts were being signed. This seems like Billy has been far more productive in making decisions than he's let on.

'Decided to grab the bull by the horns, at last,' says Richard, patting Billy on the back with a huge grin on his face.

'Am I the bull or the horns?' Rhonda asks in a measured tone as she turns to him with her eyebrows raised.

For the first time I've seen since meeting him, Richard is speechless. He stands open-mouthed while the rest of us try our hardest not to laugh.

'Richard put me in touch with Rhonda,' Billy explains to me. 'They go way back.'

'But not too far back,' Rhonda adds, unable to stop a smile forming. 'Now, Billy tells me you own a shop in London.'

'Just outside,' I nod, guessing she won't have any idea where Kent is, but enjoying the fact that she's taken an interest in me and what I do, despite being here on her own special business. 'It's a teashop, so there's lots of tea and cake.'

'Sounds charming.'

'Thank you.'

'Business is good?'

'Really good,' I nod, feeling like I'm being interviewed but not entirely sure what for.

'Is it the sort of place you can franchise? Or have other shops within your control open up?'

'I've never even thought of it,' I admit with a shrug. 'It's not the sort of shop you can replicate. I wouldn't want to. It's too special . . .'

'Plus you've got all sorts of plans for the place,' encourages Billy.

'Exactly. One shop is enough to keep me busy,' I laugh.

'Lovely. And you've never thought to try your hand at acting?' she asks, tilting her chin ever so slightly into the air as she waits for my response.

Her question catches me so off guard that a loud laugh

pings from my mouth, surprising us both. 'Sorry,' I manage, controlling myself.

'What's so funny?'

'I'm not . . . no. It's not for me,' I say, manically shaking my head at the thought, whilst my arms seem to take on a life of their own, bashing the idea away.

'Such a shame. With your looks and that adorable accent we could've made magic. People are screaming out for authenticity and normal folk. Stars they can instantly connect with,' she continues, looking at me sadly in a longing manner that almost makes me feel as though I'd say yes to anything she asked of me. She clearly knows how to work people in an endearing and friendly fashion to get what she wants. 'There's a reason Jennifer Lawrence has made such a splash, you know,' she continues. 'Obviously her talent is a huge part of it, but all that goofy behaviour and falling over on every red carpet she treads? Well, that's the work of a genius and can't be fabricated. She's a normal girl living in a fantasy world. People love that. It's easy to connect to.'

'Well, you'll have no luck with that one,' Billy tells her, gesturing towards me with a broad smile on his face. I'm relieved he is finally coming to my aid before I lose my mind and sign my life away.

'So I see,' Rhonda says, looking at me from the corner of her eye while talking to Billy. 'Still, can't be greedy. At least I have one of you.'

'So, what's the plan moving forward?' asks Julie in her newly found meek voice, eager to get in on the conversation and, no doubt, hear that Rhonda has huge things lined up for Billy already.

'We take one movie, one role and one project at a time,'

Rhonda shrugs, as though it's an obvious way to manage things. 'I know Billy's last manager worked him to the bone, but we don't want people getting bored of his face and feeling like they're seeing too much of him. Sometimes less is more.'

'Pick and choose your projects to maximize your potential,' chimes in Richard, eagerly nodding along to what we're hearing. 'You're more than a fad.'

'Quite,' says Rhonda, turning to Julie. 'I know a lot of people are interested in working with Billy right now, but *not* working with them will make them hungrier for him in the long run.'

'I see,' Julie nods, sucking in her bottom lip at the statement that's the total opposite of the one she used to try and persuade Billy back into the studio.

'Although he's definitely right to be working with Richard right now,' she laughs, making Julie smile at Billy in an 'I told you so' fashion.

'But moving forward, sustainability is what we're after,' Rhonda continues smoothly, her tone serious and business-like. 'We're working on a lifelong career, not putting Billy into a fleeting popularity contest that can have a million different variable outcomes.'

I look over at Billy and watch him listening to Rhonda's every word. I can see why he decided to be looked after by her. She's smart, direct and really seems to know what she's talking about.

'What about him living in London?' Julie asks, looking up at Clive who, rather uncharacteristically, gives her a sterner expression than I'm used to seeing from her peace-keeping husband.

Rhonda screws her nose up as her shoulders bounce in response. 'I appreciate that things might've been different when Billy first moved over here with *Halo*, but now location really doesn't matter. Billy won't be going to an endless number of auditions with the rest of the LA cattle. He's at the point now where he gets to pick the roles. End of.'

'That's my boy,' Clive says quietly, winking at Billy while clenching his fist with pride.

'Quite,' Rhonda smiles, turning to Billy. 'As I said before, your base can be wherever you please. The most important thing is that you're happy and inspired. No one is that when they're forced to live in one place and their heart is off elsewhere. You'll do your best work when you're happy, Billy. I can make the rest of it fit around that.'

Billy turns to me and grins, clearly as pleased as I am with everything that's being said.

For once I feel as though it's really possible to have everything.

Now, wouldn't that be nice.

22

Rhonda and Richard don't stay for much longer. As they both seem to be at the top of their professional games, I'm sure they have a million things to be getting on with aside from making small talk with us – even if we are linked to one of their hottest talents.

Once they've gone, Julie releases a lungful of air as she places her hand on her chest, visibly relieved that the encounter went well. Seconds later, Dee enters the room with several glasses of champagne, a sight that is welcomed with a coo of delight from Julie.

'I'm so proud of you,' she sings, going over to Billy and pinching his cheeks with one hand while simultaneously downing the contents of her glass in one.

'What's he done this time?' asks Hayley as she and Jenny appear from downstairs in comfy clothing with rollers in their hair – clearly getting ready for another evening out.

'Billy's just signed with Rhonda Wilson,' Julie squeals, holding out her empty champagne glass to Clive, who silently takes it from her, refills it and hands it back without flinching.

'Now that calls for a celebration!' exclaims Jenny, looking impressed.

'Yes! In fact there's a new club opening tonight in West Hollywood. Anyone who's anyone is going to be there.

You two should totally come with us,' invites Hayley, looking as though she'd love nothing more than to turn up at this exclusive event with her brother by her side.

My insides instantly knot at the thought of going anywhere like that. I know I've never been out on the Hollywood scene (I've barely ventured on to any 'scene'), but all I can envisage in my head is dozens of paparazzi clicking away as we arrive and leave, standing uncomfortably in a loud, dark, cramped room, and having to watch while Billy gets cornered by millions of tipsy girls who look utterly perfect – like the twins. Not one part of that image fills me with the desire to go get my glad rags on.

'I've got to film tomorrow . . .' Billy says apologetically, something I'm rather thankful for.

'That's always your excuse,' retorts Hayley, her face collapsing with annoyance as she rolls her eyes in Jenny's direction.

'That's because the studio is working me hard,' reasons Billy.

'And once again that's paying off!' chimes in Julie, although I think the only people listening are Clive and I.

'But we never get to see you,' Jenny pouts.

'I know, but . . . maybe another time,' Billy suggests, uncomfortably shifting his body on the sofa.

'Promise?' challenges Hayley, giving a little jump of excitement.

'Yeah,' Billy laughs, shaking his head at them, happy he has lifted their moods and sidestepped a confrontation.

'Yes!' giggles Jenny, as though he's offering them something far more special than he has.

His promise might fill them with excitement but it does

the opposite to me. In fact, even though it's a very loose agreement, I can't help but think of the Billy Buskin the press used to love writing about – the one with a love of clubs, alcohol and women. I know he's here to work and that one night out doesn't necessarily equal a never-ending party, but still, it unnerves me to think of him back in the environment that he used to love.

Not that I'd want him to feel he can't do as he pleases here. I certainly don't want to be the nagging girlfriend from across the pond, stopping him from having fun. After all, he'd be with his sisters and I'm sure they wouldn't want him to get up to no good. Not that I think he would, anyway. He's not an impressionable teenager any more. These days he's a grown man with his own mind.

I guess this is just another case of us finding enjoyment in different things and I know there's nothing wrong with that, as long as that enthusiasm doesn't create a conflict of interest in terms of our long-term desires . . . and one night out on the town couldn't do that. Not to us.

'Rhonda, huh?' Lauren mutters, walking into Billy's room a few hours later. Looking absolutely shattered from a long day at work, she throws herself on the end of the bed where we've been curled up chatting for the past half hour. 'Mum just told me. I missed about ten calls from her today. Honestly thought someone might've died.'

'Gladly not,' Billy grins, reaching behind him and chucking his pillow at her.

'Oof!' she laughs, grabbing it and placing it under her head, snuggling down and making herself comfortable. 'Seriously, though, well done.'

'I didn't realize management was such a big deal,' I say, not meaning to voice the thought out loud.

'They can make you or break you,' says Lauren sleepily, closing her eyes.

'So they say,' smirks Billy.

'I have some news,' Lauren says, prizing one eyelid open to find us both staring at her.

'Oh?'

A cheeky smile spreads its way across her face as she enjoys holding our attention as we wait for her to speak.

'Tell us,' I say, an unexpected bubble of suspense washing over me.

'I'm going on a little trip with my editor Patricia,' she teases.

'Where to?' I ask.

'London!' she grins, pushing herself up off the bed and performing a crazy little dance in the middle of the room – her hips wiggling from side to side as she waves her arms around wildly and shakes her head.

'No way,' Billy laughs. 'How come?'

'There's some fashion event she's going to and she needs a couple of lowly interns there to boss around,' she says, happily out of breath and looking extremely pleased with the gloomy description she's just given.

'When?' I ask.

'In a few weeks.'

'That soon?'

'And I'm flying economy,' she says to Billy with a panicked expression, although the little sparkle in her eye tells us the thought of it actually thrills her. 'I don't think I've done that since I was a kid.'

'You're such a brat.'

'Totally!' she laughs.

'You'll have to come see me. You could even stay,' I offer, knowing Mum and Colin would love to meet her.

'Ah, thank you. I would've loved to but they're putting me and another intern up right next to the venue – just to ensure we'll be available to wait on Patricia hand and foot. I'll only be there for a few days, but nothing will stop me sneaking out to see you,' she says, jumping back on the bed.

'You're such a rebel,' Billy grins.

'Don't you know it!' she laughs. 'It's going to be so much fun!'

'I didn't even think you liked London,' Billy continues, raising a questioning eyebrow at her.

'I love London,' she gasps, acting shocked that he'd assume such a thing. 'I mean, the weather I can take or leave, but . . .' She stops and thinks for a second or two before continuing. 'Actually, I'm just so happy to be getting away and doing something different.'

'You'll be an editor before you know it,' Billy encourages.

'All right, Mum,' she mocks, shaking her head at his enthusiasm. 'Let's lower those expectations of yours . . .'

'Let's raise yours!'

She rolls her eyes at him before grabbing hold of my hand. 'I was just going to turn up and surprise you, but I couldn't contain it. Although it's a shame it's not for longer. It would've been lovely to have some proper time over there. Maybe next time.'

'Even catching a glimpse of you would be better than nothing,' I beam.

'Aaaaah . . .' she squeals as she dives on top of the covers and squashes my body underneath her own, making me howl with laughter.

The thought of having her in London causes a surge of giddiness to fly through me. I'm not sure whether it's because of my fondness for her, or simply knowing that a little bit of Buskin will be close by even though Billy will still be stuck over here on set. Either way, I can't wait to have her on English soil.

PART THREE

23

'Peter said he might pop in today,' says Rachel, once she's delivered a chicken salad roll to June Hearne and is making her way back to the counter.

'Oh, really?' I ask merrily, flashing a smile I've not stopped wearing since I walked in this morning. It feels so good to be back.

It's nice to hear Peter's popping in too. I'm so grateful to him for helping out while I was away. He actually ended up doing both of the Saturdays so that Mum and Colin could drop me off at the airport on the first Saturday, meaning neither of them had to do the long drive back on their own. He might have only worked two days, but having him there meant I didn't have to worry too much about anyone working a full six-day stretch, or Mum having to take time off from the library so that she could slog away at the shop. Plus, I've no doubt Mum will be wanting to save up her holiday, as she's got a honeymoon to be thinking about.

Realizing I've not heard anything about them taking a romantic getaway yet, I make a mental note to ask her about it. Depending on when they go, Billy and I could always have the kids so that they can have a proper break. I think that actually sounds like fun for all of us.

'He left his coat here,' Rachel says. 'Phoned yesterday

and said he has a lunch meeting in town today so will head back after that and get it before we shut.'

'Must've been a cold commute without it!'

'I'd say. Spring my arse!' Rachel laughs, looking out of the shop window and shuddering at the sight of the cold weather that's lingering and refusing to leave.

Laughing at her response, I pour us both a cup of hot tea.

It's my first day back since landing from LA yesterday and I'm in dire need of the caffeine. Although I'm fine when I'm doing something, it's when I stop that I get light-headed and tired. Which is funny, considering I had a week of doing half the amount I do here and managed to sleep the whole flight back.

'I probably won't be able to stick around past three today, though,' Rachel adds, grimacing, as though she's sorry for knocking off early even though she's just worked a full week without me. 'The boys made me promise I'd pick them up from school today.'

'Of course. Don't be daft. I asked enough of you last week,' I say, shaking my head at her and feeling guilty for working her so hard it's made her boys miss her.

'Thank you,' she smiles, looking relieved. 'I'm sure Peter will be happy to lend a hand if things get busy. He was great.'

'Well, he did say he has a bar back in Oz, so I guess he's used to serving and everything that comes with it,' I offer, realizing I've not specifically asked how things went with him, yet. Although I'm sure she would have mentioned if he'd been awful.

'That'll be it,' she nods, with a smile as she waves

goodbye to one of her mummy friends, who's heading out the door, dragging her uncooperative two year old along with her.

'Were the ladies all gushy?' I ask, taking another gulp of my drink and thinking about how they still act around Billy, even though they've known him for a couple of years now. I always find it funny that our dainty little shop causes any human with a higher testosterone level and a slightly deeper voice to stick out a mile and get fussed over.

'Actually, no. It was sweeter than that. It was as though they just really wanted to talk to and confide in him. And he listened,' she gushes, as though caught in the memory.

'Is it only them he won over?' I ask with a grin, finding her smitten reaction funny.

'What?' she asks, looking at me with a confused expression before the penny drops, the way she's been talking about him dawning on her. Her cheeks might redden slightly, but she brushes it off, screwing her face up in the process. 'Now, Sophie, I'm a happily married woman! That said, we all know how much us ladies love to be listened to, and to have something pretty to look at,' she laughs.

'I'm sure Colin had the same effect?' I chuckle, raising a playful eyebrow at her.

'You know what, your mum had better watch her back with him. He's just delicious with a heart of gold,' she coos, putting her hand to her chest as she turns on the hot tap and starts doing the washing up.

'Couldn't agree more,' I nod, not giving too much thought to the idea of Colin running off with one of my old dears. I know they say you never can tell, but I'm pretty certain he's not the sort to do such a thing.

'How is it that I was in LA sunning myself for a whole week, yet you're still more tanned than me?' I laugh when Peter walks in that afternoon. I'm in the middle of prepping for a big afternoon tea party the following day and making sure I have everything I need. My hair is sweatily stuck to my head beneath my headscarf and my matching turquoise apron is covered with flour . . . it feels so good to be back in my comfort zone!

'It's deeply ingrained,' Peter laughs in response, his hand rubbing along the afternoon shadow on his face before he rests his elbows on the counter and leans over to see what I'm doing. 'You've got a lovely golden glow, though. I've got that rugged, rough Aussie thing going on. If we're honest it looks a bit like I need someone to give me a good scrub.'

'No, you don't. You look great,' I say, feeling slightly mortified as the words leave my mouth. Clearly he does look fab, he's a handsome man. I just didn't mean it in the dreamy way it came out.

'Ta,' he says, shrugging it off – much to my relief. He straightens up and scratches the back of his neck, just underneath the collar of his white shirt. 'So how was it?'

'Good!' I nod, getting out a mug and filling it with tea for him before gliding it across the wooden worktop.

'Yeah?' he asks, winking in thanks as he picks up the tea and takes a gulp. He clearly has a mouth made of steel when it comes to boiling water. I prefer to let my drinks sit for a bit to avoid burning the roof of my mouth and ruining my ability to taste for the rest of the week.

'Well, the weather wasn't quite as hot as it was at Christmas, but I still managed to spend the majority of the week working on my non-existent tan and reading,' I laugh, giving an accurate account of the majority of my time over there. Even though I managed to explore a lot more than I had when I was previously there – it was great being able to do the touristy bits like the Hollywood Walk of Fame without worrying about Billy being recognized and badgered – basking in the sun's warmth was still a novelty compared to how chilly it is in Blighty right now.

'You probably needed the break. It's exhausting working here,' Peter says, before turning around and walking over to a table that's only a few feet away. He pulls out a wooden chair and slumps down on to it, as though the very thought of what I put him through over those two days here as our 'Saturday girl' is shattering enough.

'Oh gosh, was it tough?' I fret, hoping he didn't completely hate it, especially as it seems everyone else loved seeing him.

After Rachel's glowing report, every regular who came in mentioned how wonderful it was to have Peter here, many asking whether it's going to become a regular occurrence. Honestly, the way they react around and talk about Peter and Billy makes me wonder whether they'd still come in here if it wasn't for the occasional promise of rather attractive male company. Although I'm sure the temptation of cake and a hot drink helps lure them in too.

'Well, I thought dealing with drunks was bad,' says

Peter, widening his eyes and giving a little shake of the head, his mouth twitching into the tiniest of smiles. 'But your customers are something else. Boy can they natter.'

I laugh loudly at his observation and the difference between how he felt compared to everyone else. There he was making customers feel special, but in truth he was probably just too polite to end conversations and walk away. I know they love to talk, and I expect that can be quite jarring if you're not used to it.

'You should've just said you had work to do and kept things short. That's what I have to do when we're busy,' I admit, although I always feel rotten when I do it. I love fussing over them all, just like Molly used to do. It's what makes this place special and different from the chain cafés on every high street around the globe. Not only do we have heart, but we take the time to value our customers when we can. What we do here is about far more than money.

'Nah, I actually enjoyed it to be honest,' Peter shrugs, shifting in his seat. 'It was great hearing their stories. Plus, especially with the older ladies who live alone, that might have been their only bit of interaction for the day, so I'm definitely not complaining. I'd rather they chewed my ear off than felt an ounce of loneliness that day.'

'So you've not quit yet, then?' I ask, quite taken aback by his sentimentally thoughtful response and pleased that he understands what Molly founded here all those years ago.

'Nope, still here as the emergency cover as and when you need me,' he says, knocking the table with his knuckles.

'That's good to hear,' I smile, taking some glass bowls out of the cupboard and laying them out on the kitchen side, in piles according to when I'm going to need them, along with all the dry ingredients. I'm quite used to chatting while getting my chores done now. If anything, I think the distraction can actually make a conversation flow more easily for me. It always gives me something else to focus on and moves my attention away from the interaction I'm having.

'Did you know I used to know your mum and Colin?' Peter asks after taking another slurp of his tea.

'Oh really?' I reply in surprise, proving that I didn't. Funnily enough, in the handful of times that I've met him they haven't been about. Plus, this is a village where everyone knows everyone, so if anything it's more strange that me and Peter never met when we were younger. He is a little bit older, so I guess that by the time I was playing in the park or out on the street (believe it or not there was a time in my childhood where I was sociable), he'd probably have moved on to pubs and clubs.

'Well, me knowing your mum isn't a big shock. Every local child of school age in the last twenty years or so must know her from the library because we used to go in there every Tuesday for a monitored study class.'

'Don't tell me, she was always telling you to keep the noise down? Librarians are renowned for that,' I half joke. My mum is meticulous about keeping things clean and tidy, but also about adhering to rules – like only whispering when surrounded by wonderful books and others trying to enjoy them. I've no doubt my timid mum can be quite stern when faced with a library full of teenagers.

'Ha! No, not at all. She was great actually. I was useless at finding the books I needed but she always helped out.'

'Well, that's sweet,' I reply. It's great to think of all the kids Mum has encouraged with books and reading over the years. She's certainly the reason I'm an avid bookworm.

'And I knew Colin and Pauline. You know, his first wife.'

'Seriously? Your mum never said,' I say, before realizing I actually found out about Colin and Mum after I'd left for London, so he never really came up in conversation between the pair of us before she passed away. The thought makes me sad. She'd love to know Mum was now happy and has found companionship with someone as great as Colin.

'I used to wash their car,' Peter laughs at the memory, while loosening his navy tie and undoing the top button of his shirt, slowly unwinding and coming out of office mode. 'I should clarify that it was when I was around thirteen, but they used to give me a couple of quid for it.'

'Not bad going.'

'It all started one summer when me and a mate wanted to earn a few bob. He came up with the idea and was happy to do it for a day, but gave up after that – not everyone gave us hot water to work with,' he says, shaking his head at the lunacy. 'I think I kept doing it for over a year, though,' he adds, almost to himself, as he tries to recall the details correctly.

'You're a hard worker, then,' I say, leaning on the counter and resting my chin on my hand, finding myself drawn in by him.

'Knowing my mum, are you really that surprised?' he laughs. 'Plus, doing it on my own meant I didn't have to split the earnings. I was rolling in it.'

'Lucky you.'

'Exactly, I could buy all the football stickers I liked and I even managed to save up for a Game Boy,' he grins. 'Anyway, Colin and Pauline had only just started living together back then. They didn't have kids or anything, obviously. Still, it took me ages to remember where I knew him from when I saw him at the weekend. It only clicked when I left.'

'I'm not surprised. You're talking decades!' I laugh, picking myself up off the counter and looking around to see what else needs doing.

'Yeah, I might've changed a bit since then. I don't think he recognized me. I'm no longer that little lanky boy with braces and a dodgy haircut,' he shrugs, making me wonder what he'd have been like as a boy. 'Make sure you send him and your mum my love.'

'I will.'

'They're awesome folks,' he nods, thoughtfully. 'Obviously I don't know them together yet, but from what I know of each of them separately, they're a perfect match.'

'They are,' I say, beaming with pride.

We're interrupted by Georgia and her friend Danielle (two fourteen-year-olds who have recently started coming in late on a Monday afternoon after hockey training) as they wave goodbye and walk out of the shop with their heaving PE kits slung over their shoulders. I love seeing fresh faces popping into the shop. I know I'm a novice at running a business, but even I know it's important to attract new trade in a bid to keep interest up and remain current – that's a huge reason why we opened our social media accounts too. I was hesitant at first (hardly surprising, I'd definitely describe myself as a shy and private person away from this shop) but some of the other local teenagers talked me into it. I think it's really made a difference, even if it does mean my inbox occasionally gets spammed by Billy's fans. Thankfully, though, that is simmering down thanks to him being many miles away.

It's so funny having people coming into the shop asking for a slice of the cake I'd posted a picture of on Instagram earlier that day, but it seems to get people's taste buds fired up. It's like the TV advert that makes you want to indulgently lie on the sofa while munching on chocolate, or gulp down a sugary drink while gawping at the male office window cleaner – it all helps to trigger a thirst or hunger that you need to quench. It's amazing that little businesses like mine can now be a part of that advertising space for free!

'Bye, girls. See you next week,' I call after them, grabbing a round tray and heading to their table with a clean cloth.

Looking around the shop, I realize we are now on our own.

'So, how are you finding being back here?' I ask, piling up the dirty crockery on the tray that's resting on my hip, before wiping down the top of the discarded table. 'Wishing you'd never come back?'

'Not at all. Enjoying it far more than I thought I would,' he admits, his mouth slowly moving into a little smile as he looks around the room. 'Actually,' he adds, clicking his fingers as though a thought has just occurred to him. 'I'm out playing football with some old school mates on Saturday, unless you need me here, of course. But do you fancy heading out for a bite to eat afterwards? The attached ones in our group are all running off home to their wives or girlfriends, while the single ones are heading into London for a raucous one. To be honest, you'll be giving me a good excuse to give it a miss.'

'Sounds nice,' I find myself laughing, not feeling like I need to give the offer much thought. 'I'll happily be your alibi. Only if you let me get dinner, though. I owe you one.'

'You do?'

I raise an eyebrow in reply as I move past him with the loaded tray, walk it to the sink and drop the plates and cups into the soapy water. I quickly start to wash them before placing them on the side to drip dry.

'Hmmm . . .' Peter sounds dubious, clearly uncomfortable with the idea. 'We'll go Dutch. You can pay for me and I'll pay for you. That way we'll both feel like we've done something nice and generous.'

'Deal,' I laugh, smiling back at him, wiping my wet hands on my apron and walking around the counter and back into the main part of the shop.

'I'll pick you up at yours around seven, if that suits? We can just go somewhere local. Make it simple,' he shrugs.

'Great.'

'I'd love an Indian actually. One thing I've missed is a proper curry. Is the one down The Hill still good?'

'The Maharajah? That's where we get our takeaways from,' I admit.

Mum and me have had the tradition of indulgent Friday nights for some time, although now our dinner for two is more likely to be dinner for six, usually alternating between Indian and Chinese, which gives us plenty of meal options considering we're only in a little village.

'Fantastic. Well, we can go sit in and chat over a nice

'bottle of Cobra,' Peter says, licking his lips as though he can already taste the beer on them.

'Lovely,' I reply, catching myself looking down at his mouth and watching its movement. Something he awkwardly notices too.

'I'm looking forward to it already,' he smiles, getting to his feet and making to leave.

'Oh! Your coat,' I say, my cheeks going hot as I run to the clothes rack and grab the grey woolly item which is far heavier than it looks.

'Thank you,' he frowns, taking it from me. 'I'd have felt ridiculous leaving without this again.'

'It would've been another frosty morning on the platform,' I say, with a roll of the eyes – something I'm still finding myself doing thanks to my recent trip and more time spent with the Buskins.

Peter purses his lips together, as though about to say more but thinking the better of it, before heading towards the door.

'Well, cheers, Sophie,' he says, clapping at the coat between his hands. 'I'll see you on Saturday.'

'See you then,' I say, turning back to wipe down the sink, rather than watching him leave.

Monday 28th March 2016

Dear Billy,

I know it's not actually my turn to write, but seeing as you organized my tickets over to see you I feel it's only right that I send one and let you know how much I appreciated it – in case I've not told you (or shown you) enough already. Ha!

I know we're weirdly back to where we were before in that we don't know when we'll be together again, but I feel refreshed after my Billy Buskin trip. ;-) I'm certainly happier than I was this time two weeks ago when I was missing you terribly and acting like a total misery guts.

Don't get me wrong, I'm still missing you . . . I've just had a lovely top me up!

Ha!

I hope you're having a wonderful time on set. How funny that Johnny is now in the movie with you. I bet you're having a right laugh together. He seemed lovely at New Year. His wife must be pleased that he's back at home with her and the children. Does he still have that ridiculous beard? I HOPE NOT.

I do feel sorry for the other actor getting appendicitis, though. Especially when it would've been his first major role in a Hollywood film. Poor thing. He must be gutted.

All is good here. The shop survived without me, which obviously I'm thrilled about, but can't help but feel a little deflated at too. It's only a minor niggling thought, but I guess I like to think it's ME who keeps things afloat. It appears I don't. Perhaps any old Tom, Dick or Harry can run a shop . . . or perhaps I should realize that it's a good thing and that I can allow myself time off now and then. I think you'll be more than supportive of that idea.

Rachel seemed to thrive with the added responsibility of being in charge. Colin said she was great. Peter also seemed to charm everyone, although I don't think he was quite prepared for how much talking goes on here. Ha! We're going to grab a bite to eat on Saturday in way of thanks.

When I got home tonight Mum told me she's booked in 'wedding dress' shopping for next weekend. I have to say I'm quite excited, but not as much as Charlotte. She's been drawing out lots of different designs, but they're all of things her Princess Barbie doll might wear. Hopefully she won't be too disappointed when she realizes Mum is going for something a bit simpler.

I hope you're having a great week. Send everyone my love!

Love you,
Sophie xxx

'Oh yeah,' I say as I'm walking down the stairs and into the lounge, with the letter for Billy in my hand, waiting to be enveloped. 'Peter came in today to pick up his coat. I didn't know you and Colin both knew him before.'

'I did?' asks Mum, looking away from the TV screen with a blank expression on her face.

'From the library. When he was at school.'

'Oh gosh. I bet he's changed since then.'

'That's what he said. Turns out he used to wash Colin's car too.'

Mum starts laughing and holding on to her chest as though it's the funniest thing she's ever heard.

'What?'

'Poor Colin. I kept telling him to speak to you about it, as he was quite miffed that he couldn't place him. I think he thought his memory was going.'

'I think it's rather that Peter has aged over twenty years since then!'

'Oh, that'll put his mind at rest,' she sighs, calming down. 'You should invite him for lunch one weekend. Might be nice for him to have a proper Sunday roast while he's back.'

'That'll be great,' I nod.

'Maybe give him a call and ask when suits.'

'Actually, we're going out for dinner this Saturday. I can just mention it then.'

'Oh?' she asks, looking surprised.

'It's a thank you thing . . .'

'Right . . .'

'But maybe I'll suggest next weekend?'

'Yes, well . . . see if he fancies it,' Mum says, looking like she's deep in thought, and turning back to watch *EastEnders*.

As I head to the cupboard to pick up an envelope, an anxious feeling churns in my stomach. Something feels a little off kilter.

I try my best to quash it as I grab a pen and write out Billy's all-too-familiar address.

24

'And then Mum goes storming into school, not caring that the other kids will think I'm a total wimp for having my mum fight my battles for me,' Peter says, lowering his fork while shaking his head at the account and trying to stop himself from laughing as he gives it. 'Well, she finds this bully and is literally so nice to him that she makes him cry.'

'How?' I ask, laughing at the flabbergasted look on his face and enjoying his stream of stories about my past best friend.

Tonight has been wonderful. We've eaten our weight in curry, poppadums and onion bhajis while talking non-stop. Laughing as we remember little moments long forgotten, our tales somehow helping to bring Molly back to life. I've loved hearing things I never knew about her. I know how easy it is to look back and mourn, but this feels more like we're celebrating the woman she was and finding joy in all of her little idiosyncrasies that our grief might have clouded over and caused us to forget.

'I don't know how,' he shrugs with a laugh, looking just as shocked as me. 'I've no idea what was said, but the bully never bothered me ever again after that. In fact, he'd literally go out of his way to avoid being anywhere near me.'

'Killing with kindness,' I smile, thinking of how Molly used to love nurturing people to bring out their best qualities. It's hardly surprising she'd use that tactic against someone who was being mean to her son.

'Yeah, both Mum and Dad were pretty special,' he replies, smiling to himself as he recalls just how lucky he was.

'So what made you move, then? How could you leave them?' I ask, dipping another bit of naan bread into the sauce of my chicken tikka masala and placing it in my mouth before looking up at him.

It's a question I often find myself considering and it's more to do with me, my life, and my own decisions rather than Peter and his. After everything that happened when I was a child I never felt I could leave Mum and go off elsewhere. Like many teenagers, I had all these dreams of travelling and seeing the world, but then the reality of our situation, of Dad's absence and Mum's fragility, would hit me and I'd know I couldn't be so carefree and careless. I couldn't just leave her. She needed me. But now I wonder how I'd have felt leaving them behind if our lives had been simpler, more straightforward and less fractured.

'They told me to,' he says simply, his face neutral as he delivers the statement while looking straight at me. Our eyes remain locked in that way for a second or two – serious and brooding – before his expression softens, becoming more animated and colourful as he continues with an explanation. 'They were lucky. They met in this village, fell in love and were happy, but they weren't silly. They understood that things were different for our generation. That the world was a more accessible place for us and ready to be explored. They didn't want me to feel stuck or like my wings were clipped.'

'They wanted you to soar,' I say, going along with his metaphor.

'Precisely. So they set me free,' he smiles, his hand swooping in the air between us and he makes a 'swooshing' sound with his mouth.

'Didn't you think about coming back after your dad died?' I ask. It's a personal question, one that perhaps shouldn't be asked, seeing as I've only met him a handful of times, but there's this air between us – this familiarity, this openness and honesty – that propels me to delve further, to understand why my dear friend Molly, a woman with a heart of gold, was left here on her own, without the two men that she loved more than anything.

'I did,' Peter replies, a momentary frown forming between his brows at the question, or maybe my assumption that he didn't. 'I came back and mourned with Mum for a bit . . . but then what? Death is the one thing we can be certain of. We all know that saying. It's drummed into us so that we're not afraid of the inevitable outcome we all face. However, Mum didn't want my life and dreams to die along with Dad's. She made it clear that each of us had already lost enough, but that I had a life to live, and, just like before, she wanted to release me back into the world.' He pauses, lost in thought for a few moments. 'It was tough. I didn't just leave and forget,' he mutters, almost to himself.

'I'm sure you didn't,' I gasp, hoping that's not what he thinks I've been getting at.

'I knew she was happy. Eventually, anyway . . .' He stops, rubbing his lips together as he mournfully looks to one side. 'I told you when we met last year about how she said the shop healed hearts,' he continues, looking at me to see if I remember the conversation we'd had in my kitchen.

I nod to show I do.

'Well, the first heart it healed was hers. Something that became even more apparent when *you* started working there. She had so much love for you. Right from day one. I might've been the bird she set free, but you were her little songbird. You lifted her heart. The shop gave her that. It gave her you. You were what she needed,' he says, winking at me with a soft, warm smile.

A lump forms in my throat as I feel my eyes prickle.

'Now, this is going to sound like a crazy pick-up line, and it's not,' he says, swiping his hand through the air between us, his eyes smiling across as me. 'But now that I've met you I completely understand the effect you had on her. She loved you. I can see why.'

A grin warmly lifts on to my face. Hearing someone so close to Molly say those words makes my heart sing – although, obviously, his compliments also make me feel rather embarrassed too. I'm not used to having near-strangers say such lovely things about me.

'She spoke about you a lot, too,' I say, coughing the emotion away while attempting to take the focus of the conversation off me and give him comforting words back. I want to spread the feeling of Molly's timeless, unwavering love that he's shared with me.

'Oh, I've no doubt she did,' he laughs, the sentimental moment almost broken as his guffaw loudly rings out, causing other diners to look over from their dinners to see what was so funny. 'I was her golden boy off travelling the world. I know she'd have been telling anyone who'd listen all she could about what I was up to,' he admits, taking enjoyment from what he's saying, rather than seeming annoyed Molly had shared endless information about his adventures overseas. 'That's probably why they feel like they know me now, because they've been told so much.'

'True . . . plus, you're like her.'

'I am?' he asks, looking genuinely shocked to hear me say it.

'So much so,' I frown, surprised he can't see it.

'Glad to see travelling the globe hasn't rid me of my roots,' he chuckles, picking up his beer and taking a gulp as the waiter comes over and gathers up our empty plates. Something I'm thankful for as I should have stopped picking at what was left a long time ago. I'm now more than stuffed.

'It really hasn't. It's astonishing,' I gush, stopping myself from saying that part of me feels I've been with Molly all night. That would probably be a little strange for him to hear.

'I'm glad you think so,' he beams back.

'I hope this isn't too . . . harsh, or maybe intrusive,' I begin, trying to find the right words for the question I'm longing to ask. 'But did you ever regret your decision?'

'There were moments,' he nods, looking at me as he ponders what I've asked. 'I'll admit that much, but they came and went. They never clung on for too long. I always managed to see past them.'

'Right . . .' I say, wondering if that's how I'd have felt if I'd plucked up the courage to just leave when I was younger and was toying with the idea. I'm dubious that we'd have shared the same emotions. I don't think anything would have made me get on that plane and fly away. My wings didn't long to be spread. My heart had no desire to soar.

'Well, that's the tough reality when talking about regret,' Peter says, his eyes narrowing and his face becoming serious and thoughtful once more. 'I've always felt it's better to regret something you did, rather than something you didn't. "If only" is a turn of phrase I absolutely hate,' he continues passionately. 'Life is to be lived, so we have to go out and grab what we want. I know my parents agreed with that. They didn't feel like I abandoned them. They gave me life, a mind of my own and a beating heart. So it wasn't my role to be there by their side with no ambition of my own. My happiness gave them happiness, and all I hope is that my decisions made them proud.'

'I'm sure they did,' I say, knowing it to be true and feeling ridiculous for not being able to offer something more when he's given a touching and intense speech. I wasn't expecting to get such deep and profound answers from him, but then, thinking back to our previous conversations, this side of him does seem to pop up every now and then. He really isn't the rough and rugged Aussie man he falsely bills himself as. There's far more heart, warmth and compassion than he lets on. He is so much like Molly.

'Funny thing is, I know Mum always hoped the right girl would come along and pin me down. But she knew timing was everything and that I'd have to be ready for it. I don't think I realized that finding the right person would mean I didn't feel pinned, or caged at all. That it would give me a whole new level of something else, rather than just taking away what I thought was a necessity,' he says, looking up at me and seeming to deflate. 'My one big regret though – despite everything I've just said – is that I'll never see her be grandma to my children. I mean, I'm single and incredibly far away from that right now. It is not on my radar. But, I wish I'd seen her in that role.'

'She'd have loved it.'

'Yeah . . .'

A silence descends as the thought lingers.

I picture Molly running around and playing with her grandchildren, making them laugh with her silly ways and giving them naughty little treats like she used to do with any young child who walked through the shop doors.

A heavy sadness fills my heart. Once more I'm hit by the unfairness of life. I wish it could have been a little kinder to the lady who had given so much.

I take my glass to my lips and have a sip of the beer Peter poured for me earlier. Until now it has gone untouched, but that was before the conversation took this unexpected turn. Now I feel in need of a swig of something stronger than water.

As I do so, Peter taps his thumb on the table.

'So, LA was good?' he asks, rehashing the question he asked earlier in the week.

'Really good,' I nod, realizing it's the first time this evening that the chat between us has felt awkward and forced. 'You ever been?'

'Nope. Not yet. It was never a place that appealed to me,' he says, shaking his head. 'You going back?'

'I think so. Well, I will at some point,' I admit. 'Just not sure when yet, though.'

'Nice,' Peter says, raising his eyebrows at me. 'It must be difficult. Being so far away.'

'It certainly makes things harder,' I nod, smiling at the waiter as he hands me a dessert menu, even though I know I won't be having one.

'I couldn't do it,' Peter shares adamantly, his mouth screwing up at the thought as he looks around the restaurant. 'But maybe that's because I'm more selfish than you are. Or greedier. Call me crazy, but if I'm with someone I like to be *with* them, you know?' he says, his eyes landing on mine.

'Yeah . . . though sometimes life just isn't that simple,' I reason.

'Ain't never been a truer word spoken,' Peter laughs, and the sound instantly lightens the mood once more.

As agreed, we go Dutch on the bill. However, Peter insists on walking me home even though I'm adamant that I don't need a chaperone and that I feel completely safe on the streets of quiet Rosefont Hill.

Thankfully, the mood remains light and upbeat throughout our after-dinner coffees and during the short walk back to mine, leaving a friendly and warm atmosphere sitting between us.

Being out in this way, and not tucked up with a book on a Saturday night (or any night), is such a rarity for me. I think I surprised myself when I agreed to dinner without even thinking, but what's surprised me even more is the fact that I've had such a lovely time. I would say I should let my guard down and do it more often, but it definitely has more to do with the actual company, rather than me just getting out of the house and doing something different for a change. It makes me wonder if years of blocking out friendships has left a gaping hole ... although I've never felt that way before, so why should one nice dinner with a friendly man, who I'd love to see more of, make me feel any different? It's just nice to chat to someone so great (who isn't a family member) and is actually here in the flesh rather than thousands of miles away in another time zone.

'Oh, Mum asked whether you wanted to come over for a Sunday roast next week?' I say, suddenly remembering her invite the other night. Even though it's not been discussed since, I'm sure she'd still love to have him over.

'I've been gagging for a home-cooked roast!' he says hungrily, jumping on the offer with great enthusiasm.

'That's what she thought,' I laugh, getting my keys out of my pocket as we walk up the familiar driveway. 'Well, I'll text you in the week and let you know the plans, but we usually eat around one o'clock.'

'Sounds perfect,' he grins, turning up the collar of his coat in an attempt to keep out the cold that's been nibbling away at our skin the whole walk back.

'Great. I'll let her know,' I say, sliding my key into the lock and feeling the heat radiate from our home as soon as I push the door open. 'Thanks so much for tonight.'

'Pleasure was all mine,' he grins, shuffling away from me, walking backwards down the driveway with his hands wedged into his pockets. 'I'll see you next week, if not before.'

'Get home safe,' I sing.

'Will do.'

He turns on his heels and heads off into the darkness.

As I close the door behind me, I pull my phone out of my pocket just in time to find Billy calling me.

'Mr Buskin,' I grin, feeling a gooeyness swirl inside me.

'Miss May,' he softly chortles, somehow sounding relieved.

'What are you up to?' I ask, locking the door before bending down to take off my boots.

'Day off. Heading to the gym with Johnny in a bit. Yesterday was such a long day that I don't really feel like it, but I'll feel better for going.'

'I'll take your word for it,' I laugh. Having never set foot inside a gym, the very thought horrifies me. It's not just because I hear everyone ogles at each other there despite being hot and sweaty, but because my fitness levels are appalling.

'Good night?' he asks.

'Lovely. I literally just walked through the door.'

'Nice . . .' he replies thoughtfully, as though he's about to ask more but stops himself. 'Are you off to bed now?' he asks, completely side-stepping the topic.

'I will be,' I say lightly, grabbing a glass of water and a Bounty chocolate bar from the kitchen (I don't know how there's any space left but seeing it on the side made me fancy it) and making my way up the stairs to my bedroom. 'Mum's over at Colin's tonight, so I'm planning on curling up in bed with a film.'

'Not *The Holiday* again,' he softly mocks.

'I'll think about watching something different,' I laugh, knowing I was actually thinking of doing exactly that. I know what I like and I've never been one to crave variety.

'It's just odd when neither of you are here. Anyway, I can't have a late one, I'm up early with Mum and Charlotte.'

'Your girlie day!' he remembers.

'Exactly,' I nod, grabbing my pyjamas from the bed and doing my best to step out of my jeans and jumper before shimmying into my comfier clothes, all the while staying on the phone. 'We're off into town to find Mum the wedding dress of her dreams. One that probably looks almost nothing like a wedding dress but still makes her feel special.'

'Interesting concept . . .' he replies. 'So your letter arrived this morning along with an excited one from Charlotte. She sent me some diagrams.'

'Of what she wants Mum to wear?'

'Exactly as you mentioned in your last letter.'

The way he says it tells me he's grinning.

'Ah . . .'

'Can't really imagine your mum in any of them, but Charlotte's so particular about what she likes. She's even put herself into something similar.'

'Oh, I know. She's sketching nonstop.'

'It's very sweet how excited she is,' Billy says fondly.

'She's certainly got a vision for the day,' I smile, loving how creative Charlotte has been and that she's enjoyed getting involved in the planning, because as much as I know we're all happy within the situation, I can't help but wonder what it must be like for Charlotte and Aaron to witness their dad marry someone new. There are moments when I find it difficult to cope with, and my dad died many moons ago. But for them, it's all a little fresher, and they're so much younger. 'I think I might ask Mum to try one on anyway. It'll make Charlotte's day. Actually, I think I'd find it pretty funny, too.'

'It'll be a great day. Has she mentioned any more about moving?'

'No, but I think I should bring it up at some point. Just get it out there again. She's probably got so much on at the moment that she's not even thought about it.'

'Or maybe she's trying to bury her head in the sand like you?'

'I must get it from somewhere,' I agree, knowing I've not been very forthcoming with the topic. I wouldn't be surprised if she's just waiting for me to ask more about it.

'You know, *we* could buy it,' Billy suggests matter-of-factly, as though buying my childhood home is no big deal.

'Huh?'

'It'll be an investment. I know we haven't got around to finding somewhere of our own yet, but it's been on the cards for a while now. We can't always stay at your mum's, we need somewhere of our own.'

'I know,' I sigh, fully aware that most people leave home as soon as they can afford to, wanting to be free of the parents who've invested so much love and money into their upbringing. 'But it's a huge commitment.'

'Well, I'm committed,' he says defiantly, as if I've questioned our loyalty to each other.

'As am I,' I say, finding myself frowning as a million thoughts cloud my brain and stop it from functioning properly. It's a simple solution, of course it is, but something about it doesn't sit right with me and I can't quite pinpoint what that is.

'I'm just saying, it's an option. That way you don't have to say goodbye to something that means so much to you,' Billy says, although I can barely hear him through the fog. He continues, though, my silence spurring him on. 'I wish I'd bought my family home back in Surrey or urged Mum and Dad to keep it as an investment. I'll always regret not thinking that one through.'

'Right . . .' I manage.

'Either way, you've got to talk to your mum. Time to suck it up, Miss May.'

'Maybe,' I sigh, picking up my Mr Blobby from the bed and giving him a little squeeze.

I've had this cuddly toy for as long as I can remember. He's seen me through my darkest days. Most people say that about a person or an animal, yet here I am saying it about a yellow-polka-dotted pink monster . . . it's true though. I left him behind when I first moved to London and I hated it. Really hated it. I felt far better when I was back at home and we were reunited. Maybe that says more about the comfort I get from this room than the larger-than-life character from *Live and Kicking!* I'm not sure.

I usually hide my comfort teddy when Billy is around, or at least put him somewhere out of sight (he's quite tattered and grimy but I can't stomach the thought of him going into the washing machine). Whenever Billy isn't around Mr Blobby is back on my bed, lapping up the attention.

Billy cuts into my thoughts by changing the subject. 'So, guess what Rhonda has talked me into.'

'Oh God, what?' I ask, instantly worrying at what our relationship is going to have to face next.

Billy laughs at my reaction. 'Check out @BillyBuskin on Twitter and Instagram.'

'You haven't.'

'I have. Well, only just. Rhonda's team have been trying to get my name from a couple of fans who were reluctant to hand it over until they knew it was for me.'

'Bet they were chuffed.'

'I'm probably sending them loads of signed stuff in thanks.'

'Nice. So have you posted your first pic or tweet yet?'

'No . . . but I'm sure Johnny will show me how to work it all when I see him. On that note, I'd better go,' says Billy abruptly, just as I've flopped on to my bed and immersed myself under the duvet. 'I was meant to be at the gym ten minutes ago.'

'Oh, OK. What are you doing for the rest of the day?' I ask, suddenly desperate for him to stay on the phone for longer. Knowing that as soon as the line goes dead I'll have to think through some pretty big decisions.

'Learning lines. I might even go through some scenes with Johnny after our workout.'

'Great . . .'

'Miss you,' he says softly.

'You too,' I sigh, feeling deflated, which is far from how I was feeling half an hour ago in the restaurant.

'I'm always here, you know. I know that's tough to remember with the distance and everything, but I'm only a phone call away.'

'Me too.'

'Will you think about what I've said?' he asks me. 'About the house.'

'I will,' I agree, but I'm already feeling a heavy weight bearing down on me at the thought. 'Will you text me?'

It's a feeble request. One that might make me seem needy and pathetic, but I feel a bit pathetic *and* I need him. I have a sudden pang for him to feel a little more present in my life right now.

'There'll be hundreds of messages from me when you wake up,' he promises, not sounding at all put out by what I've asked.

'Good,' I whisper, already feeling comforted.

25

Billy does as he promises. I wake up to an absurd amount of texts literally detailing everything that he's got up to during my sleeping hours. Luckily, I always put my phone on silent before bed, so I wasn't woken up every fifteen minutes or so. There are even a few silly selfies of him and a beardless Johnny messing around: one in the gym, one at dinner with their scripts, one of them just driving down the freeway in an open-top car with the sun beaming down on them, and finally one of Billy in bed – again with his script, although this time it's resting on his bare chest.

It's a lovely sight to wake up to.

I know it's ridiculous, but it means so much to know I'm being thought of. Not in the sense that I worry he's off living the single life if I'm not glued to his side, which I'm guessing might be a concern for some people in our situation. But I've not found myself feeling paranoid or insecure – I just like knowing he's thinking of me.

As well as all the messages from Billy, there's one from Mum telling me Charlotte got her up super early and they will be over earlier than expected; one from Rachel saying that the boys kept her up all night with tummy bugs and that she was looking forward to being back in the shop tomorrow and regaining a bit of sanity; and then one from Peter telling me he got back home safely and that he thoroughly enjoyed our meal.

I don't think I've ever woken up to such a busy phone or felt so popular.

I thought I wasn't going to sleep very well last night thanks to a few things hanging over me. However, once I got off the phone to Billy I decided I really wasn't in the mood to watch anything – yes, I skipped on the opportunity of catching up with my favourite Jude. I didn't even get out from underneath my warm duvet to pick up the chocolate bar I'd left across the room – surely I must be coming down with something – or even brush my teeth – disgustingly lazy and means I still taste of onions. Instead, I just lay there cocooned, thoughts drifting about while I tried to keep my anxiety at bay.

Miraculously, I suppressed it and managed to keep calm. I lay there like that for a little while but ended up slipping off into a deep sleep fairly quickly with none of the thoughts managing to formulate into anything huge and uncontrollable.

In fairness, I was probably suffering from a serious case of food coma, unable to move or think coherently. That's probably why I was able to nod off and get a good night's sleep, despite there being so much to focus on.

I think back to the worries that niggled away at me the previous evening to see whether they carry the same weight now that it's daytime. I've always felt problems can appear bigger and more overwhelming in the darker hours – and it's good for me to take a step back every now and then to reassess.

This house is a big issue. I have a connection to it, a desire to never leave its safe walls nor walk away from all the memories that have been built here.

Yet. Yes, there's a yet.

A lot of bad things happened here too.

When Mum first talked about moving I was terrified of losing sight of those happier times. Worried that not actually living here would cause me to forget, or that I'd be moving further away from Dad, the man whose face and voice are shamefully becoming dimmer and dimmer in my memory. I wanted to anchor my heels into the floorboards and protest that I wasn't going anywhere, that this is my home and where I want to live for ever more. But now that Billy has suggested an alternative, a solution, a way of staying within the space that holds the past memories of the May family, I want to run. I want to escape. I want to flee from the torturous nightmares that have haunted me in this house. The bedroom I've never repainted because it held memories of the last precious moments shared between our little family; the front door the policewoman knocked at to take me to the hospital the night my dad died in a hit-and-run accident; the spot outside their bedroom where I used to sit in the darkest hours, listening to my mum howl in despair over her lost love . . .

It's all here.

I remember the love and laughter, but I'm also trapped by the constricting despair, loneliness and heartache.

I want to be here. It's my home. But at the same time, I'd love to be somewhere new. To be the bird. To be set free.

It's a sad realization, but one that becomes all the clearer when thinking about what Peter said last night about Molly and Albert, and the way they made sure he followed his own path and lived his own life, rather than purely living the life they had planned or hoped for him. They didn't want him to be too dependent on them. Likewise, they didn't want him to have the pressure of them depending on him so that he might feel like leaving wasn't possible. Instead, they gave him options. And through those options, they gave him the world.

I think I might want a bit of that.

I don't think of this house as a cage, it offers more kindness and love than that, but it's trapped me on an emotional level. Now, with Mum talking of moving out, is it possible that I can finally think of what I want without feeling an immeasurable amount of guilt?

Is it my turn to have the world?

Do I even want that now?

And if I do, where do I go?

Anywhere Billy is would be the obvious answer, but who knows where Billy will be from one year to the next. And that's the other reason why buying this house wouldn't work. Only in the last year have I started spending nights alone here. Before that there was Mum and Dad, then just Mum, then Billy. If Billy and me were to own this place, what would happen when he was gone? Would I spend months here in this house on my own? Would I want that? Could I cope?

And that leads me to another thing Peter said about wanting to be *with* the person he's in a relationship with . . .

Maybe I am tied down.

Maybe I am trapped.

Or maybe, as I said yesterday at dinner, life isn't that simple and you just have to do the best with what you've got. Last time I dropped everything to follow Billy it made me see just how important it is to keep hold of something for myself. Not only for my own piece of identity, but for my own sense of purpose and ambition. That's what Rachel mentioned, too, in her first few days of being in the shop – her newfound sense of self-worth beyond existing for Shane and her boys . . . And then there was Rhonda's talk of expanding the business. Now, I wouldn't want to have dozens of versions of my unique little shop sprouting up in different locations around the world (you can't replicate the heart contained inside those walls), but I'm definitely not ready to leave it all behind or stop wanting to help the shop organically evolve . . .

'Soph!' Mum shouts from the front door, interrupting me before I can dwell any longer on what I'm feeling or can really formulate a solid conclusion. 'You up?' she yells again.

'Yes,' I call back down, prompting the sound of little feet running up the stairs and a rather excited Charlotte to fly breathlessly through my bedroom door while still clinging on tightly to her Minnie Mouse soft toy.

'This is going to be the best day ever!' she declares, diving on to my bed and jumping on top of me.

'Ooof,' I wheeze as her knee lands on my ribs. 'Come here you,' I say, pulling her round and wrestling with her, making her laugh.

'Someone decided it was time for the day to start,' says Mum, having made her way up the stairs to join us.

'So I see,' I laugh, as Charlotte flings her arms around me for a cuddle, breathing heavily as she starts to calm down, appearing exhausted from our playful scuffle.

'You had breakfast?' Mum asks.

'Nope.'

'Neither have we . . . there's some bacon, sausages and eggs in the fridge, though, if you fancy it? Give us energy for the day ahead? Plus the shops don't all open until eleven. We've got plenty of time,' she suggests, waiting for us both to answer.

Even though I ate an obscene amount of food last night, the thought of a fried breakfast makes my mouth water and causes my tummy to suddenly feel like I've been starved for a week. 'That would be great,' I grin, already feeling naughty for agreeing to the idea.

'Can I have a dippy egg?' asks Charlotte in the sweet voice she uses when she really wants something.

'Of course,' Mum laughs. 'Now come on. You can come help while Sophie gets out of bed and has a shower.'

'Thought I could smell something,' Charlotte giggles, with a cheeky expression on her face.

'Oi, you!' I laugh, tickling her under her armpits and making her squeal.

Sometimes children and family really are the best remedy for any worries and woes . . . especially my little rabble.

Half an hour later I'm dressed and seated at the breakfast table, with a clean head of hair and newly applied make-up, tucking into a lovely salty breakfast.

'So how was last night?' Mum asks, chopping up Charlotte's buttered toast into dippable slices while her huge brown eyes look on hungrily, ready to tuck into her morning treat.

'Really nice,' I nod, sticking sausage and bacon into my

mouth and enjoying the juiciness as I munch. 'He's already agreed to come over next Sunday. Was delighted to be asked.'

'Great,' Mum says, though her mouth wriggles in concern as she puts down Charlotte's knife and turns to her own plate, loading a forkful of beans. 'Wasn't it weird at all, last night?'

'In what way?' I ask.

Mum looks at Charlotte before turning back to me and continuing. 'Well, you're a girl, he's a guy . . .'

'Oh gosh! No, Mum. No. There was nothing like that.'

'Thank goodness,' she says, expelling a lungful of air before bringing her fork to her mouth.

'Is that what you've been worried about?'

'Well, Billy's away, you're probably a bit lonely . . .' she says, a slight frown on her face, probably hearing how ridiculous the scenario sounds now that it's been voiced.

'Mum, there was no one for years before Billy and that didn't turn me into a man-hunting vixen, did it? I think I can cope with being on my own for a few months,' I say, failing to admit how great it was to have some company for a change.

'Oh, I know, but it's a long time to be apart when you're in love,' she reasons. A fact I can't argue with. 'Plus, you always hear that it's hard for men and women just to be friends – that their relationships get complicated by all sorts of chemistry and confusing business.'

Now it's my turn to look at Charlotte. When she looks back at me, I roll my eyes to the skies.

'Charlotte, please tell my mum . . . can boys and girls be friends?'

'No, they can't,' Charlotte says adamantly, with a firm shake of her head.

'What?' I squeak, expecting her to say the opposite.

'Have you met the boys in my class?' she asks, screwing up her nose in utter disgust.

I can't help but laugh at her response. I forgot she was still in the hating boys stage of life.

'OK, the boys in Charlotte's class excluded. Platonic relationships between boys and girls exist and work,' I protest, hoping my words will eradicate Mum's suspicions. I'd have thought she would just be pleased I'd been out socializing for once. 'I'm not about to become a mechanical cog in an old cliché – next thing we know Billy will be running off with his Swedish PA.'

'Does he have one?' Mum gasps, concern etching its way back on to her face.

'No!'

'Oh!' she chuckles, covering her eyes with her hands and shaking her head at being so slow on the uptake. 'Sorry.'

We immediately dissolve into a fit of childish giggles. Even Charlotte joins in, although I imagine that's down to the sight of two of the adults in her life being uncharacteristically silly.

'Honestly, Mum,' I say, wiping tears from my eyes once the laughter has subsided and I can talk again. 'Peter's a lovely guy and I enjoy spending time with him, but there's nothing more than friendship there.'

Funny thing is, as the words make their way out of my mouth, a tiny part of me questions whether they are entirely truthful. Was there chemistry? Did he flirt? Were there heated moments? Or has it all been as innocent as

I've been protesting? Am I only querying it all because Mum has? And how has Billy's silence over the non-date made me feel? Would I have preferred him to give me the Spanish Inquisition? Did he realize it was just the two of us?

'Oh, I knew there wouldn't be,' Mum sighs, tutting at herself. 'I was just being silly. It's a mum's job to worry. Not that I'm worried about you, I know you'd never act in such a way.'

'Can I have some more dippy toast, please?' asks Charlotte, even though she still has two other pieces left on her plate. I love the fact that she's so forward thinking with her food and would rather ask in advance of an empty plate than sit and wait for a few minutes once it's gone.

'Want me to open your other egg now, too?' asks Mum.

'Yes, please,' Charlotte grins, clapping her hands together.

I watch the exchange while having a gulp of my tea, which I continue to slurp on even though it's too hot. In a gorgeous way, Mum is being given a second opportunity to mother. It's strange for me to witness it, but I love seeing how natural she is at it all despite being fretful that she might somehow let them down. I know she won't. She wouldn't. She's a different woman to the one she was back then.

We both are.

Although, in some ways I'm exactly the same.

Mum's right, I wouldn't do anything foolish when it comes to Billy and me. It's not me to act recklessly like that. Plus, I highly doubt Peter is reading any more into this than me being the young girl who walked into his mum's shop a decade ago and struck up an unlikely friendship. And that's what I am, a huge link to his mum. The only one he can really share his personal memories with while knowing that the person listening loved her just as much as he did.

It's simply stupid social politics implying what we're doing has to be more than that. It's innocent. Meaningful, but totally innocent.

'Is that the time already?' I gasp, looking at the clock hanging on the wall and noticing that the morning has started to slip away from us already. 'We'd better get a move on.'

26

We wolf down the rest of our breakfast at lightning speed, throw the empty plates in the sink, chuck on our coats and shoes and head out. Even though we'll be spending the day in dressing rooms, we've clearly all made an extra effort for the special day. I've taken the time to blowdry my hair so that it's smooth and shiny and am wearing the posh boots that Mum got me for Christmas with leggings and a knitted dress. Mum still has her hair whipped back in her signature bun (with no wispy bits out on display) but has managed to make it look softer and more elegant by wearing it looser. She's dressed smartly in black trousers, brown Chelsea boots and a cream blouse, while Charlotte is wearing one of her prettiest polka-dot dresses (which apparently she insisted on this morning) and looks almost identical to her Minnie Mouse (who is, obviously, coming along for some girlie fun).

Mum drives us all into town and we head straight to the department store Magpies which sells everything imaginable, and also has a well-stocked bridal wear section. Even though Mum has said she doesn't want to go down the traditional wedding dress route, we decided there might be some simpler designs that could be worth looking at before trying anything less conventional.

Hitting the dedicated bridal part of the shop floor, we're greeted by dozens of ivory and white dresses, all containing miles of lace, beading, sequins, chiffon, organza and tulle. Every bride's dream.

Usually.

'I suddenly feel a bit queasy,' says Mum, placing her hand on her chest and taking a deep breath, holding on to a nearby rack of silky numbers to steady herself.

'I love this one,' sings Charlotte, typically tugging on the skirt of the biggest dress on display – an off the shoulder, sweetheart-neckline, princess-shaped gown. 'It's just like the one I drew,' she beams, totally in awe of the dress in front of her and completely oblivious to anything being wrong.

'Looks beautiful,' I smile at her, before looking back at Mum. 'You OK?'

'Just having a moment,' she sighs.

'It's only a dress … I know people say differently, but really, in the grand scheme of things it's one day, one dress,' I say, hoping the confidence in my voice will appease her anxiety.

'Think it's excitement, actually,' she blushes, still concentrating on slowing down her breathing.

'Oh?'

'Yes, I can't wait to play dress up.'

'Now that we can work with,' I laugh, leaning over and giving her a kiss on the cheek before giving her a hug. I'm so used to my mum worrying, being fretful and fragile that I forget she is more than capable of experiencing ups too. Plus, she should be happy and excited. She's preparing to marry a wonderful man who we both adore.

'Can I help at all?' asks the sales assistant, a sleek-looking woman in her thirties who I'm sure would look fabulous in every one of these dresses.

'I booked an appointment. For Jane May?' says Mum. 'I'm the bride.'

'Well, lovely to meet you. I'm Zoe. I'll be helping you with the dresses today,' she smiles, instantly becoming warmer now she knows we're actual customers and not just cooing over dresses we have no intention of buying. 'Can I ask, when is the wedding?'

'End of May – so not long. That's OK, though, right? I've not left it too late?'

'Not at all. I'm sure it'll be fine, Jane,' Zoe smiles sweetly, nodding her head as she thinks through the dates and makes a note on the pad in her hands. 'Now, let's start this morning off with you selecting a few looks and styles you like, and then we can take it from there. How does that sound?'

'Great,' Mum gulps, an excited squeak escaping. 'Let's go for that one first,' she laughs, grinning towards Charlotte who has now managed to get herself inside the skirt of the dress she loves, even though it's still hung up on its beautiful padded satin hanger.

'Lovely choice,' Zoe replies with a courteous smile that doesn't reveal whether she actually thinks it is a suitable match for Mum or not. But I guess that's a good saleswoman tactic: keep it neutral.

Three minutes later we're in the biggest changing room I've ever seen, with Mum and Zoe one side of a huge grey curtain getting into the mammoth gown and Charlotte and me waiting outside to see what the big puffy dress looks like on Mum's slender frame.

Charlotte doesn't say anything while we wait – instead,

she sits motionless with her hands on her lap and her eyes glued to the curtain in front of her. Her expression is a mixture of excitement and anxiousness. She's clearly looking forward to seeing Mum in the style of dress she's been drawing for her, but also worried it might not be what she imagined.

'It's so heavy!' calls Mum through the curtain.

'Really?' I ask.

'There's a lot of material,' mutters Zoe, sounding like she's still fastening it together.

Silence falls on us all again as we listen to the rustling of fabric as its layers get ruffled, fluffed and smoothed down.

'Are you ready?' giggles Mum, once their movement has come to a stop.

'Yes!' screams Charlotte, like she's at a Christmas pantomime.

The curtain is dramatically whipped back to reveal Mum looking like a gorgeous princess. I'm surprised to find the whole thing more manageable than I'd imagined it was going to be. I thought the skirt part was going to be ridiculous and more meringue-like. I thought it was going to be hideous. I thought we'd both hate it.

'Wow,' says Charlotte with a giggle.

'Oh, Mum,' I manage to say through the lump that's formed in my throat.

'It looks completely different on you to any other bride I've seen in it,' says Zoe, squinting at Mum's form in the gown while stepping to one side and holding on to the tape measure that's dangling around her neck. She looks more like an actual seamstress rather than a sales assistant in a department store. 'I've seen brides be dominated by this number, but you give it a timeless beauty . . . It looks classical and sophisticated. Maybe it's the way you wear your hair, too, but up like that, it gives the whole look an almost regal feel.' She's on the verge of gushing now, clearly getting excited by the sight of Mum in the dress she's no doubt seen on hundreds of women before. Now that she's started to share her opinion, she seems reluctant to stop. 'I'm not just saying this. Honestly, we don't work on commission or anything, but you make the dress your own!'

And she does.

I thought we were going to see it on, have a giggle and then have to explain to Charlotte that, although it was a pretty dress, it wasn't quite right for Mum who wanted something a little more understated and simple. But this is neither of those things. Instead, it's flamboyant, detailed, big and fancy. It highlights her slim figure while accentuating her curves – curves I never knew she had.

It suddenly dawns on me that I've never seen Mum in anything fancier than a plain dress (usually accompanied by thick black tights). This is so far removed from that. It's so much more. So delicious and dreamy. She's a true vision of beauty. I can hardly take my eyes off her.

'What do you think?' I ask Mum, because it's clear what the rest of us think, but she's stayed quite quiet since being confronted with the sight of herself in this dress.

'I love it,' she whispers, her hands running along the fabric draped across her tummy, her apparent elation causing her face to turn rosy and glow. 'I absolutely love it.'

'Yes!' grins Charlotte, looking incredibly pleased with herself as she punches her fist in the air. 'I knew it.'

'You did,' nods Mum, releasing a girlie laugh.

'You sound surprised that you like it?' Zoe says, no doubt wondering why Mum chose to try it on in the first place.

'I thought I wanted something less like a wedding dress. It's not my first wedding, you see. However, Charlotte has had other plans and has been begging me to try on something like this,' Mum explains, with a shrug, unable to tear her eyes away from her reflection in the mirror in front of her.

'So you wanted something more like this one you selected?' asks Zoe, her hands gesturing towards another dress Mum has brought in with her to try on. It's completely the opposite to the one she's currently wearing. I'd say it's still pretty, but rather plain and boring in comparison.

Scrap that.

It now looks dull and magic-less. It doesn't look special at all.

'Yes, exactly. And even that was fancier than what I'd imagined I'd go for,' Mum pouts, frowning at the previously preferred dress, clearly bemused by her unexpected change of heart.

'You'll be surprised how many brides come in with a set idea of what they think they want, but quickly start changing their minds when they try on different cuts and styles.'

'Really?' asks Mum, her face a little brighter, happy to hear she's not the only one to want something so different to what she'd planned.

'Absolutely,' Zoe passionately nods. 'So many women have never worn dresses like these before. Seeing a model in a design, and then picturing yourself in it is very different to the reality of having your body in one. I always think it's best when a bride comes in with no expectations at all, that way they won't be disappointed when their dream dress looks awful on them . . . it happens more than I'd like,' she admits, looking gloomy at the thought of past brides. 'You've done it the best way round, believe me.'

'Maybe you should try what you had in mind and see what you think now?' I suggest. 'There's no harm in seeing it on. It might help you make a decision either way.'

'Great idea,' nods Zoe, smiling at Mum and waiting for her to agree to the suggestion.

'Go on, then,' she sighs.

The curtain closes and once more the sound of swishing fabric is heard.

'Just like a princess,' Charlotte says to Minnie Mouse, before giving her a tight squeeze.

I can't help but grin at her pride over being right and her unashamed way of saying 'I told you so', even if it is just to her stuffed toy.

'Hmmm . . .' Mum says moments later, clearly having been switched into the other dress. It's a contemplative tone, telling us that she's not been instantly won over by the new design.

'What do you think?' I ask, eager to see it on. 'Do you like it? What does it look like?'

I'm not left waiting long. Seconds later Zoe pulls back the curtains to reveal Mum looking elegant in the simpler sheath number. She still looks lovely and every inch the beautiful bride, but somehow something is missing, and I'm not sure whether it has something to do with the dress itself or the grumpy look on Mum's face. She looks like a child who has been forced into wearing a hideous outfit given to her by a great aunt or something, not like she's been put into another special frock.

'What do you think?' I ask, having to stop myself from chuckling at this petulant side of her that I've rarely seen before.

'If I'd put this on first I'd have loved it,' she replies as she looks herself up and down in the mirror, turning from side to side and taking in the whole image from every angle possible. The sight causes her to sigh dramatically.

'And what do you think of it now?' I ask patiently, guiding her to the obvious conclusion, because I'd be greatly surprised if she decided to go for this one after all this crabby behaviour.

'All I'm thinking about is being back in that one,' Mum replies glumly, looking longingly back across the room to the first dress.

'That's a good thing!' I sing, not understanding her attitude.

'I can't go for that one, though,' she huffs. 'There's only blooming six people coming to the service.' She shakes her head sadly.

'So?' I shrug.

'You don't think it's over the top?' she asks, a sliver of hope squeezing its way through.

'I think you look absolutely stunning in it, Mum.'

'I feel it.'

'Well, the day is about you and Colin feeling special and amazing. If that's how you feel in that gown, then that's the right choice. Simple.'

'Maybe I should try it on again,' she mutters, her eyes drifting from her dream dress back to the mirror.

'Fab idea,' says Zoe, taking control of the situation. I'm sure it's not the first time she's been faced with a dilemma like this. In fact, I'm sure she's used to dealing with far worse.

The curtain closes.

Swishing.

Ruffling.

Fabric moving.

The curtain opens.

Mum looks gloriously happy again, literally her face lights up as soon as she sees herself in the reflection. It clearly makes her feel spectacular – she's even standing in a different way. She has more confidence, more poise. She's like a majestic snow queen in a fairy tale. I don't feel there's any way we could let her leave this store without purchasing the dress that's made her look this happy.

'Oh gosh, isn't it smashing?' Mum exclaims, suddenly becoming girlie and light.

'You look incredible,' nods Zoe, still on her knees having fluffed up the under-layers and smoothed out the top one. 'You'll make such a stunning bride.'

Suddenly I think of mum on her wedding day, of me holding her hand and leading her down the aisle, of Colin's reaction when he sees her in this masterpiece, as I lead her towards him, giving her over to his care . . . I'm overcome with emotion. So much so that my throat closes up, my nose burns and tears work their way to my eyes.

'It's perfect,' I blub, my words almost inaudible through the gentle sobs that can't be contained no matter how hard I try to hold them in. 'Colin is a very lucky man.'

'No, I'm a lucky woman to have found someone so special,' Mum replies, her own eyes brimming with tears as she knots her fingers together, a tactic I know she uses to steady herself when her emotions are on the wobble.

'I think we're all lucky,' Charlotte squeaks from her seat, her eyes wide with innocence and wonder. 'I bet Mum and Dean are so happy right now. I know they brought us all together from their cloud in the sky.' She smiles at us both before looking down and giving Minnie another squeeze.

What a lovely thought. Her mum, my dad, working out how to help us all move forward with love, laughter and a new sense of togetherness with others who have felt a similar loss.

'What a wonderful bunch you are,' Zoe says quietly, sniffing as she gets up from the floor and exits the changing room, leaving us on our own.

'Come here,' Mum says to me and Charlotte, gesturing us over by flapping around her hands in a scooping motion.

I slide in under the groove of her armpit, just as I remember doing as a child, while Charlotte rests her cheek on Mum's tummy while wrapping one arm around her waist and the other around mine. Mum squeezes us into her and the exquisite wedding dress she's still standing in.

'I love you, girls. You're both incredibly special and important . . .' she whispers softly. 'I don't know what I've done to deserve you, but thank you.'

We stay like that, in a hug for three, for at least a minute – absorbing the love and feeling more united than ever.

'Can I have pancakes for lunch?' Charlotte asks

eventually, her voice squeaky as she looks up at us with a cheeky little expression on her adorable face.

We both laugh.

'It's a girlie day!' Mum says back with a gasp, as though she's shocked at the question having been asked. 'It would be rude not to.'

'What are you going to have on yours?' I ask, still holding on to them both as my hand glides over Charlotte's long brown hair.

'Hmmm . . .' she ponders, licking her lips as she gives the tough decision a great deal of thought. 'I think banana and chocolate sauce.'

'Yum!' I reply, my tummy rumbling, even though it's absolutely stuffed from last night's dinner and this morning's breakfast.

'Well, I guess I'd better get out of this then,' Mum sighs, looking down at her dress as though she's reluctant to do so.

'But you're getting this one, right?' Charlotte squeaks.

'Well, it is bigger than I'd have liked *and* is a bit showier than I care to be . . .'

'But . . .' protests Charlotte.

'But,' agrees Mum, a smile working its way on to her lips. 'Sometimes you've got to listen to your heart and throw caution to the wind.'

'Does that mean you're getting it?' Charlotte asks, her face on the verge of exploding.

'There's no way I'm leaving without it,' Mum laughs. 'So, yes!'

'YES!' Charlotte shouts, gripping hold of her even tighter than before.

'The first dress you tried on too!' I smile, thrilled with Mum's decision and in no doubt that it's the right one.

'Exactly, and now we get to have pancakes and shop for you two all afternoon.'

'See, this is the best day ever!' Charlotte laughs, releasing her hold on us so she can jump up and down on the spot.

27

'So, how was your girlie day?' asks Billy when I speak to him that night.

I decided to skip dinner (it's fair to say I couldn't stomach any more food) and have a bit of a pamper night instead: hot bath, facemask, cucumber over my eyes – a chance to actually cut my toenails and paint them a pale gold colour. It's not something I treat myself to very often, but now I feel full of zen and inner peace.

'Great. So great,' I reply sleepily from my bed where I have just been relaxing with Jane Austen's *Emma*.

'Glad to hear it.'

'I was thinking I might head back out and see you,' I say, looking forward to hearing his reaction.

'Are you joking?' he asks. 'When?'

'I haven't worked it out yet. Perhaps I'll talk it over with Rachel, Peter, Mum and Colin. See when's best for them all to cover.'

'It's only been a week,' he says, his voice higher pitched than normal.

'Is that a bad thing? Would you rather I didn't come back out?' I ask, suddenly feeling like I'm getting mixed signals and that he might not want me over there after all.

'Don't be daft. I meant I thought I was going to have to bend your arm and convince you to take more time off somehow. I didn't expect you to be saying this already,' he laughs. 'So, when were you thinking?'

'Not sure. Like I said, I'll talk to the others,' I say, feeling disheartened about the idea now that his initial reaction was less than enthusiastic.

'Of course.'

'But the last day of shooting hasn't changed, has it?'

'Nope, still May 13th. Although I might have to stick around for a few days the following week – Rhonda wants me to meet a few people, but I'll try and get that done straight away so I can come home on the Thursday or something.'

'That's really close to the wedding,' I note.

'I know, but what can I do? It's not like I'm going to miss it. I said I'd be back at the end of that week and I will,' he snaps, taking me by surprise. 'I'm meeting important people, not going out and getting pissed in a bunch of clubs. Because I could be doing that, and I'm not.'

'Right . . .' I frown, taken aback by the sudden swing the conversation has taken when I thought I was calling him with good news.

'Not that I want to be doing that,' he says, sounding confused and displeased at his own argument. 'I'm just saying, I'm working really hard. I'm not off on a jolly in La La Land.'

'Of course. I know that,' I say, wanting to immediately stop his spiky tone, seeing as talking on the phone two days in a row is such a rare treat.

I don't want him to stop calling altogether because he's worried one of us will say the wrong thing and upset the other. But I can't help feeling his priorities are changing.

I know he'd say I'm wrong, but I can see his ambition and hunger growing more and more, making me wonder where he sees me fitting into the whole picture . . . Hollywood and acting are reclaiming his heart, but does that mean my hold on it is slipping? Because it definitely feels like it's getting harder to hold on.

'I've been thinking . . .' Mum says, coming into my room an hour later and perching on the bed, just as she's done since I was a little girl.

'What about? Your wonderful dress?' I tease.

'Yes,' she laughs, her hand covering her mouth as a giggle escapes.

'I'm not surprised.'

'It was me who said I didn't want a big fancy wedding. That I only wanted us six to be a part of it . . . maybe I was wrong.'

I can't contain my laughter, as I guess what's coming next.

'What?' Mum asks, looking at me innocently.

'Now you've got the bigger dress you want the bigger wedding?'

'It's not that,' she says, looking embarrassed as her cheeks flush red. 'But it *is* such a beautiful dress!'

'It would be a shame for people not to see it,' I nod, a big grin spreading across my face.

'It just made me realize exactly how special and wonderful the day is going to be and how grateful I am to have Colin and you kids in my life,' she explains, raising her shoulders helplessly.

'Ah . . .' I beam.

'I want to celebrate that. Really celebrate,' she says, clapping her hand against her thigh.

'There's only seven weeks until the wedding . . .' I remind her.

'I know,' she frowns.

'But there's a lot we can do in that time,' I say, feeling a flurry of excitement fire through me.

'Really?'

'I think so. Do you want to change the venue or are you happy to keep it as it is?'

'Well, you can get quite a few people in the shop . . .' she says, her fingers twisting as she thinks. 'I'm not talking about having hundreds of people suddenly, I don't even think we know that many, anyway. But maybe just a couple of dozen or something.'

'Just so it's more of a party and not a family get together?'

'Yes . . . maybe we should sleep on it,' she frowns, doubting herself.

'It's not me you need to convince, Mum. I think it's a great idea.'

'Thank you,' she beams, still looking radiant from earlier. It's like she's found her wedding mojo. I love seeing her like this. It makes her seem younger than ever.

'And I'm here to plan and help however I can. It'll be a busy few weeks, but we can do it. I have every faith in us.'

'You're a star,' she says, kissing the top of my head before getting up and making to leave. 'I don't know how I'm going to sleep tonight,' she giggles. 'There's so much to think about . . . Now, I'm finally going to go and stick some post-it notes in those magazines I've been flicking through for months.'

My heart sings as she leaves. This is completely what Mum deserves and I'm thrilled she is allowing herself to really celebrate the happiness life can bring instead of questioning everything. We're both reclusive characters at heart and have preferred to cut ourselves off from the community when things got too much for us, but now it feels times are changing.

I think back to my previous chat with Billy and realize sadly there's no way I can leave Mum now and go back to America. Not with only seven weeks left until she marries Colin. Not when all the plans have changed.

I take a deep breath and look at my phone, wondering if I should call him now and tell him it's looking unlikely, or whether I should wait for another day . . . I know he'll be disappointed and that it's likely we'll end up snapping at one another again if we speak now.

Rationally, I know those moments of sadness and anger that flicker between us are just signs of annoyance at being apart, but how long will we be able to cope like that before an eruption is too big to come back from? Is it going to be the same every time we're apart for filming? Will one of us always be trying to tame the other's emotions?

I don't want to think of Billy being down. And I don't like the thought of him worrying about me in that way either. Relationships should be easier than this, I know that. Everything else around you might fall apart, but the two of you should always be left standing like two strong and entwined trees, united against whatever forces might try to uproot you . . .

I just wish everything could go back to how it was at

the end of last year: simple, normal and easy in our secluded Rosefont Hill bubble. Although, even as I think it, I know it's a selfish request which would mean only one of us living the life we want.

I decide not to call Billy back straight away, preferring to bury my head in the sand, something he seems to think me and Mum are good at anyway. Instead, I torment myself about the whole thing for the rest of the night and, just like the previous day, the reality of the situation with Billy clouds the fun I've been having beforehand.

So much for being in a Zen-like and relaxed state.

28

I don't get to speak to Billy the following day, or in fact for several days. We're both busy, although despite his protests to the contrary it looks like he's having far more fun than he's letting on if his social media posts are anything to go by. Pictures that he would have previously sent only to me of him in his trailer or out with Johnny are now being seen by the millions of fans who started following his accounts as soon as they were verified. Because he knows I follow him and probably see them, he doesn't bother forwarding them on to me too, meaning his contact with me is getting that little bit less and I end up feeling more like a stalker than a girlfriend. It's weird knowing what someone is up to when they haven't directly told you so themselves, but it's also hard not to look when everyone else around you seems to know more about what your partner is doing than you do.

'Oh my goodness, you are a lucky so and so,' says Rachel one morning as she skips into the shop with a huge grin on her flushed face.

'Sorry?' I laugh, elbows deep in flour and baking dough.

'You've not seen what your hunky Adonis posted a little while ago, then?' she smirks, clearly whatever she's seen making her quite giddy.

'Do I look like someone in the know?' I ask, raising an

eyebrow at her even though I'm finding her behaviour quite entertaining.

'I'm talking about this!' she giggles, thrusting her iPhone in my face and showing me Billy's Instagram account.

She scrolls through the pictures he's posted – because he's uploaded not one but several of them in the last hour since I've been at work.

Him and Johnny obviously had a rare afternoon off and did the LA thing of tackling Runyon Canyon, a dusty and challenging track leading all the way to a summit that is renowned for its celebrity visitors. I can remember Hayley and Jenny talking about it many times when I first went over there. On hitting the peak Billy and Johnny took half a dozen sweaty selfies in celebration – all with their tops off and displaying their toned, tanned bodies as they smile away at the camera in the Californian sunshine. Billy looks every inch the movie star and not at all like he's pining for his absent girlfriend. Not that he should be moping around the whole time, but a hint of sadness in his eyes that only I could read would certainly help me. Selfish, but true.

'Seriously, I wish our Shane looked like this with his kit off,' Rachel chuckles, looking at the image on her phone once more. Really squinting at it to take in every detail. I love the fact that she doesn't care she's unashamedly lusting after my boyfriend in front of me.

'Don't let him hear you say that,' I warn.

'What? Anyone would think it was him who carried the twins for nine months,' she laughs, covering her face with her hands. 'Oh, I'm being cruel. I don't mean it in the slightest. Just saying it in jest. Anyway, I'd be too scared to take my clothes off if he looked like this.'

'Oh, shush, you,' I say, shaking my head at her modesty.

'True . . .' she muses, giving it a second thought. 'I'd still take my clothes off, I'd just make sure the lights were off first,' she cackles wickedly as she puts her phone away and hangs her coat up.

She makes me chuckle and almost takes my mind off the fact that she and everyone else who has been on Instagram that morning knew exactly where Billy was and who with, when I didn't. I haven't even received a reply to the 'Good morning!' text I sent him a couple of hours ago yet. It's not a huge deal, but surely I'm allowed to feel slightly irritated when he's decided to take the time to post these pictures rather than get in contact with me. I'd rather not be made to feel like the best way of knowing what my boyfriend is up to is to sit and refresh the home-pages to my social media accounts all day long . . .

Not that I'm stuck at home dwelling on it too much. The shop is busy with afternoon tea bookings (almost doubling the morning bake time, not that I'm complaining) and we have a rather important wedding to focus on and plan in only a short amount of time.

Yes, my mind is occupied and full. I'm not avoiding the situation I'm in, but rather am immersing myself in my surroundings and the things that are actually occurring and present in my life. That's how I've learnt to cope and keep any wobbly feelings at bay, by focusing on the here and now and not hankering after something and someone that feels distinctly unobtainable lately.

The following Sunday I'm surprised by the grin on my face when I open the front door to Peter, suddenly realizing that I've missed him over the past week since our dinner. It's silly really, as I've only spent a handful of days with him since properly meeting him, but it's the combination of his friendly blue eyes and endearing smile that echo his mother's that bring me the most joy. Rather embarrassingly, I find myself staring at him with a huge toothy grin before I remember myself and welcome him inside, my face turning pink as I do so.

As expected, he is warmly greeted by the whole family and immediately fussed over. Mum and Colin start laughing over their past encounters when Peter was just a young teenager, Charlotte becomes adorably bashful and won't leave my side, while Aaron instantly tries to drag him out to the garden for a kick around with his football. He's wrapped up in our world straight away, and from the happy expression on his face I can tell he's thoroughly enjoying being with us all. And it's not strange having him here with us. He comfortably sits himself at the kitchen table (the same place he sat when we first met after Molly passed away) while Mum makes him a cup of tea, as though it's a normal occurrence.

'So, what's new?' he asks, removing his grey woolly turtleneck jumper now that he's in the heat of our home. Spring might have arrived and started to warm up the previously icy weather, but it's still chilly out there.

'Well, we're getting married,' Mum says with a shy smile as she looks at Colin, who gives her a smitten look in return.

'I knew that!' Peter laughs. 'I've heard all about your romantic proposal, Colin. Sounds like you did a terrific job.'

'If something is worth doing, it's worth doing right,' he replies, visibly proud that he pulled the magical moment off and that it quickly became the talk of the village, and has remained so ever since.

'Couldn't agree more,' Peter grins.

'Well, sadly for Sophie, the plans have slightly changed,' sighs Mum, looking nervous about the whole thing again.

'Oh?'

'It's nothing,' I shrug, rolling my eyes at her for worrying. Now that we've made the decision to go bigger we just have to run with it and throw ourselves into getting everything ready. 'We're just going bigger.'

'And why not! It's your special day. You can do and have whatever you like,' Peter encourages.

I can't help but smile at him.

'Rachel said you're using the shop?' he continues, smiling back at me, his eyes twinkling.

'That's right,' Colin says, getting the milk out of the fridge for Mum and placing it beside her. 'Where else?'

'Actually,' I start, as a thought pops into my head. 'I know it's a cheeky request and that I'm putting you on the spot when you've only just walked through the door, but I don't suppose you'd fancy helping out, would you? Rachel was going to do it on her own when it was just us lot, but I think that'll be a bit much now. Feel free to say no . . .'

'I'd love to,' he replies, holding his hands up and gesturing for me to stop talking.

I'm gabbling because I hate asking people for things and feeling like I'm putting them out in any way. I like the fact that Peter senses this and wants to reassure me otherwise.

'I'll do all the prep, of course, so you won't have to do much more than serve and keep everyone happy,' I continue, unable to help myself.

'It'll be great.' He pauses. 'Besides, if all else fails I can use my fake Aussie charm,' he winks.

'Exactly,' I say, giggling at his idea. 'It's been working on all the ladies so far.'

'That's very kind of you,' says Mum to Peter, cutting in on the moment as she places his drink in front of him. 'It'll be lovely for Sophie to just relax and enjoy the day. I'm sure Billy will step in if need be, too.'

'So, he'll be back by then?' Peter asks, looking surprised as he glances across at me.

'I should certainly hope so. It wouldn't be the same without him,' says Colin, opening a packet of custard cream biscuits and offering Peter one, even though dinner isn't far from being ready.

A strange feeling of guilt crawls up my spine at the mention of Billy and at that look from Peter.

'Please can we go outside now?' Aaron pleads as he walks in with his football under his arm, looking bored as Charlotte bounces in after him. The two had decided to go off and play a few minutes after Peter arrived when they realized the boring grown-up chat was going to happen before they got a look in with the exciting guest. Now they're back and want entertaining.

'Come on then, mate,' Peter laughs, downing the contents of his boiling drink before standing up and following his new buddy out into the garden.

'He talks funny,' muses Charlotte, her head cocked to one side as she slides into his chair.

'Because he's lived in Australia for so long,' Colin informs her.

'Australia,' she repeats. 'Have we ever been there?'

'No,' says Colin, shaking his head. 'It's very far away.'

'Ohhh . . .' she replies, looking out of the kitchen window and watching Peter. 'Is he your new boyfriend, Sophie?'

'No!' I gasp.

'Charlotte!' Colin warns.

'What?' she retorts innocently, as though unable to comprehend our shocked reactions. 'He's a boy and her friend . . .'

'Well, when you break it down like that . . .' Colin replies, shrugging at me and Mum as though unsure how to respond. 'He's a very nice man,' he murmurs.

'Does Billy like him?' she asks, looking directly at me.

'They haven't met yet,' I reply.

'Hmmm . . .' and just like that she slinks out of her seat and disappears into the other room.

Colin laughs the incident off and busies himself by getting the plates and cutlery out for the table, while Mum flashes me a concerned and knowing look before taking the roast potatoes out of the oven and giving them a shake.

The boys come in half an hour later, just in time to see the roast lamb being plated up, and then join Charlotte and I at the table. Dinner is delicious. Mum barely cooked for years (we either didn't eat or lived off microwave meals when Dad died), but she's pulled back her culinary skills and has managed to master the traditional Sunday roast to perfection – something she usually does every Sunday with all the trimmings, as though it's Christmas day.

Peter is asked a million questions during the feast. Not just from Charlotte who now wants to hear all about the existence of kangaroos and koalas (she's never seen any, so she thinks they're as mythical as unicorns), but from everyone at the table. The conversation flows as Peter opens up about his childhood, Molly, his dad, which football team he supports, whether he thinks he'll ever move back here, what it's like living in the future and whether or not it gives him superpowers (he says not but the children believe otherwise). It's lovely seeing everyone welcoming Peter and wanting to know all about him, but it's even more magical to have an outsider come in and witness my glorious family who are being thoroughly entertaining and inclusive. Thinking back to the Buskin household and the first time I went there it's clear the attention was always on Billy and never fully on me. I was grateful for that at the time as I hate being put on the spot or having my presence anywhere highlighted, but because of my resistance and them being wrapped up in Billy, I don't think I ever experienced anything like the hospitality and love that my family are showing to our guest right now.

Watching them warms my heart.

I know how their kindness will be making Peter feel . . . because everyone in this room has experienced loss and seen the heart of their families crushed into obscurity, yet me, my mum, Colin, Aaron and Charlotte have been fortunate enough to have been given second families.

I want Peter to witness that and for him to be moved

by it. To see how wonderful it is to have those special times continuing in the absence of loved ones, and to observe how being 'pinned down' or 'having your wings clipped' can actually be something beautiful and not at all oppressive. I know it's something he's already started pondering over (he said as much when we went out to dinner), but when I think of his outlook and compare it to my own circumstances I'm made aware of how much my life has changed since I've started to let those barriers of independence down. My world is brighter and warmer thanks to my family attachments.

The smile on his face throughout the meal tells me he sees what I see, but even better than that, I'm delighted to spot a lightness within his burly frame that wasn't there before.

The hours trickle by, and before we know it we're all gathered in the hallway to see Peter off.

'Actually, I'll walk up the road with you,' I say impulsively, grabbing my red coat and throwing it on.

'Oh?' he asks in surprise.

'What for?' asks Mum, her voice squeaking on its way out.

'I forgot to see if I have enough food colouring left for a rainbow cake I've got to make first thing,' I explain. 'I'm sure I do but I'd rather go up now and stop in at Budgens on the way back rather than faff around tomorrow morning when I should be getting on.'

Mum looks back at me blankly.

'You know I like to be organized,' I say, grabbing her by the shoulders and giving her a kiss on the cheek, trying to telepathically tell her that she has to stop worrying about me. Over the last few hours she must have seen that Peter is a lovely guy, but that there's nothing more between us than companionship.

'Thank you so much for having me, Jane. Dinner was superb,' Peter says, nudging me out of the way and taking her slim frame into his manly arms before squeezing her with a hug.

'Not at all,' she says, managing to compose herself. She's far worse than me at having her personal space invaded, yet Peter comes with a familiarity that means she doesn't retreat into her shell on the spot. Instead, she keeps her composure and even manages to look un-affected by the embrace.

'Well, if we don't see you before, we'll see you on our wedding day,' Colin says, his friendly face grinning at the thought as he shakes Peter's hand while simultaneously patting him on the shoulder.

'Take care until then,' Peter smiles. 'Although maybe I'll see you soon for a bit more footy, eh, mate?' he adds, ruffling Aaron's hair.

'Yes please,' he gushes in reply, his cheeks stretched into a wide grin. He's clearly enjoyed someone being here to play with him. Even though he's started going out and playing with his friends from time to time, there's always something awe-inspiring from having that sort of inter-action with adults when you're a child – especially when they're not your boring old parents.

'See you later, little lady,' Peter says to Charlotte, who smiles up at him in response.

'I like you,' she beams, throwing an arm around his waist.

'You too, kid,' he softly laughs, his eyes crinkling in delight at her affection. He gently pats her back as she lets go and plods backwards to take hold of Colin's hand.

'I won't be long,' I call, leading us out of the house and waving goodbye to the assembled troop watching us leave.

'They're great,' Peter grins, once the door has finally been shut and we're out of earshot. 'What a rad family you have.'

'Thank you,' I smile.

'I can see why it's more than the shop keeping you here.'

His statement catches me off guard.

It's true that having a lovely family to go home to every night certainly makes it harder to walk away from than our old fractured shell of a family. Although, even then, there was no way I could leave Mum in the black hole she was living in. Now though, I love walking through the door of an evening and seeing them all milling around doing 'normal family activities' like homework, having dinner or all curled up watching TV. It's mildly depressing when Colin and the kids aren't over, especially if Mum's gone there for the night too. I don't know how I'll cope when I no longer have them to come home to, but knowing they'll still be in the same village is better than having them thousands of miles away . . . I don't think I could do what both Peter and Billy did.

'Penny for your thoughts?' Peter asks as we reach the park, which is routinely quiet for this time of year with just a few dog walkers in the distance, out in the crisp cold air.

'That is most definitely something your mum would've said,' I laugh, briefly grabbing hold of his elbow.

'Oh no, am I turning into her?' he gasps back with a smirk.

'Lucky us if you are.'

'Seriously, though, what's on your mind?' he pushes, glancing at me before looking down at his shoes on the pathway.

'Just thinking that I love living here,' I sigh, feeling rather dreamy about the matter. 'That there's nowhere else I'd rather be . . .'

'That's . . . that's great,' he grins, taking a breath.

Without warning, Peter takes his hands from his pockets. He stops walking, places one hand on mine to encourage me to do the same and then turns towards me, his free hand sliding through the hair behind my ear and to the back of my head. Before I can fathom what's happening he leans down and places his cold lips on mine, his hand moving to the nape of my neck and firmly holding my head in place.

It's horrible. Not the actual kiss, the kiss is fine, I guess, but the feeling it stirs within me is one of horror.

'What are you doing?' I ask, pushing him off me, my hands instantly flying to my mouth as though they've been bruised from the unwanted contact.

'What? I . . .' he stutters, a frown of confusion burying itself in his brow.

'What? You what?' I shriek, my body shaking at the invasion, my face turning bright red with embarrassment and shock.

'You said there was nowhere else you'd rather be,' he stammers.

'Than Rosefont! I wasn't talking about this specific moment. It wasn't about you or us.'

'Well, in that case you were very misleading,' he says matter-of-factly, shaking his head.

'How? At what point did I make you think I wanted that?'

'You never made me think you didn't.'

'Are you serious? I have a boyfriend!' I breathe, my bottom lip starting to quiver as I guiltily think of Billy and hating the fact that Peter has put us both in this situation.

'Then what are you doing out with me?'

'*Out* with you? My mum thought it would be nice to have you over for dinner so you weren't on your own.'

'I'm not a charity case,' he objects, looking hurt.

'I didn't say you were,' I frown. 'You're Molly's son! You –'

'Is that all you see me as?' he asks quickly, looking wounded as he fires the question in my direction. 'Some dead woman's son?'

'Of course not,' I hesitate, surprised by the depth of emotions swirling between us when things had been so different just minutes before. 'I like your company,' I shrug, feebly.

'Well, that's nice to know,' he laughs hollowly, taking his hand to his head and rubbing at his eyes, as though my honest and heartfelt words offer him zero comfort.

I stand and watch him. Having never been in a situation like this one before I'm stunned into silence. Part of me is reeling that he's just taken it upon himself to act like that, but the other part is searching my brain and trying to work out what's going on. Have I been giving off mixed signals? I know I've enjoyed his attention, and even lapped it up without questioning it, but from what I've heard that's just like every other woman in the village he's taken the time to talk to. I haven't seen him going around trying to kiss all of them, though . . .

'I'm sorry. I feel like an absolute idiot,' he says, his voice low and calmer as his eyes look down at me, his face contorted in discomfort.

'It was a misunderstanding,' I mumble, attempting to shake the matter off. He's not the only one feeling foolish right now and I don't really want to follow it up with an argument. I simply want to remove myself from the situation completely and go hide in my bedroom.

'You don't need to make excuses for me. I shouldn't have done that,' Peter says, shaking his head. 'I had a great day with you and your family and then I went and acted like a dick.'

'You didn't . . .' I start.

'I know you think otherwise but are being too polite to tell me so,' he continues, raising his eyebrows and challenging me to disagree.

I don't. Instead I look down at my black boots and scrape one of the soles across the concrete path.

'These things happen,' I find myself saying.

'Really? When? To who?' he asks, thankfully questioning my ludicrous statement.

'Well, so I've heard,' I admit, looking back up at him. 'Not to me, though. Never to me.'

'No, me neither,' he says, his blue eyes full of sorrow as he flicks his gaze to me before turning away again.

I take a lungful of air and slowly dispel it as I look around at the rest of the park, which, thankfully, seems just as deserted as it was before. I don't believe Peter is some horrific predator out to catch me off guard and take advantage. I usually feel more than safe in his company and know he wouldn't have acted in that way if he thought it was going to upset me. Another deep breath sees my shoulders relax and my pulsing heart calm down. Slowly the mixture of heightened emotions Peter caused to surge within me start to ebb away, making me feel less like a rabbit caught in headlights.

'That was such a silly move.'

'Tell me about it . . . can we just forget it even happened?' he pleads. 'I mean, I'll stay away for a bit, obviously, but I don't want things to be weird for us just because I turned into a gross lad for a few seconds. That's not who I am.'

'I know.'

'Good . . . because you are every bit as great as Mum said and I'd hate to lose the last proper connection I have to her. That would break my heart,' he says, stopping as his words choke him.

I clench my jaw to stop my own emotions getting the better of me. This isn't a side of Peter I'm used to seeing. I'm the one who's overly sentimental, not him.

He gives a slight cough to compose himself before rubbing at the stubble on his face. 'Please don't bar me from the shop.'

'Can you do that with teashops?' I ask, my voice almost a squeak as I try to lighten the mood and find myself wanting to cheer him up. 'I thought that was just something the pub landlords always say in *EastEnders*.'

'You can do what you like, you own it,' he shrugs, a half smile forming on his lips.

'Well I won't ban you just yet,' I say, managing to mirror the smile he's giving me.

'Thank you.' There's a slightly awkward pause. 'I'm so sorry.'

'Let's not talk about it any more,' I say. Not because he's forgiven or because I don't think he's done anything wrong, but because I don't want to stand around analysing it any further. It was a foolish mistake that meant nothing.

'Deal,' he says, pressing his lips tightly together, as though stopping himself from saying something further.

'Right, well, I'd better be heading home,' I say, my thumb pointing back the way we came.

'Don't you need to go to the shop?' he asks, bemused.

'I do, but –'

'You don't want to walk with me in case I try anything again?' he frowns.

'No, it's not that,' I say, shaking my head. 'I think I'd rather go home now, though.'

'Shit . . .' he murmurs, looking exasperated at himself.

'Honestly, I'm fine,' I say, backing away from him.

'Well . . . call me if you're not,' he shrugs.

'Yeah, maybe . . .' I reply, knowing I have no intention of doing so. 'See you later, Peter,' I say, turning and heading in the direction of home.

I don't go straight there because I know Mum will suspect something is up if I return so quickly and I'm not ready to admit she was right to be worried about my blossoming friendship with another man . . .

Instead, when I know I'm out of Peter's sight, I sit on a bench and just stare at my surroundings, hoping the beauty of nature will untie the knots that have formed in my stomach. I watch the tree branches blowing in the wind, spot squirrels and rabbits hopping about on the grass and listen to the silence around me, attempting to take some comfort from it and fill myself with calm.

Peter kissed me and I really wish he hadn't because now I find myself questioning my own behaviour and my innocence in a situation I'd been rather enjoying. I liked having a friend. I even liked having the occasional flirt – something I never do but was able to because I felt so comfortable in Peter's company.

I'm not in a love triangle.

I'm not.

I do not have romantic feelings for anyone other than Billy.

It's true I have a lot of admiration for Peter and feel a deep connection to him – but that's down to something completely out of his control. It's in his DNA, and in the characteristics he's unknowingly picked up from the woman who raised him. It's because he shares a connection to this beautiful village in Kent that I have incredible affection for. These things might make me want to spend more time with him, but they don't make me want us to be anything more than good friends.

Friends . . .

Having only had a handful of encounters with him, is it likely we'll go through the difficulty of trying to remain in each other's lives after this awkward episode? It would be far easier to just avoid each other, even though I know I'll feel like I've lost Molly for the second time . . .

No, I can't do that. I've enjoyed feeling her presence too much. Surely it's worth seeing if something is salvageable before throwing it away? Especially as it means so much! Besides, it's only us who know about the indiscretion, so what harm can trying do?

29

Early Sunday evenings seem to be the only time Billy and me are guaranteed to actually talk without fail. So as I walk into my room an hour later I'm not surprised to feel my phone vibrating in my pocket to let me know he's calling.

Even though I'm spaced out from the way my afternoon has panned out, my heart tells me I need to hear his voice – we might have spoken the previous night but communication between us has been sparse to say the least. It's been weeks since a letter has found its way to me, and it's just dawned on me how much I've come to depend on the sight of his messy handwriting.

'What have you been up to today?' he asks, sounding full of beans as he fires a normal, mundane question in my direction. It's lovely that he sounds so pleased to talk to me, but I suddenly feel put on the spot and on edge.

'Nothing. Just a roast with everyone,' I reply, sounding a little cagey as I omit to tell him that Peter joined us. It's not lying, but it's certainly withholding the truth and putting up a barrier between us. I just don't want to be talking about Peter to Billy. I don't want further questions being asked, because then I would have to lie and that would be terrible.

'Nice . . .' he replies, as though he's unaware of my mood. 'Can't wait for one of those when I get back. Mum's not attempted to cook another one since the last disaster.'

'Right,' I say shortly, realizing that I definitely shouldn't have picked up the phone when I saw him calling. It was most certainly a bad idea. He's light and lovely while I'm the opposite. It's as though I'm looking to build some friction between us. Perhaps it's the guilt eating away at me but I can literally feel myself on the verge of throwing myself under a metaphorical bus.

'So when are you coming out here?'

'I'm not,' I blurt, not even trying to break the news I've been putting off telling him all week in a sensitive way.

'You . . . what?' he asks, making sure he's heard me correctly.

'It's the wedding. Mum's changed her mind about some stuff and I need to be here for her,' I say, matter-of-factly, unsure as to why I'm being so tactless.

'So you're dropping me just like that?'

'I'm not dropping you,' I scoff. 'I never said I would *definitely* come. It was always dependent on what's happening here.'

'I know how protective you are over her, but you can't stop your own life for your mum, Sophie,' Billy mutters coldly, as though he's suddenly annoyed at the bond Mum and I share – something he's never even hinted at in the past. 'You've done that before and for far too long.'

'Excuse me?' I demand, shocking myself at the authoritative bitterness in the tone of my voice that's daring him to expand on that thought.

'I just mean . . .' he flounders, clearly looking for the words. 'You have to live your own life, baby. You can't pander to your mum all the time. She's a grown-up and not the timid woman you always act like she is. Besides, she's got Colin now. She's moved on.'

'Billy!' I shout. I'm astounded at the words that are coming from his mouth, as though I'm a full-time carer for Mum or something. Or as though I treat her like an invalid. I mean, I know I worry, but she still worries about me too so what's the difference? 'Will you shut up?'

'Pardon?'

'You know nothing about the relationship between me and my mum,' I hurl.

'No, I didn't mean . . .' he starts, but I cut him off, not wanting to hear any more.

'She's my best friend and she's weeks away from one of the biggest days of her life. So huge in fact that it affects me and my life directly,' I say, feeling the fire in my chest and unable to stop myself from continuing. 'Being with her *is* living my life. Flying to LA so I can potter around until you finish frolicking about on set pretending to be some ninja warrior, or whatever it is you're doing over there, is not living my life in the slightest. In fact I'd say *that* would be wasting my time and taking me away from the arduous task of living my own life!'

And just like that I end the call, turn my phone off and seethe at the day's events as any effort to stay calm is obliterated for good.

Who does Billy think he is telling me how to behave with my mum when I made sure not to say anything about his, even though she acted like a petulant child and I overheard her speak badly of me? If either of us needs to question the relationship we have with our mums to assess whether they're healthy or not it's certainly him and not me. My mum is nothing like the manipulative matriarch I witnessed in action in LA, and for that I'm bloody thankful. At least my mum has good reasons for being the way she is – she's not just a spoilt brat who pawns her son out so that she can continue living the lavish lifestyle that she doesn't lift a finger for.

I'm fuming so much it's a good job I got off the phone when I did. I know doing so was a childish thing to do, but if I'd stayed on the line a second longer I know I would have said something worse, something irretrievable. It's much better that I removed myself from the conversation and allowed myself to mutter profanities at my bedroom walls for a few moments instead.

Anger is not an emotion I'm used to expressing – I'm definitely more of a lover than a fighter. But my sudden outburst feels so good after months of bottling up my worries and concerns.

It feels so cathartic to let loose and get some of the tension out, even if only my bedroom walls can hear it while I bang around noisily. Billy doesn't need to hear everything on my mind – but some of those thoughts just need to be set free, because keeping them contained isn't doing me any good.

I leave my phone off for the rest of the night and unplug the landline. Thankfully, before I came up here, Mum headed over to Colin's with him and the kids to iron their school shirts for the following day so I don't have to worry about explaining myself to anyone.

Knowing I'm completely unreachable feels good. It's freeing somehow. And even though I know I'm going to have to face everything that's going on maturely at some point, I allow myself to be reckless. Because that is not who I am and, right now, I like that feeling.

30

I might have enjoyed my night free of contact, but my stupidity hits me like a huge whack over the head when I wake up the following morning. At first I think the previous day's events are fragmented parts of a twisted dream, but then I'm hit by the reality of one guy friend inappropriately kissing me, me acting like an idiot towards my boyfriend and then him insulting me and my family, causing me to hang up on him and kill all contact. Not great. In fact it's quite a disaster on all fronts.

I reluctantly throw the covers off and get out of bed even though, for the first time in a while, I'd much rather curl up under my duvet and avoid everyone and everything. But there's just too much on today to allow myself to be so self-indulgent, especially now I'm the boss.

On my way into work I turn my phone back on and head straight to Twitter and Instagram to see if Billy's posted anything. Thankfully he hasn't. I say thankfully because I'm glad he's not been in the mood to share jolly selfies with the world when things are difficult between us, although the absence of an update on what he's up to or how he's feeling also makes me feel uncomfortable and sad. I'm regretting that I wasn't able to just communicate with him and be honest. Maybe not about Peter, but certainly about other things that have been niggling away at me.

I'm about to disparagingly put my phone back in my pocket when it starts buzzing, with dozens of messages from Billy. Rather than read them I put my phone back in my pocket and decide to look at them when I can focus properly at home later. The lightness in my heart tells me that the mere sight of Billy's name popping up is enough for now . . .

The morning is busy and chaotic, meaning I don't have much time to dwell on yesterday. Instead, I let Rachel focus mostly on looking after the shop while I set about my mammoth baking session. Not only is there that rainbow birthday cake to make, but we also have a surprise baby shower booked for the following day for one of Rachel's mummy friends, so it's all systems go.

There's something therapeutic about baking and being able to make something with your hands. All of your concentration is channelled into textures, tastes and decoration and after hours of work it's lovely to be able to step back and see what you've created. It always leaves me feeling fulfilled and satisfied (unless I've had a disastrous experimental bake, of course).

I watch shows like *The Great British Bake Off* and I completely understand why it's taken the nation by storm. It's so rewarding. Plus, it doesn't matter how I'm feeling or what's going on in my life, I know a session in the kitchen will blank it all out and leave me feeling stress free for an hour or two.

Obviously, there's the added bonus that afterwards you can sit down with your delicious creation and scoff the lot while actually thinking through your problems – if you feel ready to face them by then, that is. Cake and tea are sure to cure most ills, after all.

I feel a lot calmer after a morning next to the oven, especially as the birthday cake turns out beautifully. I'm rather chuffed with myself when I watch Rachel leave to deliver it later in the afternoon once the sponge has been cooled and we've smothered it with buttercream icing and decorated it with heart- and star-shaped hundreds and thousands.

'What did she think?' I ask, as soon as Rachel returns with a bag full of shopping from Budgens.

'Hmm?' she says with a frown, looking distracted as she looks around the shop, which is empty now as it's just before the mad after-school dash.

'The cake? Was everything OK?' I ask.

'Oh yes, fine . . .' she says, pulling out some Fairy liquid from the bag and placing it next to the sink, before going back to retrieve something else.

'Are you all right?' I ask. Rachel is never dismissive or vague and she's acting entirely differently to how she was half an hour ago.

'I wasn't going to say anything because I know what this village is like for gossip,' she says, blowing air through her lips. 'But I think you should know what's being said . . .'

'What's Billy done now?' I ask, rolling my eyes at her and trying to keep the chat between us light, even though my heart feels like something has tightly clamped on to it.

'Not Billy,' she says, looking as though she's debating whether to say any more or not before she looks up at me. 'You.'

'Me?' I frown, my voice tellingly catching in my throat as I say it and unable to stay neutral. 'What's been said?'

'Oh, I don't want to repeat it,' she says, rustling through the bag and trying to avoid the conversation she's started.

'You have to now,' I say, placing my hand on top of the plastic carrier and forcing her to stop.

'It wasn't said to me and I've probably just overheard wrong,' she says, looking extremely uncomfortable.

'You can't leave it like that,' I say, feeling sick as I wait for her to tell me the inevitable. 'You've started now so you might as well say it.'

'It's so silly. I know there's absolutely no truth in it,' she says, shaking her head as though she wishes she'd never brought it up. 'But someone was saying they saw you kissing a man in the park.'

'Who?'

'They weren't sure, but it obviously wasn't Billy,' she says, her eyes narrowing as she says it because I haven't done the one thing I should have done and denied it straight away.

'No, I mean, who said they saw it?' I push.

'Does it matter?' she frowns.

'I guess not,' I say, knowing that anyone in the village would have felt like they'd hit gold seeing me in what must have looked like a lover's embrace. Not only that, but anyone being told something like that about little old me (who they all think is so innocent) would be lapping it up and eager to pass it on to the next living thing they came into contact with — human, cat, dog, hamster. They wouldn't be too fussy. Not with juicy gossip like this.

'It's not true, is it?' Rachel asks slowly, her eyes

widening as she leans her hip on the counter and looks at me suspiciously.

'No,' I lie, feeling my ears burn and unable to remove the guilty look from my face. I've never been very good at lying.

'It is, isn't it,' she states, looking shocked as her mouth slackens and she gawps at me.

'Stop it,' I tell her, not wanting to discuss it. I reach for the bag of shopping to take out a few items but Rachel stops me by snatching the bag away. It seems that if she's not allowed to use the shopping as a distraction technique then neither am I.

'I didn't even want to bring it up, but you told me to,' she says, defiantly dumping the bag behind her before looking back over at me and placing her hands on her hips.

'I know, but . . .' I start, wondering if I can afford to share what's happened, or whether it'll just add fuel to the fire to have the truth of the matter out there to be spread further. The more people who know Peter kissed me the less likely it is that things will simply return to normal. I just want the whole thing to go away.

'So who was it?' she asks, not letting go of the subject as she thinks through any possibilities. Let's be clear, the only unattached male who's walked into this shop lately is Peter, so her reluctance to jump to the obvious conclusion straight away implies she's not ruling out the village's married men, which is slightly horrifying.

'No one,' I reply, feeling hurt.

'When did it happen?'

'What, did the gossip monger fail to dish out vital pieces of information when they were whispering about me?' I snipe.

'Sophie!' she says, stopping me.

Instead of questioning me further she goes to the front door and locks it, quickly flipping the sign round to closed while she's there. It's something I'm grateful for as I really don't want anyone coming in and catching us having this conversation – although I'm sure the fact we've shut the shop will set tongues wagging if anyone notices.

'Sorry . . .' I puff when she's back in front of me. I know none of this is Rachel's fault and that she clearly thought she was just going to deliver a bit of idle gossip for us to laugh over. She hadn't banked on it being true. 'So is everyone talking about it?'

'I only heard three people chatting about it, but I expect it's doing the rounds,' she says sorrowfully. 'Although without a man in the frame to flesh the story out a bit and give it some weight I imagine it's going to quickly die away.'

'Or they'll keep digging until they know more?' I speculate, quashing her optimistic view.

'I don't think they'll do that. They'll move on to something else before too long,' she says, her voice full of pity as she takes hold of my hand.

'It's horrible knowing people are talking about me,' I admit.

There have been several times over the past couple of years when the tabloid press have picked up on a nugget of information about me or Billy and turned it into international news, but somehow, knowing that it's the people I love and care for talking about me is worse. Although maybe that's because the whole thing isn't as innocent as I'd like it to be and I hate them thinking badly of me.

'You don't think anyone would go to the papers, do you?' I ask with a sudden panic.

'And say what?' Rachel laughs. 'They've got nothing to back anything up with. Besides, I don't think that's where anyone's minds would go here.'

'I hope you're right,' I say, feeling like something minor that should have already been erased from my mind has now turned into a whole crater of potential doom – a grenade waiting to be detonated.

'It's not a regular thing, though, is it? You're not cheating on Billy?'

'Of course not,' I say, my voice shrill. 'I wasn't. Whoever saw what they saw didn't see the whole picture.'

'I don't think they saw much but your bright red coat and a stranger's arms wrapped around you.'

'Well, if they'd spied a bit longer they'd have seen the guy in question getting pushed off and put in his place,' I declare.

'Oh . . .'

'It was over before it began.'

'Does Billy know?' Rachel asks.

'No . . . we've actually had a row, too,' I admit, laughing into the palms of my hands as the ridiculousness of the whole situation hits me.

'What about?'

'Me not being able to go back over there. It all just escalated from nothing and stupid things were said.'

'Right . . .' she replies, pursing her lips at me. 'You two are under such a lot of pressure. I can't imagine what it must be like living so far apart like you are while continuing to be in a relationship. I'm not surprised you row. I'd be so resentful of the situation all the time, I'd be giving Shane earache every time he bothered calling.'

'That's what I feel I'm being like,' I say, thankful to her for making me feel like my reaction to the whole thing isn't entirely pathetic.

'But it's not you and it's not him,' Rachel says calmly.

'I just feel terrible because I pushed him into doing the film in the first place but now I'm the one with the problem,' I say, feeling a wave of emotion wash over me as tears spring to my eyes.

'I'm sure it's not a walk in the park for him either,' she says, putting her arm around me.

'That's what he says.'

'Well then . . .'

'It's just not easy.'

'You know, I don't think any relationship worth having is ever easy,' she ponders.

'I agree. In fact I think I've used similar words before. We're just in a particularly tough situation. I look at everyone else walking around the village in their little couples and I'm overwhelmed with this feeling of sadness.'

'You forget that each of us only sees what we're permitted to see – hence the old "what goes on behind closed doors" saying. Take me and Shane,' she says, putting her hand on her chest. 'Everyone always assumes we never argue, that we're always in agreement with each other and that not a stressed word is ever uttered between us. Well, bollocks to that.'

'You two are wonderful together,' I laugh, wiping my eyes with the backs of my hands.

'Yes, that's exactly what we like people to think. And

we're not lying, we're not being fake or putting on a show. We have our moments but prefer to keep them to the confines of our home. Just like every other couple out there. Honestly, I can't tell you how many times I've sat there in a foul mood throwing invisible daggers at the back of his head,' she says, squinting as she venomously stares at the air in front of her.

'Why?'

'Because he's annoyed me about something, or because I'm simply ridiculously tired from being up with the boys all night but still there in the kitchen cooking his dinner,' she laughs while pretending to strangle the air in front of her. 'It can be over the smallest, most insignificant thing, but once I've had my moment of silent hatred I get over it and go back to loving him. It's a part of life. Nothing is good all the time and absolutely nothing is perfect. That's a fact.'

'I know that.'

'My point is we all have our crosses to bear, but sometimes those struggles are worth fighting through. No relationship comes without its hardships or the need to compromise.'

'Yeah,' I nod.

'He'll be back soon. I'm sure things will make more sense then,' she says, flashing me an encouraging smile.

'I hope so,' I reply.

'I'm sure it will. You've already done better than I could've.'

'So what do I do now about the village whisperings?' I ask, my thoughts returning to Peter, that non-kiss and the repercussions that might come from it now I know we were spotted. 'What if it gets back to Mum?'

'I'd say wait it out a bit,' Rachel shrugs, screwing up her face as she thinks the matter through. 'It's all so fresh and it sounds like you're the innocent party in the whole thing. To be honest it sucks that you were spotted and not the guy.'

'Tell me about it . . . thank you,' I sigh, turning to her and giving her a hug, possibly by way of thanks to her for being so kind, or possibly because I'm in dire need of the physical comfort. 'It feels so good to have someone other than Mum to chat to. Especially with the wedding being so close, I haven't wanted to worry her about anything.'

'Well, I'm always here,' she says, gripping hold of my elbows as we part.

'Thank you,' I say, the sides of my lips rising into a smile. 'You're my new Molly.'

'Careful. She'll come back and haunt you if she thinks she's being replaced.'

'Ha!' I say, looking around the room as if to check she's not here now. 'No, you're right, no one could ever replace her like that. But until now I hadn't realized how much I've been missing having a friend. Molly was always there for me. She was my first proper friend. Possibly my only one. There's been a gaping hole left since she died.'

Without saying it out loud I think about Peter and have a further understanding as to why I felt a connection to him. The lonely woman inside of me wanted my Molly to confide in, and he reminded me of her so much it made sense for me to latch on to him. However, I hadn't thought about just how much of myself I was giving over, or whether it was entirely appropriate when I have a boyfriend.

31

'I'm such a shit,' Billy says, sounding beaten and weary as soon as he picks up the phone later that evening.

I decided to wait until I was safely in the privacy of my room before calling him back, not wanting Mum to know anything was the matter, and certainly not wanting her to hear that he'd been rude and disrespectful about her.

'I couldn't agree more,' I sigh, the anger of last night having escaped me. Instead, I feel oddly calm as I wait for him to say more, perching myself on the windowsill and looking up my quiet street.

'I was disappointed that I'm not going to get to see you for a bit longer, that's all.'

'You didn't even sound like you wanted me over there when I first said I was going to look into it.'

'What? Are you joking?' he says, sounding taken aback by my observation.

'No . . .' I say, circling the yellow blobs on Mr Blobby as I cradle it in my arms.

'It's just difficult when you won't come on set,' he says simply, without any hostility or blame. 'I understand your reasons and hate to think of you being uncomfortable, but I want you with me. It negates the purpose of you being here otherwise. Honestly, I don't care whether we're locked up in a trailer together for three hours or watching the sun set in Malibu – the only thing that's important is that we're together.'

'I know . . .' I say in agreement as I think back to the argument we had when I last arrived in LA and wonder whether I'd ever be able to combat my worries and join him in that way. 'I think I'd rather be back on that beach, though.'

'OK, you've got me there. The beach would be more ideal,' he sighs, last night still weighing on his mind. 'You know I didn't mean anything I said.'

'I know.'

'No, I feel I need to grovel some more. Don't accept my apology yet.'

'Billy . . .' I say softly. Although I know he said some awful things I'm not exactly a saint. I don't want him feeling too bad about the whole thing, even if I am fiercely protective over my mum.

'I said things I shouldn't have.'

'We both did,' I remind him, nibbling on my lip as I watch our next-door neighbour arriving home after a day at work in London – something that guiltily turns my thoughts to Peter.

'Maybe. But you and your mum share something that me and mine never have. An equality that means you face things together without one of you dictating or stepping on the other's toes. I know that's down to sad circumstances or whatever, but I've always admired the love and friendship between you both. I don't want you thinking I feel anything different.'

'I don't,' I say.

'Your mum and Colin have been nothing but lovely to

me,' Billy continues. 'And I'm the biggest idiot ever for spouting anything different. I just wanted to see you.'

'Yeah, well maybe launching an attack on the most special person in my life isn't the best way to achieve that.'

'Duly noted. I'm so sorry.'

'So you didn't mean any of it?'

'I was just being selfish and obnoxious because I wasn't getting my own way. I'm frustrated, tired and a complete arse.'

'Are you getting spoilt on those movie sets by any chance?' I ask, poking fun.

'Possibly,' he chuckles softly, clearly not feeling out of the woods just yet.

'I'm sorry too that I can't come over,' I say softly, feeling sad that I'm not going to be able to see him for another month.

'It's not your fault. Just one of those things . . .' he says, sounding equally as bummed out as me. 'Look, I've got to go. I'm needed back on set.'

'Oh, right,' I say, not having realized he was already at work. I'd been picturing him in his bedroom at the house.

'Sorry I can't talk longer,' he says, his voice sounded strained. 'Thank you for calling me back and not giving up on us . . . I know this is tough.'

'It is.'

'But I'm worth it?' he asks, and I can tell from his tone that his mouth is slowly spreading into a cheeky and familiar grin.

'Don't push your luck,' I smile back, thankful for him injecting a bit of humour.

'Too soon?' he asks. 'Got it.'

When he eventually gets off the phone I feel momentarily lighter at having resolved the tension between us, but then I'm reminded that our issues go much deeper than a few angry words said in a moment of madness.

We're together. An item. A couple. But in many ways we're strangers. Torn apart by the miles dividing us and the fact that we rarely get to talk for more than a few minutes here and there.

Something Peter said when we were in the Indian really stuck with me, and that was how he couldn't handle being in a relationship without having all the perks of them being there at your beck and call. I know I like to think of myself as independent, especially now that I have the shop, but maybe I simply need the comfort of a partner being in the same time zone as me. Saying that, I know once he's back from LA for a few months I'll feel just as wrapped up in us as ever. It's the dark times we're apart that we really need to focus on if we're to make it work beyond the summer.

We each have separate wants, needs and desires, but is there a way of achieving those while ensuring neither of us has to compromise too much? Maybe it's time for me to revisit the idea of what I actually want, and see where that leaves me. And us.

The following morning I start to understand a little more about Billy's frame of mind as a letter, written just after I'd told Billy on the phone that I was going to go back over there and see him, arrives at the shop.

Dearest Sophie,

I was shaking my head at your last letter. Stop being so modest. You certainly do more than just keeping things afloat. What you do requires real skill. You and Molly created something that completely works. It's brilliant that you can leave the business without it falling apart and it's a credit to how much love and hard work you've poured into it. If anything the shop honours you in your absence rather than mocking you by cruelly collapsing the moment you step away from it and take some well-deserved time for yourself. You've built the foundations of a strong old tree, Miss May! Now own it.

Glad the new staffing is going well, but I'll be back to claim my Saturday role in no time so tell Peter not to get too comfy. Although I doubt you'll need him too much. Sounds like he's a busy guy anyway. Saying that, hopefully he'll feel inclined to step in again in a few weeks when you come back out. I know it'll make you feel better not placing too much responsibility on your mum and Colin.

I can't wait to have you back over here, because even though I LOVE the fact you feel you've had your Billy Buskin fix, having a Sophie May fix makes me feel lonelier than ever once you've gone. But maybe that's because I can't just arrange to fly over there whenever I fancy. Sorry that the pressure is on you this time. I'm sure it's not always going to work like that. Well, take the summer – I'll be all yours!

OK, I promised myself at the start of this letter that I wasn't going to say anything because it would ultimately make me look like a first-rate plonker, but it really bugs me that Peter gets to see you when I don't. I know that's absurd and ridiculous when I'm the one who's chosen to be out here and he's just Molly's son, but I get this desperate feeling of jealousy when I know you've been together. I had it straight away when you first wrote about him turning up at the shop. I got that letter the day you arrived over here and it threw me off when I read your words saying how great it was to see him. That's part of the reason I didn't come get you from the airport, or at least why I didn't tell you I wasn't coming. I didn't want to say something I shouldn't have and knew I just needed a few hours to think rationally, because it got my back up. Then knowing that you were out for dinner with him last night – well, in my head I imagined it to just be you two having a romantic candlelit dinner, even though it was obviously a work thing and that others were there. No need to tell me I'm being ridiculous, I already think it. I'm just sad not to be the one getting to spend time with you . . . Well, it's out there now. Not that I expect you to change anything you're doing to cure me of my silly thoughts. I know I'll feel better when I'm over there and can meet him. We'll probably end up as best mates. ;-)

Anyway, Rhonda asks about you every time we talk. I think she's seriously hoping you'll change your mind about acting. Either way, you've got a huge fan in her. I think she's used to her male clients dating highly strung girls. I think we might set up a fan club in your honour. Actually, we've already recruited our third member – Lauren. She keeps going on about seeing you soon. She's doing my nut in. I've never been so jealous of that little brat. Ha!

Johnny brought Cherise and the kids on set yesterday. Gosh those kids are cute. Can't wait for you to meet them. The smallest one just kept running over for cuddles. Johnny had to physically pull her off me at one point so we could carry on with filming. Won't lie, it got me quite excited for our future . . .

Right, I'm off to bed. It's been a long week on set and I'm
knackered. Hope you realize how much I miss you.

Always with love,
Your Billy xxx

The section about Peter is, obviously, what makes my
brain freeze. Seeing as the guy tried to kiss me by the time
this was written, Billy had every right to have a problem
with me spending time with him. I feel awful knowing
that he's torturing himself over these thoughts when
they're justified, and guilty that the meal out was actually,
as he'd feared, just the two of us. I'd definitely made it
sound like it was my way of thanking him for stepping in
and helping out, but actually, it was him who asked me
out and I was more than happy to oblige. I knew how it
would look and I'd tried to avoid being made to feel like I
was doing something wrong. Truth is, I'd known all along
that it was a crappy move to make.

I guess Peter's blunder was a blessing in disguise, as it's
certainly made me re-evaluate the situation and put an
end to something that could have easily grown into something less innocent if we'd continued to spend time
together and get closer, which is not an easy thing to
admit.

People always talk about Billy being away and how
hard it must be on me knowing girls are throwing themselves at him. I'm often asked if I'm worried he'll cheat . . .
However, it's worth noting that Billy is one of the most
recognizable men in Hollywood. If he were to do anything untoward I'd know about it almost immediately – take

the incident with Heidi Black. He told me straight away, of course, but it was in the papers just hours later.

Me on the other hand? Yes, I live in a community of nosy neighbours, but if I wanted to I could still be sneaky. It would be far easier for me to be the promiscuous party, but because I'm not the one in the limelight, people assume I would never do such a thing. That I wouldn't risk what I have.

I wouldn't, obviously. But thanks to Peter, I've realized just how easy doing so could be. Not that I think I should become a recluse and shut everyone out – lord knows I'm spectacular at doing that already. But life should be lived with your eyes wide open, not shut or slightly squinted to give you the view you'd rather have of the world.

'Just got your letter,' I say softly, as soon as a sleepy Billy picks up the phone.

'I was having a moment,' he says, gently laughing at himself.

'You OK?'

'I'm just missing you . . .' His voice is filled with a sadness that I hate hearing. There are two of us in this relationship, and, unlike what I'd imagined, two of us finding the distance between us equally as difficult, just as Rachel had said.

'Why didn't you say?'

'I always tell you I miss you.'

'About Peter,' I nudge.

'Oh . . . because I didn't want you thinking I was a possessive boyfriend. Plus, you should have friends. It's not for me to tell you who you can and can't talk to,' he tuts to himself. 'Sorry this is difficult.'

'No, I'm sorry,' I say, apologizing for far more than he realizes.

I momentarily think about telling him about the weekend's events, but although I know we both value trust and honesty, I can't bring myself to do it. I've already brushed the whole thing off as ridiculous and unfortunate, so I'd hate for it to be blown up into something bigger than it has to be. I don't want Billy thinking he's got anything to worry about, because he really doesn't. Not in terms of Peter and I. Although I hope the gossip has died away by the time he comes back . . .

Once I'm off the phone I look back to the rest of the mail the postman delivered first thing and find a letter from my solicitor, informing me that the tenancy agreement for the flat above the shop is about to come to an end and enquiring about how I'd like to proceed. Either I can offer a month-by-month rolling contract, renegotiate new terms or rent it out to someone new. I've not had to deal with upstairs before. Having worked here for almost a decade, I've obviously been up there (it's a surprisingly spacious two-bed) but it was always occupied when Molly was alive. The current tenants, a young couple who work in the city and have always kept themselves to themselves, had only just moved in when the shop came into my hands and we've hardly spoken other than one time when I had to get the washing machine fixed. With so much to think about in the shop I've been happy for them to continue with whatever they'd arranged through Molly previously. I regularly forget they're even up there as they've already left by the time I arrive in the mornings and don't get back until an hour or so after I close up and leave. Even at the weekends they tend to be out, so I've rarely bumped into them. It's weird to think of myself as anyone's land-lady really, especially as they never call in for tea and cake, or cause any fuss.

I make a mental note to pop a letter through their door when I'm on my way home later and see what they'd like to do moving forward.

That thought is negated when I open the third letter – from the aforementioned couple upstairs, informing me that they'll be sadly leaving at the end of the month for a flat in town. At first I feel a little sad at the idea of having to find someone new to take it on, but then a thought pops into my head – and it's something I ponder over for the rest of the day.

As excitement builds through me and I can't shake a huge smile from my face, I realize I've independently made the first solid decision about what I want in my future and it absolutely involves me staying here, in the place I feel loved, comfortable, safe and free. Because not all of us need to fly the nest like Peter and see ourselves on the other side of the world to grab hold of our freedom and independence. For some of us it's about staying exactly where we are and being perfectly happy with that decision.

I'm reminded of a letter Molly once wrote to me – the one I received after she died, telling me she was leaving me the shop. In it she urged me to follow my heart and not to feel trapped by her leaving it in my hands. I'm pretty sure the wording she used was that she didn't want me to feel tied down. Let's not forget that this came from the same lady who encouraged her own son to move to the other side of the world so that he wouldn't feel con-fined to life in Rosefont Hill.

Molly knew me better than anyone, and I know she would have realized that by giving me everything that she did, she was also giving me my independence and unclip-ping my wings. She saw that this is where I would blossom and thrive, and she understood before I did that I wouldn't need to travel thousands of miles to find the person I want to be, because I'm happy with who I am and where I am already.

I could have left a long time ago. I could have moved to London, I could have agreed to move to LA, but I didn't. Even before that, if I'd have had the courage, I could have gone travelling or somewhere new, exploring what else life had to offer. But I didn't, and that wasn't just because of Mum. It was because of me. Because, actually, I never had any desire to be anywhere else. Rosefont Hill lights up my world in ways that nowhere else ever could. It's stamped all over my heart and all over my being – and I'm flipping proud of that.

I didn't miss out because I didn't don a backpack and slum it across South America or visit the beaches in Thai-land. I didn't fail because I didn't find a way out of here. It might have felt like that at eighteen when I knew everyone in my sixth form had exciting plans ahead, but now I see that my life is richer for the plans I did make. I found this place. I found Molly and Billy. I watched Mum fall in love with Colin and our family become whole again. I found the place where I belong.

Molly knew what she was doing when she gave me the shop, and when she wrote me that letter. But best of all, she gave me the option to work it out on my own. She was giving me the chance to go and leave Rosefont behind, but she was also giving me the gift of being able to stay if I wanted to. She wasn't forcing me into choosing (she knew I'd find such a decision overwhelming), rather, she allowed me the space to let my life pan out, and for me then to decide, in my own time, what I really wanted – in a way that felt natural and right.

And it does feel right. I feel more sure about this decision than I have about any I've ever made.

Now I just have to tell Mum.

And Billy.

32

My stomach is full of knots when I get home that night. Not because I'm nervous about telling Mum, but because I'm experiencing an unexpected wave of giddiness at what lies ahead. I've never been good with change, but somehow this feels different. It's like a new beginning in something I already know and love.

I find Mum at the dining room table surrounded by cream card, wooden hearts, glue sticks and other fun materials we found in Hobbycraft in the hope that we'd make some unique wedding invites. Having only started last night she's clearly eager to get them finished so that she can post them before she changes her mind and goes back to wanting a smaller ceremony.

'Good day?' she asks, pushing her glasses up the bridge of her nose before looking back down at the materials in her hand.

'Yes,' I smile, sitting down opposite her and fiddling with a tube of gold glitter as I think about what I'm going to say. It's a conversation I've had many times over in my head today and all the way home.

'What is it?' she asks suspiciously, her eyes back on me.

I can't help but giggle.

Mum doesn't ask again. Instead, she puts her hands on her lap and watches me with an intrigued smile on her face.

'OK,' I say, calming down, remembering that this is a huge deal for the both of us and still a delicate subject. 'Have you and Colin talked any more about where you might live?'

'Oh,' she says, taken by surprise. 'Yes. It's been discussed a few times. Actually I keep telling him to stop talking about it because I wanted to make sure me and you know what's happening before any big plans or changes are made.'

'But we've not spoken about it.'

'Exactly,' she smiles.

'Billy says we bury our heads in the sand.'

'He's always talked sense,' she laughs, her hands returning to the invite she was working on. 'Colin's thoughts are that we should be living in the same place from the wedding onwards, whether that's here or there. That would obviously be a temporary solution until we decide on what to do in the long term.'

'I see,' I nod.

'Obviously I don't want you feeling pushed out –'

'I'm not going to feel like that.'

'Because it would be understandable if you did,' she adds, not listening to what I'm saying.

'I won't.'

'We understand that it affects all of us, and even though you're older than the other two, you're still my baby girl . . .'

'I've found somewhere to live.'

' . . . you will always have a home wherever I am.' Mum stops suddenly and looks up at me, as my words sink in. 'Wait. What? You've found a place? You're moving out?' she asks, her eyes widening at me.

'I think so,' I say, my hands cupping my cheeks that are stretched wide thanks to the huge grin on my face.

'When did this happen?'

'Today.'

'Is it close by?'

'Very,' I nod. 'Above the shop.'

'What?' she asks, looking delighted and confused all at once.

'The tenants are moving out at the end of the month.'

'Right . . .' she says, taking a deep breath as she looks across at me. 'Well, I guess it makes sense for me to go to Colin's for now then.'

'If that's what you want to do.'

'Makes more sense me moving there than all three of them having the upheaval, possibly twice. Their place is equally as lovely as ours.'

'It is,' I agree.

'So we're both leaving this house,' she says, her eyes welling up as she purses her lips together.

'I guess so,' I nod, tears filling my own eyes now that it's been decided upon. 'It's been a lovely home.'

'It has, hasn't it,' she agrees, looking at the room around us and out into the back garden. 'I can remember when me and your dad first came to see it. We knew instantly that it was right for us. Actually, the previous owners were a lovely elderly couple who'd lived here for decades. Their children had already grown up and left home, but outside there was still a rickety old wooden swing,' she says, her eyes glistening as she recalls the moment. 'I can remember him turning to me and telling me we'd found the one and knowing it was purely because this couple had shared a long and happy life in it. That's what he wanted for us. And for you.'

'I don't remember an old swing,' I muse, only able to remember a plastic red and yellow one that sat in the middle of the lawn.

'Of course not,' Mum laughs. 'As soon as you came along your dad realized what a death trap that rotting piece of wood was and chucked it out.'

'Nice,' I squawk, screwing up my face and laughing with her.

'We had some lovely times here,' she smiles.

'What happens now?'

'I'll talk to Colin and then put it on the market, but obviously half of it is yours anyway.'

Death is a funny thing. Two of the people I love more than anything die and I end up set for life . . . I'd rather have Dad and Molly back, obviously, but it's lovely knowing that whatever happens they're still playing a key role in my future.

33

My newly formed plan isn't the only thing to keep me upbeat and happy. The arrival of Lauren also fills me with more elation than I thought possible for any Buskin that's not Billy!

Thankfully, Lauren is granted a little bit more time off than expected and lands on our doorstep shortly after I get in from work the following Wednesday night. She's dressed as though she's been caught in a blizzard with a woolly scarf wrapped around her head so many times that only her eyes are visible – quite an effort as she's only had to walk a few metres from the taxi to the door.

'What are you doing?' I laugh, watching her run into the warmth.

'It's bloody freezing,' she shouts, her voice muffled through the fabric.

'It's actually far milder than it has b—,' I start, although am stopped by Lauren who throws her small overnight bag to the ground and jumps on me, almost making us both topple over.

'It's so awesome to see you,' she says, pulling the material away from her mouth to reveal a beaming smile.

'You too,' I grin, pleasantly surprised by my affection for her. 'And it's only been a few weeks.'

'After the last few days it feels like years,' she admits, shaking her hair free of her scarf and taking off her black knee-length coat.

'So, how's The Dragon been?' I ask, taking her discarded clothes and laying them over the banister of the stairs.

'Who, Mum?' she replies, not missing a beat.

My jaw drops as I stammer to find a response. I find myself just staring at her, unable to speak.

Lauren cackles wickedly at her own joke.

'You're such a cow!' I declare, feeling my cheeks turn bright red.

'Patricia has been fine,' she answers, following me into the kitchen where I pour us each a glass of white wine. 'Strangely more relaxed over here.'

'Really?'

'God, yeah,' she nods, hungrily grabbing her glass and taking a sip as we sit either side of the kitchen counter. 'I'm surprised she even lets me leave the office sometimes back at home, so it's a miracle that she's let me come out here.'

'You had to ask permission?'

'I know. I feel like a teenager again,' she mutters, rolling her eyes even though she doesn't look at all put out by the arrangement. 'She's just made me promise to keep my phone on loud and not be back late tomorrow. That's it.'

'So, Dragon's got a heart?'

'Who'd have thought?' she laughs, helping herself to some olives I've put out on the table. 'So how has it really been here?'

'Fine,' I shrug, not wanting to talk about how tough it's been being apart from Billy, or how Peter overstepped the mark, or that I've finally made some concrete plans for my future. Call me crazy, but I think it's important I share certain details with Billy before I start blabbing to his sister, no matter how much I love her.

'Really? I think you're forgetting that I've seen first-hand how difficult the whole long-distance thing can be.'

'It's what you make it,' I offer back, not wanting to explain that her link to Billy is exactly why I find it difficult talking to her about it.

'Fair enough.'

'What about you? You've really turned everything around.'

'By becoming someone's skivvy?' she questions, raising a playful eyebrow.

'More like claiming some independence for yourself,' I praise, shaking my head at her modesty. I fail to believe starting on the bottom rung of a ladder can be particularly easy when everyone knows your impressive affiliations. 'Come on, you know what you've done.'

'I know, I know . . .' she admits, giving a reflective pause. 'You know what, though?'

'What?'

'It's really given me a thirst for more. I like doing things separately from the family. I love leaving the house in the morning and doing something different. If anything, I feel bummed out when it's time to go home,' she admits, screwing up her face.

'Really?'

'Yeah . . . I think I might want to get my own place too. Not easy when I'm currently in this unpaid role, but it's an idea.'

'Wow, that's quite a step,' I say, impressed by her new drive and ambition, a bubble of excitement stirring within me as I think about the little flat above the shop.

'But an exciting one, nonetheless,' Lauren beams.

'Definitely,' I agree with a grin. It's hard not to be sucked into her enthusiasm for her future and her desire to achieve more for herself. 'Do you wish you'd got a job sooner?'

'Nah,' she laughs, slowly shaking her head while looking into her wine glass, her fingertips circling its rim. 'I've had a lot of fun so I've nothing to regret there. And I don't think I was ready before.'

'So what made you get a job in the first place?'

'A couple of things,' she confides, looking up at me. 'Jay was one of them. Seeing how he's been building a life for himself away from the shadow of being a less successful Buskin was one of them, but also that horrendous meal on New Year's Day.'

'Really?' I say with surprise, sure I was the only one to keep thinking back to that day.

'It was awful,' she reflects, sounding disgusted at the memory. 'I don't want to be a part of that. I don't want to be forcing someone to do something for my own benefit. And, unlike the twins, I don't relish the thought of just being a socialite and trying to get my face pictured at the trendiest hotspots. I'm more than that. I've got substance.'

'You certainly do.'

'And I'm not saying what they're doing is a bad thing,' she adds, clearly not wanting it to look as though she's judging her sisters for the choices they make. 'But it's not for me.'

'Each to their own,' I offer.

'Exactly,' she nods. 'Actually, I spoke to Mum on the way here and she said Billy might be going out with them tonight. They've finally roped him into a night out.'

'Really?' I ask, not wanting to sound too shocked or out of touch. Billy hasn't mentioned these plans to me at all, not that I'd want him to think he has to ask permission to go out with his sisters or anything like that, of course . . .

'I'm surprised he hasn't been out more to be honest,' Lauren adds.

'He's probably been concentrating on work,' I suggest, echoing what Billy has told me previously.

'Maybe. Never stopped him before,' Lauren shrugs into her glass of wine before looking up at me again. 'A weird thing happened today . . . I've been offered another job.'

'That's amazing,' I say, trying not to let my mind dwell on her comments about Billy's partying ways.

'I know, it's paid and everything,' she laughs, oblivious to the effect her comment has had on me.

'So what's the issue?' I ask, noticing the new possibility has left her confused, which I'm guessing is why she's spoken without thinking. There seems to be something far bigger on her mind. 'You'd be able to start saving for your own place,' I tell her.

'Yes . . . while I rent somewhere else in Paris.'

'What?'

'The job is in Paris,' she shares, letting the information land.

'No way!'

'Yes way.'

'Have you ever been?' I ask, wondering where her thoughts lie on what could be a life-changing adventure.

'No.'

'Do you think you'll take it?' I continue, wanting to know more.

'I've not had time to think, it all happened so quickly,' she admits, blowing out her cheeks. 'One of the designers cornered me this morning and thrust his card in my hand, telling me he was looking for an assistant before literally offering me the position.'

'Just like that?'

'Just like that,' she shrugs. 'It's bonkers.'

'I'd say.'

'What would I tell Mum?'

'Ah . . .'

Telling my own mum that I was going to be moving out of our family home and up the road was hard enough, so I can only imagine how Lauren is feeling. And there's no telling how Julie might take the news, having seen her in full emotional swing over the comings and goings of her children, I've no doubt Lauren is nervous of the fall-out that moving thousands of miles away could cause.

'I know it might look like I despise her at times and that we don't get on, but she's my mum. I know she'll be gutted to see me go,' she says, showing an unexpected fondness for Julie.

'Your mum wants what's best for all of you,' I offer, finding my own heart soften towards the head of the Buskin household now that I know she's about to be separated from yet another of her children. I know we've had our wobbly moments, but I can't imagine how difficult it must be to have the family you raised spread so far apart. My thoughts turn to Molly and my own mum, and I find myself wondering whether it's harder watching your only child up and leave to explore the world, or having your handful of children scattered across the globe. I imagine Julie's heart must break every time she thinks of the distance between them all. No doubt it's a catalyst for her sudden breakouts. Despite what I might have thought earlier, I don't believe her actions are purely selfish, or rather, maybe her actions are actually led by more love than I've ever given her credit for. It must take a huge amount of selflessness to not get in the way of your child's dreams, especially when they take them so far away.

'Just talk to her,' I suggest, knowing Julie will find it in her heart to be pleased for her youngest daughter.

'You're right . . .' Lauren frowns, probably thinking about how that encounter might go.

We're interrupted by the sound of a key in the front door.

'I'm home,' Mum calls from the hall, cutting in on our conversation for now as she walks in and gets pulled into a hug by Lauren.

'It's so lovely to meet you,' Lauren sings happily, acting as though she's known Mum all her life.

In response, Mum laughs, instantly won over by Lauren just as I was at the airport all those months ago.

The next morning Lauren is up and out of the door before I'm even able to offer her breakfast. She literally chucks on her clothes, grabs her belongings and gives me a tight squeeze goodbye before jumping into a taxi.

It was so lovely to see her. She was a ball of energy and wouldn't stop asking Mum about the wedding plans. She was the perfect guest – continuously cooing with admiration for every detail Mum shared, as she pushed her own concerns and dilemmas away for the evening.

I know Paris is still quite a distance from Rosefont Hill, but I selfishly hope she takes the position, as I'd love knowing she was that little bit closer.

All the same, I didn't sleep well last night when we eventually turned in. And now Lauren's left, I find it impossible to stop myself scouring the news and my Twitter feed on my phone, looking for any details of Billy being out at a club. I never heard from him yesterday, but I imagine he wouldn't expect me to have heard about his plans for a night out. I consider texting him a carefree message telling him how great it was to see Lauren, but then think against it. Instead I continue to stalk the internet.

It's only when I'm checking for the billionth time on my way to open the shop that little bits of information start trickling through, firstly on his mentions on Twitter.

'@BillyBuskin You're even fitter in the flesh. Thanks for the picture. xoxo

'OMG, saw @BillyBuskin in Norish just now. He was wasted.'

'@BillyBuskin Shame you couldn't stand up tonight, really wanted to give you my number. Next time.'

There are pictures to accompany some of the tweets being sent to him. A few of him looking in control and incredibly handsome as he arrives, several of him with various girls (who I'm guessing are fans who've asked for selfies), a couple of him dancing with Hayley and Jenny, and then dozens of him falling about, passed out on a sofa and being carried out of the back exit by James and some other security men I don't recognize. It's as though I'm receiving a storyboard of the messy events.

The worst account of the night comes an hour or so later when the media catch wind of the story, with several outlets alluding to him having partied the night away with more than just alcohol.

Is Billy really the sort to take drugs? I never would have thought so, but am I being too naive to think someone from that world wouldn't be tempted? Whenever I've had a wobble over his partying ways before, I've been more focused on the way the press liked to paint him as a ladies' man. Never have I worried about drugs, or even thought to. But having said that, the last time we broke up was due to him getting ridiculously drunk with Heidi Black and her forcing herself on him – his alcohol consumption making it difficult to push her off before a conveniently placed pap caught them 'in action'. Maybe there was more to that story that I just hadn't cottoned on to? Maybe it wasn't just alcohol that had blurred his senses? Maybe I don't know Billy Buskin as well as I thought I did.

I hate myself in that moment. Hate myself for letting this piece of drivel written by people I don't know cause such a whirlwind of emotions within me, and for making me question Billy.

I go about the rest of the day in near silence, opting to remain in front of the oven as much as possible rather than venture out to the front of the shop much. Rachel must sense something is up, or maybe she's aware of the speculation being formed. Either way, she leaves me to it and doesn't try to force conversation out of me.

At three o'clock in the afternoon my phone rings repeatedly.

Rachel looks across and winks at me, gesturing she'll be fine on her own.

I go out into the little courtyard and sit on an upturned bucket, steeling myself for what's about to be said.

'Afternoon,' I say, my cold and distant voice sending a chill through my body.

'Please tell me you don't believe any of it,' he asks in a rush, sounding tormented and full of anguish.

I don't respond, simply because I'm not sure how to. I really don't know what to think.

'Someone must've spiked my drink or something.'

'So it was drugs?' I ask, shocked at his quick confession, my brain struggling at how to process the information.

'No. Yes. I don't know!' Billy stumbles, sounding awful and confused. 'I only had three drinks. I know I've been working hard on set and abstaining from everything, but there's no way I'd have been such a lightweight. And I wouldn't voluntarily take anything. I'm not that stupid, baby.'

'Have you spoken to Rhonda?' I ask.

'She's left me a rather stern voicemail or two.'

'I'm not surprised,' I admit, unable to hide the disappointment in my voice. I've never knowingly associated with anyone who's taken drugs. I'm aware that fits in perfectly with my sheltered little broken home of a life, but I don't care. The very thought of it freaks me out.

'Sophie, I didn't do anything wrong,' pleads Billy, desperate for me to believe him.

'But how can you remember? If you were as out of it as people are saying, how can you possibly remember what you did or didn't do?'

'I . . .' Billy struggles to respond before the phone is snatched from his hand.

'Sophie, it's Jenny.'

'Oh. Hi,' I say, taken aback that Billy has anyone with him.

'Look, I can assure you nothing untoward has happened. James was with us the whole night and I slept in Billy's bed when we got back to make sure whatever was put in his drink didn't trip him out and make him jump out the window or something.'

'What?' I shriek.

'You're making it sound worse than it is,' Billy's muffled voice shouts in the background.

'Wait until Mum wakes up and then tell me that,' says Jenny with a sternness in her voice that I've never heard before. 'We didn't know what you'd taken, I think we were right to be cautious.'

Billy's groan tells me he's probably dreading her reaction more than mine.

'Sorry, Sophie,' Jenny says softly into the phone. 'I just want you to know from someone who was actually there and with Billy all night that he definitely had his drink spiked. Don't read any of the crap being written, and try not to worry.'

'Right . . .' I reply, not really knowing how to absorb the information.

'James was beside himself last night. He couldn't believe someone had got that close to Billy without him realizing something was up,' she continues, offering more of an insight into the night. 'The security guards at the club didn't quite share the same level of distress, though. My guess is that the owner wanted to put his club on the map as the go-to place.'

'By drugging Billy?' I ask.

'We'd never be able to prove it, but yes,' confirms Jenny, in a matter-of-fact tone.

'Jesus!'

'Can I speak to her now?' Billy asks, sounding agitated as I hear a kerfuffle as the phone is passed between them. 'One night out the whole time I'm here and this happens. Safe to say I'm ready to live life as a hermit and never go anywhere new ever again.'

'When Mum and Rhonda get hold of you I think that decision might be taken out of your hands, anyway,' Jenny warns.

Once more Billy groans in despair.

We speak a little while longer, or, more accurately, he continues to grovel for another five minutes before we say our goodbyes and I wish him luck with having to face the other women in his life. When he's gone I look at the blank screen in my hands.

My head isn't flooded with thoughts. Instead it's numb. I can't be angry at Billy when it's clear he hasn't actually done anything wrong. He's obviously been the target of someone else's wrongdoings. Yet, once again, I'm faced with the realization of how different our worlds are. After all, I don't see any of my elderly customers slipping me something dodgy in the hope of a bit of extra gossip to spread around the village . . .

The whole thing is just so far removed from who I am as a person and the life I crave living. I have simple desires, quiet needs and humble ambitions. No less important or significant than anyone else's, but certainly I want a life that doesn't involve dramatics or people putting others in danger for the sake of publicity.

I want a life of normality.

I want to be free.

PART FOUR

34

Somehow I manage to put the whole ordeal behind me and focus once again on the here and now. For the time being at least. Luckily, the following month speeds along, thanks to the shop being busy with orders and a constant stream of afternoon tea sittings, and also with all the wedding prep for Mum and Colin. We'd all agreed that we wouldn't go overboard with the planning and that the key element of the day was for it to be understated and relaxed, but, just like with the dress, excitement has got the better of us. We've been making heaps of decorations together at home – which has reminded us of last December when Colin had us all doing the same thing but without us knowing it was for him to propose to Mum in the magical setting of the shop.

It's nice being properly involved and I've thoroughly enjoyed helping them both plan and come up with ideas (whilst trying not to take over). And we've really done our research and thought about what might work with such a short amount of time to organize, because time is something we really haven't had. It's a good job we're all hard workers.

After scouring our way through a dozen bridal magazines we decided to continue with the theme that Colin set up back in December, minus the Christmas paraphernalia. The idea is that we will bring the outdoors indoors with festoon lighting, flowers placed in jars or mismatched teacups (something we have plenty of) and a variety of homemade signs, banners and culinary delights for people to feast on. Still sticking to the premise of nothing being too fancy, perfect or professional looking. Nothing slick and exact, instead we're all about things looking a little drunk and skew-whiff.

Even though neither of us is highly skilled in floristry, Mum and I decide to tackle the flower arranging ourselves as our vision of them coming out of jugs, cups, jars and watering cans is quite simple in theory (it's just like plonking them in a vase at home, just done with a bit more flair . . . we hope!). We've practised a few times and have been happy with the results, so the last thing we'll do before going home today is collect the bunches of more wild-looking flowers like spray roses, hydrangeas, freesias, wax buds, tulips and crabapple blossom and place them delicately in their scattered homes around the room.

When we were in the florist choosing flowers a couple of weeks ago I was surprised when an old thought and dream was reignited. Years ago, on our first official date, I'd mentioned to Billy how I'd love to incorporate flowers in the shop somehow, and maybe hold weekly flower arranging classes with the locals one evening a week. I love flowers – always have since being a bucket girl in that very same florists on a Saturday during my teens – I still remember all their pretty names – and I really enjoy creating things with my hands, so it's definitely something I want to think about some more after the wedding. In fact, it's probably even more of an attainable idea now, thanks to me taking over the flat upstairs. I know it's my home and should be kept separate, but it's great to know I have a little more space on the premises to play with if I want to.

Not that I've moved yet.

The tenants have moved out and I've been in and given the place a thorough scrub, painted the walls neutral colours and moved a few little items in, but I'm still living at home and will be doing so until Billy gets back. Having lived so much of our lives through letters, phone calls and other non-face-to-face forms of communication over the past few months, I decided that the topic of me staying put in Rosefont Hill and moving into the flat should be discussed in person. I know it's a delicate subject and want to handle it carefully. Having suggested we buy my family home for us to live in I know he won't be completely miffed at the idea, but I realize I've made a decision on my own about the sort of future I'm after – even though it's a decision that actually affects both of us.

I hope he'll be as excited as me about the fresh start in the place I love, although I know it means I'm laying down firmer roots here when he wants to go off and chase his own dreams . . . something else I'm sure we'll be talking lots about when he eventually gets here. It's not exactly been the easiest few months to deal with.

In true showbiz style, or rather that should be 'Billy style', he's booked to fly in from LA tomorrow, on the morning of the wedding. Needless to say I was disgruntled as it would have been nice to have him here helping out the day before and knowing that he's definitely going to be here and not caught up with a delayed flight or something ghastly like that, but I'm thankful that he's making the effort to come back in time for it. I know he's literally rushing from a meeting straight to the airport to catch his flight. Plus, now that filming has wrapped, touching down on English soil marks the start of Billy being here for a few months solid, so I definitely can't complain.

Things have been calmer between us over these last few weeks apart. It's the busiest we've ever been while separated and it seems that, rather than adding pressure to an already stressful situation, we have both silently resolved to make life as simple as possible and work our butts off without causing the other one any added worry. Obviously, in relation to Billy, that focus also comes from a stiff warning issued from Rhonda and general nagging from Julie following the media furore that occurred after his night out with Hayley and Jenny.

The letters keep darting back and forth, something I'm amazed we've kept up when we can't even manage a daily phone call. But those little handwritten notes are so special, they help keep a constant thread of communication and a feeling of direct contact from him to me and from me to him – something I'm thankful for even if we are going to be having a few serious face-to-face conversations when he gets back here.

Things aren't perfect between us, but I've accepted that nothing ever truly is. I just want to see him here in Rosefont Hill and discover how I feel when he's in my grasp and properly in my life again.

I've heard from Lauren a lot. She decided to bite the bullet and simply tell Julie about the job offer. I'm told Julie cried lots, but more from pride than from suffering the loss of another of her babies flying the nest. For once

I think Lauren felt truly special in her mum's eyes, but this definitely helped mend their fractious relationship. I think the distance will make them closer than they ever have been.

In a bid to get everything done in time and not be rushing around on the actual wedding day, I decided to shut up shop not only on the special day, but the day before too. That way, I shouldn't need to go in at all before the service, meaning I can just be with Mum as we get ready. My old dears love a bit of routine and hate change, but on this occasion I'm forgiven. They all know Mum and Colin and are fond of them both, so I've not heard a single disgruntled whisper.

With the shop closed I start the day by putting finishing touches to the three-tiered wedding cake. We decided that two tiers didn't look quite special enough as it didn't have a lot of height. Mum and Colin left us kids in charge of flavours so each layer is different – I chose lemon and lavender, Aaron rather surprisingly went for the more traditional vanilla sponge with strawberry filling and Charlotte went for chocolate. There's a nice variety. In a bid to have it in keeping with the rustic theme in the shop, I've opted to steer away from fondant icing and have gone for a cream-coloured buttercream instead. I've carefully textured the paste on it in horizontal stripes and added a light-blue lace ribbon to the base of each layer for definition. For the top, rather than adding a bride and groom, we've made miniature bunting on little sticks with the words 'Mr and Mrs' – it looks so twee and romantic. Later on we'll add some flowers too, but even now I think it looks delicious.

'That looks incredible!' gasps Rachel as she walks through the front door. We might be closed for the day, but the plan is for Rachel, Mum, Colin and I to set everything up so that Rachel and Peter don't have too much to do tomorrow.

Yes, Peter is still helping out.

Part of me had hoped he'd forgotten so that I wouldn't be put in an awkward position, but he messaged me a few days ago saying he was still free and would love to lend a hand. Rachel had insisted she'd be fine without him (I have an inkling she managed to correctly put two and two together), but I knew it was a lot to ask of her. I texted back saying his help would be much appreciated, while trying to keep my wording as polite as possible without sounding off or distant. I just want things to be normal, although I also don't want to be disrespectful of Billy's feelings. Not that anything else has been said on the matter as I've purposefully stopped myself from mentioning his name at all. Which hasn't been too difficult, as Peter did what he promised and stayed away.

'Glad you think so,' I say to Rachel, stepping back to look at it again.

'So, where do we start?'

'That's the question,' I say, with a worried smile.

'Don't act as if you haven't thought about it. You've been writing lists for weeks,' she laughs.

'Very true,' I say with a smug smirk, lifting up my rather official-looking clipboard and giving it a tap. 'Let's get all of the food we're making today done first, then we can go about setting up the shop and making it all look pretty.'

'Yes, boss!' Rachel shouts back enthusiastically. 'When are your mum and Colin getting here?'

'In a few hours. They're moving some boxes across first.'

'Ooooh . . .' Rachel says, remembering that tomorrow night will also mark the first official night of Mum living in her new home with her new husband, meaning tonight will be the last one she'll be spending with me in ours. 'What have you got planned for tonight?'

'Takeaway and a film.'

'Sounds perfect . . .'

It was Mum's idea to have a night in, just the two of us, making it like our old Friday nights in together that have become fewer and fewer thanks to the welcome additions to our little family.

When I think about the significance of the night ahead I'm glad Billy isn't back until the morning as tonight will be as it should be: with Mum and me looking back and reflecting on the time we've shared within those familiar walls. We've shared some of the greatest moments and some of the saddest there. Yet, whether light or dark, each of them has shaped us into the women we are now and brought us to this juncture of drastic change.

'How are you feeling about it?' Rachel asks, picking up all the utensils I've had out already this morning and taking them to the sink, turning on the hot water and squirting in some washing soap. One thing I've always loved about Rachel is that she understands the importance of cleaning up as you go along and in between jobs. Working from a clean surface at the start of each new task makes everything so much easier, plus it means you're not left with hours' worth of washing up at the end when you should be all done.

'I think I'm OK,' I nod, nibbling on my lip as I watch the sink fill with bubbles. 'It's been surreal watching things get boxed up and then dividing the contents of the house between us both.'

'It's the end of an era.'

'Exactly,' I say, grabbing a tea towel and standing next to her, waiting to be passed bowls and spoons once they're washed.

'Are you still excited about upstairs?'

'Silly question,' I laugh. 'I've not stopped being giddy about it since the idea turned into a fully-fledged plan of action. When I've not been thinking about wedding decorations I've been mentally mapping out where I'm going to put the furniture or what kind of bedding I'm going to have.'

'You've a busy mind.'

'Always.'

'And you've still not told Billy?' she asks, screwing her face up at me and already knowing the answer.

'Do you think that's a mistake?'

'You know better than me,' she shrugs, reminding me that the two of them have never been properly introduced, even though he was here the day Rachel enquired about the job months ago. The thought highlights how long Billy's been away and how lucky I am to have Rachel, as it already feels as though I've known her for years. She's certainly made the transition into being someone's boss far easier for me, which is mostly because she's got a great intuition for how I like things and just gets on with it. 'He knows it's your mum's last night there tonight, though, right?' she asks.

'Yeah.'

'Well, at least that explains the boxes around the house.'

'Oh, I've been careful about that,' I tell her, feeling sneaky as I share the details of my tiny little deception. 'I've left the surface of my room the same, but packed up most of the wardrobe and drawers. He won't look in them anyway. Not tomorrow. I don't want to have to talk about it before the wedding. Not when there's so much going on and to think about already.'

'Tricky enough as it is?'

'I think it'll mostly be emotional,' I say. Funny thing is I've not paid too much thought in these last few weeks to the significance of tomorrow. There's been so much to get ready and keep my brain occupied. Although the reality is that it will almost certainly have its moments of beauty and sadness . . . how could it not?

'Well, you don't have to worry about this place,' she says, her eyes wide and sincere, letting me know she's taking her role seriously. 'I'll come in bright and early and just make sure everything is exactly as we've planned.'

'Thank you,' I say, putting an arm around her shoulder and giving it a firm squeeze. 'You've been wonderful.'

'It's nothing,' she tuts, shrugging her shoulders. 'So, what time is Peter supposed to be getting here?'

'When do you want him?' I ask.

'Oh, you've not set a time yet?'

'No, he just messaged saying to let him know . . .'

'I see. Maybe just before you lot are set to arrive, then?' she suggests, passing the glass bowl into my hands. 'No point him being here longer than he has to be . . . he's not even needed to be honest. Once everything's plated up it's just a case of carrying it all out and topping up the drinks. It's not like there are hundreds of people to serve.'

'No, but I don't want you feeling under pressure,' I frown.

'Remember, my friend. If I weren't here I'd be running around the park after two crazy little rascals. This is a breeze in comparison,' she laughs.

'I'm not sure about that,' I say, thinking of her incredibly polite boys.

'Honestly, if anyone, it's Shane you should be worried about. I think he's the one who's most likely to crack under the pressure tomorrow . . . I can picture him now stood in the middle of the field as the boys run off in opposite directions, testing him to see how he reacts.'

'What would he do?' I ask, feeling panicked for him.

'He wouldn't run after either of them, obviously,' she scoffs. 'He wouldn't even shout. Instead he'd be frozen to the spot and swivelling around at each of them in turn, his eyes pleading with them,' she says, doing the funniest impression of her poor husband and making us both howl with laughter.

'Poor Shane,' I cry.

'Honestly, it's a good job I love him,' she sighs, taking the plug out of the sink.

35

'So what do you think?' I ask Mum and Colin at seven o'clock that evening once we've finished transforming the space into somewhere fit for a wedding.

I thought we'd managed to make it look pretty spectacular for the proposal, but this is simply divine. Mum didn't originally want a sit-down meal, but when the idea of an informal afternoon tea was suggested she fell in love with it. So we cleared out the shop furniture and brought in three long, thin decorating tables (the idea came to me when I was buying paint in B&Q and wandered down the wrong aisle). Colin has made the cheap tables sturdier before beautifying them by painting their legs a light cornflower blue (they're the only bit the guests will actually see). Surrounding the long tables are thirty chairs on which we've hung individual black slate name signs as place settings, which the guests can then take home afterwards. On top of the tables we've obviously left plenty of room for the cake trays and sandwiches, but there's also all the mismatched floral crockery, some posh silver cutlery (Mum and Colin each had sets from their previous weddings hibernating in cupboards), cornflower-blue cloth napkins and miniature glass jars of flowers spread all the way along the centre – each containing delicate sprigs of higgledy-piggledy flowers. We've continued to place the flowers in cups, jugs, jars and watering-cans along the windowsills, on an old wooden ladder Colin found (it's splattered with paint but looks fantastically rustic and romantic) and any other spot where there's a flat surface. Fabric bunting of various different prints hangs across the room from the ceiling and dozens of tealights are scattered everywhere, waiting to be lit before we all arrive tomorrow.

The other area we've decided to decorate is the little courtyard out back. Having never used it properly before, we gave it a good tidy and placed two benches out there for people to sit on and get some fresh air . . . although these aren't any old benches. They were handmade by Colin, who's simply carved a 'D' into the back of one and a 'P' on the other – a lovely little tribute to their other loves. Surrounding them on the floor are buckets of flowers, and dangling above them are strings of fairylights. We've even laid out a few blankets for people to snuggle up in, especially if they're still out there later in the afternoon when the weather can get a bit chilly.

I have a sneaky suspicion I'll want all the decorations to stay out there after the wedding too. It's so lovely and might help to provide customers with a nice little outside area if they want to eat their tea and cake al fresco.

'I'm speechless,' Mum says back in the shop as she looks at our handiwork. 'I don't know how we've done it.'

'Determination, no sleep and a bit of magic,' Colin laughs, stifling a yawn.

'Tired, my love?'

'Happily so,' he replies, closing his eyes and resting his head against hers in a sweetly intimate way.

'I should probably give you guys a moment,' I say,

realizing they're about to say goodbye for the final time before they see each other at the church and probably would rather I wasn't loitering next to them. 'See you at the altar, Colin,' I say with a grin on my face as I walk away.

I head behind the counter and double-check on the food Rachel and I prepared earlier, although it's all covered in cling film and tin foil, so I can't really see much anyway. It all looked delicious earlier, though. It's so wonderful having Rachel by my side here. Not discrediting Billy at all, but it's far easier having someone who can get stuck in without me having to explain how to do each and every task. And, of course, she's so easy to get along with.

Realizing I haven't messaged Peter about timings for tomorrow I go to my coat, pull out my phone and find two messages. One from Billy saying he's just got on the flight and can't wait to see me in the morning (I'm gutted I can't be there when he walks into Arrivals, but I know he understands that I'll be getting ready with Mum) and the other from Peter.

Just bumped into Rachel and she said I'm no longer needed tomorrow as you've got everything under control. Not surprised. Hope the day goes beautifully. Send your Mum and Colin my love. See you soon. P. X

A paradox of emotions hit me. I'm disappointed that I won't be seeing him as it's been weeks, but I'm also relieved that we won't have to be in the same place with Billy and some locals who are sure to be a bit suspicious if they hear we've been spending time together. We've not heard any more whispering of rumours, but that doesn't mean they're not still lurking about or set to restart if fuel is added to the fire. I've no doubt what Rachel has done is for the best.

Instead of messaging Peter back I text Rachel a simple thank you, to which she replies with a winky face, confirming what I already knew – that she had definitely deduced that Peter was the guy I was seen with in the park.

I should have stopped Peter coming to help out myself, but I was avoiding the situation by doing nothing about it. Plus, Mum and Colin were expecting to see him there and I didn't want to have to lie or explain myself. To be honest, I was being a total coward. Rachel would have known the position I was in and how important tomorrow is on so many different levels. I bet she pounced on Peter as soon as she saw him, blurting out that he wasn't needed before even thinking.

It's nice to have a friend like her and to know that she's looking out for me.

'Right, ready when you are.' Mum reappears, hoisting her bag over her shoulder. Her little face looks a little swollen and apprehensive.

'You OK?' I ask, grabbing my belongings and going to her, giving her arm a quick squeeze.

'I will be,' she smiles, looping her arm through mine as we leave the setting of her intimate wedding party behind for the night.

'Indian, Chinese or pizza?' I ask Mum as soon as we get home. We've both been so busy all day that neither of us has properly eaten (despite being surrounded by food in the shop) and now that we've stopped I realize I'm famished.

'Indian will bloat me . . .' Mum tells me sadly while rubbing her flat tummy (which I've never ever seen bloat before). 'Plus I'll want onion bhajis and I don't think Colin will thank me for that tomorrow.'

'Fair enough, we can't have that,' I laugh.

'Maybe Chinese?'

'Fab. Our normal?' I ask, taking out my phone and pulling up the number.

'Perfect,' she nods, opening up the bottle of sauvignon blanc we picked up from Budgens on the way home and pouring out two glasses while she listens to me order. We're not big drinkers, but tonight definitely calls for a little glass of something to mark the occasion. 'Here you go,' she says, handing me a glass as soon as I've put down the phone.

'Thanks!'

'Toast?' Mum suggests, raising her glass to mine.

'Definitely,' I say, letting her take the lead.

'To Dad, our home, and our futures . . . and to us for persevering.'

'To Dad, our home, our futures and to us,' I repeat with a smile as we clink glasses and take a much-needed gulp of their contents.

What a life I've lived here . . .

Lowering my glass, I let out a sigh as I look around me. The house feels empty and cold now that Mum's belongings have been moved over to Colin's, leaving just my stuff behind.

'Odd moving out like this . . . slowly,' she says. 'I wonder when it'll get sold.'

'Does it matter that it won't be furnished?' I ask, feeling guilty because I'm taking quite a bit of the bulky items like the sofa, TV and some cabinets with me when I go into the flat. Actually the only thing I'm treating myself to straight away, while I settle in, is a bed.

'I don't think it'll make much of a difference – although it might be best that we empty it entirely once you've moved too,' she says, frowning as she thinks it through. 'Not like we're in a rush, anyway.'

'True.' There's a comfortable pause as we both quietly take it in, lost in our thoughts. 'So what's your fondest memory of the place?' I prompt after a few moments.

'Sophie, I've lived here for almost three decades. That's not the easiest question to answer!' She shakes her head with a smile at me.

'Try . . .'

Mum looks into her glass thoughtfully, as if the wine will magically make an answer appear. I sit silently, giving her time to think while searching my own brain for those little golden nuggets of the past.

'The day we brought you home from the hospital was extremely special,' Mum eventually says, smiling at me before tilting her head and frowning. 'Actually, so many other emotions were mixed in with that too. Fear mostly.'

'Thanks,' I laugh, enjoying her honesty.

'No,' she chuckles back. 'I just mean that we were new parents and we had no idea what to do with you. We were terrified we were going to break you. So we just sat there in silence staring at you and checking you were still breathing every two minutes.'

'All right, doesn't sound quite as magical as I'd dreamt.'

'It was still magical, don't you worry about that, but the day we first found out we were expecting you – now that was special,' she recalls, her face lighting up.

'Really?'

'Yep. I'd gone to the doctor's on my own because your dad had to work. But the first thing I said to him when he came through the front door that evening was "Hello Daddy". He burst into tears on the spot. Wept in the hallway for a good ten minutes.'

'Aww . . .' I murmur, a mixture of happiness and sadness swirling in my chest.

'When he eventually calmed down he wouldn't stop rubbing my tummy and talking to you – even that early on. He doted on you from the very beginning,' she muses, her eyes clouding over at the memory.

'And Christmases were always pretty spectacular,' I say, looking through to the lounge and remembering how much of a fuss was made over the occasion.

'We wanted you to believe in the magic.'

'Well, I definitely did,' I admit, because they did everything – the bells ringing outside, the muddy boot prints by the chimney, even sprinkled the presents in fairy dust (well, silver glitter), insisting that's how Father Christmas had got them down the chimney and under the tree. I fell for it all. But then I believed everything Mum and Dad told me. I had no reason not to. That's one of the reasons it was so tough when he died. We had plans, places we were set to see, things we were ready to explore.

How was it possible, I wondered back then, that those things were no longer going to happen?

'Painting your room was a pretty spectacular day . . .' suggests Mum, choosing a day that has always held a rather special place in my heart too, as it's the last time I can recall us all being together and laughing. 'Although you cried your heart out when your dad first suggested that pink wouldn't be a good idea.'

'He thought I'd want it changed within a week,' I remember.

'He'd be surprised to see it's the same colour now.'

'I haven't wanted to change it once.'

'No . . . a lot of the house is like that,' Mum nods, not at all surprised by my admission. 'Stuck in its ways. That's why I think it's a good job we're both moving and getting a fresh start.'

'So we no longer have to put up with pink walls?' I joke.

'So that we can live in our homes and not feel guilty every time we want to change something.'

'Yes, but this is the ultimate guilt, right? Leaving it all behind for good.'

'It'll always be with us. The memory of the pink walls, the brown kitchen units, the avocado bathroom set.'

'Gosh, it's all quite ghastly really,' I joke, making Mum laugh as I look at the place in disgust with my nose turned up. 'Anyone would think we were still living in the nineties.'

'I don't know how we've coped,' laughs Mum. 'Are you going to be OK here without me?'

'I'll have Billy, and it won't be for long,' I say, hoping

that I will still have Billy here with me when he finds out about the flat. Although listening to Mum echo some of my own thoughts about this house makes me even more resolute in the decision I've made.

'I have something for you,' Mum says, getting up and going to the dining room.

'I'm intrigued,' I call after her.

'For obvious reasons, I don't feel I can take this with me, so I want you to look after it,' she says, bringing in a cream box.

'Your wedding album?'

'Yes,' she grins, visibly reining in her emotions as she opens the box and takes out the leather-bound cream album I remember from my childhood, which has been delicately wrapped in white tissue paper. After removing it from its wrapping, Mum places her hand on top and strokes it fondly.

'Are you sure you want me to take it?'

'I know Colin would understand if I took it over there. You know, they've still got pictures of Pauline on the walls that I'd never ask or want him to take down,' she says, ferociously shaking her head at the idea of asking him to do such a thing. 'I know it's important for the kids to be able to see their mum and feel like she's still a part of their lives.'

'Well, you understand that better than most,' I reply, wondering if any part of Mum finds that difficult.

'I am taking some photos with me. I have my own memories to treasure,' she says firmly. 'But I want you to have this. It's special.'

She holds it out towards me. Hesitantly, I reach out and

take it, finding myself mirroring her own action and stroking the top of it. Setting it down on the kitchen counter, I open the album to the first page and instantly see a photo of Mum and Dad at the altar. Crazy to think they were far younger than I am now when this picture was taken. Like many dresses at the time, it's clear to see mum was influenced by the late Princess Diana, with shoulders puffed out to double the width of her slender frame, while the skirt and bodice of the dress are covered in frills and lace. She looks more like Little Bo Peep than a bride, but that could be because underneath her veil her hair sits in heavy ringlets, as though it's been permed. Dad looks dashing in his grey suit and light grey tie, although the dodgy moustache and shoulder-length hair make the whole thing comical.

Despite all this, though, there's one thing that stands out more than anything in the picture and that is their faces. Both Mum and Dad look young, foolish and madly in love . . . it's a beautiful sight to see.

We continue to look at the rest of the photos, of which there are about twenty. While we giggle our way through, Mum gives me funny little accounts of their day – like the fact that the car that was meant to drive them to the reception had broken down on the way, meaning they had to travel in an aunt's old blue mini (Mum had to take the hoop out of her skirt so she could fit in!).

It's lovely hearing Mum share her memories.

We never used to talk about Dad. Ever. But that all started changing when Billy and Colin entered our lives. Ever since then she's shared a little more about life before I arrived and started recounting later moments, allowing us to keep Dad's memory alive rather than be scared of the shadow he's left behind.

'Thanks for this,' I say, closing the book and delicately wrapping it back up.

'I wonder what tomorrow's going to be like,' Mum says, although I'm not sure if she meant to say it out loud or not.

'It's going to be wonderful . . . are you nervous?'

'Yes, but not in the way you might think,' she says, slowly taking a sip from her glass and placing it back on the table. 'I know what it's like to love someone with all your heart and make those important declarations of unity. It's beautiful. Truly magical and unique . . . I just hope I live up to his expectations.'

'You already exceed them,' I smile, walking around the table and giving her a hug.

'Thank you my darling. You are a love . . .' she says, planting a gentle kiss on my cheek. 'And are you looking forward to seeing Billy in the morning?'

'Very much,' I say, feeling my tummy flip at the thought.

The doorbell rings to let us know dinner has arrived, putting an end to our conversation and marking the start of us stuffing our faces while watching *Fifty First Dates*.

More than usual I find myself looking at Mum and watching her reactions to the screen, probably because I know I'm not going to be seeing as much of her from tomorrow. I know hundreds of children move away from their parents every day, but when you've been through what we have, you learn not to take the little things for granted and to savour each moment as it comes.

When the night comes to an end, when most of the

lights have been switched off and we've walked upstairs together for the last time, we turn to each other on the landing outside our neighbouring bedrooms and embrace. Tight, loving, meaningful . . . I might have lost my mum for the majority of my childhood, but I'm so glad she's back now. My mum. My best mate. My inspiration.

36

I'm wide awake and full of excitement by six-thirty. Surprisingly, I fell asleep as soon as my head touched the pillow, which was probably thanks to the manic day we had getting everything prepared. Luckily now, thanks to having a solid eight hours' sleep, I feel full of energy and buzzing about the day ahead.

I quickly dive off my bed and open the curtains. Sunshine greets me. Nothing but glorious sunshine. Not that I'd expect anything less when we have all of our angels in the sky watching over us.

I scramble back under my warm covers and reach for my phone, just in time to see Billy's name flashing up on the screen.

'Hello?' I say, a smile instantly spreading across my face.

'Guess who's back,' he chuckles, his words sending a wave of elation through me.

'Oh gosh, I can't tell you how much I'm looking forward to seeing you,' I gush, my tummy dancing at the thought.

'Well, I'm still on the plane but I shouldn't be too long getting out of here. Hoping to be with you in a couple of hours.'

'Amazing.'

'I'll probably crash out for a bit when I get there,' he

warns, suggesting he's spent another flight watching films rather than making the most of being able to lie flat and sleep. 'At least you and your Mum can have some time to get ready together without me interfering.'

'Very true . . . I'm so happy you're back.'

'Same. There's nowhere I'd rather be than on my way to you.'

His words make me giggle. They might be cheesy, but he's saying them to me – and I love him for that. No matter how difficult and full of torment the past few months have been, those negative feelings seem to lift dramatically just through knowing he's so close.

When I've put the phone down I hear a gentle knock on my door.

'Come in,' I call.

'Only me,' Mum says as she pokes her head inside my room.

'Who else would it be?' I laugh.

'Oh yeah,' she grins.

'Did you get much sleep?'

'Some,' she shrugs, her face looking radiantly joyous. 'Breakfast?'

'Definitely!' I say, getting back out of my warm bed and following Mum as she heads downstairs.

I make us a spectacular cooked breakfast of bacon, sausage, fried eggs, beans and tomatoes while ensuring Mum takes things easy and sits down with a pot of tea. Something she's reluctant to agree to, but I physically force her away from the kitchen counter and into a chair so that she has no choice.

Once breakfast has been eaten we both have showers

and start getting ready in Mum's room. Once it's blow-dried, I set Mum's hair in rollers. No, I'm not going to recreate the Little Bo Peep look she wore for her first wedding. She's still going to have her signature bun, but we're just going to soften it up slightly and add a little volume – that's the plan anyway.

I've just finished twirling in the last of the rollers when the doorbell rings.

'Billy,' I gush at Mum in the mirror, who's looking equally as thrilled as I feel.

I turn and quickly run down the stairs, taking them two at a time like an Olympic athlete, and whip open the front door.

'Peter?' I say, my body jolting to a stop rather than pouncing on the arrival as I'd planned, unable to hide the shock of him being on my doorstep. But there he is, in his Nike running gear, the sweat pouring off of him making it clear he's already been out for quite a while.

'Sorry,' he mumbles, rubbing his forehead as though questioning why he's found himself here, especially on Mum's wedding day. A look I'm probably mirroring without even realizing.

'Is everything all right?' I ask, trying to prompt him into saying whatever he's come to say while pulling my dressing gown around me a little tighter, suddenly cringing at the fact that my hair is half done (I've quickly dried it but nothing else – it's definitely frizzy) and that I've not put any make-up on yet.

I glance upstairs and pray Mum doesn't come down and wonder what's going on. Not that I have the foggiest idea anyway. I just know that I really don't want him here right now.

'I've just been out thinking about things,' Peter tells me, unable to look me in the eye.

'Right . . .'

'Obviously I understand why you changed your mind about me being there today,' he frowns at the ground. 'After the other week . . .'

'No, actually – that came directly from Rachel.'

'But you must've told her to say that?' he says, looking up at me.

'Nope. I didn't say anything,' I say honestly.

'So you do need me today?' he asks, looking confused.

'No,' I say firmly, shaking my head.

'Oh . . .'

'Look Peter, we were seen. Well, I say "we" but really I mean just me,' I whisper, feeling a hardness come over me, along with the urge to share this information even though I've kept it to myself for the last few weeks because I haven't wanted to contact him. Suddenly I feel as though I want him to know the severity of his hapless little moment and that it could still come with serious conse-quences. Especially for me. 'I was spotted in the park being kissed by a stranger . . .'

Peter's eyes widen at me. 'Shit,' he swears, looking completely taken aback and apologetic.

'Yeah,' I nod. 'I just don't need that kind of attention in my life.'

'No, obviously. Like I said it was a complete mistake and I'd never do anything like that again,' he says, his face becoming sterner, as though what I've said has given him more conviction to carry on and say whatever is on his mind.

'Glad to hear it,' I say, knowing he's unlikely to get the chance to anyway. I wouldn't be foolish enough to be alone with him again. It's odd, last time we were together I felt so carefree and comfortable around him, but now I'm aware that both of us have erected barriers. That each of us is keeping our distance. It's such a shame things have turned out this way, but having time away from him has made me see that however much he felt familiar and like a long-lost friend who had returned to my life, he wasn't. He was still a stranger. A stranger who put me in an awkward position and overstepped the mark.

'Actually, that's why I'm here,' Peter says, coughing slightly.

'Oh?'

'I would've told you when I saw you later on but seeing as that got changed . . . well, I'm moving back,' he says, his eyes finding mine once more, perhaps looking for a reaction of some kind.

'To Australia?' I ask, the pitch of my voice raising slightly higher than normal. Even though I knew it was going to happen at some point I hadn't expected it to happen so soon.

'Yep. The opening of the London office has gone smoother than anyone expected, so I'll be packing my bags and heading back to the waves pretty sharpish.'

'Back to your surfboard?'

'I can't wait.' He shrugs.

'I bet,' I say, feeling foolish that, when I first opened the door, part of me thought he was here to declare his undying love to me. 'When do you go?'

'Tuesday.'

'That soon?'

He shrugs in reply. 'As good a time as any, right?'

'I guess . . .' I say sadly, as it dawns on me that he's only come here to say goodbye.

'You know me, I don't like to stick around.'

'You like to fly away.'

'And be free as a bird,' he winks, his voice sounding cheerier than his face looks as it continues to search mine.

I'm still mulling over his sudden departure when I see a black car pull on to the driveway.

My eyes widen and my heart freezes.

Noticing that something's up Peter swivels on the spot just as the back door of the taxi opens and Billy places a foot on the driveway.

For a split second I notice the look on Peter's face, one of pure guilt and shamefulness.

'Billy,' I exclaim, trying desperately to get a hold of myself as the taxi driver jumps out and starts unloading his luggage.

There seems to be a slight pause before Billy steps out of the car and bounds straight over. Ignoring Peter, he puts his strong arms firmly around my waist and holds me tightly, kissing me hard on the mouth.

'God, I've missed you,' he says, loud enough for Peter to hear.

'You too,' I reply, glancing towards the other man on my doorstep. 'Erm, this is Peter . . .'

'Molly's son?' Billy asks, looking surprised as he looks between the pair of us.

'That's the one,' Peter says, the previous expression on his face replaced with a forced smile as he extends a hand to shake. 'Pleasure to meet you, mate.'

'You too, bro. Wow, I see what you mean,' Billy says, grabbing Peter's hand with a firm grip while glancing back at me. 'You are just like your Mum.'

'So people keep saying,' Peter mumbles.

'Soph wasn't lying,' Billy laughs, grinning at me. 'It's uncanny.'

It dawns on me that Billy is being tactical in his reaction to Peter being here. He's not shown any signs of being put out, instead he's made a huge display at being reunited with me (which I'm sure he would have done anyway) but also made a point of letting Peter know that he's aware of him. Putting Billy in a slightly better position than if he'd been caught totally off guard by the sight of me in my dressing gown saying goodbye to a complete stranger.

'Well, I'd better go,' says Peter, offering his hand out again to Billy.

'See you around?'

'No, actually. Peter's going back to Australia,' I say, sharing the information I've just heard as though it's lovely news for us all – which I guess it is, really. Peter moving eliminates all sorts of problems and possible complications.

'Already?' Billy frowns.

Peter shrugs in response. 'Work.'

'Too bad,' Billy replies, although I can't tell whether he's genuinely a little bummed out that Peter's not going to be around (I had spent weeks declaring how great he was) or whether he's just using his magnificent acting skills to make it seem that way.

'OK. Well . . . have a great day, guys. Give my love to

your Mum and Colin,' Peter says, turning and walking back down the garden path before picking up pace and continuing on his morning run.

'He seems nice,' Billy says casually, before turning back to me and lifting me up, nuzzling his face in my neck and smothering it with kisses. Continuing with the reunion we should have been celebrating right from the moment he got out of the car. It's been two months since I saw his handsome face in the flesh, melted into his safe arms and felt his soft lips on mine.

Yet, although I've been yearning for his embrace for so long, it now feels tainted and messy thanks to my mind guiding me to think about the man in dodgy lycra running away from me and my life.

The guy I'll probably never see again.

I know it's for the best. I know it's what I want.

But I wasn't prepared for the heavy feeling of guilt he's carelessly left behind.

He's gone, I reason to myself. It's over.

And with that thought I let out a long, slow sigh of relief.

I'm in the arms of the man I love and hopefully that's where I'll stay . . . if the future is kind.

'There you are,' my mum giggles as she comes down the stairs and sees Billy.

'Mrs May,' he grins, putting me down and hugging Mum instead.

'Not for much longer,' Mum says, biting her lip. 'Gosh, I'm going to be Mrs Banks. That sounds very grown up.'

It's so strange to think me and Mum are no longer going to be sharing a surname, but I'd rather it be her that changed her name first than me getting married and leaving her on her own. There's something about it that's just that little bit easier to cope with, knowing I'm not leaving her with the burden of being the last one to ditch a name attaching us to another lifetime. But perhaps that's me overthinking things. It could be that a small part of Mum is pleased to leave the name behind and feels the same as we both do about leaving our home and living somewhere new. After all, names have shadows, just like houses do.

'Interesting hair choice,' Billy says, gesturing up to Mum's rollers and making her laugh.

'I couldn't resist coming down to say hello. Feels like you've been away far too long. And just look at you,' she says, her hand reaching up and feeling his bicep (I swear I see her blush).

'All those gym sessions have paid off,' I praise, suddenly looking at his body properly for the first time since he's arrived. There's no denying he's really put in a huge amount of effort to get rid of his so-called 'Dad Bod' and transform it into something more solid and sturdy. On top of that he's also got a really healthy tan which makes his skin glow with radiance. Or maybe he looks so great because he's spent the last few months doing what he loves and it's literally caused him to light up from the inside out. He looks, quite simply, drop dead gorgeous and, despite the long flight, refreshed and fully energized. I'm sure Rachel's going to be a bashful mess when she's properly introduced to him later on.

'Now ladies, stop,' he says, holding up his arms. 'You both know I'm not good with attention.'

'You're selling that line to the wrong crowd,' I laugh,

my arm gesturing between me and Mum who genuinely aren't great with having the focus on us.

'Feeling nervous?' Billy asks Mum.

'Not yet,' she replies, really emphasizing the 'yet'.

'No need to be anyway,' I wink.

'Well, I'd better keep getting ready. I'd hate to be late,' Mum says, feeling the rollers on her head. 'Thank you so much for coming back.'

'I wouldn't have missed it for the world,' Billy says softly.

'That means more than you know,' Mum says, clamping her hands on his cheeks and pulling his head down so that she can kiss his forehead, as though he's a little boy.

It's a beautiful exchange.

As she walks away and back upstairs, I see Billy's nostrils flare as he bites on his lip. When he looks up at me I notice a shine to his eyes and know, without him having to say a word, how sorry he is for what he said on the phone last month. He loves my mum, loves my patchwork family . . . and that means everything to me.

I take hold of his hand and kiss him on the mouth, feeling so happy to have him back in my life and here for such an important day. There's no one I'd rather share it with.

37

The short journey to the church is a silent one. We sit in the back of the black Mercedes – an upgrade from the retro mini but not too flashy – holding hands and letting our thoughts take over. I know Mum probably has a million thoughts whirling through her brain so I don't push a conversation. I understand that this moment isn't about me, so it's not for me to ambush it with my own ramblings, although I can't help but wonder what she's thinking about in her last few moments as Mrs Jane May.

Pulling up outside the church, Mum waits for me to get out first, her eyes fixed out of the window and on to the building next to us. Once the driver has opened her door I carefully help Mum out and hand over her bouquet, a beautiful arrangement of the same flowers people will see in the shop later on (if they've not wilted overnight).

Charlotte comes running over in her pale pink bridesmaid dress, the colour matching my own but the cut much puffier, younger and fun than my slinkier number that hugs my figure while still being floaty and free. Our flowers are similar to Mum's but smaller, and in her free hand Charlotte is clutching hold of Minnie Mouse – obviously. She couldn't be expected to miss the big occasion.

Charlotte isn't jumpy or chaotic, instead she's giddily calm. By that I mean she's wearing the biggest smile on her face as she greets us with cuddles, but manages to keep her body under control and not fidget and jump around afterwards. She may be young but it's clear she understands the significance of the day, and that makes her look so much more grown up than she is.

The three of us slowly walk up the concrete path towards the church. It's only once we're standing at the doors, waiting for our cue to enter, that I suddenly have an urge to say something to the utter vision of resplendence to my right.

'I love you so much, Mum,' I whisper, looping my arm through hers.

'And I love you so much,' Mum responds, squeezing my arm and giving me a loving smile.

She looked incredible in the shop, but now she looks otherworldly. She's poised, calmly composed and serene – the opposite to the shell of a human she was for a huge period of our lives.

As we take our steps behind beautiful little Charlotte and start walking down the aisle towards Colin, I experience a powerful surge of honour at walking my Mum into Colin's arms. It gives me the greatest delight to be by the side of this strong woman and seeing just how much she's blossomed and been transformed by the love of a great man. It's with deep pleasure and satisfaction that I am about to give her away, and I have never and could never be prouder than I feel in this precise moment.

As I slowly guide us both down the aisle in front of Mum and Colin's closest friends and family, I notice they're all visibly choked with emotion at the sight of Mum and the promises of love they're about to witness.

Colin's face is a picture when he eventually turns

around – something he leaves until we're only a few feet away. His face pings into action as though it's been physically whacked with emotion. His chin wobbles and his mouth opens as he audibly sucks in a lungful of air.

Darling Aaron puts his arms around his dad and pats him on the back of his smart navy blue suit. He might only be a young boy, but the gesture of support is incredibly sweet and touching.

When Charlotte gets to Colin he bends down to kiss her. However, she wraps her arms tightly around his neck and then pulls his face to hers, gently rubbing their noses together before she kisses him on the cheek and stands next to her brother, where the two of them hold hands.

Colin takes a deep breath and, when he finds himself back on his feet, stands taller than before as he lovingly gazes at Mum. He glances at me with smiling eyes, but his attention is all on her. As it should be.

I take Mum's soft hand and place it into his, feeling tears run down my cheeks as I back away from the altar and go to my seat beside Billy, who is looking extremely smart in his tailored three-piece suit. He protectively puts an arm around my waist and pulls me into his warm body.

I'm so thankful he's here. Not just so that I don't have to sit here on my own, but because I realize he understands me more than anyone else ever has before. And that's important in any relationship. We all come with our quirks and idiosyncrasies – it's inevitable. But the key to having anything long lasting is finding someone who doesn't mind the twisted traits you possess. Or who sees them but loves you anyway . . .

*

The service is beautiful. What stuns me most is the out-pouring of love in the room, and not just between the bride and groom. Everyone here is radiating love from their core, and it creates such an intimate and special atmosphere inside the large, cold church.

There are tears, there's laughter (sometimes at the same time), but I have a smile plastered on my face throughout, echoing the same expression that's on the faces of each member of my patchwork family. As the vicar speaks, as Mum and Colin say their vows and declare their love, I feel us all being stitched together and becoming one. Officially becoming unified and whole.

I couldn't be happier.

38

'Thank you, Rachel, you're such a star,' says Mum, smiling up at her in the same euphoric state she's been in since we left the church.

Rachel has been wonderful, we really couldn't have asked for more. As planned, she handed out glasses of bubbly as we arrived at the shop and then, once the guests were seated, brought out the platters of sandwiches and neatly displayed cake stands filled with treats that she put together this morning. They're scattered along the tables, in between the flowers and candles, and look deliciously enticing. Once everything is laid out and people are happily tucking in, Rachel starts laying out the tea.

'She's like a duck,' I laugh, making room for her to place a pot down our end of the table. 'She looks totally unfazed at having to look after so many of us.'

'No wonder I've lost my job. You're a pro,' Billy tells her.

'Oh, it's nothing,' she gushes, her cheeks reddening at Billy's attention.

'I'm surprised you didn't get Peter to help out, though,' says Billy, looking at me.

'Oh . . .' I say, the statement catching me by surprise.

'He was meant to be helping out, wasn't he?' asks Colin with a concerned frown. 'You asked him.'

'I guess he's probably too busy packing,' says Billy with a shrug, coming to his own conclusion.

'Packing?' asks Rachel, looking at me.

'He's going back to Oz,' I say calmly, not liking the fact that we've already spent far too long talking about him.

'Oh, that's a shame,' Mum sighs, her voice light and colourful.

'Hmmm . . .' Rachel sounds, walking back behind the counter to continue distributing the tea to the rest of the wedding guests, although now she's frowning as she does so.

'Peter's really good at football,' Aaron tells Billy with a knowing nod. 'Although he's not been back to the house like he said he would. Probably won't now either,' he adds, looking dismayed.

'Did you know there are animals as tall as humans in Australia that bounce around like rabbits?' asks Charlotte, her eyes wide and full of wonder, as though she's telling him about something magical and unheard of.

'She's talking about kangaroos,' explains Aaron, grabbing a hazelnut macaroon from the cake stand in front of him and jamming it into his mouth.

'So I guessed,' Billy replies.

'I don't think they're real though,' Charlotte sighs, looking bitterly disappointed at the prospect. 'I think Peter was making it up.'

'Well, adults do and say silly things sometimes,' Billy says, looking across at me with a troubled expression on his face.

The look sends a shiver down my spine and causes my jaw to tense up.

'So when was he over at the house?' he asks Aaron, clearly trying to piece together whatever I've not shared and going to the most loose-tongued of the gathered group.

'Few weeks ago,' shrugs Aaron.

'I treated him to a roast,' Mum admits, her innocent face smiling at Billy. 'My idea.'

'Oh . . .' Billy says, glancing back at me.

I'm not sure whether he believes her or not, but the conversation is thankfully dropped.

An hour later, once everyone's tummies are being rubbed and people are declaring they've eaten too much, Mum stands up from her chair and taps her teaspoon against the side of her china cup.

It doesn't take long for her to grab everyone's attention and for the room to stop talking and look over. After all, this is so out of character for my mum.

'You all know I'm not one to make public speeches or whatnot, but when Colin asked me if I wanted to say a few words today the word "Yes" came out of my mouth so quickly I dared not question it,' she says, causing her gathered guests to laugh.

Mum gazes over at Colin, who looks back encouragingly. She takes a deep breath, smiles and continues.

'First, I want to start by saying a huge thank you to you all for being here on this special day. Obviously you all know this isn't the first time Colin and I have said our "I dos", but that doesn't make them any less special, or lessen the importance of our previous vows we made to two special people who we'll always continue to cherish and admire,' she says, her hand finding my back and giving it a rub, while Colin places his arm along the back of Aaron and Charlotte's chairs. 'So on this day I'd like to make a promise to Colin's Pauline and to my Dean. I promise to honour your memories, and go forth in the knowledge that your love guides us through the dark days, and joins us through all the good times yet to come. You will always be a part of this family,' she says, her gaze lingering on us three children. 'Gone will never equal forgotten.'

'Hear, hear,' someone shouts out, causing a little laughter to join some discreet sniffs in the room.

'Colin and I have been blessed with three precious gifts in Sophie, Aaron and Charlotte,' Mum continues, her grip pulling my shoulder into her hip. 'Sophie, what a remarkable girl you are. You will never know how much you touch those around you with your kindness and unwavering heart. I'm so proud to call you my daughter. I can't thank you enough for making this day simply perfect.'

She bends down, cups my face and gives me a kiss on the cheek.

'I love you,' I whisper back.

'Aaron and Charlotte, what a joy you are to be around,' she adds, talking to the two little cherubs who are listening to her every word. 'You're complete credits to your mother and father and I promise to love and support you both as much as I can. And finally, to Colin I'd like to say thank you,' she says, her eyes welling up as she looks at him to find him dabbing his face with a napkin. 'Thank you for giving me light when I thought there was only darkness. Thank you for giving me laughter when I was sure there were only tears. And thank you for giving me a future when I thought there wasn't one.'

A silence lands on the room as her beautifully thought-through words settle in.

'So if you'd all like to raise your glasses, I'd like to make a toast. To Colin. My husband. My shining star.'

'To Colin,' we all chorus before erupting into applause at Mum's eloquent speech.

'How on earth can I follow that one?' Colin sighs as he gets up from his chair, causing us all to laugh. 'I feel like saying "what she said" and then sitting down again . . .' he says, his fingers wiping the sides of his mouth. He stands there, collecting his thoughts while waiting for the crowd to fall silent again. 'Life is a strange thing. Just when you think you have it all figured out something happens that throws all of that into oblivion. I don't know what tomorrow will bring, but I know that today, right now in this moment, I'm where I should be. That I'm the luckiest man alive to be able to call Jane my wife and these three our children . . .'

Unexpectedly, my nose stings and tears spring to my eyes.

I knew Mum had her own thoughts about Aaron and Charlotte and her role as their step-mum, but I hadn't thought about Colin and the part he'll now play in my life. To hear him, kind, loving, loyal Colin, refer to me as one of his children hits me harder than I expected. It fills me with love and further appreciation for the man who has unconditional kindness in his heart.

39

Once the guests have gone I send Rachel home, despite her protests. I also demand Mum, Colin, Aaron and Charlotte leave so they can enjoy their first official night of having Mum live with them. I think Mum wanted to argue, but thankfully decided against it. After all, it's her day to enjoy.

For a minute or two I think about clearing up and taking down the romantic decorations, but it seems such a shame to do it while I'm wearing my pretty dress, so resolve to come back in the morning to do it. Instead, I take Billy by the hand and lead him into the romantically lit courtyard.

We each grab a blanket and collapse on one of the benches Colin made, wrapping ourselves up and getting snuggled into each other.

'It already feels like I've not been away,' Billy muses, his head back looking at the stars above.

'Funny, I was about to say it feels like you've been back for ages,' I note.

'We're so in sync,' Billy chuckles.

'Are we?' I find myself asking, placing weight on his comment that was clearly meant to be a casual throwaway.

Billy turns to me, his face contemplative. 'You tell me . . .'

Whenever I look into his eyes my troubles seem to melt away, but on this occasion, perhaps it's best to voice how

I've been feeling over the last few months and come clean about a couple of things. After all, how can a relationship last anyway if it's not built on the solid foundations of trust and honesty?

'Peter kissed me,' I say sadly, surprised at myself for diving in and starting the conversation, especially when we're in such a romantic setting on our first night together in months and after such an emotional day.

'Thought so,' Billy replies instantly, his voice low as he closes his eyes and tightens his jaw.

'You were right to be worried and put out by the whole thing,' I continue, shaking my head as I think back to the moment in the park. 'I was an idiot. I wasn't expecting it . . . I didn't reciprocate,' I say, wanting to clarify that fact in case he's thinking otherwise. 'It was weeks ago. The first time I saw him since then was this morning.'

'Ah . . .'

'It didn't mean anything.'

'You sure about that?'

'Yes,' I say adamantly, my voice strong and determined.

'You know I trust you more than anyone else in my life,' Billy says, looking over at me with a hurt expression on his face.

'I didn't want to say anything on the phone or in a letter,' I explain, feeling like I'm letting him down even though I am trying my best to be honest. 'Actually, I didn't want to have to say anything at all, but I think we need to talk about things anyway and that little moment is so insignificant that it suddenly felt like a good place to start,' I admit.

'So there's more?' Billy puffs, his eyes looking worried

as they widen in concern, looking at my face for clues as to what's coming next.

'I've found it really difficult.'

'So have I . . .' he frowns.

'But I've felt like the pressure has been on me to adapt and change my life so that I can fit around yours,' I explain. 'And when you're over there our lives are so different.'

'I'm sorry you've felt that way,' he says, looking even more concerned about where the conversation is heading – something I can relate to. I'm also troubled about the outcome now I've started.

'For a long time I plodded through life with no sense of direction,' I say slowly, wanting to be sure to speak the right words and only say what I mean. 'Then you came along and the world became a bigger place with more opportunities and more possibilities . . . I hadn't thought of life outside a six-days-a-week job in Rosefont Hill, not since my teens anyway, but suddenly there you were throwing up the question of dreams, ambition and the future. I followed you to London, I changed my life for you, but that didn't make me happy.'

Billy listens quietly as I speak, sometimes looking at my lips as they move or woefully searching my eyes. Sometimes, though, his gaze is off me entirely, absentmindedly looking at the space ahead of us. But I know he's listening. I know he's absorbing my every word, and that spurs me on.

'Obviously we had our problems then, but when Molly died and left me this place I was rooted back here . . . thankfully with you by my side,' I continue, not wanting to hash up old problems, yet needing him to understand where my head is at now. 'But I still took all of what I had for granted. It's only you being gone this time and watching you actively fulfilling your dreams and being so focused on those ambitions that has caused me to question what it is I want from my life.'

I pause, and think for a second. Wondering how to communicate what I've discovered about myself in his absence. When I start talking again my voice is softer. 'I've loved the letters. A few weeks ago I found myself re-reading them all, as well as an old one from Molly. It made me realize that I'm not tied down by the shop. I'm not. If I wanted to I could just up and leave and follow you anywhere you went in the world. But. I don't want to move anywhere. This is my home. It's where I belong. It's where I want to be.'

'I know that,' Billy sighs. 'That's why I suggested buying your house.'

I look at him and sigh. It feels good to be here talking with him and getting everything out in the open, but man alive, does it take some courage to share everything I want to. 'I actually made some other decisions too.'

'There's more?'

'Yes . . . But let me show you this one.'

'OK,' he frowns.

I take Billy by the hand, grab my keys from the kitchen side, and lead him to the front of the shop.

'Actually, wait here a second,' I say, leaving him by the front of the counter while I dash outside, unlock the flat door, run upstairs and turn on the lights to make it look more welcoming and friendly.

I take a deep breath before running back down the stairs. At the shop door I usher Billy towards me, holding out my hand for him to take.

'What's going on?' he asks, perturbed, looking completely downtrodden as he complies and takes my hand.

'You'll see,' I say, trying to sound upbeat.

After a momentary pause, I guide him out of the shop, lock the door and then walk a few paces to the left where the door to the flat is still wide open.

'What's this?' he asks when we start climbing up the stairs.

I resist replying until we walk through the main door upstairs.

'Welcome to my new home ... potentially, *our* new home,' I say, holding my arms out wide and looking at the space around us, gesturing for him to look around and explore.

I watch as he takes it all in.

Interestingly, I see it with fresh eyes being here with Billy, which allows me to really absorb the space and see all of the hard work and effort I've poured in over the last few weeks. The lounge, although still sofa-less, is cosy and inviting. I've painted the walls a warm cream, hung white curtains at the windows (which are embroidered with very faint stars) and placed some rustic hearts made of entwined twigs in the window frame. On two shelves I've arranged some photo frames containing prints of quotes from my favourite books, each of them uplifting and inspiring. There are also chunky vanilla-scented church candles and a small selection of my most-read and loved books. I'll eventually get a book unit for the rest once I properly move everything over from my old room, but for now this is enough. In the centre of the room, on the floor, I've laid a shaggy rug, on top of which is a gorgeous coffee table that Colin had stored in his garage and wasn't using.

The rectangular kitchen has white units and a wooden work surface to match the wooden doorknobs, with a small wooden table and chairs set, also donated by lovely Colin, in one corner. Again, I've hung things that make me smile, like a set of six hand-painted heart mugs that dangle from hooks from underneath a display shelf which is home to my ceramic pots and glass jars of flour, sugar and other necessary cooking ingredients.

I've not done much with either of the bedrooms yet, except paint them and hang curtains, as I've been waiting to move over the furniture I'm bringing from home. However, I can't help but smile when I walk into the main bedroom and see three cream walls, alongside one pink one. My plan being to have a wall that's just like my one at home – pink and filled with happy pictures and memories . . . I'm taking the essence of the wall without all the pain and heartache.

I glance at Billy and see the corner of his mouth lift at the sight in front of us, which causes a feeling of hope to surge within me.

'So?' I ask. 'I know I've done it without consulting you.'

'It wasn't what I was expecting to come back to,' he admits, his eyes fixed on the pink wall.

'I don't want either of us to feel like I'm pinned down to the shop. I know your mum said it would make life more difficult, but I think it'll actually make things easier if we understand we're both chasing and living our dreams. I think we might be able to have the best of both worlds if, with the help of Rhonda, we play it right . . .' I say, feeling myself rambling but unable to stop, wanting to get the words out. 'But I also know that priorities and plans change. People change along with their wants and desires. I'm not going to be forcing you to live a life with me here if you'd rather be elsewhere, pursuing a different life in some Hollywood Hills mansion.'

'When did my mum say that?' Billy asks soberly, looking across at me.

'I overheard her talking to you. Telling you that she didn't want you throwing your life and dreams away for a girl,' I admit, realizing I might as well get it all out there while I'm at it.

'Ah . . .' he nods, clenching his jaw.

'I'd never want that for you. I wouldn't want that for me either . . . And although I understand that I probably do offer you a sense of normality, I've decided that's not a bad thing. I'm proud of the life I lead. I love it,' I conclude.

'Why didn't you tell me you'd overheard her?'

'Things were bad enough without me adding to the drama.'

'She really does like you.'

'I'm not so sure about that,' I chuckle.

'No, seriously,' Billy says, taking hold of my hand. 'That was such an odd time . . . I hate that you had to see my mum like that, but that's not who she is. In time you'll see that.'

'No one's perfect,' I shrug, not wanting to argue about

something completely off topic when there's already so much to talk about and sort through.

'She loves you.'

'Come on,' I say, rolling my eyes.

'Seriously . . . they all do,' he says, placing an arm around me and pulling me into his chest.

I tentatively place my hands on his hips and take a deep breath, enjoying the feeling of his strong arms around me, but also scared of what's to come. Now that he's here, in my new home, I understand how much I'd hate to lose him.

Eventually Billy pulls away from me and walks back into the kitchen.

'Let's sit down,' he says, pulling out a couple of chairs, sitting and resting his arms on the table.

'You must be shattered,' I say, remembering he only flew in this morning.

'Yeah.'

'We can talk about this tomorrow if you'd rather?' I suggest, my voice cracking as I say it, knowing it's not what I want.

'I've travelled five thousand miles to see the love of my life,' he says, his lips pursing together. 'I want to make sure I'm not about to lose her . . .'

'I thought I was about to lose you,' I confess, feeling my face crumple.

'Sounds like we've both been a bit scared, then.'

'Maybe,' I nod, nibbling on my bottom lip.

His hand cups one of my cheeks while his lips find the other.

He places his forehead against mine, and there we rest

with our eyes closed for a few moments. Silently in thought.

'OK,' he whispers eventually, opening his eyes and taking a deep breath. 'Now it's my turn to do the talking . . . I know I made a bold statement last year about leaving acting behind and opting for a simpler, more fulfilling life with you. Though please notice I said nothing about chasing normality,' he says intently, looking me in the eye to make sure I know his mum's choice of words is not his own.

I give a modest nod.

'I know I've backtracked on what I said and can see that it might have made you feel like my priorities have changed or that I'm suddenly not as into you as I was . . .' he says, placing a hand on my knee. 'But that couldn't be further from the truth, baby. It makes me sad to think you think that. If anything I'm doing all of this for you, for us, for our future.

'I've fallen back in love with acting – that's true. But performing is for me what the shop is for you. I wouldn't want you to have to choose between me and your life here, and I know you wouldn't ask me to do the same with you and acting. I know we've had a couple of wobbly patches while I've been out in LA, but we're both learning how to cope and adapt,' he states, his thumb gliding along the fabric of my dress on top of my kneecaps. 'It's not easy, we knew it wouldn't be. We do have to compromise, but I don't want that compromise meaning either of us is left unhappy. It's about finding a balance and realizing that having something else in our lives doesn't have to mean we love each other any less.'

'I know that . . .' I frown, wishing it were as simple as it sounds.

'You'll always be my top priority when it matters.'

'But how can you distinguish when it matters and when it doesn't?' I ask calmly.

'Well, I hope I'll be intuitive on that, but I'm bound to get it wrong occasionally. I know I did this time round.'

'You're not the only one,' I groan, thinking back to Peter.

'And if that happens again we have to be honest in the moment. Call each other out on it,' he says, gripping hold of my hand. 'Rhonda is on our side. Three months on, three months off, that's what we've got planned. And if that doesn't pan out then we'll scrap that idea and come up with a new strategy. Nothing is set in stone and making sure we're both happy is more important than anything else,' Billy says firmly, a frown forming along his brow as he says it. 'Don't forget, Rhonda wasn't involved when I signed this deal. It'll be different next time.'

'With Rhonda cracking the whip?' I joke.

'Exactly, she'll make sure it's not as demanding or strenuous.' Billy smiles, taking a deep breath as his eyes well up, emotion getting the better of him. 'You spoke earlier about how I changed your life. Well, before you came along I'd lost my way with acting. I know people will think it's the BAFTA that gave me focus and drive again, but I think they'll find I went off the rails after that too. *You* taking over this place reignited my passion and love for the craft. Watching you in the shop, in a place where you visibly shine and thrive, working so reverently and relentlessly to make your vision work. Watching you made me realize I simply needed a fresh injection of energy, like the kind I've seen you pour so lovingly into this business,' he smiles, stroking my hand. 'Can't you see you inspire people, Sophie May? You should. Because it's not just me you've had an effect on. Take a look at that crazy little sister of mine. Lauren's about to start chasing her own set of dreams in Paris and seeing as she's talked nonstop about you and everything you've achieved since the first day she met you, there's no denying you've been a positive role model to her.'

It's lovely to hear him talk this way and to hear he understands how much the shop has given me, but I'm startled by him saying it's my focus that's inspired him and Lauren. That I really wasn't expecting. I can't believe I warrant such huge praise. When I think of the difficulty I've had trying to depict what I want from life and how long it's taken me to find a place I feel secure and stable, it's hard to imagine others have looked on and been compelled to act.

'I just want you to see that my world is a brighter place with you in it,' he declares, his hands sliding on to my bare arms. 'You make me work harder. You stop me from slinking off into a dangerous place. Do you know how nice it was being in LA and not being led by the night scene or column inches? Ironic I know, seeing what happened on the only night I did go out. But I need you to understand that I feel great because of the motivation you encouraged me to have . . . I want you to see I'm still the same guy you fell in love with, but mostly I need you to accept that you are the only girl who has made me question myself, doubt myself and then build myself into a better person.'

'But what about all the time we're going to be apart?' I whisper. No matter how much we love each other, living separately is going to be a normal occurrence for us.

'I get it. You need a sense of permanence, of future security. Right?' he asks.

'Yeah . . .' I mutter, shocked he's able to see it in such simple terms.

'I'm not angry that you've decided to fortify a life here,' Billy shrugs, shaking his head as he looks around the room. 'I actually love what you've done. I love that you've created somewhere that makes you content, because that's how I want you to feel. I want to share it with you as much as I can . . .'

'Same.'

'This can be our base. Our home. We might just have to be a little flexible with it.'

'How?' I ask. I'm not trying to sound difficult but I want us to find a solution where we can both have what we want and stay together.

'I'll be here as much as I can be and we'll juggle around the times I have work,' he sighs, his eyes pleading at me not to give up. 'My jobs are not always going to be in LA. Those working periods aren't always going to be thousands of miles away or even in film. I can do another stint in the West End and still come back here every night. It can work,' he insists.

'You make it sound so easy.'

'I know it's not and I'm not saying we have to live this way forever, but for now let's make it work so that we can build the future we want together. Because none of this means anything without you by my side . . . You're the one

I want to share it all with, whether we're together in the same room or thousands of miles apart. Love makes the world a better place and I want the life I lead to be one that's driven always with love. With you.'

'That's how I feel,' I say, feeling tears spring to my eyes and hearing my heart sing at his words.

'I know I offer unpredictability when all you want is stability. I appreciate how difficult that must be for you, but I also promise to love you for as long as you will allow me to. We're not going to have a conventional life together, but I hope with all my heart that we have a happy one.'

'I hope so too,' I laugh with a sob.

And then, slowly, Billy slides from his chair and on to the floor in front of me.

With one knee bent in front of him, his fingers gently stroke the bottom of my chin, bringing my eyes up to his. 'Sophie May, I've thought so much about how this moment would play out and doing it like this didn't enter my mind once,' he laughs, shaking his head as his beautiful brown eyes fill with tears, prompting my own to do the same. 'But now I see that I don't need an over-the-top setting to tell you that I love you with all my heart. That you are my one. My only.' He pauses. 'I'm not perfect, but I'm all *yours*. Will you marry me? Will you let me be your husband?'

I'm rendered speechless. Never in a million years did I expect that question to fall from his lips. Not tonight.

But as I sob, something clicks into place inside me. A house is only bricks and mortar, just as we discussed all those months ago, standing in his LA mansion. Yet what turns those man-made materials into a home is the people it houses, the people we surround ourselves with and those we let into our hearts.

As Billy kneels on my kitchen floor offering his own heart to me, I realize my own desire for a piece of rubble isn't what I've actually been craving. Instead, I've needed to know that I'm unequivocally and unquestionably loved, and that whoever I choose to give my own fragile heart to can be trusted to house it and keep it safe alongside their own.

I'm left in no doubt that Billy will do his utmost to do just that.

And slowly, I nod my head and accept.

Acknowledgements

This book wouldn't have happened without a lot of great people encouraging me and giving me a little love when needed/necessary.

Huge thanks to:

My wonderful agent, Hannah Ferguson, who's still continuing to reply to my emails even though she's welcomed gorgeous Nell into her life and should be on maternity leave. HELLO, NELL!

The fabulous teams at The Marsh Agency and Hardman & Swainson – thanks for spreading the book love far and wide.

My waddle of Penguins – namely Maxine Hitchcock, Kimberley Atkins, Ellie Hughes, Claire Bush, Nick Lowndes and Fiona Brown. But also everyone in the multiple departments who continue to make me proud to be part of the colony.

You, the reader. Without you devouring my work and showing your support there really wouldn't be any books! I hope I never disappoint you.

My friends who I love and adore. It's taken me three decades to realize how important it is to have positive people in my life and to banish the negative plonkers. You all rock!

My super family who grow bigger by the year – Mum, Dad, Giorgie (and bump, AKA Little McClane), Chickpea, Mario, Debbie B, Debbie F, Bob and Carrie! You're all brilliant humans. I'll forever be thankful for the love you show me.

Tom, Buzz and Buddy – my forever loves. No matter how busy life gets, finding time for you guys will always be my priority. I love you to the moon and back . . .

'Warm and romantic, this charming read will
certainly brighten up your day'
Closer

Billy and Me

'A gorgeous, gloriously romantic read with
buckets of charm – I absolutely loved it!'
Jill Mansell

Giovanna Fletcher

The gorgeously romantic story of one small-town
girl and the world's most famous movie star . . .

'A heartbreakingly beautiful story about friendship and unrequited love. I was totally and utterly captivated'

Paige Toon

Giovanna Fletcher

You're
The One
that I want

It's Maddy's wedding day but has she made the right choice between the groom and his best man . . . ?

'Saucy, fun and full of heart.'
Heat

Giovanna
Fletcher

Dream
a little
Dream

From the bestselling author of
Billy and Me and *You're the One That I Want*

Because people never really find the
person of their dreams... do they?

He just wanted a decent book to read ...

Not too much to ask, is it? It was in 1935 when Allen Lane, Managing Director of Bodley Head Publishers, stood on a platform at Exeter railway station looking for something good to read on his journey back to London. His choice was limited to popular magazines and poor-quality paperbacks – the same choice faced every day by the vast majority of readers, few of whom could afford hardbacks. Lane's disappointment and subsequent anger at the range of books generally available led him to found a company – and change the world.

'We believed in the existence in this country of a vast reading public for intelligent books at a low price, and staked everything on it'
Sir Allen Lane, 1902–1970, founder of Penguin Books

The quality paperback had arrived – and not just in bookshops. Lane was adamant that his Penguins should appear in chain stores and tobacconists, and should cost no more than a packet of cigarettes.

Reading habits (and cigarette prices) have changed since 1935, but Penguin still believes in publishing the best books for everybody to enjoy. We still believe that good design costs no more than bad design, and we still believe that quality books published passionately and responsibly make the world a better place.

So wherever you see the little bird – whether it's on a piece of prize-winning literary fiction or a celebrity autobiography, political tour de force or historical masterpiece, a serial-killer thriller, reference book, world classic or a piece of pure escapism – you can bet that it represents the very best that the genre has to offer.

Whatever you like to read – trust Penguin.